THE LANCE AND THE VEIL

AN ADVENTURE IN THE TIME OF CHRIST

12/7/14

Merry Christmas!

Kevin Rush

For my parents,
who started me on my journey
towards Christ

THE LANCE AND THE VEIL

AN ADVENTURE IN THE TIME OF CHRIST

KEVIN RUSH

Chapter 1

19 A.D.

Veronica could not remember the moment that she knew her father was dead. There had been a flurry of activity, grownups crying like children, then hushed conversations that ended abruptly when her mother walked into a room. Gradually an awareness grew of something permanent and terrible: the man mother spoke of so often will never return. The *but why?* would be answered succinctly with a word she could barely comprehend, but which disallowed further inquiry: *death*. No one comes back from *death*.

Did it matter that her father's death may have resulted from something other than the normal course of battle, under the inherently dangerous circumstances of defending the empire? Assassination. Conspiracy. Such concepts are beyond the reckoning of a four-year-old, especially one stunned by a household thrown into tumult over a cloudy event, weeks ago, in a distant part of the world.

What Veronica did remember, and remembered very clearly, was her mother as a portrait of agony, red-faced and shrill, defiant and defeated. Her nails dug into the face of the stranger who had brought the news, until Demetria, the old Greek house slave, pried her fingers loose and eased the lady back to her cathedra[1]. Blood ran from cuts above the man's eyes, which he dabbed with a cloth one of the slaves offered. Veronica would retain total recall of the scene and the words, although it would be years before she could decipher their meaning. Dumbstruck, she watched tears stream from her mother's bloodshot eyes, as she declared herself a martyr to justice.

"I shall swallow fire like Portia[2]."

Demetria dipped a cloth into cool water, wrung it out and raised it to her lady's forehead. Veronica watched the gnarled hands stroke her mother's flushed face. But her mother's passion only rose. Striking the crone's hand, she struggled to her feet and paced the tile floor.

"I cannot say that My Lady is not in danger." The messenger remained attentive, though careful to avert his eyes. "But Prefect Sejanus[3] advises that quiet mourning — as befits modesty — might mollify the Emperor[4]."

A hiss and she bared her claws to him. "I should be silent? My husband was murdered. I should care that his murderer sits on a throne?"

"You might care to stay alive," Demetria cautioned. She took her lady's hand and urged her again to the cathedra.

---

[1] A throne-like chair
[2] Brutus' wife, who committed suicide after her noble husband assassinated Julius Caesar
[3] Lucius Aelius Sejanus (20 BC –31 AD), a confidant of Emperor Tiberius Caesar
[4] Tiberius Caesar, Roman Emperor from 14 AD to 37 AD

"For what? If I had a son, I'd live for vengeance."

"Be grateful you've a daughter," Demetria whispered. "Tiberius would kill your son. Even that young."

Veronica detected no gratitude, only a trembling, wrenching sorrow. Her mother's eyes locked onto hers, and her face contorted. With sobs that had no breath, her shoulders heaved until a spasm seemed to break and a wail from deep in her anguished soul poured forth. Veronica screamed. From fright, confusion, frustration, she cried, hoping to be gathered in her mother's arms, but instead was lifted by Demetria and carried out, despite thrashing and kicking in protest. Her mother hunched forward on the cathedra, head bowed, her face obscured by tangled, chestnut hair, wringing her hands as though she'd tear skin from the bones. It was the last time Veronica saw her mother alive.

*   *   *   *

The horses came that night. Veronica was awakened by them, but was not afraid until Demetria burst into her room, lifted her off the bed and ran with her wrapped in a blanket to the servants' quarters. The cheek pressed against Veronica's forehead was wet. Demetria's voice was hoarse as she whispered that Veronica must stay hidden. She placed her in a storage alcove, drew a curtain and padded away. For a while the only sound was Veronica's heart. As it slowed, her eyes grew heavy and she slipped into sleep again.

Heavy footsteps and deep voices woke her. Shadows crossed the curtain. A violent smack startled her, then a thud as something hit the wall, followed by a slap on the floor.

A calm voice intervened. It was deep like a man's but lilted slightly like a woman's. "Separate the other servants. Beat each in turn until one talks. Then strangle whoever brought her the poison."

Veronica was wide awake now. She curled into a tight ball to make herself as small as possible, but her breath ran away from her, and she let out a tiny squeak. A monstrous shadow fell over the curtain, sweeping it aside. A man towered above her, then crouched low. His face glistened, lit on one side by a flickering lamp.

"Ave, daughter. I am Sejanus. A friend of your father and mother. What is your name?"

"V'ronica."

Sejanus leaned into the alcove and lifted Veronica out. As her head bobbed over his shoulder, she spied Demetria, lying on the floor against the wall.

"'Metria."

"Yes," the man whispered. "She's sleeping. We mustn't wake her."

He carried her past Demetria out to the garden, where servants of the house were spread out and stripped naked. They whimpered as men dressed like this Sejanus beat them with rods. Sejanus carried Veronica into the main house, where there were more men standing with the girls of the house. A cauldron of embers behind the line of girls filled the room with an acrid smoke that stung Veronica's eyes and throat.

"They claim it wasn't poison," a man told Sejanus. "Only the coals. And she took them herself."

What's wrong with mother? Veronica thought, as she wriggled a hand free to rub her itching nose. Her mother lay on her back, staring wild-eyed at the ceiling, her mouth opened in a wide O, as a wisp of grey smoke wafted upward from her throat. Veronica would wonder for many years about the symbolism of her mother's death, but on that night she didn't know what death was. She only felt an eerie separation, awe and a reverence for a scene where she shouldn't intrude.

So she didn't object when Sejanus carried her away. That is, until they reached the front door. Suddenly a chill hit her and Veronica saw, not landscape and sky, but utter blackness, eternal emptiness. She was gripped at that moment by what must have been the fear of death. Oblivion from which there is no return.

Veronica shrieked and grabbed the doorjamb. All of her strength went into that grip, to keep from falling, from being lost forever. Sejanus tickled her at the ribs, chiding her gently, but the girl only became angrier, kicking and screaming, until, his patience expiring, Sejanus pried her fingers loose.

"Off we go," he sang as he bounced her in his arms across the portico[5], and trotted down the steps to a waiting chariot. It was then the driver's task to restrain the girl as Sejanus untied his cape and wrapped Veronica tightly.

"Whom have we here?" his driver asked.

"Mistress Veronica."

"Curious name."

"*True image*." Sejanus dabbed at her tears with a corner of the cape. "True image of your mother, clearly. Let's hope you meet a happier end."

The driver snapped the reins and the team broke forward. The loud wheels of the chariot drowned the world out.

*   *   *   *

Prior to that night, Veronica had visited her Uncle Theodosius' home, but it was not entirely familiar. She only had a vague image of him as someone distant, lofty, much like the man referred to as *father*. He stood on the portico and greeted Sejanus as he climbed the stone stairs with Veronica in his arms.

---

[5] An open porch without a railing

"Ave, Sejanus."

"Ave."

Theodosius' hand, extended in salute, seemed to stop Sejanus below the portico. He placed Veronica down and unwrapped his cape. He folded his cape over his bent arm, then took Veronica's hand and urged her to climb the last couple of stairs. Her uncle's dark countenance and the line of servants behind him formed an imposing barrier. Veronica hesitated until she saw Claudia peeking around the maids in the doorway. Her older cousin had been friendly and affectionate the few times they'd played together. Now Claudia skipped forward and hugged Veronica, and walked her back to the house. "Ave, Veronica," she whispered. "Did they tell you? We're going to be sisters."

With a flick of his wrist, Theodosius dismissed the servants, who scurried past the girls. Veronica hesitated at the threshold. Somehow, crossing into this home had a weight of permanence she wasn't willing to accept. *But why? Death?* She listened to the men for some clue, but the meaning of their words escaped her.

"A pity," Sejanus sighed, "we didn't arrive in time to save her poor, distraught mother."

"Perhaps your arrival was the precipitating event."

Sejanus wagged his head. "That would have been a tragic misinterpretation of our interest."

"Such misunderstandings have become common."

Sejanus donned his cape. "So good of you, Theodosius. To give the girl a home." But before he could turn to depart, her uncle continued.

"What details are there of my brother's death?"

"Few, I'm afraid."

Her uncle paced a few steps before responding, "As with Germanicus[6]. Seems this is an age when Roman officers die mysteriously."

"Even a good soldier can get dangerously close to the enemy."

Theodosius raised his voice. "Enemies of Rome, or of Caesar?"

The question lingered in the air, before Sejanus broke the tension with a wry smile. "Is there a difference?" Then, more forthrightly, "Good night, Theodosius. The Emperor will note well your charity."

Theodosius stood rooted as Sejanus returned to his chariot, then turned back to the door. His eyes flashed annoyance at the girls loitering in the foyer, and they scampered away. As she ran with Claudia across the cold tiles, Veronica desperately wanted to hide. A curtain had been pulled back from her world, and she'd seen terrible things. She dove under the covers of Claudia's bed and veiled her eyes.

---

[6] Germanicus Julius Caesar (15 BC –19 AD), a prominent Roman general

26 A.D.

The clack of hickory batons striking reverberated through the atrium. Veronica's arms were tiring, and Claudia was taking advantage. She swung her rudis[7] in a slashing motion, crossing Veronica's just above the leather bell, sending a shock up Veronica's arms. All Veronica could do was lean back and point, hoping Claudia wouldn't knock the wooden sword from her two-handed grip. In a few strokes it was over. Veronica's arms sank under the force of the blows, until she could no longer keep her hands firm. Claudia smacked the rudis and sent it skittering across the stone floor.

"No fair!" Veronica whined.

Claudia stomped her foot. "If you're going to cry every time you lose, you shouldn't play."

Theodosius picked up the rudis, slicing the air with a flick of his wrist. He took a step toward his daughter. Claudia responded by raising her weapon. A swing and a loud crack sent Claudia's rudis into the reflecting pool. She huffed and stomped, not daring to offer a verbal complaint. She waded into the piscina[8] and plucked her weapon from the surface of the water.

"The point of training," Theodosius stated calmly, "is not to embarrass your partner, but for each to do what is necessary to improve his skills."

Claudia tried to shake the water off her rudis, only to have it slip from her hand, bouncing again into the piscina, scattering the fish. She flopped down on the lip of the pool and began to pout.

"If you're going to cry every time..."

"Shut up, Veronica!"

Theodosius took a deep breath. "Perhaps that's all for today." He signaled for Claudia to retrieve the rudis from the pool. Adrianna, the Greek slave who tutored the girls, appeared in the doorway, and remained standing until Theodosius acknowledged her with a curt nod. "Time for your lessons."

The girls left the atrium scowling at each other. When Adrianna didn't follow, Veronica turned back to listen.

"It is not my place to be critical, Master Theodosius," Adrianna almost whispered. "But it seems this activity raises passions in the girls. Makes them difficult to manage."

"They're difficult by nature."

"Perhaps, but activities which discipline boys only seem to make girls more willful."

"What makes a girl willful is having attendants to order about. To sit while three slaves paint her fingers, toes and face and a fourth brushes her hair. Idleness and entitlement."

"But is swordplay the antidote?"

---

[7] A wooden stick used to practice swordplay
[8] A shallow indoor pool filled with fish

"She should mind her own business," Claudia whispered. Veronica agreed; Adrianna had complained when Uncle Theo first taught the girls to ride horses at their estate in Tuscany. But swords and horses were what her uncle knew, and even though he'd retired from the military, and like other Senators[9] made his living as a gentleman farmer, he was in great demand to train the sons of wealthy patricians[10] in various martial skills.

"Clearly, I'd do better with sons," he admitted. "But let me ask you, Adrianna. When you look at Claudia, do you see Julianna?"

Adrianna hung her head at the mention of Claudia's mother. "You cannot blame yourself, Master."

"But I can act upon knowledge. I can make a reasonable judgment that Julianna died in childbirth because she was not strong enough to handle it. Because her life of privilege had made her soft." He clacked the two wooden swords together, then continued. "Now, I don't want to see my girls playing harpastum[11] on the Campus Martius[12] any more than you. But I want them to be strong."

"As you wish, Master," Adrianna acquiesced. "Perhaps you might consider keeping them in the country?"

Veronica's heart swelled. She loved the summer estate. She'd spend hours with her greyhounds racing through its open fields. By contrast, Rome was close and congested, filled with foul odors and rude people. But Theodosius banished the possibility with a shake of his head. He would not discuss his reasons, but Veronica knew that his Senate duties weighed upon him lately. He dawdled in the house before leaving for the forum, and always returned exhausted and distracted. And there was Claudia. At fourteen, she was eligible for marriage, and it was customary for the father to settle on a husband before the girl turned fifteen. While Theodosius did not seem anxious to have his only true daughter leave his home, everyone in the household was growing tired of the tedious introductions to young men who fell way short of expectations. Unfortunately for Claudia, her father was too diplomatic to refuse any Senator's request that his son should meet the lovely Claudia. Her afternoons had become tightly scheduled, and exceedingly boring. Boring for Veronica, too, because as much as the two girls squabbled, Veronica was desperately dependent upon her cousin.

In the seven years she'd lived with her uncle, Veronica had not made friends out of the home. Claudia had several, and would be invited for lunches and parties, but those invitations were rarely extended to Veronica. Theodosius

---

[9] The deliberative body of the ruling class in Rome. During the Republic, it had significant power, but after Julius Caesar established a dictatorship, the Senate lost most of its influence.

[10] In the Roman caste system, the patricians were the wealthy ruling class, represented in the Senate

[11] A violent ball game of the Roman Empire

[12] Field of Mars, open land where young men trained and competed

blamed the difference in their ages, but that did not explain why Veronica did not receive invitations from girls her own age, or why it seemed so much more complicated getting her guests to attend a luncheon than it did Claudia's. Again, Theodosius stressed how girls of marrying age needed to be trained in social graces, and so there were more parties. Still, Veronica suspected some other force at work.

She also suspected that, as bored as Claudia was by the awkward boys who appeared on her doorstep bearing flowers, aromatic oils, pewter statuettes and bolts of fine cloth, she was not bored by the prospect of marriage. In fact, it seemed to inflate her sense of self-importance. Claudia was — as always — dreamy, lazy and petulant, but suddenly, at least where Theodosius was concerned, no longer willful. She listened to him at every opportunity, asking questions, not simply about facts, but about his attitude toward things, his opinions. She wanted to know how men thought and felt. Rather than resisting the idea of marriage, she seemed to be looking forward to it. This frightened Veronica, who couldn't imagine this home without her "sister." The fear spiraled downward to shame as Veronica realized she still didn't much feel like Theodosius' daughter. She was an orphan, an object of charity, the friendless girl who needed a lofty Senator's political machinations to ensure attendance at her play dates. Veronica feared what might happen when she came of age, whether Uncle Theo would be as meticulous in choosing a husband as he seemed to be for his own, true daughter, and even if there would be any interest in a girl who'd been dropped on a doorstep after her mother's suicide.

Veronica sought distraction with her dogs, the birds in her aviary, and occasional trips to the theatre. On evenings when Theodosius had other Senators to the house, Adrianna would take the girls to one of the many free performances. But while it was a chance to laugh, listen to music and see other children her age, the focus would invariably come back to Claudia, as all the older boys loitered nearby, hoping to get a chance to converse with *her loveliness*.

Veronica imagined they all ran home to their fathers and begged them to arrange introductions, because not two days would pass before the same boys would appear, one by one, laden like Greeks bearing gifts, and stammering about the horses their fathers owned and planned to race in the circus. Not that they would ride; they'd pay some poor plebeian[13] to do that. They'd quote some oration of Cicero[14] they had memorized. They'd recite Homer, in Greek, which, to her tutor Adrianna's disappointment, Claudia could barely follow.

After several weeks of this, Claudia's willfulness reemerged. She vowed to fight her father if he suggested she marry any of the soft, slack-chested boys. She and Veronica lost their desire to go to the theatre. Instead, the girls would

---

[13] The Plebeians were the working class in Rome
[14] Marcus Tullius Cicero (106 BC –43 BC), a Roman philosopher, politician, lawyer and orator

creep onto the veranda overlooking the courtyard, and spy on the men who came to dine with Theodosius. Their talk was filled with intrigue and crises in the empire. And, from what little the girls could understand, the gravest threat to Rome was Emperor Tiberius himself.

For one thing, Tiberius was a recluse. He trusted very few people whom he met only in private; first among them was Sejanus, who had removed Veronica from her home. Tiberius was extremely paranoid. He jealously held onto power, and was suspected of having killed Germanicus, with whom he had jointly ruled. Most of the men who visited Theodosius seemed to think that if Germanicus had been planning a revolt, he'd had good reasons. They sympathized with the old Republicans who had assassinated Julius Caesar when he'd started acting like a dictator.

Veronica found this all very tedious. There were too many names to keep track of, and too much history going back too far. She was not fond of raking up the past, or considering that painful episodes might repeat themselves. She had a good home now, and wanted it to remain that way. But Claudia was spellbound. "When I marry," she'd said, "it's going to be to a man of the world." Veronica didn't understand: all men were in the world. "I want a husband with ambition. Who wants to shape the empire. Not sit back and be a bystander. Who matters more? The man in the arena, or in the grandstand?"

This startled Veronica. She sat up in bed and asked, "When did you go to the arena?"

"I haven't."

"I heard men die there."

"I know. They fight to the death."

"With swords?"

"With all kinds of weapons."

"Did Uncle Theo ever fight there?"

"No, silly, he's a free man. It's only slaves."

"I don't want to see it," Veronica cried. "I don't want to see anyone die. Ever."

Claudia became quiet. "Anyway, that's not the point. The point is, I'm tired of being bored, and I want something to matter."

Thus, none of the boys who called measured up: nothing they talked about seemed to matter. So, on this day, flush with the passion of swordplay and tired from three hours of lessons, Claudia decided to rebel.

"Tell the boy I'm not available."

Adrianna's mouth dropped open. "What excuse shall I give?" she asked, and after Claudia tossed her head impertinently, added, "Consider how your response will reflect upon your father."

"Tell him I have a headache. Or a stomachache. A toothache. Whatever illness will cause father least offense."

Adrianna stood motionless for a moment, then nodded. "Very well, Mistress."

Free from the shackles of courtship, Claudia spent most of her "sitting" time on the veranda, tending to their aviary. At one point, she took one of the brightly colored finches from the cage and tossed it to the wind.

"Fly, pretty bird," she called. "You're free!"

Confused, the bird circled the courtyard twice and landed back on the aviary. Veronica sensed an omen, but Claudia resolutely ignored it. She fanned her fingers at the bird, scaring it off the veranda. As it disappeared over the rooftops, Claudia giggled, "Let's follow it!"

Now it was time for Veronica's jaw to drop. For two girls to leave the house unescorted, to wander from the front of their property, was nothing short of scandalous.

"Oh, Claudia, I don't think we..."

"No, not we," Claudia shot back. "You would only slow me down."

So Claudia trotted inside to the landing and sneaked down the stairs to the front door. Veronica clung to the marble railing and watched as Claudia waited for a servant to leave the door, then made her break. In a blink of an eye, she was gone. It was nearly sunset when she returned.

Claudia joked upon returning that she couldn't find the red finch. According to her, she'd looked everywhere: the Hippodrome[15], the Circus[16], the Campus Martius, all the way to the Tiber River. So intoxicated was Claudia with the freedom and audacity of wandering aimlessly through Rome, that she repeated her escapade not once, but twice. On the third day, a prodigious knock at the front door at dusk shook the household to attention.

Veronica teetered at the rail of the second floor landing as a servant opened the door, revealing a tall, broad-shouldered officer of the Praetorian Guard[17]. Beside him slunk Claudia, her cheeks crimson with shame. Adrianna scurried to the door to reclaim the wayward Mistress.

"A thousand pardons for the trouble she's caused," Adrianna bowed. "You'll have the Senator's thanks."

"I would much prefer," the guard begged, "that this service remain anonymous."

That evening, Veronica witnessed for the first time her uncle's wrath. The crash of his fist threatened to splinter the table.

"You are a princess of Rome, not some weed in the gutter! You will comport yourself with dignity! Have I raised you to roam the streets like a slave shirking his errands? Like a runaway concubine?"

Claudia listened stoically until her father's storm dissipated.

---

[15] A stadium for horse racing and chariot racing
[16] A large open-air venue for public events
[17] The force serving as the Emperor's bodyguards

"When a man comes to call, he will find you here, and you will sit with him graciously for a respectable period. Is that understood?"

"Yes, father."

"You will not leave this property without Adrianna to escort you. Is that understood?"

"Yes, father."

"I'll have no more scandals attached to this home." Theodosius cut himself off abruptly. But in a slip of the tongue he'd revealed what Veronica had always suspected. Her uncle had paid a price for her. The children, who would not speak to her, who would not invite her to play or answer her invitations, had been warned by parents who feared the taint of scandal. But more than the price itself Veronica now knew that he harbored some resentment. Theodosius made a feeble gesture to stroke her hair, then thought better of it. He took his seat at the head of the table.

"May I be excused, Father?"

The Senator nodded. Claudia pushed her stool from the table and left the dining room. Veronica watched her uncle dip a crust of bread into olive oil and wine. "Are you finished?" he asked her.

Veronica nodded.

"You're excused. Go, be with your... sister."

"Yes, sir."

Veronica found Claudia in the atrium, lying on her stomach on the lip of the reflecting pond. She splashed with her fingertips, scattering the fish.

"You're not crying?" Veronica asked.

"Why?"

"He was so angry at you."

"It doesn't matter," Claudia sighed. She rolled to a sitting position; Veronica crouched beside her. Claudia was completely serene as she stated, "I've already met the man I'm going to marry." Veronica could have fainted dead away. Unfazed, Claudia continued, "He's handsome and tall. He's lean, but has muscles like thick rope. He can throw a pilum[18] farther and more on target than any man on the campus. And he's going to be very important. He has all sorts of plans for the provinces, to develop them and increase trade for the empire."

"You've spoken to him already?"

"I've spoken to him every day this week."

"Is he coming to see you?"

"He will. When he can arrange an introduction. It's complicated, but he's not quite a patrician. Though he will be someday. He'll be the most famous Senator in Rome."

"What's his name?"

[18]A Roman lance made of iron and wood

Claudia looked up through the skylight, as though announcing his name to heaven: "He's called Pontius. Pontius Pilate."

Chapter 2

"I first met him in my dreams," Claudia whispered. Veronica tossed and turned toward the wall. The endless confessions of love were becoming tiresome.

"I dreamed him so vividly," she continued. "At first, he was far away in the middle of this wide field. He had a horse he was training that he trotted in a circle. A muscular, white horse, and you could tell it wanted to break away and gallop, but he kept it under rein. It was afraid of his whip. The horse was cloudy white, and then I saw it was marble, and I realized the horse was Rome, and he controlled Rome by cracking his whip —"

"Go to sleep, Claudia!" Veronica groaned. Claudia always did this. Something would come about that affected the house and Claudia would claim she had dreamt it. She had dreamt Adrianna would sprain her ankle on the stairs. She had dreamt Veronica's greyhound would have three live puppies and a fourth would be stillborn. But she never predicted anything! She didn't warn Adrianna about the stairs, or intimate to Veronica that her dog's delivery might not be entirely joyous. Now she was doing it again: claiming after the fact to have had some mystical prior knowledge that seemed only to reinforce how she wanted to feel.

"Well, it's true."

"Ugh!" Veronica grunted.

"Jealous," Claudia huffed, but at least she was quiet the rest of the night.

The next day, Theodosius announced that the girls would attend a party. Senator Catullus was trying to arrange a match for his son, Marius. Veronica was excited to go, but Claudia pouted.

"I don't like him," Claudia whined. "He's got huge pimples, and his breath smells like a rat curled up in his mouth and died."

"That's enough," Theodosius declared. "You will attend and you will behave graciously. If you find one afternoon sniffing his breath is unbearable, imagine a lifetime."

"You wouldn't!" Claudia shrieked.

"No." Her father couldn't suppress an arch smile. "Just keep in mind that I could."

Veronica was elated at Claudia's defeat; not simply to see her cousin knocked down a peg, but because a party meant new clothes. If Theodosius was in a particularly generous mood — which Veronica had reason to hope, since she had been so cooperative all through Claudia's rebellion — Veronica would not simply get a new woolen tunic to replace the drab child's garments she daily wore; she would get a brightly bleached linen tunic. Perhaps with a colored sash to belt it at the waist.

Under Rome's Sumptuary Laws, the styles and colors of clothing were regulated, according to one's status in society, so anyone could tell an individual's rank on sight, whether he was a free man or a slave, a Senator or an Equestrian[19]. Only the Emperor, a general celebrating a triumph or high-ranking magistrates could wear purple. Theodosius, as a Senator, wore a *tunica lanticlava*, a simple, white garment with broad crimson stripes down each side. His white toga also bore a crimson stripe indicating his function as a priest. Though there were fewer restrictions on the colors a woman wore, the style of her garment indicated whether she was married or single, slave or free, of good or ill repute. Only the very lowest class of woman wore a toga. Upper-class married women wore the palla and stola, a simple dress with or without sleeves adorned with a broad sash. Girls were relegated to tunics, either knee or ankle length, with sleeves or without, and of course, they always wore their bulla. This was a medallion the girls wore on a string around their necks. It indicated their single status and was meant to protect them for marriage. When a girl married, she burned her bulla.

The Proculus family, like many of the wealthy in Rome, had a slave who was a trained tailor. Paenulus also shaved Theodosius and cut his hair, a position of great trust, since this slave held a razor at his master's throat. Theodosius had the girls gather all their clothes and follow him to the roof, where the tailor had his quarters. Paenulus left the garment he was stitching and rose as the Senator entered. Out on the roof itself, a pair of boys, each barefoot, marched in place in a shallow basin and slowed until they stood at attention.

"Ave, Master," Paenulus bowed. One boy, who looked maybe a year older than Veronica, bowed too deeply and nearly tumbled out of his basin.

"Ave, Paenulus," the Senator began, "the girls will be attending a party at the Catullus home."

Paenulus snapped his fingers and the boys went back to work. Each stepped out of his basin, reached down and pulled out a sodden wool tunic and began wringing it out.

---

[19] In the Roman caste system, the Equestrians were the middle class, those rich enough to own a horse

Theodosius continued, "They both seem to be growing like weeds. And they're not terribly careful in the kitchen." He showed Paenulus several of Claudia's tunics that were spotted.

"I can get that out, Master Theo," he smiled. Then he gestured to a clay pot, just outside the doorway. "If you'd be so kind?"

"Certainly."

Veronica giggled as her uncle stepped out and straddled the large bowl, hitched up his tunic and relieved himself. Claudia turned away, blushing slightly. The Senator spoke matter-of-factly as his water cascaded into the clay pot.

"See what you can do about the stains. It will do for the house. But for the party, something new. Your finest linen."

"Sleeveless, Father," Claudia chimed in.

Theodosius shook himself and stepped back from the pot. "Very well. And the lines should be flattering. Not to do away with all modesty, but if Claudia's to be married, her clothes might as well admit she's a woman."

"Understood," the slave nodded. "I've crimson dye, Master."

"For the sash. The tunic should be white. As for Veronica..."

Paenulus had already sifted through Veronica's things.

"I've plenty of wool, Master."

Paenulus held up a skein of unbleached wool. Veronica thought, *What am I, a Barbarian? Next he'll be dressing me in skins,* but held her breath as Theodosius squinted in thoughtful deliberation. "No," he said finally. "Not a child's tunic. White linen as befits a young lady."

"Very well."

"And a sash. Nothing ornate or conspicuous. But give it color."

Colors were restricted less by the Sumptuary Laws than by the sheer expense of the dyes. Upper-class colors like purple and crimson were very expensive. Purple came all the way from the eastern edge of the Mare Nostra[20] and was said to be worth its weight in gold. The dye was extracted from seashells by crushing them, and it took around ten thousand mollusks to produce enough dye for just one purple toga. Needless to say, Paenulus didn't have any purple dye on hand. The rich crimson dye also required an elaborate process: a very particular kind of female insect was gathered from a very particular type of evergreen oak. The insect bodies were then dried and fermented. No doubt it took as many bugs as seashells to produce the cake of dye Paenulus had on his desk; Veronica eyed it greedily, imagining a vibrant sash from her shoulder to her hip.

Theodosius brought her back to earth, muttering, "Anything but red. She's eleven years old."

---

[20] In Latin, "Our sea," the Roman name for the Mediterranean Sea

The younger of the boys poured the pot of the master's urine into an empty basin. He added water and white clay powder, then dropped Claudia's old tunic into it. He hopped into the basin and began stepping, grinding the powder into the fabric. As Veronica watched him, he smiled at her. He commenced high-stepping, arching his back and bringing his knees all the way to his puffed-out chest. This caused a great deal of sloshing and got Paenulus' attention.

"Sabinus, stop that now! I'll put the rod to you!"

The boy returned to his mundane march, then mimicked his boss when his back was turned. The second boy hung wet clothes on a line and brushed the fabric. Afterwards, he'd stretch them out on a wooden frame, with a pot of sulfur burning below them to whiten them like new. Standing in the doorway, Veronica caught a whiff of the rotten-egg smell and she retreated. *No wonder Paenulus had the boys work on the roof.*

Paenulus returned to the subject of Veronica's sash. "Maroon?" he asked. "Subdued and modest."

The Senator shook his head. "Green. To set off her eyes." Her uncle tipped Veronica's chin upward, turning her face toward the light from the doorway. "Those are your mother's eyes. Your father so admired them. Flecks of hazel in a field of green."

Looking from her uncle, who seemed lost in distant memories, to the show-off boy, who seemed to have lost interest in his work, Veronica felt oddly at the center of something over which she had no control. Something elusive, but powerful, that was not her, but somehow contained her. At that moment Veronica realized she might, in fact, be pretty. Claudia ended the moment abruptly.

"Father," she groaned. "What about my hair? It's dark and drab and I hate it."

"Well," Theodosius sighed, "Paenulus is a skilled barber. I'm sure he can treat your head as he's treated my chin." The master rubbed his smooth skin as the slave laughed heartily.

"No, Master," Paenulus roared. "But there's a fine, skilled lady who can bring a red glow to her crown. The right mix of tallow and ash, and Mistress Claudia will shine like cherry wood."

"And makeup?" Claudia insisted.

"She'll paint you like the sunset."

"Or blue as a Barbarian!" Theodosius chuckled.

Paenulus made the appointment, and on the day of the party, Claudia's transformation was astonishing. The lady Paenulus had suggested was Domitia, a plebeian wife whose formula for hair dye had been passed down three generations. It was said to burn less than other treatments that might leave a girl's hair broken and gray. Not only did Domitia bring an auburn glow to Claudia's dark hair, but using hot oil and irons, she curled the tresses tight as a lamb's fleece. While the makeup borrowed some purple from the sunset to line her eyes, it was mostly copper and bronze for the lids up to the brow, then a pink blush applied to the cheeks, and scarlet for her lips. Claudia rose stiffly from the chair where she'd been sitting for hours, discarded the bib that had protected her tunic, and strode to the three-quarter-length mirror that stood against the wall. Lifting her chin, she tossed her hair forward onto her collar bones, smoothed her sash and declared herself pleased. "It's exactly how I dreamed it."

Veronica groaned.

Theodosius was allowed in. Opening his purse, he sighed wistfully, "My daughter is now a museum piece." He placed a few coins in Domitia's hand, and the plebeian bowed graciously.

Veronica received no makeover. Too young for such vanity, she kept her walnut hair straight, her beige skin unadorned, and her lips their natural pink. Far from neglected, she felt free of the trappings into which Claudia seemed to have disappeared. Veronica was content to have a beautiful white tunic with an emerald sash, and to finally be going to a party.

The Catullus home was rather grand. They were an old Roman family who'd built their house before the city closed in. It was set back from the street and separated on the sides from the surrounding homes by a rich lawn and shrubbery. Veronica's eyes opened wide as she stepped into an atrium large enough to convene the Senate. A servant led them through the house to the back garden, where they would be formally announced.

Veronica gazed from the veranda to the lush garden, its many shades of green made bolder in contrast to the white marble statues of Catullus patriarchs going back to the founding of the Republic.

"Senator Theodosius Proculus and his daughter, Mistress Claudia Procula." Polite applause followed as father and daughter descended the stairs to the garden. Veronica waited a breath to be announced, but Adrianna nudged her toward the stairs.

"Looking for a husband, are you?" she whispered. "Come along." Veronica was stunned for a second, then quickly padded down the stairs. So was that it? She was invited, only to be invisible? To trail behind Claudia like a slave? Veronica stood frozen on the periphery as Theodosius introduced Claudia to his colleagues from the Senate.

"Go on, now," Adrianna urged. "You can talk to the girls."

Veronica didn't budge. "They don't want to talk to me," she muttered. Then, turning, she discovered Adrianna was gone. Of course, slaves had few chances to socialize, to hear the gossip of another household. Adrianna had immediately pitched in with the Catullus servants, no doubt hoping to learn something she could use to curry favor with her master. So, summoning up her courage, Veronica waded into the party. She searched for familiar faces: girls she might have seen at the theatre, the circus or the plaza. But they were all older. And they talked like conspirators in close circles, shoulder to shoulder, giving their backs to the rest of the gathering, occasionally glancing over the shoulder of a cohort, before diving back into the circle like a gopher.

Suddenly Veronica was distracted by laughter, *oohs* and *ahhs* coming from an area near some low shrubs. Veronica saw a boy in his late teens, very thin and tall. His arms and legs were extremely hairy, but the hair on his head was already thinning. His teeth were slightly bucked, and his chin almost unformed. A wispy attempt at a beard made him look unkempt. Everyone seemed to be watching him, because he'd caught a sparrow. The bird fluttered its wings and hopped from one of the boy's hands to another, but could not get airborne.

"I haven't hurt it," the boy rasped. "It's an old trick. A little salt on the tail, and it can't fly." He held the bird's legs between his thumb and forefinger. It pecked at him, but the boy distracted the bird with the index finger of his free hand.

"But if it can't fly, it can't live," Veronica objected.

The boy craned his long neck toward her. "It's alive."

"But a cat will get it. It won't stand a chance."

"All the better for the cat," the boy laughed. "Of course, I agree with you. A bird that can't fly is perfectly worthless." With that the boy closed his fist around the body of the bird, and with his free hand snapped its neck. The girls groaned almost in unison. Some of the boys laughed, but still shook their heads in disapproval.

"By all the gods," Veronica cried, "that's the cruelest thing I've ever seen!"

"Then you've seen very little," the hairy boy sneered. He tossed the lifeless carcass into the shrubbery. "What do the gods care about a sparrow?"

"Gaius," a deep voice called. The crowd parted and Veronica recognized Sejanus, the Prefect of the Praetorian Guard. She'd encountered him occasionally over the years, and each time she'd felt the chill of the dread night he'd removed her from her family home.

"Have you had enough revelry?" he accused more than asked. "This seems almost calculated to get you sent home."

"Yes," Gaius snapped. "I'm tired of boring parties with boring people. Especially the pretenders. They're the most boring of all." Then he eyed Veronica strangely, as if expecting her to take his part. He scowled and stomped past her.

"Don't let Little Boots upset you," Sejanus said softly. "Since his father passed, he imagines enemies everywhere. Our poor Caligula." Sejanus tapped a finger on Veronica's chin and strode toward the stairs.

By now Veronica was almost sick to her stomach. Looking around for a place to sit, she noticed that Claudia was not faring much better. Marius was practically standing on her toes, huffing down on her with his stinky breath, causing her eyes to water. *Just like the sulfur on the roof*, Veronica thought.

But Claudia couldn't turn aside, and as she batted away the mist with a flutter of her lashes, her makeup started to run. Veronica watched Claudia reach her arm behind a girlfriend and dig her nails into the poor girl's shoulder blade. The afflicted girl mouthed a silent, but plaintive, *"Ow!"* But she took the hint and grasped Marius by the arm, directing his attention to a nearby statue and peppering him with inane questions about his ancestors. Claudia looked desperately about for Theodosius, and with limpid eyes implored: *Release me!*

Theodosius, leaning on the rail of the veranda, was caught in a similar bind with the elder Catullus. "Tell me, as a priest," the Senator asked, "would you divine them a good match?"

"The ways of the gods are a mystery," Theodosius replied, lowering his stern brow at his daughter. "I'd be more inclined to ask my daughter her preference."

Catullus laughed, incredulous. "Friend Proculus, isn't marriage too important to leave to the whims of girls? Remember, Virgil has written, '*Alas, it is not well for anyone to be confident when the gods are adverse.*'"

"*And* Virgil has written, '*Love conquers all, so let us surrender to love.*'" Theodosius attempted to change the subject. "Anyway, can we be sure the gods themselves don't act upon childish whims?"

"Has the priest lost his faith, Proculus?" Catullus chided.

There followed a moment of tense silence and Veronica sensed a chasm open between the two men. Theodosius looked down to the garden again in time to see Claudia tug at the girlfriend's arm, and bolt around the hedges with friend in tow. Theodosius froze, his daughter's defiance catching him completely off guard.

Veronica felt tempted to follow. No one was talking to her anyway, and she was certain that whatever the punishment, Claudia would get the worst of it. She waited for her uncle to turn his head, and darted out.

Dashing through the garden maze of the Catullus estate, Veronica had a faint sense that the girls were heading toward the river, where the Campus lay. Veronica could only catch up by taking a shortcut, left through a grove of pear trees. Running full out, Veronica kicked a fallen pear, then screeched to a halt when she spied soldiers flanking an old man, bowed under a purple cloak. The pear skipped, striking the old man's ankle. He let loose a muffled groan, and all eyes snapped to her.

"Kneel before Caesar!" a man barked.

Veronica swallowed hard. *Caesar? Here? Five feet away?*

The old man turned slowly toward her. Veronica dropped to her knees and kept her eyes down. Twigs snapped as the Emperor stepped closer. *What had she done?* She had kicked a pear. The pear had struck Caesar. She had struck Caesar! Would she be executed? Would she at least get a trial, where she could explain it had all been an accident? Surely, Caesar would understand. She was only a girl and accidents happened all the time, especially with children. Surely the man who ruled Rome would be wise, would understand. He was probably smiling about it right now. He probably was amused at how frightened she'd become over nothing. He would be looking down on her with mercy and compassion. His face would beam. By now, feeling herself altogether too silly, Veronica sighed, ready to laugh with the Emperor and his men. She lifted her head to greet Caesar and saw... an absolute horror!

The blistered skin of his face was raw meat, covered with yellow film. His rheumy eyes blinked away flies as his lip curled in a snarl revealing yellow teeth and bloody gums. Veronica yelped and ducked her head.

"Arise," the Emperor coughed. Veronica stood slowly, keeping her head down. She stared at their feet; Caesar's were wrapped in linen beneath his sandals, the wraps rising to his knees. Other men wore military boots. "A simple curtsey would suffice. A daughter of Rome should not lie in the dust."

Veronica brushed dirt and dry leaves from her legs.

"Th-thank you, Cae-Caesar," she stammered. Caesar turned away. His shoulders seemed hunched even more. She'd embarrassed him, she knew. She'd shown fear, not because he was Caesar, but because he was monstrous. Yet how could she apologize for reacting without causing more offense? Desperate for a clue, she looked to the military man who'd ordered her to kneel. He was broad shouldered and tall. His hair curled in tight ringlets on his forehead. His features were handsome, but weathered; the architecture of his face had shifted under the buffets of many battles.

"Well, be gone!" barked the military man. "Caesar has no use of you."

Veronica nodded and scurried past. She resumed running, although now she knew not where. At the far edge of the pear grove, a path led along a low stone wall. The trees became sparse, and Veronica saw the Campus Martius opening before her. This was the practice field, where several weeks ago Claudia had first glimpsed the man she claimed to love. Claudia would not watch the games in the open; any girl who publicly showed interest in boys would bring shame on her family. Veronica knew she'd find her cousin hunched in the midst of a thicket, peering through branches and brambles.

That's precisely where she was, squatted shoulder to shoulder and ear to ear with her friend from the party. Veronica stooped under some low branches and duck-walked towards them, rustling leaves and snapping twigs, until the girls spun around.

"Oh, your cousin," the girlfriend yawned.

"She follows me everywhere," Claudia griped.

Veronica stifled her objection. It wouldn't do any good to argue that she never followed Claudia on the one occasion she had. Instead she tried to impress them.

"I saw the Emperor," she whispered dramatically.

The girlfriend gasped. "How close?"

"As close as you are."

The girlfriend's jaw dropped. Claudia moved immediately to reclaim focus.

"Oh, tell us another. At home we call her Aesop. A story for every occasion."

"That's not true," Veronica huffed. "I did see him, and I saw his face!"

"Is he as bad as they say?" the girlfriend asked.

Veronica had no idea what "they say," but still chimed, "Worse!" Then piled on the drama as Claudia rolled her eyes. "Oh, he's like a dead person back from the grave. Swollen and decaying."

"They say it's leprosy," the girlfriend whispered. That disease could not be spoken of with a full voice.

"I don't care," Claudia groaned. "Who cares about sick, old men, or what they're dying from? Or silly little boys with rich fathers? Did you see all those statues Catullus had? How much did he pay the sculptor to add muscles and straighten their spines? Ha!"

The girls ducked, covering their mouths. A troop of young men ran across the field, kicking a leather ball along the grass. They bumped shoulders and hips, tangled arms and legs, jabbed with elbows. The ball soared to the far end and they chased after it.

"Was he there?"

"No," Claudia pouted.

The girls remained in the thicket for another half hour. Finally the game with the leather ball ended, and the young men yielded the field. Across the way, two men set up a mannequin shaped from a tree trunk. It held a wooden sword and shield. The men then crossed the field towards the hiding place. They stood within earshot, as Claudia blurted out, "That's him!"

That was the first look Veronica had of young Pontius Pilate. He was tallish and lean, the hair on his large head dark and straight. His nose and chin were sharp, but delicate. His shoulders were broad, his waist and hips narrow, and his chest tight rather than expansive. He took a javelin from his servant and balanced it in his hand. Leaning slightly back and trotting forward, he raised the lance high, and whipping his lithe frame toward the target, cut a straight line through the air to the center of the mannequin. The javelin pierced the dumb foe with a hollow *"thunk!"*

Claudia turned to the other girls and beamed. "He's the best on the field."

Veronica had never seen a spear thrown before, but could not imagine it being done any better. A servant yanked the javelin from the mannequin and trotted it back to its owner. The girls chittered with excitement as Pilate grasped the javelin again. He must have heard, for Pilate glanced over, a flash of recognition forcing a half-smile. *Did he know it was Claudia*, Veronica wondered, *or would any wayward girl's attention have pleased him?*

"Ave, Pilate!" a voice boomed. Pilate snapped to a military posture and the girls recoiled into the thicket. Two men approached, apparently his superiors, and Veronica recognized both: Sejanus and the military man from Caesar's escort.

"Afraid I've bragged too much about you to Macro[21]," Sejanus joked. "Now he demands visual evidence."

Macro, broader and more muscular than Pilate, nodded to the servant holding the weapon. The servant offered and Macro gripped the javelin, weighing and balancing it.

"Not that I distrust the word of a Prefect who's conducted his affairs with such scrupulous honesty," Macro mused. "But shouldn't all in Rome rejoice when Caesar's body grows another strong arm?"

Macro lifted the javelin above his shoulder, trotted a few paces and let the spear fly. It found its mark, striking and sticking in the mannequin's neck. The men acknowledged Macro's impressive throw, and he bowed, graciously if not modestly. Pilate breathed deeply and gestured to the servant for a javelin. All he had to do was duplicate his last effort, but how easily could that be done under such intense scrutiny? He lifted the lance and loped forward, coiling back and springing forward, unleashing such force he nearly fell to his knees.

The girls craned forward following the high, arcing flight until it landed square in the mannequin's chest. He'd hit the heart.

Pilate smiled broadly, revealing a row of straight, white teeth. Macro gave only a stoic nod of approval. Sejanus clapped the protégé on the shoulder, bowing his mouth to Pilate's ear.

"Bravo, Pontius. You'll do well."

Claudia's sigh was audible. It startled Sejanus and made Pilate blush. Sejanus peered into the briar at the girls ducking from sight. Veronica could tell he recognized Claudia, but he had to; he knew her too well. The Prefect's face turned stony, and his voice was cold and measured: "But not that well."

That brought a halt to the exercise. Sejanus signaled the servants to clear the field, and marched Pilate away with Macro.

The girls relaxed. Claudia and her friend dissolved into giggles.

"Claudia's getting married!" her friend teased.

"Shh!" Claudia warned. "You'll jinx me. The gods will hear, and they'll be so jealous, they'll say, *No mortal girl should be so happy!* And they'll send thunderbolts down to smash the Earth between us. They'll split the Earth in two, because only that will keep us apart!"

"Oh, why do you think the gods should care?" her friend laughed.

"Because," Claudia lectured, "when we're happy, we're not afraid. And they want us to be afraid. Especially of them."

Veronica couldn't tell if Claudia had lost her mind or found some terrible wisdom. However, her cousin did seem to realize that arranging her marriage to Pontius Pilate was not going to be easy. Veronica didn't know why there was

---

[21] Quintus Naevius Cordus Sutorius Macro (21 BC – 38 AD) became a prefect of the Praetorian Guard, serving Emperors Tiberius and Caligula

a problem, but clearly there was. If Sejanus had reacted so sternly, how would Theodosius react when he found out?

Chapter 3

It was several weeks before Veronica learned how her Uncle Theodosius would greet the news of Claudia's romance. In the meantime, she had to deal with his reaction to their disappearance from Catullus' party. By the time the girls had returned — exhausted — from the Campus, the only people left in the garden were the slaves cleaning up. Adrianna ushered the girls inside at once and started cleaning them, picking the leaves and grass off their tunics and washing their legs, feet and hands. Claudia's makeup could not be salvaged; Adrianna scrubbed her face clean. After several minutes of intense activity, Adrianna sent word upstairs that the Proculus ladies — who had been generously assisting in the kitchen to demonstrate the worth of their domestic skills — were ready to say their good-byes to the gentlemen. Adrianna hoped to plant the notion that these serious-minded girls preferred service to supercilious socializing. The gentlemen, who'd been wondering for hours what had become of the runaways, accepted this explanation as not the truth, but a fiction that would cause less offense. Thus, the girls would not be ridiculed for rude, wild behavior, and Marius Catullus would not be held up as an odious bore.

However, the fiction did not suffice at home. Theodosius demanded the truth and got — not the whole story of watching Pilate from the thicket, but — enough to convict Claudia. At first she maintained that her father had projected enough sympathy for her plight that she was reasonable to extrapolate permission to flee. But under stern interrogation, Claudia conceded her father would never have condoned behavior he'd admonished her for just a few weeks earlier. The offense earned Claudia five stripes across the back of her legs with a rod cut from a sapling in their backyard. Some skin was broken, and dabs of blood were drawn. Claudia sat for a week on the very edge of her stool. Veronica had earned two lashes, which raised pink to purple welts, but did not draw blood. She also got a strict warning that this was the last time her punishment would be mitigated because of her age and Claudia's influence. Theodosius himself seemed to suffer worst from the strokes. Throughout all the time the girls recovered, he sat bolt upright on his stool, and never smiled during any of their meals. It was only after Claudia started sitting comfortably that her father seemed to relax, and the household appeared to return to normal. But then one evening Sejanus came to call, and the whole affair was brought back to the surface.

"I have attempted to reason with the boy," the Prefect intimated. "He has talent, intellect. He has the carriage of Roman nobility."

"But not the pedigree," Theodosius proffered.

"Unfortunately, no."

The two men circled the garden in silence. Theodosius laced his fingers together behind his back, and rocked from one foot to another. His nostrils flared as he considered the dilemma. From her vantage point, crouched behind the rampart of the veranda, Veronica could not discern his attitude. Clearly, he was annoyed, but at what or whom was unclear.

"The Samnites[22] have lived under the yoke of Rome for three centuries," he said. "We call them citizens."

"From citizen to Senator is an Olympian[23] climb," Sejanus lamented. "Your office might welcome a soldier who distinguished himself on the battlefield. But a veritably unknown youth, climbing in rank because his smile wins the favor of a Senator's daughter? It will incite jealousy. It will create enemies for him, and for you, Theodosius."

"You're hardly making a case for him, Sejanus."

"I vouch for Pilate's talent and character. But I cannot ignore the consequences of his request."

Theodosius nodded. "I am inclined to agree. But when I look at the boys of our station, I see slack limbs, curved backs and thin, craning necks. Where is the vitality that once was Rome? I fear we've wasted our best on the battlefield, while those who stayed at home, safely in bed, bred an elite but bloodless class, which shall be the ruin of Rome. New blood may be necessary."

"What you're saying," Sejanus mused, "would be heresy to your colleagues in the Senate."

"Let my colleagues in the Senate breed sons worthy of Rome." With that Theodosius bid Sejanus good-night. He walked the Prefect to the front door. Veronica and Claudia scurried inside and watched the visitor depart. As Theodosius closed the door he turned and lifted his eyes toward the second floor.

"Claudia," he spoke effortlessly, knowing full well she'd been eavesdropping, "come down, please."

Claudia rose, showing herself above the railing. She walked down the stairs and stood before Theodosius.

"Yes, Father?"

---

[22] An Italian ethnic group conquered by Rome
[23] Referring to Mount Olympus, the mythical home of the gods

"I've received a request for your hand in marriage. I have every reason to believe it will create difficulties for you and the boy. You will be scorned for marrying beneath your class. He will be ostracized for marrying above his."

"But I love him, Father."

Theodosius shook his head. "More important than the easy affection of love is the firmness of duty. Love is variable. Duty is fixed. Love may be the heart of marriage, but duty is its spine." He turned away from her and paced over to the reflecting pool. He gazed at himself, perhaps searching for the certainty on his face that he could not sense in his voice. "I must question the boy. We'll speak no more of this until I do."

Agonizing days passed. Each night, Theodosius paced the atrium, the garden and the veranda. Each morning at breakfast, his stony face greeted the girls and another round of silence began. Little did the girls know that Theodosius was himself being forced to wait. A butcher's apprentice, a young plebeian who delivered meat to the Proculus kitchen, told Adrianna what he'd heard at the Catullus home.

"Senator Catullus has petitioned Caesar to intervene, to prevent Mistress Claudia's marriage to Pilate." He placed a bundle on the kitchen table and unwrapped a leg of mutton. He mopped his brow with a rag as Adrianna assessed the freshness of the meat. The young plebeian cast an eye toward Claudia. "It seems Marius has his heart set on you, Mistress. Senator Catullus insists rank should determine the issue."

"As it well should," Adrianna snapped. "If only to keep your likes from addressing a child of this house." She pressed a coin into the plebeian's palm and urged him toward the door. He objected, asserting that even he might someday marry a lady. That earned the upstart a shove out the door.

"The gods forbid!" Adrianna gasped. "This is what comes from social climbing. Insolence from the rabble."

But Claudia was angrier at Adrianna than the too-forward apprentice. "You'd have me wed to Marius?"

"Oh, your father would never..."

"But if Caesar commands?" Claudia grabbed a huge knife from the counter. She gripped it with both hands and with a broad sweep placed the tip at her sternum. "If Caesar gives Marius my heart, I'll cut it out!"

Adrianna rolled her eyes and extended her hand, demanding the knife. "Perhaps you should wait until your father's had his audience with the Emperor?"

Claudia handed the weapon over. "I'll fall on Father's sword!" she declared.

Adrianna started slicing the mutton down to the bone. "If you must commit suicide, please choose a bloodless method! You know I'll be cleaning it up."

"I'll hang myself!"

"That's my girl!"

Despite the playful teasing, Veronica was apprehensive. She'd had something terrible on her mind all week. "When is Uncle Theo meeting with the Emperor?" Veronica asked.

"Today," came the answer, from behind her head.

Veronica spun to see her uncle in his finest toga. He was newly shaved and his hair was oiled. He glowered at Claudia, "Do you think you can delay killing yourself until I return?"

Claudia crossed her arms over her chest and puffed her cheeks. "I don't know."

Veronica needed to say her peace. She had to warn Theodosius. "Uncle," she asked, "have you seen Caesar before?"

Theodosius raised an inquisitive eyebrow. "What are you asking, Veronica?"

"It's just," she hung her head guiltily, "I saw him. You should prepare yourself."

His eyes bored into her. "When did you see the Emperor?"

Veronica shut her mouth. She tried to keep it shut, but somehow the words came gushing out. "The day we ran away. I ran through a pear tree grove. He was there. I saw his face."

Theodosius swallowed. "You didn't... react, did you?"

Veronica felt her eyes brimming. "Well... I might have, maybe, *yelped*."

Theodosius smacked the heel of his palm against his forehead. Veronica could feel the rod coming down on her bare legs again. But, after expelling a breath, Theodosius simply muttered, "What's done is done." He adjusted the toga on his shoulder, and strode for the door.

"Wait, Father," Claudia whined. "What about Senator Catullus? How are you going to stop him from demanding me for Marius?"

Theodosius snorted. "Perhaps I should offer Veronica."

Claudia smiled, delighted with the idea. Adrianna shook her head and chuckled. Veronica sank onto her stool. Suddenly, a few strokes of the rod looked comparatively good.

The hours that passed were miserable, anxious and worrisome. Veronica fretted that Caesar would punish Theodosius (and by extension Claudia) for how his snotty, little niece had reacted in the pear grove. Adrianna worried Claudia might become hysterical and hurt herself. And Claudia was absolutely panicked. *Lose Pontius and have Marius forced on her?* Veronica asked if she'd gleaned any comfort from her dreams, but Claudia snapped back, "How can I dream if I can't sleep?" True enough, Claudia's agitation had kept them both awake all week. Both girls were now so jittery and short-tempered, Adrianna had to separate them, keeping Claudia in the kitchen and sending Veronica to her room, where she finally fell into a deep sleep. ·

She awakened to hear horses trotting up the street and wagon wheels rumbling before grinding to a stop. She stood on the second-floor landing overlooking the atrium as Claudia and Adrianna came running from the kitchen. The tall door was thrown open and a smiling Theodosius clapped his hand on the firm shoulder of Pontius Pilate. "Ladies," he beamed, "I finally have a son!"

Speechless, Claudia ran to Pilate's arms and hugged him tightly. She took his hand and led him out to the garden. Then Theodosius raised his eyes to Veronica and playfully admonished her.

"Oh, Veronica, you've got to pack. Senator Catullus expects you." Veronica stuck her tongue out and crinkled up her face. As she padded out to the veranda, her uncle's laughter reverberated through the atrium. Out on the veranda, Veronica crouched behind the railing, spying between the posts at the young lovers. They walked hand in hand as Pilate unburdened himself of the afternoon's drama.

"Caesar called me in and fired all manner of questions at me. Accusations, really. That I was a schemer. A social climber. An opportunist. That young men with no worlds to conquer will rise through intrigue."

"What did you answer?"

"As Sejanus had coached me, *Some men rise to serve.*"

Claudia hugged her future husband around the waist. His face suddenly went dark. "Catullus was vicious," he whispered. "Said I was creeping close to Caesar to plunge a lance through his heart."

"Oh, don't pay any attention to that old serpent," Claudia said. She soothed Pilate's brow with a delicate wipe of her fingertips. He closed his eyes, then laughed and sprang forward.

"That's when Sejanus said, *Have you seen Pilate throw a lance, Senator? He needn't be so close!* So Caesar had me demonstrate, and I think hitting the target from across the piazza, I guess that won him over. That and your father."

Claudia seemed a little afraid, but nevertheless inquired, "What did my father say?"

"When I was there, he only said that he believed I loved you. But then he asked that I and the other men be dismissed, so that he could speak to Caesar privately. I don't know what he said then," Pilate beamed, "but obviously, it worked."

Pilate caressed Claudia's face, lifting her mouth to his, and they kissed. Then Veronica was startled by a sharp tap on her head.

"Rome has enough intrigue," Theodosius whispered, "without you spying on your cousin." Veronica scooted away from the railing, stood and headed for the house.

But a thought occurred to her, and she turned back to ask, "Uncle, Caesar's face, can't anything be done?"

Theodosius only shrugged, "Some things we must leave to the gods," which sounded very much like simply giving up.

That night Claudia was full of talk about her upcoming nuptials. At first Veronica shared her excitement, but as the hours wore on and Claudia wouldn't stop talking, Veronica needed to sleep.

"This is turning out just as I dreamed," Claudia sighed.

"I thought you weren't dreaming," Veronica groaned, "because you couldn't get to sleep!"

"I don't mean *'dream'* dreamed," Claudia huffed. "I mean how I hoped."

"Well, I was hoping we'd both go to sleep!"

With that Claudia rolled over, grumbled about Veronica being jealous, and soon fell asleep.

*   *   *   *

Claudia's wedding fell on a bright April day, evincing that spring had routed the lingering forces of winter. Remnants of dark clouds receded to the very margins of the sky, and what opened was a dome of the purest blue. Theodosius, despite his occasional disparaging comments, was still a temple priest and still performed rituals of divination when an occasion called. He sacrificed several birds to the gods, and, examining the entrails, pronounced the day auspicious.

Claudia herself outshone the sky. Dressed in a pure white palla and stola, her auburn hair adorned with white roses, she looked ready to ascend Olympus. Pilate was handsome in a shining breastplate, red cape and olive laurels. Veronica tossed flower petals before the couple as they ascended the temple stairs. There, Theodosius burned incense to the gods, white smoke that rose triumphantly, and wound a cord around the couple's wrists symbolizing their bond. Their promises to each other were sealed with a kiss, and then the whole party descended the stairs, anticipating several nights of celebration.

However, a commotion arose on the street. Passersby scattered, opening a path for a racing chariot leading an ornate carriage. Carved into the carriage's wooden flanks was the seal of Caesar, the profile image of Emperor Tiberius, or at least what his profile might be, were his face not so ravaged with disease. The pennants of the Emperor whipped in the wind, then fell limp as the carriage stopped.

The crowd fell to their knees, and Veronica felt a sudden pressure on her shoulder: Theodosius urging her down. As she knelt, Veronica tried to peer into the carriage, but its windows were covered with heavy drapes. Suddenly one of the drapes was pulled aside.

Caesar's charioteer called toward the kneeling assembly. "Pontius Pilate. Caesar commands a word."

Claudia gripped Pilate's hand tightly; he had to peel her fingers off, patting her hand gently, before she let him step forward. As Pilate approached Caesar, he kept his head bowed slightly in reverence. Caesar's cowled head was now visible past the drape. Veronica had to strain to make out what the Emperor said. His chilling whisper made the hair on her neck stand up.

"Pilate, after much consideration, I've chosen a post that matches your talents."

"Thank you, Caesar," the young man answered.

A gnarled, pink hand emerged, clutching a wax tablet. Pilate opened the tablet and read. His face dropped. "Judea?"

Caesar chuckled in a dry, mirthless tone. "Beastly place," he said, then cast a jaundiced eye at Claudia. "Unfit for a flower of Rome. But for a young lion? A place to distinguish yourself. If you love your Emperor, you can prove yourself a noble Roman. If not, you'll do us no harm."

The curtain dropped again, and a thump was heard from within. The charioteer snapped his reins, again clearing a path for the imperial coach. The crowd stood as the vehicles rumbled past. Veronica rubbed her sore knees. Her uncle consoled the newlyweds.

"Come," he said, "let's not allow this news to dampen our celebration. We can deal with all this tomorrow."

Pilate shook his head, staring again at the tablet. "My orders. I leave tonight."

Chapter 4

29 A.D.

Veronica tried to stand still. She imagined herself a marble statue, high on a pedestal. Then the needle jabbed her side. She flinched and nearly teetered off the stool.

"So sorry, Mistress," Paenulus winced. "Forgive me. Again."

It was the third time the tailor had stuck her. If the palla were not such fine cloth, if Veronica were not absolutely sure she was going to be the envy of every girl in Rome when it was finished, she'd have stormed off after the first prick. But she also felt sorry for Paenulus: the grey cataract that had covered his left eye with that revolting film certainly was not his fault. How tragic that a craftsman who relied on his vision should lose it so suddenly. So thoroughly. Claudia insisted it was further evidence that the gods were capricious and cruel, and mortals were just their playthings. She'd held this opinion for three years, since Pilate had been ordered to Judea on their wedding night.

Veronica often recalled the tumult of that day. After Pontius had received his orders, the family had returned home. Adrianna had labored, and Theodosius insisted that the great feast proceed. Musicians played, jugglers performed, servants poured wine and passed trays heaping with food. But few of the guests had any appetite. Only Catullus seemed amused, and beamed beside his shame-faced son as the two greeted the newlyweds.

"As I've often said, *Alas, none can be confident when the gods are adverse,*" he gloated.

"Father, must you quote Virgil now?" Marius groaned. For what it was worth, Marius seemed deeply embarrassed.

Pilate shook Senator Catullus' hand — a collection of twigs he could easily have snapped — and remarked dryly, "There is something to be said for meeting adversity. And recognizing adversaries."

The excruciating party plodded through several courses, until Veronica noticed that Claudia was gone! The stress must have been too much and she'd had taken to the streets again. Pontius had to be told; it was now his duty to discipline his wife. But she didn't see him either. Veronica searched from room to room, before plowing directly into Little Boots. His bony elbow caught her right on the jaw, setting off sparks before her eyes.

"Ow," she groaned.

"My, you're in an awful hurry," he laughed, rubbing his elbow.

"What are you doing here?"

"Your uncle couldn't hold a wedding without inviting the whole family," he sneered. "So for the sake of good manners, I have to spend an entire afternoon and evening bored to death."

Veronica didn't want to believe they were even distant relatives. "You weren't at the temple."

"The gods and I had a falling out. Around the time my father was murdered. Which was just before your father was murdered." Little Boots peered at Veronica as though he were studying an insect.

"My father died in a battle," she huffed. "In a war far away."

"The battle was far away," he whispered, then checked each direction down the hallway before adding, "but the war is here at home."

"What are you talking about? And why am I even listening to you?"

"You're listening," he hissed, "because my words could save your life."

Veronica felt her head getting cluttered, and shook it hard, like one of her greyhounds come in from the rain. She remembered Claudia. "I have to go. Enjoy being bored."

Veronica left Gaius Caligula in the hall, but somehow she felt him stick like spiderwebs draped across a garden path, making her skin crawl. Did he really have secret knowledge? Was the world so dangerous that what had happened to her parents could happen to her? No wonder Claudia would run away, and no wonder Pilate would agree. He'd want to protect her, even if he had to defy Caesar. He'd take her somewhere safe. But was anywhere safe when Caesar's arm reached everywhere? Even to Gaul[24] and Hispania[25]?

In the kitchen, Veronica found Adrianna. "We've got to stop Claudia!" she blurted out.

Adrianna paused over a pile of scraps she'd swept up. "Why would you want to stop her?"

"She's only going to make things worse!"

"Make what worse?" Adrianna grunted.

"What if Caesar finds out?"

Adrianna straightened and stretched her back. "I imagine Caesar expects it. But if you must stop her, you should hurry. Off to the bedroom."

Veronica blinked and wagged her head. "She's here?"

"With her husband. One chance to conceive before he's gone to Judea. But I'm sure she'd welcome your interruption. Considering she'll see him soon enough, in four or five years."

"Well, you don't have to be sarcastic!" Veronica snapped.

"Don't have to," Adrianna shrugged, "but occasionally I enjoy it."

Veronica spent the next hour slumped on the stairs, watching Senators who'd had too much wine lurch toward the door and wondering if Claudia would actually conceive a child. All the time she'd talked about marriage, Claudia had never mentioned wanting a baby. Her own mother had died in childbirth. Veronica imagined pregnancy would frighten Claudia terribly, and,

---

[24] Modern-day France
[25] Spain

even if she survived, she'd still be afraid. How could she be a mother if she'd never known one?

Eventually, Claudia and Pontius came downstairs, looking uncertain and sad. Veronica wondered if they could know whether their attempt at a child had failed. Or did they know they'd succeeded? And did that make parting even more painful?

Sejanus was still there; he'd arranged a wagon to take the family to the dock to give Pontius a proper farewell. Not a word was spoken as the horses clopped, hoof on stone, and wooden wheels ground toward the river. It might have been a funeral procession, and Pilate's quinterime[26] a barge whose pyre[27] they'd light and set adrift. Only Sejanus, driving the team, tried to lift their spirits. He bantered about the sea, the reach of the Empire, how Pilate was sailing to the very rim of the world. Veronica strained to see the ship: the bronze ram at its bow gleamed with the last rays of the evening sun. Behind it, three massive, wooden decks lolled, row upon row of oars dipped into the water, and a huge mast rose up to the sky. Sejanus halted the wagon and the party hopped down.

Sejanus hooked Pilate by the elbow and led him toward the ship. "The Jews are thick-necked people," he whispered. "Wretched, obstinate vermin. A few lucky accidents in the past have convinced them their god will deliver them. He can't prevent them from being conquered, but he'll aid any petty revolt. Remember, you are the face of the Empire. Show strength. Grind them into the sand if you must."

Pilate nodded. He took Claudia's hands in his. "I'll leave my heart here."

"Good boy," Sejanus smiled. "You'll do well." He then drew Theodosius near and continued. "Caesar has intimated he may leave Rome. His appearance makes it quite impossible to rule from home."

"I heard it's leprosy," Claudia said.

"Shh," Pilate warned her.

Sejanus pressed on, "Most likely he'll reside at Capri. He'll have to appoint a regent. It's possible that if the regent were well disposed toward you, Pontius, you could return at the end of the standard term." All held their breath for a beat. "Four years."

Claudia wailed, "No!" and Pilate hugged her close. "What kind of king punishes love? It's wicked. Wicked."

"Hush, Claudia," he whispered, "We've a long life ahead. Years and years to love."

"Now," Sejanus pursed his lips, "I am prepared to offer my services to Caesar, as his regent. But I will need allies. Influential Senators."

Claudia wiped her eyes and looked to her father. Theodosius leaned against the rail of the pier, a crouching sphinx[28], his thoughts an unknowable

---

[26] A warship of the Roman navy
[27] Bonfire used to burn a corpse in lieu of burial

riddle. Then, as if a cold splash brought him back to consciousness, he coughed, "Of course. Whatever I can do, Sejanus." He extended his hand. Sejanus smiled, as he formed a tight grip around the Senator's wrist.

It had been three years since Claudia had held Pilate, kissed him and whispered, "Vale[29], my love." And even though their separation had been ordered by one man, Tiberius Caesar, on the instigation of another, old Marcus Catullus, Claudia's flair for the dramatic had extrapolated her misfortune into a theory of the universe: the gods hate it when humans are happy.

Her dreams offered confirmation. Six months after Pontius left, Claudia dreamed he had built a great aqueduct across a chain of mountains in Judea. It was wide as a river and deep as an ocean. Pontius stood before its straining gates and called upon the gods to bless the water he'd brought to Jerusalem. The Jews came forward with jars. Their skin was dry as papyrus. Their eyes swollen shut. They begged for water and Pontius laughed. "Here, drink!" he exclaimed, "Living water!" and threw open the gates. A torrent of red rushed forward. The frightened Jews flailed about in a city flooded with blood. To Veronica's mind, the dream had no basis in reality. Nothing in Pilate's letters hinted at any difficulty. But Claudia still suspected the gods were conspiring against her husband's success. Then his letters stopped.

Claudia's dark ruminations started to color Veronica's worldview. Now fourteen, Veronica was eligible for marriage. She hoped to find a boy she could love, but love had not brought Claudia happiness. Claudia's one evening of love had not even yielded a child. And now it had been months since she'd received her last letter from Pontius. *What good was love?* And what good was Veronica's standing — getting jabbed by a blind tailor — simply to have a dress that might attract a husband whom Caesar could then send to the rim of the world?

"Ouch!" Veronica cried and pulled the cloth away. She'd been jabbed enough for one day and, against Paenulus' protests, jumped down from the stool.

"Please," the slave implored, "don't tell Master Theo. I can't be put out to beg!"

Veronica pulled the palla over her head. She grabbed her tunic and dressed. "Do you really think he'd do that? Set you free to wander the streets?"

"Some do. A slave only has value when he can work." Paenulus' lip trembled, and he wept.

"You don't think you're worth more than your labor?" she asked. "You're part of this house." But the old man would not be consoled. Veronica tightened the sash around her waist and slipped out the door.

---

[28] A mythical creature, a fierce guardian of sacred places, that posed impossible questions that mortals couldn't figure out
[29] Farewell

As she descended the stairs, she heard voices in the kitchen: Adrianna and Claudia were at it again. They fought often these days. Since her marriage, Claudia imagined herself lady of the house, but Adrianna was loath to relinquish her authority. Each tried to enlist Veronica to her side, but when their voices rose, she simply stayed away. Now, as she tried to scoot by the kitchen door, Claudia burst through, stared at Veronica with clenched jaw and, without so much as a word, marched past her toward the atrium. *She's leaving*, Veronica thought; *that should buy us an hour or two of peace*. But then she heard music, a piper playing low from the atrium, and remembered Theodosius had planned a sacrifice. She walked quietly into the atrium and took a seat near Claudia on a marble bench between the reflecting pool and the family altar.

Many of the household servants were already seated on the floor. Adrianna and Paenulus answered the call of the piper. Veronica watched the kitchen maid place a cushion down; the tailor helped her onto the floor before easing himself down beside her. When all were seated, Theodosius approached the altar and, with his back to the assembly, offered a prayer to Janus, the god of beginnings, the guardian of gates and doors, and the caretaker of the universe. His image hung over the left side of the altar, showing two faces: a bearded man and a clean-shaven youth. On the right side of the altar hung the image of Vesta. She sat upon a cathedra, holding a scepter in one hand and a bowl from which a serpent ate in the other. The ceremony would conclude with a prayer to her, for she represented the survival of the family from generation to generation. But first there would be a sacrifice and, from the entrails of that animal, Theodosius would attempt to divine what may have happened to Pontius and why his wife had received no word for months.

The piper brought forth a crow. A hood had been placed over its head to make it docile. Theodosius sprinkled grain over the bird then dabbed his fingers in a chalice of wine and flicked several drops onto the crow. After he took a sip of wine, Theodosius took a sharp knife and slit the bird's throat. He drained the bird's blood into a pan and laid the body out on the altar. Theodosius then slit the carcass, exposing the entrails. He sifted through the organs, attempting to read some portent regarding Pilate or Claudia. He then tossed the entrails onto the flames of the pyre, causing a billow of grey smoke. After a moment, he tossed the limp crow onto the fire as well. Then without a word or a glance to Claudia, Theodosius signaled for another bird, this time a white dove. He repeated the ritual and slaughtered the dove. Again he attempted to read the entrails, tossed them onto the pyre and waited for the smoke to rise before dispatching the dove's carcass.

Then Theodosius turned slightly toward Claudia and, looking more towards the floor than her, muttered, "He is well." A general sigh of relief went up, and Theodosius offered a quick prayer to the *lares familiaris* — household gods, who were ghosts of the Proculus ancestors — before ending with the prayer to Vesta.

Veronica was relieved to stand after sitting so long on the hard bench. But Claudia didn't move. She continued to stare at her father, who puttered around the altar. He drained the chalice of wine, his face flushing as he swallowed. He handed the cup to one of the servants, then gave the pan of blood to another. A slave came forward with a bowl for Theodosius to wash his hands. He washed and dried them, handed the towel back to the slave, and walked out of the atrium. Not once did he look at Claudia.

After a breath, Claudia popped from the bench, turned away from Veronica, and without looking back demanded, "Come."

"Where?" Veronica asked.

"Shopping."

Veronica felt her shoulders tighten. This was not going to be fun.

Since she had gotten married, Claudia had enjoyed more freedom to move about the city. So, whenever things got too tense between herself and Adrianna, or herself and Theodosius, or herself and any of the household slaves, Claudia would march down the Via Sacra[30] towards the forum, where numerous shops catered to the wealthier Roman classes. Though Pontius had not written in many months, he had arranged through Sejanus that Claudia be given an allowance. Since she still lived under her father's roof, Claudia had no household expenses, so she could spend her allowance on anything she desired, and Claudia seemed to desire anything she laid eyes on. Veronica thought her spending sprees frivolous: how many rings should a woman own, when she only had ten fingers? How many gauntlets, bracelets and necklaces could a woman wear before the sheer weight made her limbs immobile? And yet, as frivolous as Claudia's sprees were, they were never lighthearted. There was always a sense of grim determination, as though Claudia could work some magic by acquiring trinkets that pleased her senses. It never had much of a lasting effect; Claudia's troubles returned as soon as she reentered the home.

Still, Veronica indulged her cousin, because it got her out of the house more often, and because Claudia, on occasion, would buy a trinket for her. Of course, Claudia would choose something for her that suited Claudia's taste. Veronica might admire an amber necklace for the way the sunlight played upon it, but Claudia would order her to "Leave that for the plebeians." Only gold and gems were fit for the Senatorial class, to which Claudia insisted she still belonged, despite having married down to the Equestrians.

Today, Claudia marched with special urgency, past the spice shops, where she'd often buy incense and perfume, past shoe shops, where she'd usually try on thirty pairs of sandals before finding the perfect fit, past book shops, where she'd listen for hours to poets reading from their latest works.

---

[30] The Sacred Road was the main street of Rome passing the most important religious sites on the way to the Forum

"Where are we going?" Veronica finally asked.

"To buy something I don't have," Claudia said. Then, amused at the puzzlement she must have read on Veronica's face, she laughed. "And to fix my problems in the kitchen." Veronica was at a loss. They had passed the food stands. Passed the artisans who sold knives, pots and bowls. They had wandered to the farthest point of the commercial area. Veronica's mouth dropped open. "No."

"Yes," Claudia smiled. "I'm going to buy my own slave."

"Did you ask your father?"

"I don't have to ask Father," Claudia laughed. "I informed my husband. If he'd wanted to forbid me, he should have written back."

"You're going to buy a slave because you're angry with Pontius?"

"No."

"Because you're angry with Adrianna."

"No," she stated, but with a tone less sure. "Father hasn't bought a new slave in fifteen years. Now they're all old and broken down. Those boys who used to work for Paenulus? They were someone else's slaves, but we trained them as fullers and tailors. Now they work for their masters, and we have a blind, old fool who can't sew a stitch without drawing blood."

"So," Veronica concluded, "you're going to buy a slave because you're mad at Uncle Theo."

"Look, cousin," Claudia stated coldly, "Adrianna is constantly complaining about her aches and pains. Soon she'll be no good at all. It's time to get a young girl and have Adrianna train her, so we can be done with her."

"Be done with Adrianna? She practically raised you. Like a mother."

"Please! If she's like a mother, I'm glad I never had one." Claudia clamped her jaw shut at that point, opening her purse and taking inventory of her coins.

"Do you even know what a slave costs?" Veronica asked.

"How much can they be?" Claudia answered vaguely. "The city's full of them, and more arrive every day."

The girls then looked at the long bench on which several male slaves, shackled at the legs, sat. They were northern barbarians with sandy hair. Their fair skin was red and peeling in places where the harsh Mediterranean sun had burnt and blistered them. They were heavily muscled, destined to be sold as laborers for the many construction projects in the city. Farther down was a bench of young girls who hung their veiled heads. A Roman, slightly older than Theodosius, but wearing the narrow striped toga of the Equestrian rank, gestured toward one of the girls, and the slave merchant bid her to stand.

She was taller and broader in the shoulders than a Roman girl, but had a young face, which, aside from a dusting of freckles, was pale as milk. Her hair was the color of straw. "She's so white," Claudia remarked.

The Equestrian gestured again, and the slave merchant pulled at the back of the girl's tunic. He tightened it against her chest, waist and hips, allowing the man to assess her figure. The merchant permitted him then to squeeze her shoulders, arms, thighs and buttocks. The girls winced, but did not resist.

"Buy her," Veronica said.

Claudia snorted, "What?"

"Buy her. Now."

"Are you so sure she can cook?" Claudia huffed.

"I'm very sure he doesn't care." Veronica glared at Claudia and practically groaned at her obtuseness, until her cousin looked again at the man pressing the inside of the girl's thighs.

"Excuse me," Claudia blurted, stepping toward the merchant. "How does this work? Is there a set price? For this girl here?"

The slave merchant narrowed his eyes at Claudia. "This girl? I've offered her to this gentleman for 800 denarii."

Claudia looked askance at the coins in her palm. Still she declared, "I'll give you eight-twenty-five."

The merchant tipped his head back to the Equestrian, who tightened his jaw and said flatly, "Nine hundred."

Claudia immediately countered, "Nine-twenty-five."

The slave merchant smiled and pressed his palms together, delighted at the bidding.

"Show some sense, Mistress," the Equestrian grunted. "Nine-fifty."

"Nine hundred eighty."

The Equestrian stroked his grey chin stubble with the back of his hand. "I'm not a bad man, Mistress. I recently lost my wife. I'm too old to remarry. Should I suffer in loneliness?"

"Should she suffer in your embrace?"

"One thousand denarii!"

"Thousand fifty!"

The Equestrian was now quite red in the face. His mouth frothed. "Will you buy all of them? Because I'm determined to take a girl home today. Unless you buy every girl on that bench, I'll have one!" Having made the point about the firmness of his desire, he softened his tone and lowered his voice. "Now, if pity for the girl is what motivates you, Mistress, consider this. If I get the girl I want, she'll be treated well. If you force me to take another, well, then none of us will end up happy." He breathed deeply through his flared nostrils, and bid again. "One thousand eighty denarii."

Veronica studied Claudia's face: she chewed on the inside of her cheek, seeming to weigh the man's argument. Even if Claudia bought every girl today, which she certainly could not do, there would be more barbarian girls brought in tomorrow, and next week, and next month.

"You'll be kind to her?" Claudia asked.

"Yes, Mistress."

"And you'll never beat her?"

"I can't say never."

"You'll never beat her in anger, only if she is deliberately bad."

The Equestrian nodded. "Yes. Ask any man on the Via Sacra. He'll testify to my character."

Claudia nodded, then turned abruptly and grabbed Veronica's hand. She tugged her cousin away, convulsing in sobs after a few steps. Swallowing air, she braced herself, and said, "Let's go home. This place disgusts me."

After a few steps, Veronica got the nerve up to ask, "How much money do you have anyway?"

Claudia laughed, snorting from her tight throat. "About eighty denarii."

A little farther along, they were nearly swallowed in a current of bodies streaming toward the center of the forum. A loud commotion filled the streets as everywhere rushing citizens speculated about the cause. Veronica heard, "Caesar has called the Senate!", "Caesar's returned to Rome!", even, "Caesar has died in Capri!" The girls were bumped on all sides by adults hurrying toward the Basilica Julia, the huge administration building which operated as a court. Just as Veronica thought they'd be trampled, the crowd of commoners slowed, giving way for a group of Senators, Theodosius among them. The girls dashed to him, realizing too late they'd given him another cause for concern.

"This is not a good time for you to be out on the street," he reprimanded.

"Why?" Claudia asked. "What's happened?"

"Sejanus. He's arrested my mother!"

Veronica recognized the raspy voice of that awful, hairy goat-boy, and sure enough when she looked left, there was Caligula, at her uncle's elbow.

"This is very serious," Theodosius insisted.

"Caesar killed my father, now he's going to kill my mother!"

"Gaius!" Theodosius barked. "Hold your tongue! If you can't be quiet, I'll send you home under armed guard. And you girls, this is no place for you. Not with tempers high as they are."

"What, Father," Claudia needled, "would you prefer we pick our way through the mob?"

Theodosius relented. "Go with Gaius to the upper level. Wait there for me. I'll get you when it's over."

Caligula and Claudia hustled into the Basilica and Veronica followed reluctantly. She still wanted nothing to do with the sparrow killer. Inside the Basilica, they climbed to the second level. They darted to the front of the balcony and slid onto the wooden bench just behind the rail. Down at the rostrum stood Sejanus. He held a scroll in his fist and conferred with an officer of his Praetorian Guard as the Senators streamed in, taking their seats. There were two wooden chairs at the rostrum, occupied by two women. Veronica had seen the elder many times before, but had never associated her with Little Boots. She was sure she'd never seen the younger.

"That's my mother," Caligula whispered. That matron, who Veronica learned later was named Agrippina, looked frightened, but defiant. She nudged the younger woman (who bore her a passing resemblance, except that she was very homely) trying to get her to sit straight and stop crying. But she sat hunched with shoulders heaving, her arms crossed over her round belly, the top of her breasts jiggling as she sobbed.

"And that's my brother[31]," Caligula pointed. Veronica blinked. *Oh my, it was a boy*, maybe a couple of years younger than Caligula. But he was so plump and pale and effeminate. His hair was long and cut like a lady's. His nails were painted. Perhaps it was only that he'd been crying, but his cheeks looked as though they'd been rouged and his wet eyes seemed to be smeared with makeup.

Sejanus gripped the lectern and the chamber grew silent. He untied the ribbon on the scroll he'd been holding and slowly unrolled it. "This dispatch," he stated, "I received this morning from Caesar. It concerns sedition and treachery by a woman our beloved Caesar has ever thought of as his own daughter." Sejanus turned and extended a long arm, pointing directly at Agrippina. His scowl seemed intended to shame her, but the matron only stiffened in her chair, and fixed her eyes coldly on his. Sejanus pitched his voice up slightly as he continued, "But as constant as Caesar's love has been, so too has been her defiance." Sejanus broke off eye contact and turned back toward the Senate, thrusting a finger forward for emphasis. "Disgracing the noble classes of Rome with wanton drinking and blatant adultery!"

Objections rose from the crowd. Agrippina was not without her supporters, and she stirred them up as she pitched forward in her chair. "Liar! Show your proof!"

"As the mother, so the daughter," Sejanus hollered. "As the mother, so the daughter![32]" Veronica did not know to what that referred, but catcalls from the balcony indicated the crowd was shifting in Agrippina's favor. Sejanus must have sensed that too, for he stopped briefly, composed himself, and began again with a more even tone. "And to that, add her scheming to thwart Caesar in the Senate. To embolden his enemies at home and abroad." He picked up speed and volume, reaching a crescendo with, "Conspiring with a standing army outside the gates of Rome!"

A hush fell over the chamber, trepidation Sejanus seemed to relish. Then with a sneer of utter disgust, he looked the whining boy up and down. "While her son practices vices from which the very gods avert their eyes." He shook his head, apparently in pity for all Rome. He let the audience sit with that image, of the gods recoiling, removing themselves from Roman life, all for the sins of

---

[31] Nero Julius Caesar Germanicus (c. AD 6–30 AD), not the Nero Caesar who was Emperor from 54 – 68 AD

[32] Agrippina's mother was Julia the Elder (39 BC – 14 AD), the only biological child of Augustus Caesar. While married to Tiberius, Julia was charged with several counts of adultery and treason. Augustus exiled her to the island of Pandateria.

these indolent, idle nobles. He lifted the scroll, open in his outstretched hands, and spoke regretfully, but dutifully. "This letter contains a litany of charges, which Caesar has tirelessly researched and substantiated. Whatever proof the Senate may require, Caesar can call forth." Then he gripped the scroll and thrust it toward Agrippina, a dagger at her throat, as he pronounced, "But this woman cannot remain at liberty. Cannot be permitted to sow rebellion in the ranks! Cannot move freely through the streets which she contaminates with treason!"

The room swung back to the anti-Agrippina forces, and Sejanus was quick to take advantage. He signaled his Praetorian Guard, who flooded the rostrum and pulled the prisoners from their chairs. Agrippina fought, yelling loudly, "It's a forgery! The letter's a fake!" She struck at a guard, who fumbled to take hold of her. Their feet became tangled, and down she went, smashing her face on the wooden armrest. As the guards pulled her to her feet, the crowd roared, some even rushing forward: her broken, bloody nose too great an outrage to ignore. Now the crowd was on its feet, scrambling, pushing toward the exits. Men fought on the stairs.

Sejanus struggled to maintain control. He barked orders at the Guards to clear the rostrum and remove the prisoners, but that only threatened to send the fight into the forum. The Guard formed a barrier behind which Agrippina and the boy were ushered out. Sejanus seized his chance to duck out as well. Down on the floor, Senators milled about. They wouldn't riot, that was beneath their station, but they seemed intensely interested in which way the fight might go.

Theodosius was more interested in the girls. He called up to the balcony, "Claudia?" and showed relief as her head tipped over the rail.

"Here, Father. We're all still here."

He nodded, then turned his attention to the open side door. The last of the guards dashed out. Veronica could hear horses. Wagons rumbled. There were loud shouts and smacks, hollow thumps and groans. But as the wagons withdrew, the shouting subsided. Theodosius looked again up to the balcony, extended a cupped hand and signaled it was safe for the youths to come down.

Back at home that evening, Veronica grew more and more anxious. Theodosius had brought Caligula home with them. There wasn't much else to do; the boy's mother had been thrown in jail. Still, Veronica didn't like having to sit across from him. His eyes darted furtively around the table, stalking a few flies that buzzed about, and striking at them clumsily, missing them, but getting his fingers in all the food. Theodosius offered him wine to settle his nerves, but it only seemed to make him morose. His eyes still stalked the flies, but with cunning patience.

Veronica ate quickly, asked to be excused and took her dogs out to the garden. They immediately chased an orange cat up the yew tree, and nothing she did could get their attention away from it. They scratched at the trunk and yapped as the cat lolled on the full, soft bough and licked its paws in haughty disdain. That's when a knock came at the door, and Veronica felt a brief spasm of panic. She crept back into the atrium to see her uncle greet Sejanus and invite him to the table.

Curious, Veronica padded back through the dining room, where Caligula sat nursing a cup of watered-down wine, and into the kitchen, where Adrianna and Claudia were putting away the food.

"There's a guest for the table," she whispered, then silently mouthed, "Sejanus."

Claudia immediately hopped to the dining room, pressing with Veronica through the doorway to see the possible confrontation. But there was none. Sejanus pulled a stool up to the table and sat across from Caligula, who continued to stare into his cup.

"The most arduous part of my job," Sejanus sighed, "comes when family squabbles boil over into the public arena." Claudia took a plate from Adrianna and placed it in front of Sejanus. "Thank you," he said. "Passions are stirred. Loyalties are brought into play. Makes it hard for people to look objectively at cold, hard facts." Sejanus placed the scroll on the table and slid it toward Theodosius. "You'll see this bears Caesar's mark."

Theodosius declined to look at it. "Perhaps my family should excuse us."

Veronica curtseyed and followed Claudia out to the kitchen.

"You, too, Gaius," Theodosius said. Caligula slipped from his stool, and, still grasping the cup of wine, made his exit toward the garden.

Veronica, though she did not hang on the doorjamb like Claudia, stayed within earshot of the men. She listened intently as the conversation continued.

"So you've been making the rounds tonight," Theodosius asked, "to convince the Senators this letter is genuine?"

Sejanus shrugged. "Genuine? The divinations of your altar, are they genuine? Perhaps to those who believe. But believers will believe anything. What's genuine is action. That is how we rule."

"That sounds vaguely like a threat."

"I've no interest in making threats, dear Proculus. Only accommodations." He took a sip of wine, rolling it over his tongue before swallowing. "Call your daughter."

Claudia didn't wait. Theodosius looked toward the kitchen and she was already at the end of the table.

Claudia bowed her head in uncharacteristic humility. "Prefect Sejanus," she asked, "have you any word from my husband?"

"He doesn't write?"

"Not in many months."

The Prefect furrowed his brow a little too conspicuously. A little too empathetically. Then straightened his back with a long sigh. "Well. You'll have to bring that up when you see him."

Claudia nearly swooned. She grasped the edge of the table to steady herself. Sejanus smiled and removed another scroll from his belt beneath his cape.

"After much careful deliberation, I have... almost prevailed upon Caesar to allow you to join your husband."

"When?" she gasped.

Sejanus tapped the second scroll on the table. "This letter of transit simply requires Caesar's signature. Which I'm sure I can secure after your father and I smooth over this unpleasant business of Agrippina."

Sejanus tipped his head toward Theodosius, who pulled back slightly from the table. Whatever Theodosius might have said was lost as Claudia dropped to her knees before the Prefect and hugged him around the waist.

"May all the gods bless you, Sejanus," she cried. He patted her head and Claudia pulled away. Overcome, her tears flowed, and she dabbed at her eyes. "I've got to pack!" she joked, and called into the kitchen. "Veronica! Come, help me pack!" Veronica stepped cautiously forward, and Claudia tugged on her hand. They ran to the garden portico, before Claudia dropped the dead weight she was dragging. She turned to Veronica with hurt on her face and in her voice. "Aren't you happy for me?"

Veronica felt her throat catch. In that split second before she could speak, Claudia threw up her hands. "Fine, I've got to go alone anyway." She spun on her heels and marched off toward their bedroom. Veronica was left on the garden portico, under the dusky sky, which had not yet darkened enough to draw out the evening's starlight. Behind her she heard the men in the dining room speaking low. But her eyes were drawn to moving shadows under the yew tree. The dogs had scampered back to the kitchen for the table scraps. Now Caligula sat looking up the interior of the tree, enticing the orange cat down.

Theodosius grumbled, "Another letter from the Emperor? Aren't you pushing your luck?"

The Prefect's answer was matter-of-fact. "Pontius needs his wife. Command requires some measure of cruelty, but the Jews provoke more than any race on earth. To endure that? In isolation, without the comfort of one's wife? A man could become..."

His voice trailed off, allowing Theodosius to finish, "Like Caesar?"

Outside, the cat fell from the tree into Caligula's arms. He petted her head, then rubbed her body down to the tail.

Inside, Sejanus poured himself more wine. "You've heard reports from Capri. Caesar's behavior is as monstrous as his visage. Such blood lust."

Caligula reached his right hand behind his back for something. With his left he continued to pet the cat. As his right hand came forward, Veronica caught a glimpse of a large rock.

In the dining room, Sejanus concluded his point, "Isn't Rome safer with a strong hand moderating Caesar's passions?"

To which her uncle flatly declared, "That would seem to be a question for Caesar's heirs."

"Well," Sejanus answered, "there seem to be fewer of them every day."

Caligula grasped the scruff of the cat's neck, thrusting its head down between his knees. The rock swung up and came hurtling down with a sharp crack and a splash of red. Again. Another muffled thud and crimson splatter. Veronica screamed. The men at table broke for the garden. Veronica pivoted and dove, burying her face in Theodosius' chest. She gathered his toga in her fists and wrapped it as far around her head as she could. Still screaming and stomping, she felt his arms squeeze her. He stroked her hair and patted her back.

Claudia came running. "What's wrong?" She gasped as she took in the spectacle.

Caligula dropped the bloody rock. He smiled as a dizzy child who's just rolled down a long hill. He smeared the blood on his face with the back of his hand.

Sejanus grunted. "The final point of my visit," he informed the Senator. "Caesar believes the boy will be better off with him. Away from corrupting influences."

Veronica stared at the sick boy. She watched Sejanus coax him forward, as he had coaxed her from her hiding place a decade ago. He touched Caligula's elbow lightly and led him into the atrium. The last words she heard were a rasping exultation, "You see what I've done, Prefect? I've become a god!"

Chapter 5

The day of Claudia's departure dawned bright; the heat was stultifying by mid-morning. "Judea heat," Theodosius called it, dry and airless.

"A good omen," Claudia declared. "I shall be acclimated before I even leave!" Veronica regarded the overstuffed bundles of luggage Claudia — or rather the household slaves — had dragged from her bedroom.

"You should leave some of this," Veronica suggested.

Claudia arched one eyebrow. "Why?"

"So you'll still be connected. To Rome. So you'll come home again."

Claudia put down her cup and hugged her cousin. "I'll always be connected to Rome. And to you, sister." She tossed Veronica's hair off her shoulders and ran her fingers through the lower curls. "Pontius will not have a career in the provinces. He'll prove his worth in Judea, and Caesar will order him home. He'll be put in charge of — oh, I don't know — something wonderfully important. The Senate will welcome him, and we'll get a house..."

Veronica squirmed. "No. Don't go. Have Sejanus bring him home."

Claudia laughed. "Oh, you're still such a child. My place is with my husband. You'll understand when you're married."

"That's not going to happen," Veronica pouted.

"No?" a voice boomed. "But I'm already getting inquiries." Theodosius entered the garden with a Centurion[33] and some soldiers, Claudia's escort for the first leg of her journey. Veronica hopped over the bundles to tug on her uncle's arm.

"Who? Who inquired?"

As always, Claudia interrupted. "Father, let me sail!"

Theodosius had insisted she take the slightly longer land route down the Via Appia to the heel of the peninsula to sail from there. He judged it safer than starting at the Tiber, voyaging all the way down Italy's shin and rounding its toe. As soldiers hoisted bundles onto their shoulders and carried them toward the atrium, he remarked, "I'm fairly sure your baggage would sink a quinterime. The oarsmen would riot as soon as it was loaded."

"No," Claudia insisted. "I could calm them. I would simply show them the radiant face of a woman in love. They would be dazzled."

Theodosius was unconvinced. "Your face will *calm* sailors? You can put your theory to the test, but it will have to wait until Brindisi[34]." His wise gaze then landed upon the Centurion, who was perhaps too attentive to parts of Claudia that were not on her face. "Isn't that right, Centurion?"

The officer immediately snapped to attention.

"I-I assure you, Senator," he stammered, "the Prefect's wife will receive every courtesy."

"Prefect's wife," Claudia mused. "I like the sound of that."

Claudia passed the gauntlet of house slaves who had turned out, most probably on their master's command, to wish her well. She shared a long hug with Adrianna, which she broke off when the old woman sobbed. Claudia batted her softly on the shoulder, "Oh, you silly, old fool, why do you want to make me cry? I have nothing to cry about: I am the wife of Pontius Pilate, Prefect of Judea!"

And so, Claudia alighted — triumphant! — to her coach. She stooped to kiss Veronica one more time on the cheek, telling her, "Don't worry, Veronica. Your uncle believes in love more than omens. He'll make sure you marry well. Of course, not as well as I." Then she embraced and kissed her father.

---

[33] A Roman officer in charge of a century of troops. This group usually numbered 80 men, rather than 100.

[34] A seaport at the very tip of Italy's heel; a common departure point for the east

Theodosius pressed his daughter to his heart and, turning his moist eyes skyward, rested his cheek on her soft hair. The crushing reality was that his daughter might never return, he might never see her or hold her again. They separated without a word spoken. Claudia waved again to the household, and sat back nearly hidden in the coach. The driver snapped the reins, and Claudia rumbled forward, toward her life with Pontius Pilate.

*   *   *   *

It was not exactly a pall that fell over the household, but a respectful silence reigned for the remainder of the day. Adrianna cried quietly several times during dinner preparation. Theodosius tossed a leather beanbag that the dogs fetched again and again. But the master was mirthless in his throwing and the empathetic animals pitiful in their retrieval. Veronica lingered outside her aviary, contemplating the caged birds, remembering the red finch Claudia had freed. Did the birds in the cage ever miss the one who'd flown away? Did the free bird ever return to visit? Was the free bird happy, or had it met with disaster? Was there a cat with a tale to tell?

At dinner, Claudia's empty stool dominated the dining room. Veronica ate quietly, while inwardly ready to explode. She'd been waiting for some word from Theodosius about the marriage inquiries, but the whole day had passed, and now they were halfway through the meal. Finally Veronica cleared her throat, and muttered, "So, who...?" at the some instant her uncle opened with, "I guess you're wondering..."

Theodosius dipped a piece of bread in a bowl of olive oil. "It wasn't Catullus," he chortled before taking a bite.

"Thank the gods," she groaned.

Theodosius dabbed the bread again, holding it over the bowl as he continued to chew.

"In selecting a husband for you, I must be mindful of the family. Centuries of history unite and divide the families of Rome. I've tried to shield you girls from this. Part of my reason in advocating for Pontius was that he had no history. But that had its drawbacks." He poured a water-wine mixture from a pitcher into his cup. He held the pitcher aloft and Veronica nodded, "Please." He dropped a splash of wine into her water cup and continued. "Now that you will be marrying, you should know who your family are, and were. And how that affects how people react to you."

He remembered his bread and bit down on the crust. Olive oil ran from the corner of his mouth and he dabbed it with a napkin. "It's not that we are good and they are bad. It's just that a family has loyalties. Families like ours have clients, who are likewise loyal. So, when conflicts arise between individuals, they become conflicts between families, and the families' clients. A personal squabble can divide the Senate, divide Rome, even divide the Empire."

"Like with Augustus and Mark Antony?" Veronica offered, remembering her lessons.

"Exactly so," her uncle confirmed. "Augustus was a fine ruler. Still the empire suffered civil war over Antony's bad marriage to his sister. So, we must be careful."

"You don't think my marriage will start a war?" Veronica joked.

"No," her uncle said, in all seriousness, "but war is part of our culture, and I would prefer not to put you on the front lines." Here he took a deep swallow of wine and sat with his thoughts until Veronica spoke.

"What about our family, Uncle?"

Theodosius leaned back and interlaced his fingers behind his head. He stretched his chest forward, drew and let out a deep breath. Then, elbows back on the table, he spoke.

"We are distantly related to the Caesars. My great-grandmother (and, of course, your father's) was Julia Caesaris, who married Gaius Marius, and who was the aunt of Julius Caesar. That technically makes us Julians, and closely allied first with Augustus and now with our own Tiberius Caesar." He shrugged as if to indicate that nothing is ever easy, adding, "But we also trace our family back through the ancestors of Mark Antony."

"So, what side did we take during the last Civil War?"

"Antony did us the favor of raising his army abroad. Our family was looked upon with suspicion, but allowed to remain neutral. When Antony allied himself with a foreign queen..."

"Cleopatra?"

"Yes. He left us no choice but to fall in with Augustus."

"And fortunately, Augustus won."

"Fortunate for the world. Antony was a brilliant soldier, and very charismatic, but something of a drunk and a fool. He would have made a terrible ruler."

"Worse than Tiberius?"

"Tiberius rules by fear, but limits most of his cruelty to a secluded island and his close relatives. Anyway, to continue, Antony's grandson was a highly regarded general named Germanicus. Your father, an able soldier, was his distant cousin, his friend and his confidant." Theodosius got a faraway look, as if across the void of time and space he had found his brother and was sharing a wistful moment with him. That moment over, he strummed the table with his fingers and continued.

"Germanicus. Yes. His early career showed him to be a fine choice to succeed Augustus, who had no direct heirs. But Augustus listened to his wife Livia, who wanted her son, Augustus' stepson, Tiberius, to succeed him. Part of the deal was for Tiberius to adopt Germanicus, putting him next in line to succeed. Tiberius even renamed him 'Germanicus Julius Caesar.' But there was an incident, which I think sealed the enmity between Tiberius and Germanicus. Germanicus was completely innocent, but Tiberius never trusted him again."

"What happened?" Veronica asked.

"Soon after Augustus died, the Senate appointed Germanicus the head of the army stationed in Germania. These soldiers had been promised their recruitment would end after sixteen years, but it was extended to twenty. So they rioted, and demanded that Germanicus be made emperor. Naturally, Germanicus refused. As I said, he was innocent. But he didn't exactly crush the rebellion. Instead he led us on a two-year campaign against the barbarians. He was brilliant. Decisive."

"Wait. 'Us'?"

"Oh, yes. I was with him. After Claudia's mother died. We were married less than a year; she died in childbirth." Veronica nodded sympathetically. "I wanted to get away from Rome, so I got myself attached as tribune to a Legion under Germanicus. During the campaign, I wrote to my younger brother, your father. He had just married your mother, but my letter convinced him not to pass up the opportunity to serve, so, taking only the time necessary to bless your mother with you, he joined me."

"And how did that go?" Veronica asked.

"Incredibly well. But, for Germanicus, success brought too much popularity, and Tiberius started to fear him. When Germanicus returned in triumph..." Theodosius' face lit up. "Oh, that was a day, a huge parade down the Via Sacra to the Circus Maximus." Then he lost the glow, continuing, "Tiberius immediately sent him out again, on a campaign in Asia."

"That seems to be the way Tiberius gets rid of people," Veronica grumbled, "by sending them to Asia."

"Quite true," Theodosius acknowledged. "I stayed here, but your father had become quite close to Germanicus. He remained in Rome only long enough to bounce you on his knee a few times." He tapped Veronica's nose with his forefinger. "Then in Asia, again Germanicus was immensely successful. He defeated Cappadocia[35] and Commagene[36], turning them into Roman provinces."

"But Caesar didn't like that?"

"Apparently not. Word got to Caesar that Germanicus was acting like an emperor abroad. In Syria, he removed the Prefect, a corrupt scoundrel named Piso, and ordered him back to Rome. It seems Piso was a special friend of Tiberius. And so, during this conflict with Piso, Germanicus died suddenly. Mysteriously. Shortly after, your father, his confidant, also died mysteriously. The Senate called for an investigation. They had Piso arrested, but he died just as the trial began."

---

[35] Region in east-central Turkey
[36] An adjacent region farther east, part of the ancient Armenian kingdom

"Mysteriously?" Veronica chirped.

Theodosius tapped his head, playfully acknowledging that Veronica was using hers. "Everyone suspected Tiberius had acted out of jealousy, ordering Piso to kill Germanicus, then had someone else kill Piso to silence him. But nothing could be proved."

"Now, this Germanicus. He wasn't..."

"Yes. Caligula's father."

"So he told the truth? That our fathers had both been murdered."

"Gaius idolized his father from an early age. Even wore a full uniform in imitation of his father. When he was just three! That's how he got his name: the uniform was exact down to the Little Boots."

"What will happen to Gaius now?"

"In Capri? Caesar will keep him close, but not too close."

"Don't you worry that Caesar will have him killed?"

"Frankly, I am more worried what Caligula might do. A boy who kills animals for sport. Had he stayed in Rome, I'd have had the uncomfortable task of forbidding him to see you."

"Me?"

"First birds, then cats. He'll kill a person one day. He'll start with someone small and defenseless."

"You're scaring me, Uncle Theo."

"Good. Reasonable fear preserves life. So let me state this very clearly, if Gaius ever returns to Rome, you are never, never to be alone with him. Understood?"

"Yes." Veronica sat with the weight of that prohibition before asking, "But what else about the family?"

"Oh, we did get a little off topic. All right. Germanicus was killed, so his wife, Agrippina was widowed. She had a number of children, including Gaius. Now, Tiberius had a son, Drusus, who was his heir and would have succeeded him. Except..."

"Let me guess, he died mysteriously?"

"Six years ago."

"And Caesar doesn't know who did it?"

"And how it must eat at him. All powerful. Able to kill his enemies with impunity. Until one of his enemies strikes at the one person in the world he loves."

"Well," Veronica stated, impressed with her wisdom, "he shouldn't have started all this killing if he didn't want it to continue."

Theodosius became very somber at that moment, saying, "Men often view killing as a final act, without realizing every act is a prelude to the next." His mind seemed to veer in a perilous direction, but then he drew back, returning to the point at hand. "Anyway, with Drusus gone, and Germanicus, Caesar's adopted son, gone, Caesar's succession fell to Agrippina's children. Of which

Gaius is the eldest male. Naturally, Caesar feared Agrippina might be holding a grudge over her husband's death, and might plot against Caesar to put her own son on the throne."

"So Caesar accused Agrippina of treason. That was the letter Sejanus read at the Basilica."

"So he could lock her away from anyone who might join a conspiracy against him."

"And now he's got Caligula."

"Correct. So Caesar is either grooming Gaius to be his successor, or keeping him far away from any conspirators who might plot an assassination."

Veronica had a silly thought in that moment — that Sejanus had taken Caligula from this house, perhaps fearing Uncle Theo might conspire against Caesar. But that was ridiculous. Wasn't it?

"You don't think Caesar will harm Caligula?" she asked.

Theodosius shook his head. "That would be too blatant, even for Caesar. No, Caesar's interests are best served by keeping Caligula alive, happy and isolated."

Suddenly — perhaps because the thought of Caligula isolated made her think of an abandoned child — a great sadness welled up within Veronica. She felt emotions she hadn't allowed herself, connected to memories she'd closed off long ago. "Can I ask you... about my mother?"

Theodosius nodded, taking a moment again to traverse the distance between present and past. "A lovely woman. Her family had risen from the Equestrian ranks, so she had a sense of how the military worked. Duty. Loyalty. But she was not prepared for politics. For intrigue and betrayal. When we learned of Germanicus' death, the Senate convened. Because of my connections to Tiberius and Germanicus, I was approached from both sides. Each trying to enlist me against the other. By the time word came that your father had died, I was so embroiled in the investigation, I didn't think how the news might affect your mother. I was meeting with several Senators when word reached us that Sejanus was sending the Guard to your house."

Veronica slid to the edge of her stool. "Why?"

Theodosius sighed. "I imagine he wanted to... bribe her? Talk her into making some show of loyalty to Tiberius. And if she did that, she'd be taken care of."

"But she thought they were coming to arrest her?"

"She knew in her heart what had happened. I guess she preferred to swallow hot coals, than to swallow the truth, and hold it inside forever."

Veronica gripped the edge of the table. "Caesar is a monster," she said. Theodosius poured himself more wine. Veronica followed his example and sipped her water. The light drops of wine mingled in her cup gave the water a tart flavor that seemed to awaken her taste buds while deadening her tongue.

"At least with Caesar," Theodosius mused, "you can tell by looking at him. The real danger comes from trusting those who are only monstrous on the inside."

Veronica offered, "Prefect Sejanus?" but Theodosius did not respond. She took a slice of cheese and brazenly reached across to a small bowl of pure wine beside her uncle's plate. Theodosius raised his eyebrow, but didn't stop her. She dipped the cheese, then nibbled on it. It was delicious! She reached to dip again, but Theodosius slid the bowl away.

Veronica slumped back on her stool. She pouted a second before stating, "This is all very complicated. And sad. Why can't... I mean, they are family. Like we are. Why can't they love each other?"

Again Theodosius strummed his fingers on the table. "Perhaps because they think of ruling, rather than living. They seek to impose order. And love does not seem to be an ordering principle of our universe."

"Huh?"

"Our Empire is built upon conquest, not love."

Veronica chewed this over along with the cheese. "But Uncle," she asked, "doesn't Virgil say *'Love conquers all'*?"

Theodosius raised his cup and, smiling, finished the quotation, "'*So, let us, too, surrender to love!*'"

31 A.D.

In the two years after Claudia left, Veronica received only four letters. Theodosius received two. He reasoned that she had written more, but for some reason the letters did not get through. Veronica worried that Claudia had written some things that would reflect badly on Pontius, or Caesar, and so he'd intercepted the letters and destroyed them. But when she suggested this possibility to Theodosius, he was dismissive.

"Things get lost. The mail is not infallible."

Veronica was approaching her sixteenth birthday, and still no marriage had been arranged. She began to worry she'd never be married, and in Rome, the only thing worse for a girl than marrying badly was never marrying at all. Without a husband, she'd be dependent on her uncle, and when he died, she'd become a ward of the state — in other words, of Caesar. But whenever she broached the subject to her uncle, Theodosius treated it lightly. She was told to relax; his colleagues in the Senate were interested, but Sejanus was keeping the body occupied with other matters. There would be time in the spring, or, there would be time in the fall.

Then one day, unexpectedly, Theodosius brought a young man home for the midday meal.

"Veronica," her uncle said, "meet Valentius."

"Ave, Valentius." Veronica curtseyed and, before the man could answer, returned excitedly to the kitchen where Adrianna stood, peeping into the dining room.

"He's not a bad specimen," she stated dryly.

In fact, Veronica tacitly averred, he was a fairly good specimen. Medium height and broad-shouldered, he stood straight and had an air of confidence. He had large, brown eyes and thick brows, which did not run together, but distinctly parted above a well-sculpted Roman nose. His jawline was well defined and his neck was muscular, but not overly thick. His teeth were relatively straight and fairly white. Veronica was pleased to pronounce him, silently to herself, handsome. Adrianna handed Veronica two plates of food for the gentlemen, and Veronica returned to the table. She stood attentively as Theodosius listened to Valentius recite Homer in Greek.

"Bravo," her uncle exclaimed. "I can see you've much potential for rhetoric." He gestured for Veronica to put the plates on the table.

"Well, Senator," the younger man modestly rejoined, "There is a vast difference between reciting and arguing."

Theodosius pointed to the pitcher; Veronica lifted it and filled their cups with wine. She splashed a little clumsily in front of Valentius, who tipped his stool back to avoid the splatter.

"So sorry," Veronica cried. "I think I've stained your tunic."

Valentius tossed his head and smiled. "White wine. It's no matter." He slid his cup closer to her and added, "Please, Mistress."

But Veronica stood frozen, staring at his right hand. It was missing three fingers. Valentius chuckled, brandished his hand, then placed it on his lap. "Oh, yes, this. A shock to see at first."

Theodosius cleared his throat. "Valentius injured his hand on duty in Galilee."

Veronica shook her head, "Where? I'm sorry, I shouldn't have stared. But where...?"

"Galilee is north of Judea. We have a problem with rebels there. Always stealing supplies. One of them made off with my digits." He chuckled at his own joke, an attempt to ease Veronica's embarrassment. She appreciated the attempt, even though it didn't work: she still felt awful.

Just then, a slave beckoned Theodosius toward the atrium. "Please keep our guest entertained," he told Veronica, and she pulled a stool up to the table as her uncle exited.

Valentius continued, "So then, the end result was, I couldn't hold a sword in this hand. So I got an early parole. My superiors believed I might study the law and recommended me to Senator Proculus. Him having no heir, they reasoned he might be open to..." He must have read the shock on Veronica's face, because he stopped mid-sentence. "I'm sorry, Mistress, I... Have I spoken out of turn?"

Veronica was off her stool and fumbling back toward the kitchen. "Oh, no. Certainly not. If you'll excuse…" She halted as Theodosius returned.

"I must be away. The Senate is convened." A slave appeared with his cape and Theodosius bent slightly backwards to have it draped across his shoulders.

"Uncle, may I speak with you?"

"When I return."

Veronica implored, "I would prefer…"

Valentius rose noisily, scraping his stool on the stone floor. "Beg your pardon, Senator. I'll be off then."

"I'll accompany you," Theodosius answered, pulling tight the strings of his cape and tying them securely.

Valentius looked back to Veronica, her troubled expression perhaps prompting him to assert, "I'm afraid I'm off in quite the opposite direction." He bowed abruptly and departed, leaving the Senator slightly puzzled. Veronica seized her opportunity.

"Uncle, what are you doing?"

"I told you," he said, marching to the door. "The Senate…"

"I mean with him!" she cried, freezing Theodosius in his tracks. They stood in silence until Valentius vanished through the door. "Are you going to adopt him? Is that what you're doing?"

Theodosius strode through the atrium, Veronica trotting to keep up. "If you must know, I have agreed to consider it."

"Because you have no heir?"

"Because…" he huffed, then his voice trailed off as he straightened his cape.

"What about Pontius? Why not him?" She tugged on his arm. "What do you know that you're not telling me?"

"I don't know anything," he groaned, twisting his forearm out of her grip. "But you suspect."

He eyed the street through the open door. "I suspect nothing."

"Then it's me? You can't find anyone to marry me, so you want an adopted son to take care of me. Is that it?"

He gestured for her to calm herself. Pedestrians were streaming down the street toward the forum and anyone might overhear. "It's complicated, Veronica."

"Why? Because anyone who marries me will be sent to the farthest desert?"

Theodosius gripped her shoulders. He then tipped her forward, kissing her gently on her crown. "These days, people are fearful. They can hardly be blamed. But let's not let our fears run away with us."

He stroked her cheek with the back of his fingers and turned toward the street. Veronica watched him join a gaggle of Senators, Marcus Catullus among them. The old schemer looked more unctuous than ever. His son Marius loped at his elbow, his thin neck barely supporting his head.

"Ave, Proculus," the snake hissed.

"Ave, Catullus," the Senator responded. He greeted the others in the group.

"I trust all is well in the Proculus household? I see your niece is still with you." He tipped his glance toward the doorway and waved coyly to Veronica. She responded with a tight, closed-lip smile and a flip of her hand. "Something of a willful girl, isn't she?"

"The better to stiffen a man's spine," her uncle averred.

"Quite so, quite so," Catullus mused. The group eased its way down the street, Catullus angling for Theodosius' ear.

Veronica snapped her fingers for the slave at the door.

"My cloak," she ordered.

By the time the slave had returned, Theodosius was nearly out of sight. Veronica donned the cloak, pulling the scarlet hood over her chestnut hair. Then she skipped down the steps, losing herself in the flow of the crowd, but gaining upon the Senators in time to overhear Catullus reach his point.

"A young man must have some maturity to handle a willful girl. Your Claudia, I apologize again, there I was premature. Insisting on her for my Marius. A girl of her spirit would have dominated the boy, that is, at that tender age. And that is never good. He has, however, grown quite capable."

"Is he capable of surviving the desert?" Theodosius asked.

Veronica laughed inwardly, *Good for you, Uncle.*

"Ah," Catullus conceded the point. "Fortunately, though the larger world is always a concern, Rome is our world. And our family quite secure within it. I trust you value security for your niece?"

Theodosius changed the subject. "Does anyone know why we've been called?"

"A letter," piped one of the Senators. "Caesar has written concerning Sejanus, but not to Sejanus."

The Senators now grouped closer as they walked. Their talk was muffled and Veronica had to strain to hear. She ducked her head to further hide her face beneath her hood and crept closer.

"Praise from Caesar, one suspects," a Senator offered. "He's inveigled his way into Caesar's good graces. *Is* Caesar, here in Rome, for all intents and purposes."

"And Caesar himself is without a worthy heir."

"This is the formality we've dreaded. Caesar writing into law that Sejanus holds his power."

"Dreaded, Senator?" Catullus cooed. "One should never dread the inevitable, but ever find a way to use it to his advantage."

The Senator in question flushed crimson. "For ten years I've prayed to the gods that Sejanus might mollify Caesar's temper. Act as a bulwark against a tyrant's cruel excesses. But never has there been an instance of Caesar's barbarity that Sejanus did not happily carry out!" The red-faced noble restrained himself, realizing he'd spoken too openly and too loudly.

"How would you know that, Flavius?" Catullus prodded. "Certainly, that would remain between him and Caesar. Would it not, Proculus?"

Theodosius demurred. "We cannot know what passes between Caesar and Sejanus. Therefore we cannot know if Caesar would have been worse without him. Though we can fairly say that Rome has seen happier days. That the people have lived freer of fear than they do today."

"So," a Senator calmly inquired, "what direction do we anticipate Rome will take, when Caesar vests Sejanus in his tribunician powers[37]? Greater civility, or greater tyranny?"

"I would caution my colleagues," Catullus sighed, "against throwing about the word 'tyrant' in the open forum."

That's exactly where they were. The forum was little more than a huge open space in the commercial district. There was an elevated rostrum, and wooden benches were brought in for the Senate, whenever they were convened. Crowds would then gather around the open space to listen to speeches and debates, while the Praetorian Guard was posted strategically to keep order. Today, the forum was so packed, the Senators had to squeeze through a path created by the Guard in order to reach their seats. That's as far as Veronica could follow, and, being shorter than most of the crowd, there was nothing she could see from that point. She had two choices: worm her way to the front, or find a rooftop she could access.

As she craned her neck to assess the situation overhead — the rooftops nearly as crowded as the street — Veronica heard a loud commotion. She thought it was horses, but that couldn't be: horses were not allowed in the commercial district from sunrise to sunset. But yes, she distinctly heard the clopping and snorting of horses and the rumbling of chariot wheels. As the crowd parted, Veronica saw a chariot and a rider she remembered seeing years ago. His name she couldn't recall, but he was the military man — Caesar's escort — from the day she'd struck Caesar with that errant pear. Pushing the crowd aside were troops, but not the military. These were the Vigiles, the Roman police force.

The chariot stopped and the rider stepped down. With a flourish of his cape, he strode through the swelling crowd, so close to Veronica he nearly crushed her toes. Standing in his wake was another familiar face, one that gave Veronica chills. His eyes met hers, and Caligula smiled.

---

[37] The powers of a Tribune of the People, historically held by a Plebeian, making his person sacrosanct and inviolable and giving veto power over any decision by any magistrate, assembly or the Senate

"Come with me. This is going to be fun!"

He hooked his arm inside Veronica's elbow and marched her past the Praetorian barrier. Her stomach leapt, remembering her uncle's warning. Of course, they were far from alone, but still, walking arm in arm with someone who might enjoy killing her was not how Veronica wanted to spend an afternoon. As they got to the Senate benches, she pulled back.

"Wait. My uncle," she whispered. "He can't know I'm here." She almost added *with you*, but bit her tongue.

Caligula chuckled at this element of intrigue. "All right. Over here." He pointed to a spot behind the last Senate bench where they could stand and peer over the heads. Veronica could clearly see the rostrum now. Sejanus stood there, his tunic as white as a fuller could make it, his crimson mantle finely embroidered in gold. He appeared newly groomed with his hair oiled and his skin gleaming. He received Senators, Catullus among them, who bowed and kissed his hand. He offered his left hand to Theodosius, a cue for the Senator to bend his knee, but this Senator eschewed the obsequious fawning of his colleagues, and extended his right hand to be shaken instead.

"They think Caesar loves him," Caligula cackled. "Loves him! They think they are looking at the new tribune, the Emperor Regent of Rome!"

Veronica ducked as Theodosius returned to take a seat on the bench. Peeking from under her hood, she saw Sejanus sit also, as a distinguished Senator ascended to the podium and spoke. "This day, Caesar convenes the Senate. And presents this letter to be read to all of Rome." He held aloft a scroll, and let the crowd see him break the seal. He unrolled it, and began reading. Caligula giggled, and Veronica hushed him.

"Shh, I want to hear."

The letter began with the usual litany of greetings to distinguished citizens and to the Senate as a whole. It spoke flatteringly of the Roman people, as good and noble, but vulnerable to evil influences. Then it wandered through a history of Tiberius' reign, making weak arguments for Caesar's cruelty, his reliance on informers and spies, and his persecution of citizens he believed disloyal. The crowd grew impatient; Caesar could repeat his justifications as often as he liked; that didn't change the fact that he was a tyrant. Moreover, he could not bore his subjects into loving him. Even the reader seemed dismayed, and hurried through, perhaps hoping to hit upon a passage that would redeem the diatribe. The letter reached a turning point, citing a pivotal moment in Caesar's reign: his alliance with Sejanus.

Sejanus swelled from Caesar's excessive flattery, citing his loyalty, talent, industry, and his tireless devotion to the Emperor and the people of Rome. It struck Veronica as all too much for even an honest servant, but Sejanus sat like a fat cat at a milk bowl, lapping it all up.

"He doesn't even know," Caligula snickered, "He's being larded, not lauded."

Veronica shushed him again.

The reader continued, his tone adding to the exaggerated praise. "I have long relied upon Sejanus and trusted his counsel," he read. "Having no direct heirs, I thought to bestow upon him the tribunician powers."

A murmur spread through the crowd. *Thought? Why did Caesar employ past tense?* The subtle change seemed to have escaped Sejanus, who did not stir. Veronica looked left to the aisle between the Senate benches. Why were the Vigiles standing there?

The reader continued, "But why is it I have no heir? Where is my son, Drusus? How did he die so suddenly? Poisoned!"

Another murmur rolled through the crowd. That was eight years ago. *Why was Caesar bringing this up now? Just a sick, old man in his grief? Or was there more to it?* The reader became pale, his face contorted. After a quick, frightful look at Sejanus, he gulped a breath, and heaved the fateful line, "Poisoned by the hand of Sejanus."

A cohort of Senators leapt, blocking Veronica's view. She shifted right, bumping Caligula.

"Here comes Macro!" Caligula squealed, and Veronica could see the military man, the charioteer, ascending the rostrum and signaling the Vigiles. They charged up the center aisle over the rostrum and laid hands on Sejanus, dragging him from the stage. Anti-Sejanus Senators — so long silent — now released their pent-up rage. They cheered Macro and the Vigiles, and abused the passing captive.

Meanwhile, those sycophantic Senators who had stooped to kiss Sejanus' hand shrank back from the crowd, fearing a riot might engulf them — all except Marcus Catullus, who threw himself in front of the Vigiles, feigning righteous anger, shouting for the Prefect's head.

"Murderer! Traitor!" he screamed, "The traitor must die! He must die!"

But the Vigiles tossed the shrill fool aside into a pile of anti-Sejanus partisans, who tore at him, prodded and harassed him until, grasping at the threads of salvation, he clung to Theodosius' toga, crying for his help. Ever calm, Theodosius shielded Catullus with his body, while he pried the hysteric's fingers from his garments and returned him to the arms of his son.

"Come on, let's go!" Caligula shouted.

"Where?" Veronica asked.

"To the steps, silly. The Gemonian stairs[38]? That's where the executioner will strangle him." When she didn't move, Caligula extended his open palms toward her, imploring. "Don't you want to see him turn blue?"

She shook her head silently. *How could anyone want to see that?* Caligula screwed up his face and ran after the mob. Veronica slumped on

---

[38]A flight of steps in the central part of Rome, leading from the Arch of the Capitoline Hill down to the Forum, notorious as a place of execution

a vacated bench, then jerked upright as a hand touched her shoulder. Her uncle pulled back her hood.

"We should go home."

At home Theodosius retreated to his altar. He offered several sacrifices, sifting through piles of entrails, trying to divine what was in store for Rome. If the gods were listening, they were not in agreement, as each new omen contradicted the last. Between sacrifices, runners visited the home, bringing news and gossip from around the city. Sejanus had, in fact, been strangled on the Gemonian stairs. His body had then been tossed down the steps to an angry mob, which tore it to pieces. Macro had sent the Vigiles to Sejanus' home. His entire family had been arrested and the house ransacked. Senators were meeting secretly in small groups to devise a response, but feared doing anything in the open until they discovered Macro's intent. Would he and Caesar be content with eliminating Sejanus? Or would they go after all his supporters in the Senate? Veronica knew her uncle had walked a fine line, supporting Sejanus in some things in order to have influence with him on more important matters. But he may have gotten too close when he'd accepted the Prefect's help for Claudia and Pontius. Viewing Rome from far off Capri, through the lens of his spies and informers, and addled by whatever sickness disfigured him, what might Caesar conclude about Senator Proculus?

In disgust, Theodosius tossed another dove carcass on the pyre. The atrium air was thick with smoke; as if the gods themselves were tamping down on it.

"Nothing. Nothing," Theodosius muttered. "The world burns and the gods say nothing."

Echoing Claudia, Veronica conceded, "Maybe the gods don't care."

Theodosius washed his hands. "Maybe they're just tired of us."

Chapter 6

Theodosius was determined not to panic. He'd received several messengers, who'd urged him to meet other Senators in secret, but he declined and cautioned against it. "Tell your master we must meet openly in daylight. We are not conspirators who hide from the light." He advised that the best course was to sleep well and rise early. "Let us meet in the Forum at dawn. All Senators of good will, whether they supported Sejanus or not."

But Theodosius did not sleep. He paced the garden, often gazing at the moon, whose yellow, pocked face instigated shadow plays on the walls of the house. Veronica watched from her bedroom window: shadows of yew boughs shifted with the wind melding one image into another, from obscure to haunting, threatening to benign. She recalled from childhood that dangers apparent in the night vanished when dawn broke. She longed for the sun to banish fear. Instead, a loud knock reverberated from the front door.

Heavy and insistent, the pounding continued until Theodosius reached the atrium. Veronica sneaked from her room and peered around the corner. Theodosius dismissed a slave and ushered in Senator Catullus and Marius. Spotting his niece, Theodosius beckoned, "Veronica, bring wine for our guests."

When she returned, the men were seated on the marble benches between the pool and the altar. Veronica brought three cups, but Theodosius declined. Catullus gulped and Marius slurped.

"Sejanus' children?" Catullus moaned. "All gone. Junilla was... Poor girl. What with the prohibition against executing virgins, they had to violate her before she was strangled."

Theodosius pointed Veronica toward the house. She curtseyed and padded out, but lingered around the corner where she could listen.

"Well, it's done then," Theodosius stated flatly, adding, "If the gods be just."

"*If*, Priest?" Catullus' voice rose. Veronica sensed him moving about. "Is that what you read at your altar? Because I simply read men's actions. Macro? Caesar's goon? He is set to purge the Senate."

"You've no reason to believe..."

"He has the Vigiles. He's taken the Guard. What force can the Senate muster against him? A divided Senate! You know he'll have support from half our ranks."

"I don't know that," Theodosius insisted.

"As close as you were to Sejanus —"

"No closer than you."

"Not true!" the schemer shrieked. "I opposed him on Pilate's marriage to Claudia."

"And kissed his hand for three years after."

"It was Caesar's hand!" the shrill voice rang, then held, until the echo died. Catullus continued in a hushed, conciliatory tone. "Yes, Theodosius, we're both vulnerable. Separately. But together we can outwit Macro. He's a common thug. And we know the real traitors. Who truly aided Sejanus. Abetted his crimes."

There followed a moment of tense silence, as Veronica heard only the pant of the old Senate dog. Her uncle had heard enough. "You're going to inform."

"I'm going to survive!"

"Get out," Theodosius ordered. "I said, 'Out!'" His voice boomed and Veronica heard a scuffle. She peeked into the atrium to see Theodosius grapple with father and son, dragging them around the pool and tossing them to the door.

Catullus yelped like a kicked dog, "Caesar will decimate the Senate. One in ten will have the life choked from him. Can you survive, Proculus? When Caesar has ever expected you to avenge your brother? Don't be a fool!"

Theodosius batted the coward's hand off the door and slammed it shut. He spun around and exclaimed, "Veronica!" She was there in an instant. "Pack, now. Everything!"

"Everything?"

"All essentials. And anything of value that might be sold."

He roused the house slaves, all of whom had been listening attentively. A mad scramble ensued as the household mobilized. Slaves dashed to the livery for horses: two saddle horses and two teams hitched to wagons. Every item of gold, silver or bronze was brought forth. Food stores were packed. Water. Clothing. Veronica climbed to the veranda, and with a heavy heart threw open her aviary and shooed the birds away. She rounded up her dogs and led them down to the atrium, where Theodosius barred her from the door. "We can't take them," he said.

Horses thundered to the front of the house. Slaves tossed bundles into the wagons and carefully placed valuables among them. Theodosius didn't wait for the wagons to be packed. As he tied a sheathed sword and javelin to his saddle, he barked orders to the servants.

"Take the wagons down the Via Sacra to Florian. Sell everything." Then he handed Paenulus a hastily written scroll. "This letter frees all the household slaves. With the money you get from Florian, first, pay the livery for the horses. Then divide it equally. Do you understand? Florian is an honest merchant, a good client of ours; he'll give you a good price. You will never have to beg, my friend." Paenulus took his master's hand and kissed it. His grey-filmed eyes filled with tears. Theodosius turned to Adrianna. He kissed her cheek, then took some bundles she'd prepared and lashed them to the saddles.

Adrianna kissed Veronica. "May the gods be with you."

Theodosius hoisted Veronica onto a mare and himself mounted a gelding.

"You remember how to ride?"

"Of course!" Veronica's mood had swung from fear to exhilaration. She brought her crop down upon the mare's flank and cantered up the hill. Theodosius urged his mount forward, and the two raced through the dark streets.

Thready fingers of sun were lifting the shroud of night when Veronica reached the top of Quirinal Hill, the northernmost spur of the high ground that defined Rome east of the Tiber River. While Veronica looked back at their home, Theodosius focused on the low ridge that connected this mound with the Capitoline Hill. He pointed to a file of Vigiles or perhaps Guardsmen, marching from the Capitol.

"Macro," he said. "Catullus went straight to him."

Seeing their torches, Veronica gasped, "Will they burn our house?"

Theodosius nodded, "Most likely, but I'm more concerned with the wagons getting through."

They couldn't see the street itself, so they didn't even know if the wagons had left. They'd be slow, heavily laden. What would happen if Macro intercepted them? Would he torture the slaves? Adrianna. Paenulus. They had nothing to do with Caesar or Sejanus, but would that matter in the heat of a purge? Sejanus' daughter was an innocent child, but she'd still been tortured and killed.

Veronica looked at the Proculus home. In a short time it would belch smoke, then burst into flames. Images of her first home flashed through her mind, violence in the night, her mother's terrified face emitting a curl of smoke.

"Come." Theodosius reined his horse around, pointing it away from Rome. Veronica was suddenly gripped with terror. She clutched the reins the way she had the portal of her childhood home. She squeezed her thighs against the barrel of her horse. *I can't leave. I can't.*

Theodosius tugged the mare's halter and got its neck around. He showed no fear to his niece, only determination. "We can't stay here. But we'll be back. I promise you, Veronica, I will bring us back home."

With that, he cracked his reins across the horse's shoulders and galloped. Veronica followed, squinting into the orange, morning light.

*　　　　*　　　　*　　　　*

They rode all morning without stopping, a few times ducking off the road to avoid the military posts along the route. All of Rome's roads had official way stations, *mansiones*, located twelve to eighteen miles apart, where an official, provided he had a passport, could change horses, have his wagon repaired, purchase food or stay for the night. Theodosius did not want the mansio attendants to inform their pursuers.

- 58 -

Macro would likely use the *Cursus Publicus*, the public mail system established by Augustus, to alert the outposts. This system, running mansio to mansio along every Roman road, allowed for a change of horses every fifteen miles, and even a change of riders. Thus, Macro could send an urgent message as far as five hundred miles in a single day. If the mail carrier got ahead of them, they'd not only face danger from pursuers, but from forces ahead, lying in wait.

Around noon, they sought shade and water for the horses. A tree-lined creek not far from the road provided both. Theodosius hobbled the horses and let them drink as Veronica sifted through Adrianna's bundles. She was delighted to find enough food for several days, so she and her uncle lunched as the horses inched their way up a flowery knoll to graze on pink cyclamen. That they would come across a tapestry of beautiful wild flowers as they were fleeing for their lives struck Veronica as phantasmic, a scene Claudia might claim was prefigured in her dreams. Veronica decided it was a good omen. She unlaced her sandals, stretched her cramped legs out and dipped her feet into the creek.

"Don't get too comfortable," Theodosius warned. "We're racing men who spend half their lives in the saddle."

Veronica cooled her toes, curling them in thick moss that undulated beneath the surface of the water. "What do you think happened with the wagons?"

"That's in the hands of the gods." Theodosius drained the last drops of water from a leather pouch and crouched beside the stream to refill it.

"Do you still trust the gods, Uncle?"

Theodosius shrugged. "I have no choice. Those wagons would never have gotten up the hill. And they'd have given our direction away to Macro. I suppose I didn't have to free our slaves. And I could have told them to bring the money to me. That would have been a fine test of loyalty, don't you think?"

"I think they'd have done it. Then we'd all be together." Veronica pulled her feet from the water, shook them dry and laced her sandals up again.

"Ah," Theodosius cautioned, "you're thinking like a family member, when you've got to think like a soldier. If I'd told them where to meet us, and they were captured, they'd have given Macro our position."

"No. They'd never." Veronica stood, straightening her tunic.

Theodosius removed the hobbles from the horses' ankles and led them down from the knoll, back across the creek to the road. "Under Macro's torture, they'd have had no choice."

Theodosius checked the saddles, tightening the cinch beneath the mare's belly. She didn't like it, and blew her barrel full against his efforts. Theodosius waited for the horse to release her breath, then pulled the strap tight.

"What road are we on?" Veronica asked.

39 An ancient route used to transport salt from the eastern coast to Rome

"This is the Via Salaria.[39] It's the most direct road to the coast."

"Won't Macro expect us to take it?"

"Perhaps you'd prefer the Via Flaminia? High mountains, twists and turns. Canyons well suited to an ambush."

Veronica felt a creeping sadness come over her. "You'd have taken that road if it weren't for me."

Theodosius eyed his niece. Veronica sensed he was weighing which insult would be worse — to admit she was slowing him down, or attempt to hide that truth from her when it was so obvious. "Yes," he said. It leads northeast to the port at Ancona."

Theodosius mounted the gelding, soothing the testy horse with a pat on his neck. "It's less direct to the coast than the Salaria, but the people of Ancona are of Greek lineage, and they've never been friendly to Rome. Less chance of betrayal there."

"We should go there, then."

Theodosius smiled confidently, putting her at ease. "We'll have to. The Salaria terminates at a major naval base. We can't loiter there waiting to ship out. We'll have to skirt by that town and take the road north along the sea."

Her uncle's confidence was contagious. Perhaps that's why he was such a fine leader. At any rate, Veronica was happy to follow him. "And where are we shipping out to?"

Theodosius kicked the gelding's ribs, spurring him to a trot. "Across the Adriatic."

"We're going to Greece?"

"Our best choice at this point. Provincial governments tend not to get swept up in the petulance of Rome's politics. They take a longer view of policy. And, they have a history of welcoming exiles."

"Like Cicero? He fled there when he was falsely accused."

"You've learned your history," her uncle commended. "Good. And I'll bet you're glad now that I forced you to study Greek!"

Veronica groaned, remembering the long hours studying, and Adrianna's impatience with the way she misplaced her accents. Once, blinking at a mangled sentence Veronica had written, she joked, "You sprinkle accents on words like salt on a boiled egg!"

"What will we do there?" she asked.

"I will practice law and you will keep the house. And we will wait for Caesar to die." He reached over and gave her a playful tuck under the chin. "It shouldn't take long. He's already had more years than a sick, old dog deserves."

They trotted at a moderate pace, sensitive to the effect of the afternoon heat upon their horses. As the day wore on, Veronica tired and started to bounce uncomfortably on the mare. Theodosius, having not ridden in a long time, also suffered, so he suggested they walk for a distance. Veronica climbed down from the saddle onto wobbly legs.

"Uncle," she piped, "If you don't mind me asking, do we have any money?"

"Not much," he admitted. "But this day was not unexpected. I've been putting away what money I could. The problem is, the wealth of a patrician is in his land, not in a strongbox. So, here is one nobleman who is presently poorer than his former slaves."

"Is there enough to get us to Greece?"

"Provided we don't encounter any highwaymen." Then perhaps regretting he might have frightened her, Theodosius added, "We should be fine."

Veronica had more questions, like, *How far away is Ancona? How many days of riding? Where shall we stay at night?* But she knew a flurry of questions would sound like complaints, and that was the last thing her uncle needed to hear. She appreciated that he was talking to her like a grownup, instead of a child, and she didn't want to say anything that would make him change his mind.

"Are you ready to get back in the saddle?" he asked.

She absolutely was not, but nodded nonetheless. "Sure."

So they rode until the sun was setting at their backs. The low fuchsia light cast elongated shadows up the stone highway. Veronica, from head to foot, was one tight cramp. Though pleased with having demonstrated some measure of toughness, she knew she'd reached her limit.

"We have to consider where we'll stay tonight," her uncle said. "There are the mansiones. We'd have comfort, but risk betrayal. There are the tabernae[40]. They're often loitering places for thieves and prostitutes. We'd stand out like sore thumbs. And Caesar has made spying an industry among the lower classes."

"We can sleep under the stars," Veronica laughed. "Am I thinking like a soldier now?"

"Just in time," Theodosius warned, spotting something over his shoulder. "Now ride like one!"

The Senator kicked his mount into a gallop, leaning forward to urge the tired horse on. "Fly now, fly!" The horses thundered across the hard stones, jolting their riders. Veronica leaned forward and clutched the mane to steady herself, but feared she couldn't keep the pace without bouncing off. Theodosius sensed she was in trouble and slowed beside her. He gripped her reins, passing them to his left hand, then with a deft, backward sweep of his right arm, lifted Veronica off the saddle. "Swing your leg around," he commanded. She lifted her left leg, and scooted onto his horse behind him.

"Hang on!"

Veronica gripped him tightly around the waist as he spurred the horse into a gallop. Her mare ran alongside.

---

[40] The public houses, i.e. taverns, inns

"Who are those men?" she cried.

"Either the Guard or highwaymen. Neither is good for us."

Veronica looked back at the riders. It was too dark to make them out, and while she couldn't judge the distance, she could tell by the rhythm of the hoof beats that the pursuers were traveling faster. When she sneaked a second look, they appeared larger.

"They're gaining!"

Theodosius nodded, and Veronica read what she knew must be his thoughts: *Of course. They have fresh horses. They are expert riders and aren't slowed by a feeble girl!* Veronica felt the strain of his sinews; her uncle's back and abdomen were like rocks. The way ahead was increasingly dark. It seemed that they were racing into the cover of night; if they could maintain distance until the sun was extinguished, they might have a chance to hide in the shadows. Yet, over her uncle's shoulder she saw the cratered mask of the rising moon and felt exposed in the sinister light of a false dawn.

There came a sudden bend on the road, and Theodosius sprang into action. He released Veronica's mare, and brought the gelding to a skidding stop. He handed Veronica a rope and pointed to a tree. "Tie the end to that trunk, good and tight, at your eye level." She jumped from the horse and dashed to the tree, tying a knot as tight as she could. Her uncle gestured to toss the rope. He caught it and whispered, "Now, hide!" Reining his horse across the road, he circled a tree, passing under the rope and letting it sag. Then, as the hoof beats grew louder, he yelled, "Yah-yah!" and spurred the horse forward.

As the riders rounded the corner, the rope sprang high and tight across their path. It caught them across the chests, knocking them off their horses and backwards onto the stone road with a loud crack. They rolled and groaned, fighting to refill their lungs. These were not Guardsmen at all: they were Legionnaires. Theodosius leapt from his horse, drawn sword in hand. He poised his blade at one soldier's throat and demanded, "Who sent you? Who?"

The soldier struggled to breathe, then replied, "Macro."

"What were your orders?"

"Kill. You and the girl."

A cold shock ran down Veronica's spine. Who was she that strangers would ride through the night to kill her? And what was Rome that its leaders gave such orders and Legionnaires — the pride of Rome's military — would carry them out? Her uncle stood with arm extended, his sword point creasing this soldier's throat.

"You dishonor yourself and the Legion when you make war on children."

The soldier nodded hastily. Veronica shared his fear that her uncle would plunge the sword into his neck. Instead Theodosius pulled it away.

"We will take your horses. That's the price for your life. And you will report back to Macro that you met with an accident."

"Yes, Senator."

"And that you never saw us."

"Yes, Senator."

The soldiers then helped each other to their feet. They limped gingerly. Their breathing was labored. Undoubtedly, several ribs were cracked. They'd have a painful walk back to the nearest mansio. Theodosius waved Veronica out of her hiding place. He boosted her onto one soldier's horse. The stallion was enormous. She wondered if she could manage such a powerful beast. Theodosius wrangled the remaining horses and roped them together. He then ascended the other stallion. As they trotted from the scene, Veronica asked, "Do you think they'll keep their word, about not telling Macro?"

"I doubt it," he answered.

"Then why did you let them live?"

"Not for their sake; for mine," he answered. He gazed at the moon, hanging low above the hills; the reddish hue of its ravaged surface seemed to mock his mercy. "The moon lends enough light to commit the crime, but never so much to expose its shame. Yet, even by moonlight, it's murder."

They rode in that moonlight, and as she suspected, Veronica couldn't command the stallion. After that long sprint, he was not in the mood to move anywhere quickly and didn't respect Veronica's feeble kicks or slaps with her crop. Finally, Theodosius took her whip away.

"Forget it. He knows he has you beaten. It's best we find a place to camp."

"Over there," Veronica pointed. A clearing was lighted by several torches, revealing half a dozen tents pitched in a circle. There were three large wagons and about a dozen mules grazed in tall, dry grass. Theodosius looked uncertain.

"Let's see who they are," he said, and nosed his horse toward the field. Veronica's mount, sensing a meal break, followed happily toward the grass. Theodosius waited for Veronica's stallion to pull a snoutful of hay from the earth, then grabbed its halter and pulled the stubborn beast forward.

A watchman saw them coming and alerted the camp. He called out in a language Veronica couldn't understand. An older man came forward. His head was covered, and he was dressed in layers of flowing robes. A full, white beard fell upon to his chest. Speaking a common form of Greek, he welcomed them. Theodosius returned the greeting as they got down from their horses.

Veronica whispered to her uncle, "Who are they?"

"Merchants. Probably Jews."

Veronica clutched her uncle's cloak, stopping him. He furrowed his brow, questioning her fear. "Sejanus called them vermin."

Theodosius chuckled, "And look what happened to him."

A servant stepped forward and bowed, extending his hands for the reins. Theodosius gave them to him, and the servant led the horses toward the grazing area.

The older man spoke again. "You've come from Rome?"

"Yes."

"We were headed there, but heard of unrest. Now we're waiting to see." The old man led them to the center of the camp, where members of his party were seated around a fire. Though younger, the men were nonetheless bearded. Two of them rose, making room for the visitors. "My wife thinks it prudent to leave immediately. But I've wanted to see Rome for many years, and this may be my last chance before I die."

"It's a magnificent city," Theodosius said. "We take it too much for granted."

"My name is Joseph, by the way." The old man gestured for them to sit; an older woman, whom Veronica took to be his wife, brought a tray of fruit and pieces of cheese. Her uncle introduced the two of them by name. Veronica saw the servant who had taken the horses lead them to a trough of water. He removed their saddles and set them aside. The old man continued, "I worry it's not a good time in Rome to be a Jew."

Veronica was struck by the ease of his admission, his comfort with labeling himself in a way others found odious. Theodosius was nonchalant, offering, "It's not a good time to be a Roman."

Joseph received bread from his wife. He tore a piece for himself and passed it to Veronica. She ate ravenously, drawing a reproachful glare from her uncle, who, though he must have been hungry, ate at a moderate pace, politely conversing with their host. Veronica listened as the men talked of politics and power, philosophy and wisdom. Theodosius finally let his exasperation show.

"The Senate is the last vestige of the Republic. Where rhetoric — reason — can triumph over brute force. When that is violated, Rome is no better than... well, it's not worth the marble pillars that prop it up." As if to punctuate his complaint, Theodosius returned to his plate, picking at some morsels and eating quietly.

The old man stroked his beard, weighing his words carefully before responding.

"If I may, Senator, it seems to me that men arguing to persuade other men is much like — as one young Rabbi puts it — 'the blind leading the blind.' At their core, men need to be led, but not by other men. By God."

Theodosius waved his hand dismissively, "Yes, the gods. Not blind. But at the moment they're deaf and mute."

"As befits stone idols. But," the old man leaned forward, his bearded face illuminated by flame, "there is a living God."

Theodosius stopped chewing. "And you've seen him?"

Veronica expected a positive answer, so much did his wizened visage in firelight resemble an elder of Olympus. But the old man leaned back out of the light, admitting "No," before gently asserting, "But I've felt — known — Him."

Theodosius sipped wine from a wooden cup, savoring it, before responding. "I have heard, and perhaps I'm mistaken, that your people claim a special kinship to a god. That is, one you claim is the only true god. Who, though he created everyone, loves only you."

The old man shook his head, "No, it's not that the Creator loves us only or loves us more. It's just that for some reason, He has chosen to reveal Himself to us. Though he whispers to all men, through reason and conscience, to us He has roared. That is a blessing, but also a tremendous responsibility."

Theodosius nodded, seeming to mull over the premise and its conclusion. "Sir, your hospitality does that responsibility justice."

"Thank you, Senator."

Theodosius let a servant refill his cup. Joseph's wife poured Veronica more tea. The Senator asked, "So, Joseph, if you don't go into Rome, where will you go?"

"Home. We are from Arimathea. A small town in Judea."

Veronica perked up. "We've relatives there. The Prefect. Pontius Pilate."

"Pilate?" Joseph gasped.

"My daughter, Claudia, is his wife," Theodosius explained. Then, alarmed by the horror deep in the old man's eyes, he implored, "Why? What's he done?"

A hollow whisper followed. "He's a butcher."

Veronica dropped her cup. Tea splashed at her feet. She looked across the fire at her host, silent as death.

"What have you heard?" Theodosius asked.

"I was there." The orange fire cast broad, black shadows, deepening Joseph's age lines. His face appeared like a carved totem, set against wind and time, where later generations might come and beg the story he now bowed his head to speak.

"Pilate's arrival was trumpeted. He marched with broad banners and streaming pennants, all bearing the images which declared Caesar a god. He marched those false idols into Jerusalem, and took occupation of the Palace. The Palace that had belonged to Herod the Great, the Palace that overlooked the Temple. Our people, coming to the Temple, saw images of Caesar. Jews who treated with the Prefect had to do so under images of Caesar. For people, who regard reverence to idols as the seed of our soul's destruction, this was unbearable. Efforts were made to have the young Prefect understand. He mocked our beliefs. Ancient superstition. Caesar was the reality we must accept! But our men could not accept. When our petitions fell on deaf ears, we gathered outside the Palace. Pilate declared he would not remove the images; he would remove our heads. So we lay in the dust and we bared our necks. Pilate's soldiers strode among us, prostrate on the ground, and waited for his command. They drew their swords. They raised their weapons. When not a man stirred, nor begged mercy, Pilate relented. The soldiers sheathed their swords. The images were struck."

Theodosius let a breath escape slowly. "A grim episode, Joseph. But if Pilate relented, how is he a butcher?"

The old man rolled his heavy head. "That was the first sign. Later, after Pilate had constructed an aqueduct to transport water to the city, he argued with the Sanhedrin, our counsel. He wanted Jerusalem to pay for it, on top of our regular taxes. Caiaphas, the High Priest, argued that we were already heavily taxed. Pilate wouldn't listen. He raided the Temple treasury. He mocked the idea that those funds should be used for holy purposes, the care of widows and orphans. He had a point, to a certain extent: the High Priest is notoriously corrupt. Temple priests are well paid for performing sacrifices. In fact, some suggest the Temple has become more of a commercial enterprise than a house of worship. But for pagans to enter the Temple and take the treasury by force, it was an affront. And so again, the men of Jerusalem gathered to protest. But this time, Pilate was ready.

"He sent Legionnaires, their uniforms covered in Jewish dress, into the crowd. The disguised soldiers mingled with unarmed protestors. Pilate berated the crowd, inflaming their passions. He mocked the High Priest, provoking more anger. He approached the crowd, daring them to act, belittling them as men. Mocking the Almighty, he chanted, *"Caesar is my god! Hail, Caesar!"* He brought these men to the brink of riot. Then he signaled his soldiers, who threw off their disguises, drew their swords, and hacked. Hacked until the forum was bathed in blood. Pilate himself — so close to the carnage — was spattered with the blood of the men he butchered. And he laughed."

Veronica sprang to her feet, unable to take any more.

"Liar! You lie about Pontius! Sejanus was right, you are vermin! Vermin!"

She tore from the fire circle and dashed through the darkness to the horses. She startled the hobbled beasts, which bucked and snorted. She heard her uncle call, "Veronica! Veronica!", as she fumbled in the dark for the halters and saddles. Images assaulted her mind: Claudia's dream of blood flooding Jerusalem, Pilate at the pier vowing to leave his heart at home. Had he done that? Abandoned his heart?

Veronica found a halter and approached her mare. The horse resisted, throwing her head up and down wildly. Just so, Veronica's imagination ran wild. She saw Pilate standing atop a pile of butchered corpses, pulling Claudia to him and laughing. Veronica screamed and the mare bolted, knocking her to the ground. Theodosius pushed his way between the horses and pulled his niece from the dirt. She fought, determined to saddle her mare and ride.

"No. Let me go!" she cried. "I'm going to Claudia! Let me go!"

But Theodosius took Veronica in his strong arms and rocked her gently. "Hush. Shh. We'll go."

She choked on her tears, "If he's become wicked, if he's hurt her...!"

"No. Hush, now. It's all right. All right." The Senator stroked her hair. "We'll go to Claudia. Tomorrow we'll set out. You'll see that she's well."

Theodosius led Veronica back toward the camp. She felt humiliated as they approached Joseph, but the old man said nothing reproachful or unkind.

He simply led them to a tent his servants had prepared. He held up the flap for Veronica to stoop and enter. A lamp burned low in the center of the tent. Veronica found a bedroll laid out for her, and reclined as she heard the men talk outside.

"He was not prepared to govern," her uncle lamented. "He listened to bad counsel."

Joseph concurred, adding, "The counsel of men. Not of God."

"If yours is a god who speaks," Theodosius said, "I should like to talk to him."

Veronica rolled over, wanting no more talk of gods. No more talk at all. She wanted to ride. She wanted to be with Claudia. She wanted to know that her cousin wasn't married to a butcher.

Chapter 7

Veronica awoke at sunrise to find the camp already in motion. It took considerable effort to straighten her sore legs from their tight fetal position, and she reeled slightly as she hoisted herself to her feet. She slipped on her tunic and felt along the wall of the tent for her sandals.

When Veronica emerged from her tent, she found it was the only one standing. Women immediately entered to strip it, as men stood by to dismantle it. Joseph's wife waved her over to the smoldering fire and served her a plate of loose cheese, dates and bread. Veronica thanked her and stood nibbling the food, watching the men pack wagons and hitch up the mules. She saw her uncle in the grazing area, apparently dickering with Joseph over the horses.

"I wish I could help you, Senator," the old man said, "but stallions make poor draught horses. Especially these, branded by the Roman Legion."

"The mansio will pay to have them returned."

"Perhaps, but if we are stopped before the mansio? I doubt the Legionnaires would believe our intent was to return them."

"Then one hundred denarii. For the two. The mansio will pay four times that."

"Sir," Joseph cautioned. "It may be better for a righteous man to trust in providence than to seek profit selling what is not legally his."

Theodosius reacted sharply, "I don't need a philosophical lecture! I need money!" Veronica could see, as her uncle turned his back to the camp, that he immediately regretted the outburst.

Joseph bowed his head, apparently sympathetic to the Senator's plight. After a second, he offered, "I can use the mare. She looks to be four years old. It's possible she'll breed with my jack. I might need another mule before my journey's done."

Theodosius muttered, "I can't sell the mare. It's the only —"

"I can ride the gelding, Uncle!" Veronica called. She skipped toward the men, snatching a halter from the ground, shaking the morning dew from it, and carrying it toward the horse in question. "He's only slightly larger than my mare. And he's very gentle." To demonstrate, she hooked her right arm around his neck and took hold of the halter, just behind his low snout. Sliding her arm down his neck while he grazed, Veronica slipped the halter easily over his nose, and slid the bit to the back of his mouth. He snorted and wiggled his head, but did not greatly protest. "See. He's not like the stallion. He'll listen to me."

Theodosius nodded and turned to Joseph, who had already commanded a young man to bring his strongbox, from which he pulled a full purse. He placed it in the Senator's hand. Theodosius peeked inside.

"This is too much," he objected.

"I see many mules in that mare's future," Joseph chuckled. "And on a philosophical note, none can trust in providence unless some are willing to help it along."

The two men shook hands and parted. Joseph strode to his caravan, supervising the final preparations for departure. Theodosius saddled their horses, then removed the hobbles from their front ankles. He boosted Veronica onto the gelding and patted her approvingly on the thigh. He chose to ride Veronica's stallion, remarking that if he didn't, the horse would be spoiled. "We can't let the beast go on thinking he's the boss." He tethered the second stallion to his saddle.

Veronica tried to relax her tight muscles so they'd stretch comfortably in time with the undulation of her horse. She dreaded the full day of riding ahead, but wanted desperately to keep a brave front for her uncle.

"Are we still going to Ancona?"

"Yes. We may not be able to sail directly to Greece, but it gets us out of Italy faster. The sooner we're in the provinces, the better."

Veronica paused, not sure she wanted to broach the next subject. But her uncle had spoken frankly to her, so she ought to be frank with him. "Uncle Theo. Yesterday you said we had enough money, but..."

"Yesterday, we were going to Greece," he said. "Today, we're going to Judea."

At the road, the horses accelerated to a trot without prompting. Veronica bounced tensely at first, but her sore muscles warmed to the equine motion and she was able to relax. And knowing that they were truly on their way to Claudia lifted her spirits even further. The sharp morning sun promised a sweltering day and the road seemed to extend forever. By her uncle's calculation, they'd have three more days of riding before reaching Ancona. So she wasn't very happy when Theodosius ordered another detour, taking them off the road as they approached the next mansio.

"We're taking the most efficient path," her uncle declared. "Even if it isn't the straightest." Veronica didn't think picking their way through the woods was efficient. Each branch that grabbed at her hair confirmed it.

Suddenly, the brush before them exploded, and a frenzied horse broke across their path. Theodosius' stallion reared as the riderless horse swept past. The Senator brought his mount under control and immediately pulled his javelin from its sheath. He had the spear poised on his shoulder and his horse angled in front of his niece as the brush erupted again.

Two riders, cloaked and masked, halted before them. One raised a crossbow, but before he could fix his aim, Theodosius had flung his javelin into the archer's chest. This caused his horse to break sideways, bumping the second rider and pinning him against a tree. He had to toss his companion off before he could raise a sword. By that time, Theodosius had circled behind him, sword high, ready to lop off a limb. Renewed good sense then met innate cowardice, propelling that rider down a deer trail, his dying comrade trailing after.

Veronica released a breath she didn't know she'd been holding, and relaxed her grip on her saddle, allowing some color to return to her knuckles.

"Who were they?"

"Highwaymen. Cutthroat robbers. Come."

Theodosius led her through the thick brush into a clearing. It was soon apparent what he was after: a man lay sprawled face-down on the ground, an arrow protruding from beneath his left scapula.

"I doubt there's any hope for him," her uncle said. "Wait here." Theodosius swung down from his horse and handed Veronica his reins. He stooped to pick up a leather cap with an official insignia. Tossing it aside, Theodosius knelt beside the man and felt his wrist, but found no pulse. He then paced around the area, poking briars, searching.

"What are you looking for?"

"He's a rider for the mail. I'm looking for his bag."

"Wouldn't the highwaymen have it?" Veronica asked. Her uncle returned to the corpse. "Or it would be tied to his saddle."

"All except," Theodosius reasoned, rolling the corpse over, "the most urgent messages." He reached inside the man's tunic and pulled out a scroll. He untied the ribbon and read. "The gods be praised!" he exclaimed. He ran back to the horses.

"What is it?"

"Our friend's bad fortune is to our good. Macro's letter. Alerting the military of a Senator, a conspirator against Caesar — that would be me —

fleeing Rome with his *daughter*." He shrugged. "Close enough. He's commanding that we be arrested and returned for trial."

"So, we're safe?" Veronica sighed.

"Well," her uncle responded, again mounting his horse, "it means we don't have to fear what lies ahead, only what comes from behind."

"So the highwaymen did us a favor."

"Clearly, that was not their intent." Theodosius reined his horse around and urged him toward the road. Veronica kicked her mare after him. She ducked branches and snapped twigs, then straightened as they gained the road. Trotting beside her uncle, she posed a question.

"Could this be what Joseph said, *providence assisting the righteous man?*"

"The mail rider might argue the point. If he could."

"But, Uncle," Veronica persisted, "don't you want to believe in the gods? You said, *The gods be praised.*"

"I did." Theodosius admitted. "And I hope they continue to earn my praise. Meanwhile, that man's wife and children will not have much praise to offer."

Veronica huffed. Her uncle's ambivalence was so frustrating.

"Uncle Theo," she asked. "Considering how you wouldn't kill those soldiers, how you regret the mail rider's death, are you sorry at all you killed that highwayman?"

Theodosius rolled his shoulders, as if letting the incident slide off his back. "I'm sorry I lost my lance."

*   *   *   *

That night they camped in a pine forest. Veronica made a comfortable bed of needles over which she placed her blanket. Theodosius scoured the area, searching for broken knots oozing sap. He scraped this pine resin off with a knife and into a cooking pot. He added chips of bark and set the pot on glowing embers to cook. The pot smoked horribly, and Veronica had to abandon her comfortable bed, which unfortunately was down-wind of the fire. She watched as her uncle scooped up some droppings from behind the horses and added them to the pot.

"Oh, that should make it smell better!" she grumbled.

Theodosius chuckled. "Go back to sleep."

The last thing she remembered that night was seeing her uncle take a knife to the gelding's mane and scrape off some hair, which he also dropped into the stinking pot.

When she awakened, Veronica saw her uncle scraping his knife along the rump of a stallion. His cloak was over the stallion's head, making the horse docile, so he could trim away at the dried paste of tar and hair he'd applied over the brand of the Roman Legion. The brand was now virtually invisible.

"Oh," Veronica smiled, "now no one will know they're stolen."

"Shush," her uncle corrected, "they're not stolen. What we did, *appropriating* these horses from those Legionnaires, is perfectly legal."

"Really?" she asked doubtfully.

Her uncle, satisfied with his work, removed the cloak from the stallion's head and placed it over his shoulders. He assumed the posture of an orator in the forum.

"The highest law is the law of necessity," he averred, "which states: *'That which is necessary is legal.'* It was necessary to take these horses to save the lives of two innocent people."

Veronica turned back to the fire. As she rummaged through the bundle of food, she pressed her uncle further, "And does that make them ours?"

"It makes our *use* of them legal. It does *not* make them ours." He hoisted a saddle from the ground and set himself to toss it over the stallion's back.

Now Veronica thought she had him. "But," she prodded, "you tried to sell them to Joseph."

Theodosius held the saddle. "No," he insisted, "I simply tried to get from him a share of the reward he would get for returning them."

Veronica scraped some mold off a piece of cheese and flicked it onto the fire. "Hm," she pretended to think deeply. "I'm not sure a person who takes a horse is entitled to share the reward for returning it."

"In truth, I'm not sure either." Theodosius placed the saddle on the stallion, and reached underneath its belly for the strap. "But we needed the money, so—"

"Law of necessity?"

"I'll admit it stretches the law," he said, tightening the cinch. He then took his knife and cut the stitches that fixed the Legion's insignia to the saddle. "But stretching the law is often what a lawyer is hired to do."

*   *   *   *

"I can't sail if there's no wind!" the shipmaster barked. "You think I've got galley slaves to row across?"

Veronica inched back up the pier as Theodosius fumed. It had been two days since they'd arrived in Ancona. For two days pennants had drooped, sails had sagged and ships all along the wharf had remained idle, as the sea failed to serve up even a light zephyr. And in that time, Veronica knew, they'd lost their advantage over Macro. Had he sent more soldiers, they might arrive at any moment to find their quarry trapped against the blue abyss.

"I am simply anxious to reach Dalmatia[41]," Theodosius insisted.

But the wily mariner snarled, "Perhaps. Though you give the impression of a man more flying from than to."

"I'm paying you for passage," the Senator reminded him.

"And you'll have it, as soon as passage is possible." The shipmaster turned his back and skulked away. Theodosius hefted their bags onto his shoulders, as he'd done the previous two days, and walked from the dock toward their lodgings.

Ancona was a seaport town. Built upon and below two vast hills — forming something of an amphitheatre around the harbor — Ancona seemed almost to have its back to Rome. It had been settled centuries ago as a Greek colony, and the townspeople, including this shipmaster, spoke Greek. In fact — Veronica had to laugh — Ancona in Greek meant "elbow," after the bent shape the two hills and sea inlet gave to the town. Since the Empire's expansion east, Ancona had lost most of its strategic importance, so there wasn't much of a military presence, except for a mansio and the occasional naval ship patrolling against pirates. Its people fished, maintained coastal trade and infrequently crossed the Adriatic for silver, which was about the only item Dalmatia produced that couldn't be gotten more cheaply in Italy. Finally, it kept up its most ancient purpose, supplying salt for the city of Rome, though the sprawling Empire had discovered (and conquered) many additional sources of that mineral.

"What should we do now, Uncle?" Veronica asked.

"Are you rested?"

"Yes, of course," she replied. They'd done nothing but eat and sleep since arriving in Ancona.

"It might be time to get the horses from the livery. We can ride up the coast to the next port."

"Where is that?"

Theodosius puffed his cheeks and sighed. "That I don't know."

They walked from the wharf towards the mansio. Theodosius had thought it safe enough to stay there, in view of the poor reputation of the local taberna, their fortunate interception of the mail, and their lead over their pursuers. But nature had squandered that lead and, even if they remained in the vicinity of Ancona, they couldn't remain at an official Roman outpost.

They crossed the street diagonally toward the mansio, when the sudden clopping of hooves on stone put them on alert. A horse had rounded the corner, and now veered to cut them off. Its rider, a slender youth, wore a nondescript tunic and cloak. A short sword hung in a scabbard at his belt.

"Senator Proculus?" he called.

The Senator froze. He lowered the bags to the street, deftly uncinching one bundle before he straightened up.

---

[41] A Roman province comprising modern-day Croatia and Bosnia

"Yes?"

"I've found you!" the rider called triumphantly, and swung down from his horse. Landing, he placed a hand on his hilt and adjusted the belt. In a flash, Theodosius was on him: he pulled his sword from the loosed bundle and — lunging — planted its point at the youth's sternum.

"If Macro wishes me dead, he should not send boys to do it!" The Senator prepared to lunge again.

"No! Senator!" the youth cried. "I'm Sabinus." He dropped to his knees. "I trained in your house as a fuller. Under Paenulus. He sent me to find you." Veronica suddenly knew him as one of the boys — now grown — who'd filled the tubs and danced upon their garments.

Seeing the recognition on Veronica's face, Theodosius lowered his sword.

"He told me to say, *Your slaves have done as you commanded. Your belongings have been sold. But we* — they — *cannot obey your last order.* They cannot take your money." Then, holding his hands high, he rose from the ground and went to his horse. From a bag he pulled two sacks of coins. He handed them to Theodosius. "Your servants request that you tell me where you are heading, that they may meet you there and continue in your service. They've kept only enough money for that journey."

Veronica then saw something she'd never seen before: a crack in her uncle's stoicism. His eyes moistened. He batted the lids to tamp down tears before raising a hand to his face. As the youth waited for the Senator to compose himself, he looked at Veronica, and seemed almost to swell.

He continued, "But, sir, I've a request of my own."

"Speak it."

"I pray that you don't send me back. That instead you send a letter. And allow me to stay in your service."

"I hardly need a fuller," the Senator joked.

"But you may need an extra sword!" Sabinus hopped to his horse again and, reaching behind the saddle, pulled a broadsword from its sheath. He brandished the weapon — obviously too heavy for him — showing off what technique he'd learned. His movements were leaden and awkward, but Theodosius indulged the youth as he lunged and parried an invisible opponent. Then the Senator abruptly ended the demonstration with a downward sweep of his own sword that crossed the youth's at the hilt and snapped it from his grasp. The loud clang of iron on stone did more injury to Sabinus' ego than the sudden wrenching did his hand. Flushed red, the boy stood rigid, until the Senator conceded, "You'll do." Happily, Sabinus snatched up his sword and returned it to its cover.

"All that money and they sent you alone?" Veronica wondered. "You're lucky to have gotten here at all. The Via is crawling with highwaymen."

"Well," the youth blushed. "I wasn't exactly alone."

"What do you mean?" Theodosius asked.

The youth became agitated, speaking rapidly without breath or, it seemed, much thought. "Well, you remember Valentius? Of course. Paenulus didn't know where to find him, so he asked me, and I fetched him to the market. And Paenulus told him the story, and asked him to take the money to you, and I pleaded to go with him."

Theodosius raised an eyebrow as the story shifted, like blown sand exposing a rocky ledge. "And where is Valentius?"

Sabinus either ignored or didn't hear the question, so involved was he in his recitation of events.

"He didn't want me along," Sabinus admitted, "but I said, 'I've purchased my liberty. I'm a free man, and I will go with you!' Not as a protector — I didn't want him to think, even though he can only hold a sword in his left hand, that I thought he needed protecting — but two on the road is a deterrent to attack. Wouldn't you concede that Senator?"

It was her uncle's turn to ignore the question. "Where is he?"

"Well, that's the funny thing, sir," the boy meandered. "Because all this time he's determined to impress me with how well he rides — and wouldn't you know — his horse comes up lame! And not two miles from town. So he's walking his horse."

"And he gave you the money?"

"Well, Senator," the boy puffed. "That was my idea. I figured the sooner we got secure lodging, and put those coins in a secure place, the better for all concerned. And since he begged me to ride ahead to catch you before you might sail, I figured I might just as well take the coins, to surprise you."

"You took the money from him?"

"No, sir." Sabinus vowed. "I took it from his horse."

Veronica giggled. Theodosius was less amused. "How did you manage that?"

"Well," the youth hedged, "Valentius took a moment. That is, he turned. He had to pass water, sir."

Theodosius' eyes rolled straight back. Veronica couldn't stifle her laugh.

"I suppose," the Senator muttered, "we should go find him."

"Now, Senator," Sabinus hopped in protest. "You've given your word I can stay in your service. I don't want his testimony influencing that."

"His testimony?" Theodosius asked. "What would that—"

"Thief!" a voice bellowed.

Veronica snapped her head around to see Valentius, overheated from temper and a long jog in the hot sun, dragging a limping horse down the street. He tugged hard on the reins, but his horse had had enough. It shook its head and snorted furiously until Valentius relented and dropped the reins. His hand free, he drew the short sword from his belt and chased after Sabinus, who scooted to the other side of his horse, then circled nose to tail, trying to keep the beast as a barrier between them. Wanting no part of the conflict, the horse scampered away, leaving Sabinus unguarded. He chased after the horse, pulling his sword from the saddle scabbard, in time to cross his blade with Valentius'. Thus engaged, they continued: Valentius clumsily swinging with his left hand at the wiry youth, who, though too thin to keep his sword aloft, was too agile to be struck.

"Uncle," Veronica cried, "won't they kill each other?"

He pursed his lips. "Only if we're lucky." Then after her glare had singed his eyebrows, he relented. "Understood."

When the combatants crossed swords again, a third blade intersected, locking the others in place. "Enough," the Senator commanded. "You're creating a spectacle." In fact, a few townspeople had stopped to watch.

"This boy's a thief!" Valentius roared.

"Possibly," the Senator allowed. "But you can't prove it on his actions today. He merely returned to me what was mine. The only thing stolen was your chance at adulation. Please, Valentius, put up your sword, and be content with my gratitude."

Valentius nodded, sheathed his sword, and said, "I am at your service, Senator."

"Get your horses to the livery," Theodosius instructed. Regarding the lame one, he added, "See what can be done. We have an extra stallion, if we have to ride."

His horse had not gone far: it stood three doors down, its front leg curled, with only the very tip of that hoof touching the pavement. Valentius took a step toward it, but stopped to settle his mind on its most pressing issue. "You'll be sending the boy back?"

Theodosius set his jaw. "He's requested to stay in my service."

"Senator, you can't seriously... That rascal?"

Theodosius squinted at the youth, now coaxing his horse toward the livery. "He may well be a rascal. Or simply a boy looking to prove himself. At any rate, I'd rather keep him happily with me, than send him unhappily back toward my enemies."

"Understood, sir," Valentius bowed.

The baggage went back to the mansio. Theodosius then composed a letter to post through the tabellarii[42], rather than risk the official mail which had to pass through government hands. Sabinus had prearranged for a letter to be sent to Crassus, another client of Theodosius, rather than Florian, who might already be under suspicion for having purchased the stock of the Proculus home. He had also devised a code, whereby Theodosius could tell his former slaves where and when to rendezvous.

"He's quite crafty," the Senator remarked.

"He's a rascal," Valentius scoffed.

---

[42] A private mail service which employed slaves as runners

Veronica found him a little endearing. He was a bit of a goose, in the way he kept honking about himself, but she understood how someone her age might be eager to impress. She also sensed, dating back to when he worked for Paenulus — and lit up every time she visited — that he wasn't so much interested in serving the Senator as he was in accompanying the Senator's niece. Beyond the obvious flattery, Veronica wasn't sure how she felt about that. On the one hand, it would be great having someone her own age on the journey. On the other hand, she couldn't possibly share such feelings with a freedman, a boy who used to earn his keep sloshing through urine and breathing sulfur. Oh, and there was a third hand: she got the feeling Valentius had his eye on her also, and that did not sit well with her. Maybe because it was all too possible: Theodosius could adopt him, making him a patrician and clearing the way for them to marry. That seemed like too much of her life being decided without her input. And, having seen him in a temper, Veronica now thought him less handsome — and much more gruff and uncultured — than when she'd first spied him. So, she welcomed having the rascal under foot. Especially since, in his deviousness, he seemed capable of thinking like a soldier, and that was the kind of thinking that just might keep them alive.

The party of four gathered at the taberna for lunch and, in hushed voices, recalled their adventures of the last few days and discussed their plans. Valentius proudly revealed how they'd tracked the fugitives, and Theodosius was visibly concerned that it had been so easy. The Senator let them read Macro's letter, then tucked it away again in his belt. Veronica wondered why he'd kept it, but as her uncle had given her no reason to doubt his judgment, she assumed he had a purpose. Theodosius decided they'd try waiting until the end of the day to attempt crossing to Dalmatia. From there, they would sail down the coast to Dyrrhachium[43]. Dyrrhachium was a major destination from the port of Brindisi, where the house servants were headed on the Via Appia, and from where they'd sail across the Adriatic.

If the day passed without any wind, — since they could not risk another night in Ancona — they would fetch the horses from the livery and start riding north. If they did sail, they would simply leave the horses. Sabinus insisted they sell the horses to the stable master, but Theodosius overrode him: if they offered the horses for sale, potential customers would inspect them, and likely discover the tarred-over brands. Considering that Valentius' horse had split a front hoof, the cash they could get for the horses did not seem worth the risk. The debate continued as they went out to the street.

"Let me deal separately for my horse," Sabinus argued. "The stable master won't connect me with the stallions. It could fetch three hundred denarii."

"Three hundred? Your horse is vulture food," Valentius snapped.

---

[43] A port city at the start of the Via Egnatia, a Roman road that proceeded east across Macedonia to Asia

"My horse?" the youth retorted, "You mean the one with four working hooves?"

Valentius took a swat at Sabinus, who ducked away.

"This will be a fine sea voyage," Theodosius remarked wryly.

"Sir, sir," a high voice piped. Veronica stepped back as a young boy presented himself to her uncle. "You are the Senator?"

"Yes."

"Ave, Senator," the boy bowed. "My master begs me fetch you to the ship. He says wind is favorable."

So it was! Veronica held her arms out and spun, enjoying the breeze. Theodosius regarded his cloak rising from his back. "Thank you, boy. Here's an as for your trouble," he said, flipping the messenger a copper coin. The child scampered off as the foursome strode across the street. "Let's get the baggage down to the pier."

Valentius halted the Senator with a touch of his arm and pointed to the hills with the remaining finger of his bad hand. "Senator. There." Between the hills, high upon the Via Flaminia, rode an Officer of the Praetorian Guard and more than a dozen Legionnaires.

"No time to lose."

But before the Senator could take a step, Sabinus, hurrying who knows where, bumped him from behind. Embarrassed, the youth hung his head and clasped his hands behind his back, sheepishly.

"Keep a cool head, boy," Valentius cautioned. Having kept his saddlebags with him, Valentius hefted them onto his shoulder and headed for the pier. Veronica and her uncle dashed to the mansio, reclaimed their luggage, then sprinted down to the pier where the shipmaster stood waiting.

"Nag me for three days, then make me wait?" the seaman scoffed.

"My apologies," Theodosius said, as he tossed the baggage to a deck hand. "We've two more for passage," he added, pointing to Valentius.

"Hope they've brought their own provisions," he grumbled. "Come, let's not lose this wind." He took Veronica's hand and helped her into the ship.

"Senator," Valentius asked, "where's the rascal?"

The deck hands untied the lines, getting ready to cast off.

"He may be at the livery," Veronica winced. She'd caught him from the corner of her eye heading up the street.

"What?!"

"I thought he went for his bags," she cried. "He must be arguing over the horse."

Theodosius strode up the pier, ignoring Valentius and the shipmaster.

"Leave that fool, Senator!"

"I can't continue to hold!"

Veronica was tempted to jump from the ship, but watched silently as her uncle ran up the main street. The mounted soldiers were charging toward the town, only a couple of minutes away. As Theodosius reached the livery, the door burst open and Sabinus fell into the street. The youth scrambled on all fours, as the stable master snapped a bullwhip after him. Dodging several quick cracks of the leather, Sabinus hid behind the Senator who found himself in the grip of the wrathful stableman. Muttering some quick mollifying phrases, the Senator freed himself, and fled back to the wharf.

"They're coming!" Veronica shouted. The sail went up and flapped noisily as it filled, but not loud enough to drown out the rumble of hoof beats: the horsemen had reached the mansio. The ship drifted wide of the pier as it plowed forward. Suddenly Theodosius and Sabinus gained the wharf. They flew up the pier. Theodosius, not hesitating, leapt onto the mounds of piled bagged aft of the sail. Sabinus continued to run alongside; he soon ran out of pier.

"Jump!" Veronica yelled.

The youth launched himself from the last plank, a six-foot arc into the ship. He only jumped five. Veronica recoiled as a plume of seawater erupted off the starboard. A deck hand tossed Sabinus a line, but it uncoiled on the churning surface for several seconds before he resurfaced. He flailed after the line and finally gripped it.

"Slacken the sail!" the master called.

"No. Make haste!" Theodosius commanded. The deckhands froze.

"I give the orders aboard this ship!" raged the master.

"Then give orders that will save it."

The master's eyes went to the town. "So you *are* fleeing!"

"To preserve our lives," Theodosius pleaded.

The shipmaster regarded Veronica briefly, then bellowed, "Full sail!"

The Senator hurried aft, his attention to Sabinus — a flounder in tow — holding tight to the line as Valentius attempted to haul him in.

"He'll lose his grip," Valentius spat.

Theodosius untied his cloak and handed it to Veronica. His belt hit the deck, then he pulled his tunic over his head. Naked but for his linen loincloth, Theodosius tied a line around his waist and dove from the stern. Just then Sabinus let the line slip, and Valentius tumbled backwards onto the deck. But Theodosius caught the youth, grabbing him from behind and rotating to keep their heads above the waves. The crew scrambled to the second line and heaved the two men in.

Veronica looked to the wharf, expecting that any second the Legion would rumble onto the pier and assail the ship. As her uncle placed a hand on the rail of the stern, the Legion finally charged onto the wharf. But the horsemen didn't storm the pier or assail the ship. The stable master was among them, bullwhip in hand, pointing emphatically south along the shore. So, the dozen horses thundered down the road, toward the next seaport.

Theodosius shook salt water from his head, and slipped his tunic back on. Sabinus hacked, spat and belched up water he'd unhappily swallowed. Veronica handed her uncle his cloak.

"Why didn't they come?" she wondered.

"I could answer that," Sabinus coughed. "But you won't like it."

"I should say we won't!" Valentius scowled. "You going back to argue over a horse! Putting us all in jeopardy!"

"I didn't go back for my horse." Sabinus shuddered, ringing cold water from his tunic. "I went back to show him this." He reached inside his tunic, pulling out a soggy scroll. Veronica recognized immediately Macro's letter. He must have taken it when he'd bumped her uncle!

"Why," Valentius roared. "Not only a thief, but a traitor! We should have let you drown!"

"Not a traitor! By all the gods not!" Sabinus swore. "I saw the cavalry. I knew how soon they'd be upon us. I knew we needed to divert them or they would capture the ship. So I presented this letter to the liveryman. I told him I was hunting the Senator on Macro's orders. Then I offered him money to be my confederate. I told him I'd lie in wait and kill the Senator when he reclaimed his horses. He called it murder and wanted no part. But I pressed him further. I said I couldn't try to take the Senator all the way to Rome, as I was sure he'd escape. I wanted only to kill him, so I could take his daughter." He looked briefly at Veronica, explaining, "The letter calls you his daughter, Mistress."

Veronica crossed her arms, wary about being drawn into his fabricated drama.

"He asked me what I wanted with the girl, and I told him I would," — and here he looked again at Veronica, begging, "pardon, it was part of the ruse," — then with an air of bravado, asserted, "but I said I'd take my pleasure with her." Veronica's jaw dropped. The brazen youth punctuated the insult, "All the way back to Rome."

Veronica wanted no more of his story, but neither did she want to admit her sensitivity to mere words. Sabinus went on about the stable master, accelerating to the story's climax.

"He said I was a rogue and a scoundrel and he would not help me. I informed him that a cavalry of twelve was approaching the city, and if I did not take the girl, they would, and whatever she might suffer by me would then be multiplied by twelve, because Macro had countenanced that punishment. He then chased me out with the bullwhip." Here he laughed, very pleased with his success. "Swearing by the gods that neither I, nor Macro's guards, would ever find that girl if he could help it."

"It would seem," Theodosius concluded, "that he could help it."

Valentius growled disapproval. "It was still too great a risk. What if it hadn't worked?"

"Perhaps you didn't notice when you put up your horse," Sabinus said, "but all the stable boys are girls. The man dotes on his daughters. It was a foolproof plan!"

Silence fell over the group and Sabinus basked in his success, sporting a smug grin — until Veronica rattled his jaw with a slap across the face. She abruptly turned and marched to the bow. Furious, she gripped the rail and stared out at the sea. Behind her, Valentius made sport of Sabinus until Theodosius demanded the matter be dropped.

The afternoon sunlight played on the rippling surface, producing a mosaic of blues, greens and golds. The rocking of the bow combined with the sparkling colors to soothe Veronica's mind and take some pressure off her sunken heart. This was a beautiful world, she knew, as even this maddening flight confirmed. There had been pastel hillsides of cyclamen, aromatic pine forests and now this vast expanse of shimmering light. But this was also a brutal and violent world, in which evil seemed to hold the upper hand. To survive, must good scheme and deceive, lie and manipulate, even kill? Veronica had never felt as vulnerable as now; she was a target for this world's violence, with no more protection than the poor sparrow Caligula had snapped in two.

She thought of Claudia, even more vulnerable, sharing her life and bed with a brash youth, whose desire to impress the demigods of Rome, had impelled him to choose terror over reason. She trembled for Claudia. In a desert bereft of wild flowers and trees, far from any blue ocean, would she forget that beauty existed? Would the absence of beauty make her apathetic to goodness? Or was there some goodness even in Judea that might lift her out of evil's grasp?

"I'm coming," Veronica vowed, leaning forward over the water. "I'm flying to you."

Chapter 8

Galilee, 31 A.D.

Gaius Cassius Longinus lifted the *lorica musculata*[44] from its peg on the outside wall. The silvered breastplate presented only a slight exaggeration of his own physique, and indeed could have been cast from life just a few years ago, before the desert heat and meager, Syrian diet had taken their toll. The food at his new post in Galilee was better, but his appetite had slowed, so he was not regaining his lost weight. Yet, this morning his sculpted armor was necessary, not to project an illusion of strength, but to camouflage a heavy heart. He slid the armor over his head, the dorsal plate slapping him on the back, as if urging him to recall his pride in service to the Empire. As he tightened the straps, he caught a whiff of stale smoke, the stench of yesterday's funeral pyre.

Longinus knew from more than a decade in the Legion, followed by this junior command in the Auxilia[45], that no incense could sweeten flames that consumed a fallen youth. Arsenius, a mere twenty years old, was a Samarian recruit who'd so distinguished himself that his Decanus[46] had given him a Roman name, meaning *manly*. But Arsenius had died without a chance to demonstrate his martial skills: he'd been ambushed, likely by a band Zealots, the religious fanatics who ran like rabbits throughout Galilee, striking when they had a momentary advantage and disappearing into the hills. As Longinus stooped to buckle the metal greaves[47] to his shins, he could taste the combat to come.

"Gaius!" The voice crept from a dry, morning throat, and Longinus discerned it was his commander, the Centurion Hastatus Prior, known to the men as Primus Pilus, or *First Spear*, of the garrison.

"Primus." Longinus stood at attention.

The veteran officer limped over to him. He wore the scarlet cloak over a graying tunic. He was shod in light sandals to accommodate a swollen foot.

"Beastly hot night, wasn't it?" the Primus noted. "Havoc with the gout."

"My sympathies, sir," Longinus stated. "If the commander cannot ride, I am more than happy to lead the detail after those murderers."

"I am quite sure, Longinus," the Primus uttered vaguely, "Into the fray? Commendable."

"Thank you, sir."

---

[44] Armor breastplate formed to resemble hyper-developed chest and abdominal muscles
[45] In contrast to the Roman Legion, composed of Roman citizen soldiers, the Auxilia enlisted native peoples to serve as peacekeepers in the conquered provinces. Officers were generally Roman.
[46] Noncommissioned officer, the equivalent of a corporal
[47] Armored shin and ankle protectors

"Unfortunately, there's, well, the business first. Grease for the wheels of empire, you understand?" Longinus did not understand, but his commander explained, "The censor in Syria is rightly concerned that Zealots will target tax collectors. And the publican will make his rounds this morning."

"Let them attack," Longinus scoffed. "It will save time in the saddle if the cutthroats come to us."

"Right you are, young man," the Primus cheerily agreed. "Less time in the saddle." He shifted weight off his engorged foot, adding, "More time to bleed the old hoof. They say it's fire in the blood that causes this. Gout. I know you think it's an old man's sickness, but fire in the blood is a young man's symptom. Yet, I would hope that whatever passions swim in an officer's bloodstream, they'd be harnessed for the good of the Empire, which this morning would manifest in the collection of taxes, rather than killing rebels."

"And this afternoon, sir?"

"This afternoon," the veteran muttered, "is this afternoon."

Longinus adjusted his helmet as the old man tottered off. He breathed deeply through flared nostrils, like a stallion held back by a timid hand at the reins. The Primus had been too long at this post. He'd mixed too freely with these Jews, emboldening them with his religious and cultural tolerance. He'd gone so far as to build a synagogue, having the Auxilia cut basalt stones from the surrounding mountains to lay the foundation. The Primus had hoped to improve relations, but his familiarity had only encouraged contempt, which Longinus knew would embolden their cunning enemy, so there would be more sneak attacks, such as the one that had claimed Arsenius.

Longinus marveled that a blighted town like Capernaum[48] could seduce any officer of Rome. True, it was not much different from his home, Pyrgi, a sleepy port on the Mare Nostrum, along the Via Aurelia[49], northwest of Rome. The inhabitants here, like his father and uncles back home, were primarily fishermen. They set out in small vessels with meager, often tattered sails. They dropped their nets, trusting in providence that the last fish they'd caught had not been the last fish in the sea.

Yet these Galileans cultivated long hair and beards suited for cool, barbaric Germania. Longinus couldn't see how, in this balmy climate, men could go around like that, and in layers of robes as well. The women were so thoroughly covered that, aside from a rare, exceptionally pretty face, their forms were not the least distracting. Which was for the best, because only the worst sort of Jewish woman would mix with foreign troops. It made for a lonely existence, but such was the soldier's lot. Most Legionnaires understood they'd have to wait until their enrollment was up, and marry upon returning to Italy. That, too, was ultimately for the good; these Jews were so deeply rooted

---

[48] A fishing village on the northwest corner of the Sea of Galilee
[49] Constructed c. 240 BC, the road ran from Rome northward, along the western coast of Italy to Pisa.

in their backward mythology that outsiders were not welcome. So, Longinus reasoned, as long as the business of the Empire went on unmolested, he could endure the shortcomings of a soldier's life for the rewards he'd enjoy later.

Longinus did not regret his decision to enlist at fifteen. For a plebeian, the military was a chance to move up in life. He'd been tall, with a prematurely deep voice, so the recruiter never suspected he was underage. That gave him an early start on his twenty-year term. He'd been elevated to Decanus at eighteen and given charge over an octet of men older them himself. He soon became a watch officer, and, after transferring from the Legion to the Auxilia, a rear guard commander in a cavalry unit. It was only a year ago that the governor of Syria had promoted him to Centurion Princeps Prior, first below the Primus, and sent him here to Capernaum. Now, if he met his goal and rose to *First Spear* within the next five years, he could retire an Equestrian, and still be young enough to farm the land he'd be granted and to raise a large family. He had no desire to tarry in the service like his current commander, wasting himself in a pitiless climate, among vulgar clods too primitive to imagine the grandeur of Rome.

Longinus strapped his sword to his side. Again, he thought of Arsenius, a youth denied his future. As he gripped his weapon, he imagined venting his wrath, not only at the Zealots responsible, but at every Jew in Galilee who viewed the murderous Zealots as liberators tossing off the yoke of Rome. That yoke had brought them roads and aqueducts, improved their commerce and put an end to the constant, internecine, eye-for-an-eye warfare. No, Rome had required them to pay taxes for a more peaceful, orderly life and had somehow offended their silent, invisible god.

A soldier walked the Centurion's horse to him. The sleek, black Arabian swung his head; he hated to be handled by anyone but his master. Longinus took the reins and rubbed the stallion's nose. To the Centurion, he was meek as a lamb; to everyone else he was, as his master had named him, *Noctu Formido*, The Night Terror. He'd bought the regal beast at two years old, paying half a year's salary.

"Is the detail ready?" the Longinus asked.

"At your pleasure, Princeps," a soldier replied.

He handed the reins back. "I'll be on foot with the men this morning. Have Formido ready to ride this afternoon."

Longinus strode to the barracks, where the squad of eight men fell in line. The Decanus raised a hand in salute, and Longinus pointed his vitis[50] toward the sea.

The shore of Galilee at Capernaum had no wharf to speak of, only two wooden docks the Auxilia had built to moor a pair of slim galleys. Fishermen hauled their boats up the sandy mud and unloaded their catch. The publican

---

[50] A meter-length vine staff that signified a commanding officer's rank

set his custom table up on the nearest street — a Roman road, of course — that opened up into the market where the fish would be sold, and waited for the recalcitrant laborers to come to him. He had a group of thugs to persuade the locals that cooperation was in their best interest. The unpersuaded would receive a visit at their homes later in the day.

Longinus deployed his men strategically at the custom table and in pairs about the market. They had standing instructions to stop any Galilean in possession of a long dagger, the weapon of choice for the *Sicarii*[51], ultra-Zealots who stood ready to assassinate collaborators. While they operated mostly south in Judea, a few had been creeping north into Galilee, radicalizing the already troublesome hill Zealots. Longinus suspected them of ambushing Arsenius; only the most brazen rebels would attack a soldier of Rome. The Centurion had no sooner positioned his men when a heated argument broke out at the customs table.

"You're demanding blood!" a fisherman yelled. He slapped a pile of coins onto the table. "That's my whole catch!" When the publican reached to brush the coins toward him, the fisherman grabbed his wrist, demanding, "What do I feed my children?"

The bodyguards stepped forward, but Longinus barred them, extending his vitis. The publican wrenched his wrist free and dropped the coins into a strong box.

"You ought to catch more fish," he scoffed.

"How?" the man asked, "When I can't even buy flax to repair my nets?"

The publican smirked, "Your want of flax is not Caesar's concern."

A rumble passed low through the men waiting on line. The fisherman had murder in his eyes, and the musculature to accomplish it. But his eyes were those of a father who'd have to look at hungry children and a sad wife, and be judged a failure. Longinus reached into the strongbox, retrieving several coins. He shook them in his cupped hand, then placed a neat stack down on the table. The Centurion nodded to the fisherman to take them back. Immediately, the startled Galilean scooped them up and bowed. His thanks were lost as the publican bellowed.

"This is outrageous!"

Longinus, pressing the vitis heavily upon the tax collector's shoulder, pinned him to his stool. He spoke in a voice low as the grave. "Assess him fairly, he'll buy a new net. He'll catch more fish, and pay more tax. Assess him harshly, he'll sell his boat to buy a sword. He'll kill you first, then he will kill me or I will kill him. Either way, it's a loss for Rome."

"So, I am to take orders from a Centurion?"

"The gods forbid."

---

[51] Literally, "the Daggermen"

Longinus lifted his vine staff, and pointed it around the market at his men. "But these men follow my orders. And if I send them into the hills to chase Zealots as you make your rounds, you may encounter an unfortunate accident." Then, with a wry smile, he continued, "Of course, I'll avenge you. If that's what you wish."

The publican grunted and called the next fisherman forward. Longinus stood over his shoulder for several more transactions, but as the fishermen grumbled, an outburst erupted in the market. Soldiers bolted through the crowd to apprehend a fleeing man. Women were knocked to the ground and tables collapsed. Auxilia troopers tackled the man, then pulled him to his feet, bleeding from the mouth, and cursing in very Judean Aramaic. Longinus stripped the captive of a sheathed dagger the length of his forearm.

"Sicarius?" the Centurion calmly inquired.

"Your pronunciation needs work," the captive spat, blinking away blood that was filling his right eye. "The word is 'Iscariot.'"

*   *   *   *

It was approaching noon when Longinus and his squad quit the marketplace. The townspeople had retreated from the heat of the day, and the publican did not seem under any threat. The Centurion was anxious to speak to his new prisoner. He'd ordered twenty lashes to loosen the man's tongue, and so hoped to find him talkative. Longinus tallied the crimson stripes on the prisoner's back, already crusted over in the blistering sun. He was shocked to find no more than ten and demanded an explanation.

"The Primus," his Watch Officer muttered, "countermanded the order."

Longinus wrested the whip from the Officer's hand and, gripping the handle tightly, let the leather coils roll out to the ground. He paced off the distance from the prisoner's back.

"Princeps, stay your hand!" a throaty voice cracked. Longinus turned to see the Primus spit into the dust. "Come here."

Longinus wound the whip up again and handed it to the Watch Officer as he passed toward his commander.

"You do understand rank, Princeps?"

"Yes, Primus. Which is why—"

"You say do this, and it is done. You don't have to check to see that it is done, you know it is done because you have commanded it be so."

"Yes, Primus."

"Unless of course, your superior has commanded that it be done differently." His superior turned his gaze toward the prisoner. "I know you think of me as a fat, old man, lying in bed waiting to die, but experience has taught me that ten lashes make a man talkative; twenty make him stubborn. Thirty shut him up entirely, after which you must go to forty, the point at which he'll say anything to make it stop. All lies he thinks you want to hear. Thus, any more than ten lashes is a waste of time, unless you intend to kill the man."

Longinus nodded.

"You may proceed, Princeps." The Primus turned, leaning heavily on his vitis, and limped back to his office. "By the way," he called back, "you'll have the full century for your mission. No sense taking chances with those rebels."

The full century: eighty men. Certainly enough to avenge Arsenius, if only Longinus knew against whom. He marched back to the Watch Officer and took back the lash.

"Judea Sicarius," Longinus called. "What is your name?"

"That's close enough," the prisoner muttered.

"I'll ask again," the Centurion said, poking the whip handle into a gash across the prisoner's scapula. "What is your name?"

The prisoner winced, then snarled, "Judas. Iscariot."

"Well, Judas Iscariot, what is your business in Galilee?"

"I came to fish."

This time the Centurion smacked the wound. "Are you sure you didn't come to recruit? That you aren't fishing for men?" The prisoner shuddered and was silent. Longinus circled the post. He unfurled the whip, letting his prisoner see its full length.

"I'm not a Daggerman."

"But you have the dagger. And call yourself *Iscariot*."

"A traveler needs a weapon to defend himself."

"And I'm sure, in your twisted mind, assassination is a form of self-defense."

"You wouldn't understand."

"I understand perfectly, Iscariot. You are a conquered people. You could be assimilated into the greatest empire the world has ever known. You could benefit from Roman engineering, commerce, law—"

"We have our own law."

"Right. Which is why some Judeans would rather die than submit. And others would rather kill. I don't trouble myself with the former; if they'd rather die, I'll oblige them. But those who'd kill—"

"That's not me!"

"Prove it!" The Centurion punctuated his command with a crack of the whip in the dust.

The prisoner rasped, "How can I prove I'm not going to do something? Except by not doing it?"

The Centurion curled his wrist, twisting the whip like a serpent. "You can prove your affection for Caesar."

"I have none."

"Unfortunately, that leaves you at a disadvantage."

The Centurion heard hoof beats. Looking to the front of the mansio, he spotted the black-and-white-plumed helmet of Juvenal, his garrison's Optaio[52], third in command. Judging by the sound, he'd brought with him four octets of cavalry from their morning patrol. Six octets of infantry would round out the full century. Longinus wound the whip up again.

"All right," he returned to the Zealot. "We've only just met, but perhaps you've taken a liking to me."

"Why?" The prisoner nearly laughed.

"Because you received ten lashes, not forty. Because they were given with a whip and not a scourge[53]. Because I haven't had you hoisted. Yet."

Longinus gave the signal and a group of soldiers came forward. They unchained the Iscariot's wrists from the post, opened the shackles and bound his hands again behind his back. They marched him to the flagpole in the center of the yard and tied the rope to the shackles. They pulled the rope taut, extending the prisoner's arms behind him. The Auxilia chuckled as the prisoner hunched forward, buckling under the stress up his arms and across his back.

"Have you ever been hoisted, Iscariot?"

The prisoner didn't answer.

"I thought not, given that you seem to have good use of both arms. Basically, what my men will do is pull on that rope, lifting you off the ground. Your arms will be stretched upward, behind your back, and eventually over your head, in such an unnatural motion, that your sinews will tear. The damage is quite irreversible, so you'll basically be a cripple for the remainder of your life. Oh, and it hurts like hell unleashed. Are you ready to play?"

A tug raised the prisoner to his tiptoes. He tottered, grimacing from the pain.

"What do you want?" he shrieked.

"Oh, that's right," the Centurion quipped, his men laughing along. "There's hardly any point if you don't know what I'm after." He then turned deadly serious. "A man of mine was killed. A man who mattered very much to me. Certainly more than your worthless life. I want to know who killed him."

"I don't know anything," the prisoner pleaded. "I only arrived today."

Longinus nodded, and the soldiers tugged. The arms went higher behind the prisoner's back, and he unleashed an agonized scream. Still, he balanced on his toes.

"Please, I'll explain. Let me tell you who I am! Why I'm here! Please."

Longinus tipped his head sideways, and his men slackened the rope. Judas Iscariot fell to his knees. Longinus signaled for the water bucket to be brought, and he ladled out a drink for his prisoner. "All right. Tell me."

---

[52] Equivalent to a Sergeant
[53] Unlike a whip, a scourge and many leather strands, each tipped with an object (metal bead, metal hook or sharp piece of bone) meant to damage the flesh

The Iscariot swallowed, took a few shallow breaths, and began his story.

"Judge my tale[54]. You'll find a man violated. Cursed from the womb, conspired against by fate or gods or whatever power's averse to men's souls. You'll find I came here to escape evil, not to cause it."

The Centurion dipped the ladle again. "Such a promising introduction. I can hardly wait."

"I grew up in a nearby kingdom, the eldest son of a queen, or so I thought."

Longinus poured water over the prisoner's back, cooling his wounds. "So you're a prince, Iscariot?"

"So I thought," he stressed. "But when that queen conceived and gave birth to a second son, she admitted her crime: she'd found me as an infant in a basket upon the shore, and, then childless and thinking herself barren, had taken me, a foundling, into the palace. For years, I continued to live within the palace, under a bitter king who thought me a usurper. He increased the abuse year to year, hoping to drive me away, since I resembled more of royal issue than his own son, and his subjects favored me."

"Well, that much is obvious," Longinus mused.

"He's every inch a king!" Juvenal laughed.

Judas Iscariot continued, undeterred, "Eventually, I feared I would do violence against this king, whom I still viewed as my father. So, I fled that home, leaving behind my mother."

"Truly sad, Iscariot. Stop or you'll make me weep."

"I crossed the salt sea, which is aptly named, *The Dead*, and starving, parched, I came upon an orchard. What else should a dying man do, than to partake in the fruit of the earth?"

"You ate."

"It was only a few apples. Any man in my state would have the right."

"But the orchard's owner didn't see it that way?"

"He came from nowhere, with fury. Again, I acted on the right of any creature."

"You struggled," Longinus noted. "And, even in your weakened state, prevailed?"

"After I buried the orchard owner," the Iscariot continued, "— Ruben was his name — I walked the length and breadth of his land. It was a rich farm. Well maintained. And there was a woman."

"His wife. Recently widowed."

"Cyborea. She was beautiful. I appealed to her to hire me. When her husband never returned, she was deeply grieved, and in her sorrow turned to me."

"Lucky you."

---

[54] Judas' story comes from The Golden Legend, compiled by Jacobus de Voragine, 1275

"I had done nothing wrong, but still my actions had left her desolate. The least I could do was comfort her."

"And help yourself to her land."

"What man, in my same circumstance, would have done differently?" the Iscariot wailed. "Yes, she was much older, but still a beauty. I went to her chamber. In the morning, when I awoke, Cyborea was weeping. Never had a woman been so bereft. Her husband gone, she knew not where, and... She told me she'd had a son; that in a dream she'd seen that he'd grow into a monster, an adversary of all goodness. So she'd placed the baby in a basket and sent him out to sea. She was certain he'd drowned."

"And so our narrative comes full circle."

"I realized, I'd committed the crime I'd fled my home to escape. Not only had I killed my father, but I'd taken my mother, defiling both our bodies. How could I absolve myself?"

"You could have hanged yourself," offered the Optaio.

"Would have saved us some trouble," Longinus nodded.

The Iscariot persisted, "Cyborea told me of a prophet, baptizing Jews for the remission of sins. I went to the Jordan. There the holy man immersed me, praying, but his dark countenance was troubled. He acknowledged the limits of his power. But, he told me, there was a greater prophet."

"This land produces prophets like carrots," Juvenal scoffed.

"He'd have the power of the Most High! He could save me. The Baptist said he would start his mission in Galilee. That's why I came here."

"That is quite a story," the Centurion averred, then tipped a glance to the Optaio and sighed. "Hoist him up."

Soldiers pulled on the rope. Judas shrieked and screamed, "No! No! Why do you torture me?"

"Consider it part of your curse," Longinus shrugged.

"I've told you the truth! As it happened!"

"You've retold the plot of *Oedipus Rex*. As Sophocles wrote it."

"What?"

"Four hundred years ago."

"I swear it's the truth!"

"And I swear I'm going to kill you."

The soldiers strained and hoisted the Zealot off his feet. He kicked and screamed as he dangled inches off the ground.

"Stop it! Stop! I beg you!" Then tearfully, he blurted, "I know who killed your man!"

The soldiers let go the rope, and Judas fell face down in the dirt. His abdomen hit hard, almost bursting, and he struggled for air. Longinus grabbed his hair and pulled him onto his knees.

"Who?" he demanded.

Judas spat dirt from his crusted lips. "I risk my life by telling you."

"You forfeit it by not telling."

"They'll kill me instantly."

"I'll kill you very, very slowly."

"You must promise to free me. And with enough money to leave Galilee."

Longinus released the knot of hair. "You'll sell me the information?"

Juvenal grunted, "Everything's for sale in Capernaum."

The prisoner rolled his stiff shoulders. "How much? You can continue to break me, or you can ride off now to find the guilty party."

The Centurion weighed his options. "Ten silver denarii."

"It's worth three times that."

"Perhaps. But you're hardly in a position to haggle."

The Centurion knew that another hour at the post — deprived of water, under this sun — and the wretch would tell him anything. But Longinus didn't want to wait another hour. Fortunately, neither did the prisoner: he wagged his head furiously; flies were gathering and biting around his bloody eye.

"Ten denarii then. Agreed. His name is Joachim Ben Nasir. From the town of Chorizan."

"Is he there now?"

"If he's not, I'll wager half my fee: you'll find him in a granary owned by his uncle."

The Centurion handed the whip to the Watch Officer and reclaimed his vitis. "You seem to know a lot about the north. For someone who's just arrived from the south."

The prisoner tilted his head back, and smiled wickedly. "People tell me things. They trust me."

*   *   *   *

The march to Chorizan was short, a mere three miles. Longinus would have ordered it at double time, except it was mostly uphill. Chorizan was situated on the face of a large mound, created centuries ago by lava flow that had formed the grey-to-black, columned mountains behind it. This sun-exposed hill with its dark, volcanic soil warmed in the springtime more rapidly than the surrounding areas. That gave Chorizan an agricultural advantage: its wheat harvest came earlier than any town's in the vicinity. Thus it was the breadbasket of the triangle it formed with Capernaum, which supplied fish, and Bethsaida, whose grassland supported the pasturing of sheep.

Longinus knew that even though it was mid-summer, the granaries would already be full. This gave him a strategic advantage; he needn't threaten violence against anyone. All he had to do was light a few torches. Longinus sent his cavalry to circle the town. They galloped at a furious pace, raising as much dust and noise as possible, as Longinus marched his infantry directly to the synagogue. The spectacle of thirty-two Roman Auxilia, thundering on horseback, while two-score marched in tight columns, incited panic among the townspeople. The leading citizens ran to the synagogue to head off what they feared was an attack on the town.

A Decanus barred the town officials from approaching as Longinus dismounted. Juvenal, at the head of the cavalry, called to him.

"Princeps," he pointed. "Over there."

Longinus looked at the wall of the synagogue. Built of gray and black basalt stones, the synagogue was a simple, almost cubical structure. But these Galileans had learned at least a little from Roman engineering; the front façade featured an arch over its three doors. What the Optaio cleverly pointed out, however, was that the wall had been defaced. A prominent, high stone, with some ornamental carving, had been smashed, opening up a crater the size of a man's head.

Longinus strode past the officials to examine the vandalism. He noted by the sharp, unweathered surface that it had been done recently. Traces of curls around the periphery of the hole suggested there had been an image of Helios, the Greek sun god. Such images were not uncommon on synagogues, though they technically violated the Jewish prohibition against idolatry. The images evinced a desire of Jews living along trade routes established by the Greeks — and subsequently claimed by Rome — to accommodate travelers, merchants and officials. Someone had objected to this gesture of solidarity, someone determined to bring the countryside into line with radical views of religious and political purity. In other words, the Zealots.

"People of Chorizan," the Centurion announced, "your law says, *Thou shalt not kill.*' But one of you has killed. He's killed one of my men. Your law demands a life for a life, and that is all I intend to enforce. Nothing but your own law. I stand before your synagogue, a symbol of your law, to say I will hold you to your law. I also point to this wall. Here was a symbol of peace. A symbol of understanding between different peoples. See the destruction. This was not done by anyone from this town. It was done by outside agitators, seeking to turn this town against Rome. You must reject these outsiders. Resist their calls to war. You must observe your own law, which says, *Thou shalt not kill,* and *For your own life, I shall demand an accounting.* Now," he concluded, scanning the crowd, "I want you to bring forth the murderer."

There was a long moment of silence, as eyes darted back and forth throughout the crowd. Finally, a finely dressed elder spoke.

"Do you have a name for this person?"

Longinus set his jaw. He was hoping he wouldn't to have to use the name the Iscariot had given him. He doubted he could trust the scoundrel.

"Joachim Ben Nasir."

Several gasps shot from the crowd. A woman collapsed. Others wailed. As protests swelled, Longinus signaled his men to draw their swords. The crowd recoiled. He looked at the officials, now straining against the Decanus to get to the commander. Longinus marveled at the fuss over a cowardly ambusher. *At least*, he thought, *they can't deny knowing him*. He ordered the Decanus to let the well-dressed elder through.

"Surely, Centurion, you can't be serious," the man objected.

"Let me tell you how serious I am," Longinus said. "If I do not leave this town in fifteen minutes with that man in chains, I will burn every nut of grain in every crib on this hillside."

"This... man?" the elder stammered.

"Take me to the man!"

The elder stood frozen, apparently stupefied. Then coming to his senses, sputtered, "Yes, as you wish. Come with me."

The elder led the Centurion and his Auxilia from the heart of town, along a narrow path up the hill. They passed several wheat fields, whose stalks had recently been decapitated — where oxen and donkeys now grazed — to a farmhouse. Looking past the house, he saw the granaries. Several men were working. On one section of the threshing floor, a tall man used a switch to drive oxen over ears of wheat, while several yards away men with wooden pitch forks tossed the trampled grain in the air, allowing the light chaff to float away on the breeze. Then there were boys sweeping the buds of grain into sacks for storage.

"Please, wait here," the elder asked.

"Which is he?"

"Please, wait."

The elder scurried toward the threshing area, over to the tall man with the oxen. *That's the one*, Longinus surmised, as the elder whispered in the man's ear. They began to argue. The tall man shouted orders and the workers grabbed up plowshares.

"Fools," Juvenal said. "Half a dozen plowshares against eighty swords?"

The tall man barked at the boys. He pointed up the hill, ordering them to flee.

"What's going on?" Longinus wondered. "Hold the men here," he ordered, and spurred Formido to a sudden gallop. The elder came running, waving his arms.

"Forbearance, Centurion! Forbear!"

Longinus reined Formido to a stop, but as the elder clutched at his greave, he raised a leg and kicked him in the chest, toppling him to the ground. Longinus spurred the stallion forward, and drew a lance from its scabbard. The threshers made no move toward him, but just in case, he hurled the lance at their feet, scaring the plowshares from their hands. He swung down from his horse and drew his sword, leveling it at the tall man's throat.

"Joachim Ben Nasir?" he demanded.

"As you wish."

Longinus cocked his arm high, ready to end this tedious play and taste the revenge he craved.

"No!" a voice shouted. A boy dove under the blade.

"Out of the way!"

"No," the boy cried. His moist eyes locked on the Centurion's; his beardless cheeks flushed red.

"I only want him," the Centurion stated.

"No," the boy wept. "You want me."

Chapter 9

Again Longinus threw the Iscariot against the wall. He slammed hard and tumbled to the dirt floor.

"You should have told me he was a boy!"

"You should have asked." The prisoner laughed until he wheezed, then wheezed until he coughed. He crouched on his haunches and extended an open palm for payment. "A deal is a deal, right, Centurion?"

"I should slit your belly and shove the denarii inside."

The stockade door creaked open. The Primus bowed his head and stepped inside.

"Have we concluded our transaction?" he asked.

Longinus threw the coins at the prisoner's head. "Don't let me see you again in Galilee."

Judas Iscariot got down on all fours, like a jackal sniffing for carrion, and picked the silver coins off the clay. Longinus slid past the Primus at the door, and into the glare of an unforgiving sun. He was tempted to throw the Iscariot to the crowd surrounding the mansio. Let them sate their anger against the Zealot informer instead of his men, who were only doing their duty. But, as the Primus would surely remind him, a Centurion's job was to maintain Pax Romana, not to incite mob violence, even against vermin who should be eradicated.

The crowd had swelled even in the brief time Longinus had pummeled his prisoner. The men and women from Capernaum had been joined the men of Chorizan. Longinus looked through the slot in the wooden door of the stockade's other cell. The boy sat forlorn on the dirt floor.

The Primus limped over and leaned against the stockade wall.

"A nasty business we've gotten into, yes?"

The story the boy had told was that he and his younger brother had gone to Capernaum early in the morning to purchase fish for the family dinner. Walking down the hill, they saw a soldier training his horse to charge. On one of the downhill runs, the boy had impulsively picked up a stone and thrown it at the rider. But his aim was off, and the stone had struck the horse in the eye, causing it to panic, roll and throw Arsenius forward onto a boulder. The boy described Arsenius after the impact: completely limp, his face bloodied, head tossed awkwardly to his shoulder, one arm bent as if it now had an elbow in the middle of the forearm. The blinded horse rolled back to its feet and dragged Arsenius, one foot caught in a stirrup, off the dusty road and toward the open country where he'd later been found.

Shocked and sickened, they had proceeded to Capernaum to complete their errand. However, unable to keep their emotions in check, they quarreled and, when a stranger intervened, they wept over their calamity. The stranger promised no ill would come if they'd simply keep their composure. He said a group of men who despised the Roman invaders would guard the boys to the end. The boy said he did not know the man's name, but that he'd been wearing a long knife.

"Frustrating for you, I imagine," the Primus mused. "Where do you vent your rage?" Indeed, his fury had dwindled to impotence, but surfaced again as the old warhorse muttered a tired cliché, "'Boys throw rocks in jest, but frogs die in earnest.[55]'"

"Arsenius was more than a frog!"

"Indeed." The Primus raised an admonishing eyebrow at his subordinate's outburst, then continued philosophically, "Yet, he died from a child's prank. No malice, yet the most malicious result. Little harm meant, but the greatest harm done. The only thing worse than the incident will be exacting justice for it. A life for a life. A youth for a youth." As he lurched away, he sighed, "I'd much prefer to crucify that Iscariot."

After a moment's reflection, Longinus trotted after him, urging, "Primus, sometimes the way to clear rats is to catch and free one, then follow him to the nest."

"Is that the assignment you want, Gaius?" the Primus chuckled. "Tailing this Iscariot all over Galilee?" He waved his subordinate off with a chubby hand. "That doesn't address the pressing question of the boy. Justice demands execution; mercy commands forbearance. Would mercy embolden our enemies more than justice would enrage them?" The Primus lowered and wagged his large head before continuing. "There is no way to handle this case without causing the Empire grief." He faced the garrison's gate, attended by a handful of men. "We must therefore cause it the least amount of grief."

"And justice for Arsenius?"

---

[55] Quotation attributed to Bion of Borysthenes (c. 325 – c. 250 BC), a Greek philosopher

The Primus ignored Longinus and signaled his guard to throw open the gate. They allowed a pair of synagogue officials, the one from Chorizan and his counterpart from Capernaum, into the yard.

The Primus leaned heavily upon his vitis and declared, "We shall take the boy to Herod Antipas. The Tetrarch will judge him by your law."

"Herod is only a tool of Caesar," the Chorizan official objected.

Longinus put his hand on the hilt of his sword. "This is a tool of Caesar. And thus far we have refrained from using it."

The Primus interposed himself between Longinus and the Galileans. "Tell your people, that the boy will be taken south to Tiberius to be judged in Herod's court."

"How will you go? By land or sea?"

"I fail to see how that is your concern."

"However you go," the Chorizan official warned, "our men will insist on going with you. To assure the boy's safety."

Longinus tamped down on his anger, but did not remain silent. "If that mob follows the Auxilia, we'll hold it as a provocation."

"These men are not political," the Capernaum rabbi interjected. "They only want the boy treated fairly."

The Primus hummed through his nose. "Even if that were true, gentlemen, their numbers give cover to Zealot rebels. Can you promise that no Zealots are in that crowd? That they will not strike and retreat into the mob? You know the Zealots thrive on violence; whether Romans die or Jews, they don't care. It feeds the hatred they use to win converts. There are more lives to be lost through mishandling this moment than through the trial of one boy."

"I fear the Centurion is right," the Capernaum rabbi said. "Men of good intent, when joined in a mob, will act from their basest passions. One or two Zealots could easily subvert them."

"That should answer that," Longinus said. "I'll have the oarsmen prepare the galleys."

"Hold your place, Princeps," the Primus ordered.

"Sir," Longinus argued, whispering lowly so the rabbis would not hear his concerns, "if we march, that mob which already outnumbers our men six to one, will swell as we pass through Gennesaret and Magdala. Such numbers will embolden the Jews to attack."

"I am aware of the risks, Princeps," the warhorse snorted.

"By sea we leave all danger behind."

"The danger, Longinus, is in the sea itself." The Primus pointed past the mansio's gate to the steep mountains on the opposite shore. "On beastly hot days such as this, the winds come over those cliffs, brewing tremendous storms. Our galleys, built for speed with little ballast, get tossed about and easily capsized. Our soggy Auxilia would either drown in their armor or swim

THE LANCE AND THE VEIL

to shore in their tunics, there to be hacked to pieces by an opportunistic enemy."

"I'd rather trust the gods and take my chances on the sea."

"You forget, young man, whose gods you must contend with." He chuckled and wagged his head. "The one out here has a reputation for using the sea quite effectively against enemy soldiers. Prepare for the march." The Primus then turned and glowered at the two rabbis. Before he could chastise them, the Chorizan official capitulated.

"We will entreat with the men to follow at a distance. A quarter mile? Would that be adequate?"

The Primus raised an eyebrow at Longinus, who nodded.

"Have them clear the Via Maris[56]," the Princeps commanded. "Go down to the water and wait. When the last of my column has passed from town, they may begin to follow."

The Primus dismissed the officials, then thought better of it. "Wait." He had his guards bring the boy, whom he ordered to strip in front of the officials. "Not a mark on him," he said. "Tell that to the concerned citizens."

The officials left the yard, and delivered the message to the crowd, which grumbled and protested, but eventually moved off towards the water. Longinus weighed how they should deploy the men.

"Will you accompany us, sir?" he asked the Primus.

"That hardly seems necessary, Gaius. You've my utmost confidence. And someone has to stay behind so the upstarts don't burn our mansio to the ground. I'll hold an octet here. Best of luck, young man." With that the Primus tottered off toward his quarters, no doubt to elevate his swollen foot while fattening himself on wine and figs.

Longinus would have seventy men at his disposal, against a crowd that numbered in the hundreds and would grow with every town they passed. He had no choice but to ask for support. He dashed to the Primus, reaching him at the door of his quarters, and asked if he would dispatch a pair of riders to Tiberius with a message for Herod: send troops in all haste to Magdala. The Primus felt it prudent and set about drafting the letter. Longinus assembled the remainder of his men, sixty strong, who would either march or ride eight miles down the Via Maris. He hoped that by the time they reached Magdala, Herod's troops, starting four miles from the rendezvous point, would at least be visible on the horizon. That might be an adequate deterrent to attack. Of course, too much would depend on Herod Antipas, a vacillating, pusillanimous puppet, so addicted to sensual gratification that he'd stolen his own brother's wife. Apparently, he had come to regret that little conquest and spent most of his time attempting to wriggle out from under the woman's thumb. Longinus hoped that when word reached Herod, his queen would be otherwise occupied.

---

[56] The Sea Road, a trade route dating back to the Bronze Age, linking Egypt to Syria

Longinus put his plan into motion. He would split his cavalry between a forward position under his command and a rear guard led by Juvenal. In between, the infantry would march, escorting the boy who would ride bound on a donkey. They would march through Gennesaret to rendezvous with Herod's troops at Magdala. They would water the horses there, but if Herod were tardy, they'd push immediately for Tiberius.

A Decanus announced that the crowd had moved down to the water. The rabbis seemed to have placated them, at least for the moment. Longinus mounted Formido and ordered the gate thrown open. He led his column of cavalry out onto the Via Maris, and turned south. The infantry fell in behind. Looking back over his shoulder, Longinus saw the Optaio trot his cavalry detail out of the garrison to guard the rear.

The Sea of Galilee was shaped like a harp, with a long, broad eastern shore forming *the column*. Longinus would march his Auxilia on the Via Maris along the curving eastern shore, down the *harp's neck* to Gennesaret[57], and southwest along *the harp's shoulder* to Magdala. From there the path making up *the harp's soundboard* ran almost directly south-southeast to Tiberius, close to *the feet* of Philoteria. The Auxilia kept the sea on their left, while the sun drooped ahead on their right. As the sun descended, the western cliffs would cool, and cold air would cascade down upon the water, perhaps provoking a sudden storm.

After an hour of brisk marching, the Auxilia reached Gennesaret. The town was basically a farmers' market, since the western Plain of Gennesaret was the most fertile area in Galilee. It boasted thick, loamy soil and abundant water that flowed from the freshwater sea through gorges and underground springs. Here, nature in all its ambition competed throughout the four seasons, producing in one locale a variety of crops, which usually required diverse conditions: walnuts, palms, olives, grapes and figs all flourished together.

Word of the boy prisoner had evidently preceded them, as a crowd of men loitered in the market, holding plowshares and walking sticks. The Centurion scanned the townsmen, who surveyed the column of soldiers. Longinus trotted Formido up a low hill, and turned the stallion so he could inspect his line. The formation was tight. The infantry stepped in rhythm. The boy rocked gently on the donkey, seemingly resigned to his journey.

Longinus looked across the sea and reluctantly admitted that the Primus had made the best decision. The cliffs on the eastern shore, generally visible even from this far point, were already obscured by a gathering storm. Threads of electrum wove through coal black clouds, shimmering, then vanishing, as a low rumble clambered onto the shore. The blue-green water turned to rolling slate, capped with white shards that slashed the surface. Any mariners were in for a rough ride. Longinus hoped the storm would dissipate before it hit shore:

---

[57] The town is named after a Hebrew rendering of the Greek word for harp.

marching in light rain would refresh the men, slogging through torrents would be utter misery.

A boy ran among the soldiers, trying to sell some figs. The troops were disciplined enough to ignore him, until he got too close to the prisoner. Then a Decanus grabbed him by the scruff and tossed him off the road. A murmur ran through the crowd, but a pair of horsemen cantered up and ordered the Galileans back, so the column continued unmolested. As the rear guard cavalry passed, the Gennesaret men fell onto the road and waited for the Capernaum procession. Longinus held his position until the Optaio reached him.

"How would you number that crowd?" the Princeps asked.

Juvenal looked back and squinted. "Five hundred?"

"Eight to one," Longinus calculated.

"There's fuel for a fire," the Optaio offered. "It only wants a spark."

Longinus wiped the beaded mist from the visor of his helmet. "We should be grateful for the rain."

It was five more miles to Magdala. The rain beat steadily, but was more of a relief from the heat than a hindrance to the march. The crowd started to fall behind; the rain had not only cooled the air, but tempers as well. Half a mile out of Magdala, though the wind was still heading steadily westward, the town's signature stench arose, reminding every nose that Magdala's name meant *Tower of Fish*. The town's major industry was preserving sardines through salting and pickling. Again, Longinus reined Formido off the road to a high embankment and observed his line. To his surprise, the Galileans had closed upon his rear guard, and were moving at a brisk pace.

"They might just be hungry," the Optaio suggested.

Suddenly the line halted, and Longinus spun around to see the reason. He could make nothing out, and spurred Formido toward the point. The gathering crowd retreated into the market as Longinus reached the lead Decanus, looking like he'd seen a ghost. In the middle of the road was a woman, lying on her back, stiff as a board, but vibrating like a plucked harp string. Her mouth foamed. It was clear the Decanus had ordered a halt to prevent her from being trampled.

"Who claims this woman?" Longinus called.

The murmuring crowd stepped back almost in unison, all averting their eyes. The woman continued to twitch and shake. Her head hammered on the stones.

"Get her up!" the Centurion barked.

As two foot soldiers stepped forward, the woman went limp. She lay motionless for a moment, then as the soldiers reached her, she sprang up, eyes and mouth gaping, and emitted a throaty growl. She pitched from a sitting position to all fours, snarling and gnashing her teeth at the soldiers who warily backed into line. The crowd laughed as the woman paced like a cornered panther, spooking the Auxilia.

Longinus shouted orders to his ranks, but their discipline vanished. Confident as they were to fight armies and insurgents, his men cowered from this unworldly horror. Longinus kicked Formido and swept toward the hag. Pivoting left and dipping his torso, he snatched her by the shoulders and hefted her over and across his horse. He pinned the wretch down with his elbows as he spun Formido around and trotted into the crowd. Now the townspeople were scared: they broke in all directions, opening a wide circle at the mouth of the marketplace. The troops spread out, ringing their commander and sealing off the mob.

Longinus flinched as the hag dug her nails into his thigh and bit down on his knee. He couldn't help but smack his knee into her face, not noticing until he'd jumped down that his greave had bloodied her nose. He hoped none in the crowd noticed either; assault on a woman, even this pathetic harpy[58], might set off the mob. He kept her pinned to the saddle, even as Formido scratched at the ground and bobbed his head in protest. The wretch continued to growl; she cursed in every language Longinus knew, and a few he didn't.

"Who are you?" he demanded.

"We are Septimus!" she hissed. The voice sounded low inside her, seeming to slither from her throat. "There are seven of us."

"Well," Longinus countered, "I don't care to meet the other six."

"We are all here!" she growled.

Longinus turned back to the crowd, again demanding, "To whom does this woman belong? Someone!"

"That's Mary," a voice called. "She belongs to anyone!"

A snicker ran through the crowd, cynical and cruel. Longinus signaled, and two soldiers pierced the crowd, pulling out the loudmouth joker. Longinus pulled Mary from his saddle and propped her in front of the shame-faced Magdalene.

"Today she belongs to you."

"But. No, I have a wife…"

The crowd roared with laughter as Longinus pushed her against him. "Today you have two. And if any harm comes to her, I'll personally slit your throat. Now—"

He never got to finish. A phalanx of Galileans had struck the center of his line. Sticks and plowshares battered shields. The Auxilia responded with clubs, not swords. Longinus dashed through the chaos, knocking aside several Galileans, and diving into a tangle of limbs beneath the braying donkey. The prisoner was on the ground. Longinus saw a knife flash, heard the clink of metal on armor. Suddenly, the thunder of hooves signaled the rear guard was circling the line, driving the Galileans back. Longinus grasped the hand clenching a long dagger and peeled the arm back. A few hard punches to the

---

[58] An evil creature from Greek mythology that is part woman and part bird

ribcage left the assassin writhing and fighting for air. Longinus handed him to his Decanus to place in custody.

"Ho! Herod's troops!" a voice rang out.

Longinus sensed the Galileans pulling back. He reached for the boy, lying motionless on the road. His clothing was shredded. Longinus pulled him to his feet.

"Well played, Princeps," Juvenal called. "You know these Zealots well."

Longinus fingered the holes in the boy's tunic, poking at the breastplate underneath. The boy took a deep breath and wiped the sweat from his brow.

"Thank the Primus," Longinus said.

"The old dog is wise to their tricks," Juvenal laughed. "A boy prisoner, killed in Roman custody? They'd make him a martyr to incite the country against us."

Longinus whistled across the market; Formido snapped his head up and trotted over. The Centurion swung himself onto his saddle and looked around. The crowd hadn't entirely dispersed, but they'd backtracked. Sitting on the wet stones of the plaza was Mary. Sad and bereft, no longer enflamed with demonic passion. The joker from the crowd was not joking, but gently cajoling her, trying to get her onto her feet. She shook her head from shoulder to shoulder and muttered like a drunk.

"Seems fish aren't the only things they pickle here," Juvenal quipped.

Longinus nodded wryly, though it occurred to him there was something more to this woman. No doubt she was dissipated, wasted, but there was a skeletal beauty about her. An elemental nobility of the tragic, suited to an Homeric epic or Greek drama. *What fatal flaw had brought her low*, he wondered, *and whither would come her redemption?*

Chapter 10

The city of Tiberius was perennially under construction, the result of miscalculations by the Tetrarch, Herod Antipas. Renowned for centuries on account of its hot springs, the site had long been a resort for the wealthy and a pilgrimage site for anyone seeking physical or spiritual revival. Herod the Great had been a frequent visitor to the baths. After he died, his kingdom was divided into Tetrarchies, three of which went to his sons, Archelaus, Herod Antipas and Philip. However, the sons soon realized how tenuously a titular monarch held his fiefdom within the Roman Empire. When the Jews under Archelaus complained loudly and often about his abuses in Jerusalem, Rome —for the sake of Pax Romana — tossed the petty despot from his petty throne[59], and installed a Roman Prefect over Judea. Hoping to escape the fate of his nasty brother, Herod Antipas had renamed Galilee's capitol after Tiberius. But, then it became necessary to turn this out-of-the-way seaside resort into a metropolis worthy of an emperor.

Slaves had cut granite from the eastern cliffs, loaded the stones into merchant ships, rowed them across the tempestuous sea, and finally assembled them in the low hills of Tiberius, constructing a fine castle with a deep and spacious dungeon. Heavily in debt, Herod might still have enjoyed the illusion of opulence, but for his fatal miscalculation in appropriating the hot springs for his private use.

Removed from the Via Maris, which veered sharply west at Magdala, Tiberius did not benefit from any commercial route. The city needed the baths to produce revenue, but Herod had reserved them exclusively for his special guests, who alone could delight in the steamy, relaxing waters, even as they cringed at the tortured wails of the prisoners shackled on the other side of the wall. Thus Tiberius' economy dwindled to that of any fishing village on the Sea of Galilee.

On the few occasions Longinus had partaken in the baths, he'd found that worse than the ghostly moans of the convicted were Herod's self-pitying lamentations. Having taken his brother's wife as his own, Herod was David after Bathsheba, Samson post Delilah, and Ahab subsequent to Jezebel. In short, he was a ruined man. Dominated by a woman whose bitterness increased as her beauty ebbed, and threatened by a capricious overlord who could unseat him at any time, Herod had bankrupted himself placating those twin nemeses.

Longinus led his Auxilia past several half-finished edifices, down a road partially blocked by building materials so undisturbed they'd taken root in the landscape. One granite pile was currently a stage for a semi-naked madman bellowing at the top of his lungs. The emaciated fool, no doubt delirious from sun exposure, was little more than a leathern scarecrow of bones and wild hair. The leonine effect of his tangled mane and overgrown beard was accentuated by a deep growl. And while the theme of his rant was the coming of the god of Israel, his target was deeply personal: he was slandering Herod.

"You, Herod! You have defiled your body! With your brother's wife! Repent! Cast the woman out! Your city suffers for your sins! Your people starve because you have polluted their home!"

"How long's he been at that, do you think?" Juvenal asked.

"It's a wonder Herod hasn't slit his throat," Longinus said.

---

[59] In roughly 6 AD

"Perhaps Herod too much respects the truth."

Longinus chuckled along with his Optaio. "That would contradict my experience of him."

By now a few of Herod's guards had approached. They stood idly as their leader spoke in measured tones. It struck Longinus as a performance by bored actors who had played the scene too many times before.

"Come on down, Baptist," the leader called. "Your cart is waiting." A mule stood hitched to a two-wheeled cart with an iron-barred cell atop. "Herod wants you back down in Jordan."

"Behold! The day of the Lord is coming! Make straight his path!"

"Straight to the river. You know the routine."

The guards started climbing the granite pile and the Baptist retreated. He tossed a few loose bricks their way as he yelled, "Every valley shall be exalted! And the mountains made low!" He scampered a few levels higher and took hold of the wooden scaffolding surrounding an unfinished building. He gripped the lumber braces as the guards tugged on his limbs.

"The mighty will be toppled from their thrones! The dead wood thrown into the fire!"

The scaffolding creaked, and the crowd of onlookers scampered to the far side of the road. The tug-of-war continued: a guard tried to peel the wild man's fingers off the beams, but the brute chomped his hand. That bit of rudeness got the Baptist clubbed on the head. He slumped, and the guards lifted him and gently carried him down the granite pile.

"Regular customer?" Juvenal wondered aloud.

Overhearing, the Captain of the Guard responded, "Once a month or so, he gets lonely out in the desert. No converts line up at the river, so he wanders into town. The people regard him as a holy man, so Herod doesn't want him hurt. We just take him back down to the river. By now I could find his cave in the dark."

"Zealot?" Longinus asked.

"More of a harmless crank. Unless the Lady Herodias is around. He gets under her skin and she lashes out at us. There's no peace when those two collide."

"Where's the queen now?" Longinus asked.

"The Tetrarch has a vineyard outside the city. The queen has taken to... *cultivating* grapes."

Longinus nodded, approving the Captain's subtlety, though it was fairly common knowledge that the Tetrarch and his queen drank. If Herod began early in the day, he was often asleep on the throne during afternoon audiences, or his pronouncements, slurred and muttered, had to wait until morning for clarification.

By now the guards had loaded the Baptist into the wagon, and the detail set out to deliver him back to his desert haunts. Longinus eyed the setting sun and wondered in what condition he would find Herod. A herald greeted him at the steps of the palace, announcing that the Tetrarch would not hear the case that day, but would give audience first thing in the morning. Guards escorted the boy prisoner inside, to be held in Herod's dungeon. Longinus was ordered to board his troops at a barracks down the road. The structure looked amenable enough from the outside, but upon entering, the Princeps discovered a similarity with most of Herod's construction projects. Looking upward towards the rafters, Longinus saw remnants of storm clouds and stars.

"Entirely unacceptable," he told the herald.

Reading irritation on the Princeps' face, Herod's minion responded with feigned sympathy, "Unfortunately, these are the only quarters sufficient for so large a force." Then cheerfully he piped, "The Tetrarch welcomes the officers to lodge in the Palace this evening."

The Princeps exchanged glances with his Optaio before answering. "Our thanks to the Tetrarch, but please express our regrets. Our desire is to share the hardship of our men."

"As you wish, Centurion." With a bow, the herald excused himself.

Juvenal scanned the sky, and held out an open palm, testing for raindrops. "Let's hope the Tetrarch's payment for our sleepless night is a clear-headed judgment in the morning."

*   *   *   *

Herod did seem clear-headed, or at least sober and eager to please. He rose from this throne and strode to the center of the chamber as Longinus was announced, clasping the Princeps' gauntlet with a firm grip.

"Centurion, you honor me with your presence. Any servant of Caesar will always find himself welcome in Tiberius, Caesar's Asian capitol."

Longinus and Juvenal exchanged raised eyebrows. Was this the Tetrarch or some jester's parody? The fawning was excessive even for Herod. Behind them, the mob of Galileans streamed through the portal into the vault of the Tetrarch's palace, held back by a line of his guards. Herod waited, his chest swelling along with his audience, then with a flourish, he continued his performance. He gestured broadly toward the boy prisoner, kneeling in shackles against the far wall.

"This sad miscreant you have brought me. And you seek justice. You do us the honor of allowing that justice be determined under our law. Of course, kings of this land from Solomon onward are renowned for wisdom in matters of law. Your humble servant can only aspire not to be a blemish on that timeless record—"

"Oh, get on with it!" a shrill voice interrupted. "Unless your sentence is that he should die of old age."

Longinus recognized the queen, Herodias, leaning lazily against the Tetrarch's throne. She flicked the back of her hand at her husband, like she was shooing a fly off her plate. Herod seemed to chew the inside of his cheeks for a moment, then reclaimed his throne, his icy stare forcing Herodias back a foot or two.

"State the Empire's case," he said.

Longinus recounted what had happened, and Herod quickly seemed to become bored with the recitation. His eyelids became heavy and his face tightened as though stifling a yawn. Finally, he cast a jaundiced eye toward the boy and ordered the Guards to bring him forward.

"Have you anything to say which contradicts the Centurion's report?"

The boy's eyes fluttered. Tears streamed. He shook his head.

Herod leaned on an elbow and stroked his beard.

"The facts are simple. But the case complex. Moses decreed that he who killed deliberately should be put to death. Yet, Moses created exceptions in the law for instances where death came accidentally or was unintended. Moses established cities of refuge, where a slayer who killed unawares might flee and escape the revenge of blood. In this case, the stone was thrown deliberately, but the death was unintended. Since the death is unintended, the boy is not a murderer. But since the stone was thrown deliberately, he is not without guilt for the death. Thus he may not be put to death, nor may he be freed. But if not freed, what punishment, short of death, approximates justice? This is a question worthy of Solomon." He stiffened, drawing himself up in his throne, then struck his hands together, clapping twice.

"Here is my ruling. The boy has killed and so his life is forfeit. But was not intended, so he must leave his home and find refuge in another. Therefore, the boy shall leave Chorizan and go to Capernaum, where he shall serve out his life as a slave to the commander of the century stationed at the Capernaum garrison. The boy is remanded to the custody of the good Centurion."

With that the palace guards thrust the boy toward Longinus. The Princeps stood stunned. The crowd of Galileans behind him groaned their objections. In the cavernous vault, the din was deafening. Longinus darted toward the throne.

"Excellency, please reconsider." He tipped his head over his shoulder toward the grumbling crowd, already pressing forward against Herod's guards. "These men will dog my Auxilia all the way back to Capernaum. The boy, living at the garrison, will be a constant sore, festering, inciting discontent and rebellion."

Herod leapt up, yelling at the Galileans, "Be grateful! Be grateful he's not to be stoned!" Then he slumped on his throne, sulking that his Solomon-like ruling had proved unpopular.

"You can't compel gratitude, Tetrarch," Longinus continued. "Send the boy to Syria. Send him to Pilate in Jerusalem."

"You oppose me, too?" Herod's eyes widened, the shock of betrayal clear on his face. "When I've given you what you want?"

"What I want?"

Herod clapped again and the herald brought a box forward, opening the lid. Herod dug out a letter, written in the Primus' hand. He handed it to Longinus, who scanned it quickly.

"I've given the verdict your commander requested. Go!" Herod barked. "And take the rabble with you!"

Longinus stood for an exasperated moment, watching the Tetrarch shrink in his robes. He'd get no help from this spineless reptile. He rolled the letter up and stuck it in his belt. He bowed and turned in a crisp about-face. Juvenal already had some Auxilia assembled to escort the boy out. Longinus pointed his vitis to the door, and the detachment marched. Herod's guards were just able to push the Galileans back, creating a narrow gap to the door. The Auxilia slipped out single file and reassembled outside.

Longinus and Juvenal trotted down the steps to a Decanus who held their horses.

"Crazy decision," Juvenal remarked. "Did he wake up drunk?"

"It was the Primus," Longinus whispered, and he hoisted himself onto Formido.

"What?"

"In the letter I requested, asking Herod for troops, the Primus also requested the boy be sentenced to serve him."

"So this whole march was a farce?"

"Apparently." Longinus surveyed the scene. The Galileans were streaming from the Palace, spreading the news like a brushfire. "Get your twenty best oarsmen," he told Juvenal. "The boy goes back by sea."

Juvenal nodded and set off through the ranks, alerting the Decanus of each octet to send his best rowers to the water. Longinus had the boy hustled down to the pier, to an imperial galley. The Auxilia walled off the crowd from the sea, as the oarsmen took their places and the sail was raised. Within minutes, the ship was on its way, and Longinus turned his attention to the march home.

*   *   *   *

The march northwest was uneventful. Unhindered by concern for protecting his prisoner, Longinus was able to maintain a brisk pace, which opened up a lead over the despondent Galileans. In the Princeps' mind this illustrated the cultural divide separating the two peoples: while Romans marched, Jews moped. Whereas the Western empires, Greece and Rome, held "the gods help those who help themselves," these backward Asians were forever petitioning their god to act in areas where they had not the ambition or backbone.

Meditating thus, the Princeps' chest swelled with pride for his country, while at the same time his stomach churned over the treachery of his commander. Once a fine officer, the Primus had obviously been corrupted by two decades of intercourse with these foreigners. He'd been too solicitous, cared too much about the niceties between the Empire and the conquered. There were rumors that the Primus had several women he visited. Young widows, who no doubt struggled, who were not above accepting a few denarii in exchange for favors to an old man. Longinus couldn't fault the man for taking comfort where he could find it, but those women had turned his head. Instead of assimilating the Jews into the Empire, officers like this Primus were Judaising Rome.

By the time the fishy stench from Magdala had reached his nostrils, Longinus was itching to call out the Primus for his underhanded treatment. The Primus trusted too much, when he should be vigilant for signs of duplicity or false dealing. Instead, he dealt falsely with his own officers. That's exactly what Longinus would tell him. Surely, Juvenal would back him. The other noncommissioned officers as well.

The road took them through the marketplace. The midday heat was just starting to dissipate; shops were reopening and townspeople returning to the open space. Longinus ordered a halt and allowed his men to fall out for food and water. He dismounted and gave Formido's reins to a Decanus who led the stallion to a trough near the central well. Longinus removed his helmet and wiped the sweat off his brow.

"She's looking much better, wouldn't you say?"

Longinus followed Juvenal's tip of the chin across the plaza to a crowded storefront. Several donkeys were lined up as men strapped goods to their backs and stuffed saddlebags until they were bursting. In command of the operation was a rather assertive woman. She moved among the men, inspecting their work, chastising them and demanding greater alacrity.

"Is that...?" Longinus started.

"It's either our convulsive hag, or her saner twin."

Longinus replaced his helmet. He ambled toward the well, hoping to get within earshot. He drew some water and drank as he listened.

"How many skins of wine?" the woman asked. Getting the answer from a stooped laborer, she assented. "All right, send the rest after. Flour. Olive oil. Mutton." She dealt authoritatively with her underlings, took her place at the head of the convoy and gave the order to proceed.

"Interesting evolution," Juvenal smirked. "From possessed to self-possessed."

Indeed, Longinus reflected. This was the tragic heroine revived. Cleopatra victorious at Actium[60]. A Dido[61] who'd convinced Aeneas that herself plus

Carthage was worth more than the founding of Rome. But if she were a woman of means and station, why had she played the Mad Hag of Magdala, in a cheap ploy to assassinate a child? What was she planning, and who were her allies? Longinus poked his vitis at a laborer bringing up the rear of the donkey train. The young man fell to his knees in front of the Princeps, hands ready to shield his head.

"Ave, Master. How may I serve you?"

"Who is your mistress? The woman giving orders?"

"She's called Mary. Her family owns half of Magdala."

"We passed through here yesterday," the Princeps stated, "and that same woman bore every mark of a lunatic." He pointed to reference an exact spot in the road. "Was it not she, who lay there twitching and croaking like a rabid animal?"

"I did not witness it, sir. But what you describe would not have been unusual. For Mary. For these past few years, she's been given to fits."

"And today? The woman is quite composed."

"A startling transformation. Some say a miracle."

Longinus grabbed him by the scruff, pressing him close. "Confess. That was an act yesterday. A ploy to distract us, so zealots could attack our prisoner."

"I can't answer to that, sir. As I said, I was not a witness. But if it was Mary, she has a history."

Juvenal then tapped the fellow on his shoulder. "Has she any contact with Zealots?"

"What, the rebels? No, absolutely not."

"Then, if we were to follow that train of supplies, it would not wind up into the hills, there to feed an army of outlaws?"

"No, sir. On my life."

The two Romans exchanged glances, at which point Juvenal drew a dagger.

"If those are your terms."

"Please, sir!" the man slobbered, "these supplies are bound for Capernaum. For the Rabbi and his troupe."

"What Rabbi?" Longinus demanded.

"The teacher who freed her. Released her demons. Again, I wasn't there, but they say he touched her head and her mind cleared — whatever spirits tortured her — and they're saying now there were seven — they vanished."

"Seven demons?" Longinus remembered her croaking the name Septimus. "When?"

---

[60] Her loss with Marc Antony at Actium drove Cleopatra to commit suicide

[61] Queen Dido of Carthage fell in love with Aeneas, but could not convince him to stay with her. When she realized that he would leave and found Rome, which would one day destroy her city, she committed suicide.

"Just last night. So, she feels a certain gratitude. And duty. These supplies are to support the Rabbi's mission."

Longinus released the man, who bowed and scurried after the caravan. Longinus mused for a moment, then slapped a palm against the front of his helmet. "Another prophet? Or a guise for a Zealot?" He headed back to reclaim his horse.

Juvenal strode at his side, inquiring, "You think it was all staged?"

"I think," Longinus averred, "we're dealing with crafty foes." He took Formido's reins and swung into the saddle. As he nudged his heels into the stallion's ribs, he focused on what would be necessary to counter a crafty foe: not the credulity of an aging Primus, who'd forgotten what it meant to be Roman. Rather, decisive action from a rising leader with the strength to crush a rebellion; someone who could see through this *Rabbi* and expose him as a fraud and a traitor. Every soldier in Caesar's service knew there came a moment when he must rise or fall in performance of his duty. Longinus knew his moment had arrived.

*   *   *   *

Joachim raised his head again and vomited into the bucket. The Primus dabbed at the youth's mouth with a dry cloth and eased him back onto his pallet. The mansio's medical officer, crouched on the other side, began again to palpate the boy's stomach. The patient gave little indication of abdominal pain that Longinus, standing at the door, could notice, but started to drool again from the side of his mouth.

"Did we quarantine him in time?" the Primus asked.

The medic stared into Joachim's wide, black pupils and shrugged dismissively. "This boy needed to be isolated before he got sick." He paused to sift through his assortment of remedies, then explained. "It's not disease. He's been poisoned."

"Poisoned!" the Primus gasped, then shot his eyes to Longinus. "Outside, Princeps. And you, Optaio, out!"

Longinus lowered his shoulders and stooped through the door into the harsh morning sun. Juvenal followed keeping his eyes down. Longinus couldn't discern if he was having trouble adjusting to the light, or if his friend simply didn't want to look at him. The door burst open and the Primus lumbered out.

"Does Rome make war on children, Princeps?" the Primus barked.

"Rome makes war on its enemies, sir."

"Not even war. Murder. Deceitful, cowardly poisoning!"

Longinus answered coolly. "Such a description matches neither the Auxilia nor its officers. It's a method employed by Zealots."

The Primus scoffed, prompting Juvenal to interject, "They tried once to kill the boy."

But Longinus had lost patience and scolded the old fool. "How can you suspect your own officers before those scoundrels?"

"I suspect anyone and everyone who bears the boy ill!" the Primus bellowed. His reddened eyes brimmed. "But I also judge opportunity. The boy lives within the mansio. He hasn't left its walls since he returned from Tiberius. Who had opportunity, Princeps?"

Longinus chose not to dignify the accusation.

"It's clearly hemlock," Juvenal offered. "Not an uncommon plant in this part of the world."

"I'm not asking who could get the poison!" The Primus stomped. His gouty foot kicked up a cloud of dust; the pain made him wince. "Who could deliver it? Who could have put it in the boy's food?"

"The logical place to start," Juvenal suggested, "is the kitchen. We'll question the men who prepare the food."

The infirmary door creaked open, and the medic emerged. "I've done what I can," he said, "but I doubt the boy will survive."

"What can be done?" the Primus demanded.

"Medically, nothing."

After a deathly moment, Juvenal commented. "I suppose the Jews have religious rites for the dying. Useless in a practical sense, but it may reflect better on the mansio if you permit the exercise."

Longinus objected immediately, "You want to open the garrison to them?"

"We could take the boy to the synagogue."

The medic waved the idea off. "Moving the boy will hasten his death. And death is coming fast."

"I'll go," the Primus groaned, then shot a look at Longinus. "And you, Princeps, with me. Ready our horses. Optaio, investigate the kitchen. I want a report when I return."

Juvenal bent his head in assent, then strode off. Longinus had saddled Formido earlier, so he called to the livery for one additional horse. It took three soldiers to hoist the Primus into the saddle, but once mounted, he rode steadily. It was only a short canter to the synagogue, made shorter by the fact that the streets were deserted.

"It's not the bloody Sabbath, is it?" the Primus muttered.

Longinus wagged his head, "They've gone to see a show."

"What's that?" the old man grunted. Longinus pretended not to hear; he didn't want to discuss the conspiracy he'd discovered out in the open street. They arrived at the synagogue, where the only person to greet them was the wife of the proprietor, who bowed her head and spoke as if to the dust.

"May I assist you, Centurion?"

"My servant, Joachim Ben Nasir, is ill. He may die. I mean to invite you, your people, to... well, to... perform whatever service for the dying..."

"Sir," she interrupted, suddenly showing some spirit. "We are indeed fortunate. Among us today is a healer. A Nazarene they say has authority over illnesses of all kinds. He's worked many cures."

Longinus knew of whom she spoke: the alleged Rabbi the Mad Hag of Magdala had provisioned. He was tempted to spit in protest of such nonsense, but the Primus shot forward like a frog's tongue snapping at a fly. "Where can we find him?" he begged.

"I know where," Longinus flatly stated.

"Then find him and bring him to me." Then, reading the eagerness in Longinus' eyes, the Primus added, "And not in chains. With all due civility."

They rode briskly back through Capernaum, the Primus moaning in pain, but refusing to slacken his pace. He rode with such urgency, Longinus wondered if the old man really thought curing the boy was possible. At the mansio, they parted company, Longinus heading northwest out of town. About half a mile out, the ground sloped upward and the fringe of the crowd was visible. Longinus saw two octets he'd ordered to surveil the event, sitting their horses in tight formation, observing the crowd and listening intently for hints of sedition. He reined Formido to a halt alongside the Decanus.

"All peaceable, sir," the Decanus reported.

"What have you learned?" Longinus asked.

"Seems this Rabbi never met my father."

Longinus raised a quizzical eyebrow and the Decanus expounded, "He asks which of you evildoers would hand his son a rock if he asked for bread, or a snake if he asked for fish? Implying no father would do that. So I conclude, he never met mine."

The soldiers chuckled, and Longinus allowed himself a slight smile.

"It's mostly in that vein, Princeps," the Decanus joked. "Though I enjoyed the bit about the plank in the eye." He mimed tottering from the weight of an enormous log jutting out of his eye, holding it aloft with his right hand, while reaching out into space with his left. "Here, friend, let me get that speck for you."

The men in the ranks laughed, until the Decanus broke them off abruptly, pointing to the top of the hill. The Rabbi rose from a sitting position. He handed a skin of water back to one of his acolytes, wiped his mouth and turned to the crowd.

"Here we go," the Decanus alerted them. "Intermission's over. Act three."

Longinus had already seen the act, but on smaller stages. The incidents in Magdala had raised his suspicions, so he'd investigated this Rabbi. At night, Longinus had cloaked himself in Galilean garb and listened outside homes where the Rabbi had been invited to dine. Longinus had uncovered several disturbing facts. Firstly, though this man claimed to be a religious teacher, the most learned, religiously observant Jews held him in low regard. These scribes and Pharisees informed Longinus that this Rabbi was a simple mechanic — a carpenter — with no formal education at all. Likewise, his followers were ignorant. He'd gathered an inner circle of blunt-minded and impressionable thugs — mostly fishermen — who were content to let someone else do their thinking. Even worse, the Rabbi seemed to be courting the most corrupt elements in Galilee. He dined with tax collectors who'd squeezed blood from their countrymen. In fact, the same greedy viper Longinus had reproached in the market had joined this Rabbi's entourage. Finally, the very Zealot who'd informed on the boy prisoner had joined the group and was managing its finances. He and the Mad Hag fought like cats in a sack, belying any notion that this group had peaceful intentions. Longinus could see a plan taking shape: this Rabbi would stir up discontent among poor, downtrodden laborers and dupe them into doing his fighting. Meanwhile, he'd get financial backing from wealthy rogues, whom he'd promise favors once he tossed off the yoke of Rome.

The Rabbi spoke in a clear and rich voice, but did not hold the Centurion's interest: *prophets, the kingdom of heaven, a Father somewhere in that heaven?* The only father Longinus had known beat him so badly, military life seemed light in comparison. And prophets were only con men looking to separate fools from their money. If the Primus believed this charlatan could cure the boy, it was only further evidence that he'd been thoroughly seduced by this backward culture. The man desperately needed to get back to Rome, and back to reality.

Longinus was already trying to make that happen; he'd complained vociferously about the Primus rigging Herod's verdict, and creating a situation that exacerbated the bad blood between Capernaum and Rome. When the Primus had chosen to ignore Longinus, he'd felt compelled to appeal to the territorial governor of Syria. Unfortunately, that legate, Aelius Lamia, was administering the territory from Rome. It would be months before the dispute was adjudicated, and in the meantime the conflict festered like a sore on the garrison. Longinus was determined not to let that happen. He would control events; he would seize his moment.

*　　　　*　　　　*　　　　*

When the Rabbi — or prophet, whatever he should be called — finished, a path through the crowd opened up, through which he and his followers headed down the hill. Longinus ordered the octets to pull out, trotting their horses down the slope on an arc that would intercept the Rabbi's entourage. But suddenly the procession stopped. A vagrant in rags blocked the Rabbi's progress. He knelt, bowing his head.

"Leper?" the Decanus speculated.

Longinus nosed Formido to the mouth of the crowd.

The leper bellowed, "Lord, if you are willing, you can make me clean."

Longinus watched as the Rabbi reached out his hand and touched the man. The crowd let loose a low gasp, but the Rabbi remained placid, utterly assured.

"I am willing," he declared. "Be clean!"

Immediately the leper started to peel his rags away. His skin was smooth and unblemished. The crowd applauded wildly. Then the Rabbi leaned close to the vagrant and Longinus thought he heard him whisper, "See that you don't tell anyone. But go, show yourself to the priest."

Longinus jerked Formido's reins and pulled the stallion away.

"What was that all about?" the Decanus asked.

"Showmanship," Longinus replied. "This man's a master of manipulation. Tell me, Decanus, if you wanted to spread a rumor quickly, what would you do?"

"I would tell this girl I know in Bethsaida, and swear her to secrecy."

"Exactly."

They cantered briskly back to the garrison, and Longinus dismounted on the infirmary steps. The Primus was in high anxiety; no doubt the boy was failing. He barked at Longinus, "Where's the healer?"

"He's returning to town," Longinus said, then drawing close, lowered his voice. "I thought you should know what we witnessed before you approached him." As the Primus shifted his great girth off his sore foot, Longinus explained. "His healings are clearly staged to fool the superstitious and ignorant. After he preached, he was approached by a man wrapped in rags. An apparent leper. And a fair disguise it was, right down to the stench. But follow me: the leper knelt before him, called him *Lord* and begged to be cleansed. Whereupon this fraud said, *Be clean!* And that was it. No process, no... The man could not have been a leper; he was an actor. Covered from head to foot in rags, no one could see his skin until he peeled off his clothes, and then, magically, he's clean. Do you understand? Why I couldn't bring him here?"

"I understand," boomed the Primus, "that I ordered you to bring him. That I am commander, and when I tell a junior officer, *Do this,* it is done. That, Princeps, is what I understand."

"Well," Juvenal interrupted, with his customary tact, "whether he was brought or came on his own, he is here." Juvenal pointed to the gate, still open, through which they could see almost the entire population of Capernaum returning from the hills. The Primus grabbed his vitis, swung down from the infirmary porch, and landed awkwardly on his bad foot. Grimacing, he rasped, "Princeps, attend me."

Longinus marched alongside his limping superior. "Respectfully, I must caution the Primus, he is making a great mistake. This man is seditious. You cannot bring him into the garrison. You cannot show him our weaknesses."

"Silence!" The Primus clenched his jaw tight. "When I desire your counsel, I'll ask for it. Simply point the man out to me." Longinus nodded. He scanned the slow-moving crowd for signs of the Rabbi or his henchmen. He locked eyes with the Iscariot, begging donations from some ignorant dupes. The scoundrel immediately dove into the crowd, leaving a trail of tottering townsmen as he knifed through. Figuring the coward would flee to his leader for protection, Longinus spied the ultimate end of that trail, and surely enough, there was the Mad Hag of Magdala perched beside the Healing Carpenter of Nazareth.

"Over there," he told the Primus, and the two waded into the crowd. Longinus was impressed at the respectful wake granted the Primus. Heads bowed and townspeople stepped aside as the garrison commander plodded down the street. Again, the Primus moved with grim determination, as if this petition was anything but folly. Finally, drawing a deep breath, the Primus braced himself and addressed the Rabbi.

"Lord," he said — the title sent a shiver up Longinus' spine — "my servant lies at home paralyzed, suffering terribly."

The Rabbi effectively mirrored his concern, with sunken breast and tilted head, eyes almost glistening. Longinus wanted to applaud such artful manipulation, but remained silent as the Rabbi asked, "Shall I come and heal him?"

The Primus, perhaps playing to the crowd, replied, "Lord, I do not deserve to have you come under my roof. But just say the word, and my servant will be healed." Then he looked at Longinus, open scorn, "For I myself am a man under authority, with soldiers under me. I tell this one, *Go,* and he goes; and that one, *Come,* and he comes. I say to my servant, *Do this,* and he does it."

At this, the Rabbi looked amazed. He laughed and said to his followers, "I have not found anyone in Israel with such great faith." Then he clapped the Primus on the shoulder and declared, "Go! Let it be done just as you believed it would." With that, he turned his back and walked off with the Mad Hag at his side. Several fishermen formed a V ahead of him, splitting the crowd like a wedge through a log. The Primus nodded, did an awkward about-face, and lumbered back toward the garrison.

"More chicanery," Longinus scoffed. "He'll be well out of town when the boy expires."

"I do not see guile in that man," the Primus huffed.

"It's not obvious," Longinus retorted, "that's what makes it guile. I'll admit, this Rabbi is different from the common rebels. His mind is supple, his wit is quick. He draws people toward him gently, but powerfully. One night, I saw a woman fall at his feet, wetting them with her tears and wiping them dry with her hair. Such fanaticism makes every one of his followers a potential soldier. He might be talking religion now, but once he's amassed numbers, he'll shift his rhetoric and set off an assault that our forces cannot match."

"Perhaps," the Primus granted. "And perhaps I am an old fool." He wheezed heavily as he trundled, speaking short phrases as he exhaled, then sucking hard for his next breath. "Perhaps I've become too soft for command. And ought to retire. What's clear is that you and I differ radically. In how we see these people. How we would treat them. And our approaches cannot be reconciled. Waiting for Rome to decide is fruitless. Only adding to discord in the garrison."

"Then perhaps," Longinus posited, "this should be the test."

The Primus stopped and drew a deep breath. His rheumy eyes bid Longinus to explain.

"If the boy is healed, your trust is vindicated. If not, a seditious rebel has just played you for a fool. Let the boy's fate decide ours."

The Primus placed both hands at the small of his back and stretched his great girth upward through his sternum. After a mighty groan, his weight resettled about his midsection, and leaning forward on his vitis, he leveled his gaze at Longinus.

"What you've said is true enough. We'll be ruled by the boy's outcome."

The garrison was less than a stone's throw away. Longinus could feel his prospects rising with each step. But the Primus, too, was confident; he strode upon the stony road without a hint of pain. Longinus felt a pang of pity for the man; he had served Rome for decades, and though he had hung on past his prime, he still deserved a measure of respect. Longinus wished his superior had chosen to retire while he was still a formidable, rather than pitiful, figure. Longinus vowed he would avert his eyes when the Primus was told of the boy's death. He would withdraw to his quarters and let the old man grieve in dignity. No one would ever learn of their bargain from him. He would never be accused of gloating, or taking pleasure from his superior's downfall. In fact, Longinus was sure that, after the sting of reality faded, the Primus would thank his junior for delivering this hard slap, before the old man's decline had led to tragedy.

The gates of the garrison opened and Longinus prepared to ask leave to return to his quarters. But before the words left his mouth, the youth came running across the campus.

"Primus!" he cried. "I'm well! Look!" The boy fell on his knees in front of the commander, who slumped over his vitis and began to weep. "Thank you, sir. The men said you went to a healer for me. I'd never been so sick, and now it's like it never happened!"

Longinus was stunned. He watched the Primus gather the boy in his arms and hug him tight. After what seemed an eternity, the commander dispatched the boy to the kitchen with orders to bring dinner, and turned to his junior officer.

"Gaius Cassius Longinus, you may tender your request for transfer at your earliest convenience." The old man then trundled off towards his office.

Before Longinus could move, Juvenal was at his elbow. His friend spoke low, a quaver in his voice.

"There was hemlock in the pantry. And one of the kitchen staff has run off."

Longinus simply stared at the ground. "Oh?"

"An Assyrian. No one has seen him since last evening. Apparently, he's deserted."

"Then that explains it. One of Arsenius' countrymen. Obviously he harbored resentment..."

But Juvenal cut him off. His normally diplomatic tone gone, he practically barked through clenched teeth. "You realize, desertion carries the death penalty. That makes two deaths to square one."

Longinus started to answer, but stopped himself. Words were useless. They were two warriors; they had seen, faced and negotiated with death. Those negotiations, to be honorable, must go according to a code. Deceit was not part of that code.

"Of course, now, the boy did not die," Juvenal conceded. "And no one really cares about a stray Assyrian foot soldier, right?"

"I suppose we can agree on that."

"Good luck at your next posting," Juvenal said. "I hope you take some wisdom from Capernaum with you."

With that his friend turned and walked across the yard. Juvenal's back spoke volumes about what Longinus had risked and what he had lost. He still believed he had been right. About the boy, the garrison, the Zealot threat. He had been right to go over the Primus' head to the superiors in Rome. As for the boy, and the Assyrian deserter, time in this rebellious snake pit would vindicate his methods. Leadership depended upon decisiveness, and Longinus had been decisive. He had risked much in the last few days, and he had lost much: his post, his best friend, and perhaps most painfully, his moment.

Chapter 11

Longinus leaned forward onto the stone parapet and stared out at Mare Nostrum. He felt suddenly wistful with nostalgia for his youth. At his fishing village on Italy's west coast he'd first gazed longingly at "our sea" and imagined what lay beyond. In the evenings, as his father and his uncles had stretched and flexed their muscles hoisting the full nets onto the deck of their boat, he'd pictured them as galley slaves, straining at the oars, driving a warship into battle. In the mornings, as they dug in the wet pits, extracting red clay that the women would press into molds and fire for tile, he dreamed the men were drenched in barbarian blood.

When he was fifteen and already longing to see the world, rumors charged up and down the Via Aurelia that the Roman Legion, under the command of the great general Nero Claudius Drusus, had won a crushing victory against the rebellious wild men of the north. Longinus then went with his family to Rome to see the Triumph of Germanicus, as Drusus had been renamed[62]. Young Longinus had been inspired by the pomp, pageantry and military splendor, by the adulation heaped upon the soldiers, and by the strange, almost ghostly, beauty of the German prisoners. Huge, broad and white as milk, the prisoners towered above their captors. The men were impressive enough, but what really stunned the would-be Legionnaire was the sister of the rebel chieftain. Thusnelda could have been a marble statue, except for her hair, the color of spring wheat, which flowed down her straight back to the very bend in her knees, and her piercing blue eyes, proud and defiant even in defeat. If such creatures existed elsewhere in the world, Longinus must find and conquer them for the glory of Rome.

He ran away that week. There was no thought of leaving a note, since no one in his family could read. He was big for his age, so no one questioned his enlistment in the Legion for the standard term of twenty years. He was thrilled to be placed under the command of Germanicus. He trained hard, refining the fighting skills he'd learned at the hands of his older cousins, hoping that someday he would distinguish himself and garner some attention from his commander. It wasn't long before he got a measure of his wish, in combat against Cappadocia and Commagene, which Tiberius had decided should become Roman provinces. Longinus found warfare exhilarating, as if life finally made sense: existence was not some random accident, but a reward for courage, strength and endurance. The unworthy perished as the mighty prevailed. His superiors noted his bravery and groomed him for command. He rose through the ranks, becoming a Decanus by age eighteen. He traveled in a detachment with Germanicus to Egypt and then to Syria, where the great man died suddenly and suspiciously.

---

[62] In honor of his deceased father who had also been militarily successful in Germany

How sordid and wasteful the great man's death now seemed. Germanicus had accused the Syrian governor, Gnaeus Calpurnius Piso, of corruption and had ordered him back to Rome to stand trial. Piso objected that Germanicus was exceeding his authority, and in the midst of this political bickering Germanicus died. Many suspected that Piso, on instruction from Tiberius, had done away with his pesky rival, who'd surpassed Caesar in accomplishment and popularity. The truth could never be proven, because Piso died while awaiting trial in Rome, perhaps at Caesar's instigation.

A shake-up in the ranks followed. Rome was justifiably concerned that someone loyal to Germanicus might seize command and cause grief for Tiberius. Longinus had always been apolitical, and carefully limited his comments to regret at his general's passing. While most of his comrades were transferred to other units, Longinus was promoted to Watch Officer. But seven years passed without further promotion. Younger men surpassed him; their only distinction being they'd never known Germanicus. Frustrated by petty politics, Longinus had transferred from the Legion to the Auxilia, ironically serving under the Syrian governor.

The Auxilia seemed to harbor no grudge; Longinus was immediately made Optaio Centurion, rear guard commander in a cavalry unit. There he served ably for four years before winning a promotion to Centurion Princeps Prior. A year later he was assigned to the mansio at Capernaum, where he'd expected to succeed the aging Primus, serve five years in Galilee and to retire with a generous pension and elevation to the Equestrian ranks. But all he'd achieved could have crumbled, a few months ago in the incident with that Jewish boy. A lot of bother it had been, Longinus reflected. He'd never anticipated so much interest in the health of such a troublesome speck. When the Primus transferred him here to Ptolemais, Longinus worried he'd face a reduction in rank and pay, and that the duty would be onerous. To his surprise, just the opposite had transpired.

As he reported for duty and his orders were unsealed, Longinus learned he'd been promoted. He was now Centurion Hastatus Prior, the Primus Pilus, with command of the garrison at this crucial, strategic harbor. After he'd recovered from that shock, Longinus had toured the high, stone ramparts that lined the northern shore of the crescent-shaped inlet. Ptolemais was the best natural port in the region, the crossroads of traffic from Europe to Asia, and Asia to Africa. The centurion pounded his fist on the stone rampart. He flared his nostrils and his heart fairly hammered when he considered that he, Gaius Cassius Longinus, had been chosen to defend it.

Though completely secure today, Ptolemais had been a site of much contention as far back as anyone could recall. The Jews told stories of a thousand years prior, when, out of captivity in Egypt, they'd conquered Judea under a general named Joshua. This region had been granted to one of their various tribes, but they were unable to wrest the stronghold from the

Phoenicians. Seems the Jewish god, who made fortresses crumble at the blast of a trumpet, couldn't shake the bulwarks of Ptolemais. Over the ensuing centuries, the Jews had been mere spectators as the harbor changed hands from the Phoenicians to the Greeks, then to the Seleucids and the Egyptians. Now Ptolemais rightly belonged to Rome, as did every city on "our sea."

Longinus stared again at the glistening water. It was now fifteen years since he'd left home. In all that time, he'd never once returned to the center of the Empire he served, and truly, Rome had become more of an idea than a physical reality. In fact, though he'd traveled the world and earned this awesome responsibility, the physical reality of his life was rather meager. He had some small savings, a good horse, fine armor and a well-crafted sword, but no other possessions of consequence. His pension would consist of some land in Lombardy, where he hoped to farm and raise horses, to marry and have children. Such thoughts naturally led his mind back to the village and home of his youth.

It was as if the sea, which like a siren had tempted him to venture out, was now seducing him homeward. He thought of his mother and wondered if she might still be alive. She had been a good woman — unremarkable when weighed against the vastness of empire, but virtuous, steadfast and dutiful in the confines of a home. Perhaps it was just a melancholy spell — understandable since leaving comrades in Galilee, especially given his falling out with Juvenal — but Longinus suddenly felt a deep loneliness, which struck at his core and seemed in this moment to define his life.

Military life had offered many opportunities, but introductions to marriageable women had not been among them. In his younger days, Longinus had imagined there'd be some version of Thusnelda waiting for him: an exotic beauty whose hair of spun gold would dazzle his eyes and leave him weak in the knees. But the women he encountered were often primitive, grimy creatures dressed in skins and barely distinguishable from domesticated animals. Matted hair, leathern skin, crooked teeth. If by chance he did come across an attractive girl, she was probably nursing a grudge over him having killed her father, brother or boyfriend. The women of Galilee, when he could make them out under all their veils and heavy robes, seemed to be among the more attractive of the foreign women he'd encountered. Galilee had a fairly good climate, not so dry as to crease the skin, and temperate, so the girls needn't put on too much weight to combat the cold. Unfortunately, these Jewish women were hateful of foreigners. They clung to their silly belief in their god — who, though *almighty*, watched and did nothing as Egypt, Greece and now Rome conquered his people — and they only married their Jewish men, a sorry lot who hadn't won a military victory in two hundred years.

Well, Longinus mused, he had five years before he was paroled. Then he might return to Italy to find a modest woman like the mother he'd so underestimated. In the meantime, he was out of the backwater of Galilee and at the crossroads of intercontinental commerce. If he could not go to his Thusnelda, perhaps she would come to him!

The Centurion punctuated that hopeful thought with a sequence of rapid slaps on the parapet and prepared to meet the magistrate. The man, thin-boned and mealy-mouthed, had an effeminate manner that put Longinus on edge. Having to take orders from a civilian was hard enough. Taking orders from a debased youth who'd done nothing to build himself into a man was insulting. Longinus would admit that smacking the heel of his palm against the solid rock was a silly, juvenile preoccupation, but it reminded him that he had risen in rank through the rigors of combat, not political scheming.

"I have seen to your request," the magistrate yawned. "Regarding personnel."

"My thanks."

The magistrate gazed deeply at Longinus. The stones received a quick round of punishment, until the Centurion's hand ached.

"I'm told officers should not get too close to their men, nor develop a particular fondness for any one man."

Longinus rubbed the pain out of his hand. "There are exceptions," he said.

The magistrate tilted his head, and a wry smile played across his weak mouth. "Truly, for exceptional relationships. With exceptional men."

Longinus chose not to dignify the remark.

The magistrate continued after another yawn. "He has arrived."

Longinus followed the magistrate's grandiose gesture, feeling his heart rise as he glimpsed a figure ascending the steps to the rampart: Juvenal. Then instantly Longinus was crushed with shame. In a fit of loneliness, he'd requested Juvenal be transferred to Ptolemais. Longinus needed a trustworthy Princeps, but had he overstepped propriety in making such a particular request? Seeing Juvenal, stiff-backed and square jawed, Longinus feared he may have imported a problem into his ranks that could fester. Should he have simply conceded their friendship was over? Had the first decision of his first command invited disaster?

Juvenal touched his chest and thrust his fist forward in a pro forma salute.

"Primus," he acknowledged.

Longinus returned the salute. "Princeps."

"That will take some getting used to."

"It's well earned," Longinus asserted, perhaps too forcefully. He immediately wondered if it showed weakness. Leaders do not curry favor with subordinates.

The magistrate scrutinized the two men, then, perhaps mercifully, changed the subject. "News from Rome. Another dispatch from Macro concerning the Senate."

"Good news, one hopes," Juvenal offered. His willingness to speak put Longinus more at ease.

"That depends how one views it. I'll tell you the news; you can say if it's good."

Juvenal raised an eyebrow. "You mean to discover my politics?"

"A soldier has no politics," Longinus stated. "We only serve Rome."

The magistrate chuckled. "You serve Rome? Though you haven't been there in two decades? No Centurion, like me, you serve power. And in Rome very lately, power has skewed towards Caesar. The empire, the power and the glory are incarnate in one man, Tiberius. The patricians hold to their shreds and even dream of restoring the Senate, but shall we let them?"

Longinus wished to dismiss this line of questioning. "Again, that is politics," he said.

The magistrate pushed forward. "I'll answer for you. We must not. As long as we serve power, it benefits us to have power consolidated. In one man, beholden to us."

Longinus cleared a knot forming in his throat. "To the matter of Macro then?"

"Yes," the magistrate nodded. "The campaign to purge the Senate has yielded positive results for Caesar, with many prominent members pledging their fealty. Some have retreated into the obscurity they so richly deserve; while hiding they will not be missed and should they reappear will not be noticed. There is one, however, one about whom Caesar is terribly exercised. A Senator Proculus."

The name jarred something buried in Longinus' mind.

"Caesar does not trust men who think too deeply or too long," the magistrate continued. "This man Proculus has had some fifteen years to think about his brother's unfortunate death."

"Yes," Longinus remembered. "He died in an ambush, shortly after Germanicus."

"A strange coincidence," admitted the magistrate, "but Rome insists the deaths were unrelated. Our deep thinker may disagree and may want revenge. Or," the magistrate closed his eyes to mere slits, "he may want what Germanicus wanted. Reform. Some restoration of that delicate balance of power that once existed between the Senate and Caesar." After a pause for effect, the magistrate waved his hand dismissively. "He's a dreamer who's doomed to fail. The girl is infinitely more important."

"What girl?" Juvenal asked.

"His niece. Daughter of the dead officer. Veronica."

"Odd name," Juvenal mused.

"The *verus icon*. True image. And she is something of a symbol. The daughter of an officer serving a general who would challenge Caesar. She must never again show her face in Rome."

"Well," Longinus shrugged, "if she's coming here, which seems to be what you're implying, she isn't heading back to Rome."

"And if she's going back to Rome," Juvenal smiled, "she won't come here."

Longinus again felt a measure of relief, as Juvenal was allowing his customary good humor to surface. The magistrate was not charmed.

"Antony led his rebellion against Augustus from Egypt. If this Veronica were looking to enlist foreign allies, she could well pass through Ptolemais; her cousin, the Senator's daughter, is married to the Prefect of Judea." Then as if firmly pressing his words in place, the magistrate nodded several times before walking away, and leaving Longinus and Juvenal standing awkwardly in each other's presence.

*   *   *   *

"Actually," Juvenal mused, "the soldier should be the most political of creatures. The soldier bears the brunt of failed politics. Putting down revolts. Crucifying rebels. The soldier is the emperor's spine and the diplomat's teeth."

Longinus swirled the wine in his cup and drank. Though he was sure the junior officers at the other tables couldn't hear their discussion, he was careful not to show annoyance. "Neither the spine nor the teeth are charged with thinking."

Juvenal tilted his head in half-begrudged assent before continuing. "Our magistrate wishes to serve Caesar."

"As do we all," the Primus reminded his Princeps.

"Of course. However, he wishes Rome's power to be consolidated in the person of Caesar. Political power is only the smiling façade of military power. The more Caesar gains politically, the more dependent he is on his armies. The more dependent on his armies, the more Caesar must deliver to those armies what they want. So you see, it's not really a consolidation of power at all; it's a shifting of power. From the patrician Senate to the plebeian mob."

"The military is not a mob," Longinus stated flatly. He meant to end the discussion, but Juvenal wasn't done.

"It's a mob when it serves a man rather than the law."

Longinus pushed back from the table and rose. "Caesar is more than a man." That statement Juvenal should have read as his dismissal. No longer was his old friend indulging his philosophical ramblings; his commanding officer was telling him to hold his tongue.

Juvenal wiped his hands on his napkin and rose slowly. He leveled his eyes at Longinus. "Every man is merely a man." Juvenal dropped his napkin on his plate, turned and exited the commissary. Longinus looked down at his own plate. Disgusted, he decided he'd eaten enough, or rather, what was left wasn't worth sitting for. Not under the eyes of junior officers who might wonder about the rift between their Primus and his newly arrived, highest-ranking subordinate. Longinus headed for the door.

He burst forth into blinding sunlight. Squinting, he spotted Juvenal in discussion with a groom about a horse. Longinus stood impatiently until the groom led the horse to the stables, then he crossed to Juvenal and, tamping down his anger, spoke.

"Princeps, you need to guard what you say in front of the men."

Juvenal rolled his shoulders slightly, opening his chest and assuming a formal stance, apparently registering Longinus' use of his rank in the address. "How have I offended my Primus?"

"I take no personal offense. I simply wish no discussion of politics to incite the men."

"I merely wished to point out..."

Longinus cut him off. He spoke at a rapid clip, but checked his volume. "I need no pointing out. I'm not naïve about our magistrate. I know he's driven by envy. He'll never be a patrician, so he wants them destroyed. His kind would reduce the empire to rubble simply to punish the wealthy. He's a venal snake who elevates his base desires above the law. But his desires are not our issue. We serve Rome. Whether that is Caesar, the Senate or some combination."

"May I suggest, Primus..."

"No," Longinus barked. "You may not suggest!" He was now jaw to jaw with his subordinate. "You may not opine or insinuate!" Longinus stepped back and composed himself, but still couldn't control his frustration, which had been building all the time since Juvenal had arrived. "By all the gods, man, I don't know what's gotten into you. You are a soldier. You receive orders and you carry them out. That should be the extent of your philosophy. And if it isn't, I'll send you back to the gouty old Primus, and you can spend the next five to ten years helping him on and off of his horse."

Longinus was four paces beyond Juvenal when he heard him call out. "He won't take me."

Longinus halted. Stunned. The Primus had always held Juvenal in the highest regard. Longinus stood rigid as Juvenal crept closer. Neither attempted eye contact.

"He questions my suitability for command," Juvenal smirked.

Longinus' eyes widened even as his throat constricted. "Why?"

"He sent me to find the cook. The one who'd run away after the boy was poisoned."

Now Longinus looked squarely at his friend. Juvenal's eyes were moist. His expression hit Longinus like a fist to the solar plexus.

Juvenal shrugged. "I told him he resisted arrest. And was killed in the struggle."

After a pause, Juvenal stated defiantly, "I'd do it again. For you. Because I know you as an officer, and I know you are more necessary to Rome than any garrison slave. But still."

The display of loyalty had Longinus flustered. "Still?" he prompted.

Juvenal cleared his throat. "I have gained some perspective on what happens when one chooses the man over the law. I don't know how these things are reckoned, whether by gods or men, in heaven or on Earth. I have killed many men in battle and never questioned, but now in my soul... there's a weight."

"You needn't bear it," Longinus coughed. "It's mine alone."

Juvenal shook his head. "There's a price I'll pay." He chewed on his lower lip before continuing. "In this Senate thing. Whatever you command, I'll obey. But. I hope if there is action to be taken, you will serve the law and not the man."

Longinus exhaled slowly as if lowering a boulder to the ground. At that moment he could turn nowhere but the sea. He gazed at Mare Nostrum and watched the light dance on the surface. He must settle this now for all time.

"In Caesar," he said, "the man and the law are one."

Chapter 12

To Veronica, the heavy fortifications made the port seem inhospitable, even downright hostile. She stared up at the high stone walls and imagined arrows raining down from the parapets. Catapults lobbing fireballs toward any approaching vessels. "Ptolemais doesn't seem very inviting," she ventured.

"A very old city," Valentius offered. "It's seen many a battle. Originally named for Ptolemy, a general under Alexander the Great."

"So it's a Greek city?"

"It's been Greek. As well as Assyrian, Egyptian, Roman."

Veronica wasn't asking for a history lesson; she wanted some reassurance of their safety. She raised a flat hand to shield her eyes, as the sun was peeking over the parapets. She leaned close to her uncle and whispered, "Is the garrison here at the port?"

Theodosius didn't answer. Veronica couldn't tell, because her uncle had a growth of beard — an element of their disguise as Greek merchants — but she thought she saw his jaw tighten. It had been a long journey; was her uncle finally starting to shows signs of the strain? Veronica had been so focused on her own shortcomings, she hadn't considered that her guardian might also come up against his limits.

As they'd crossed the Adriatic, Veronica had become violently seasick. She'd kept her malady to herself, not wanting to appear weak or cause needless worry. By the time they'd reached the port town of Salona, Veronica had been vomiting for nearly six hours. Still, she said nothing of her condition; she was simply grateful to be able to put her feet on dry land. A bit of sleep and she'd be good as new. But that was not to be. The men held council and decided that, the weather being so favorable for sailing, they should immediately ship south to Dyrrhachium, another three hundred fifty miles, requiring three more days at sea. Veronica gritted her teeth and marched determinedly toward the merchant ship. She could do this, she'd told herself. She'd acclimate and the pain would pass.

But within hours, she was near death, or so it seemed. She sucked hard on a piece of ginger the ship master had given her, but it only burned her throat, almost as much as the bile that kept creeping upward. Theodosius had become quite distressed and ordered the ship's master toward the shore, but he had rebuked the Senator, saying the wind, current and coastline forbade it. So they sailed on, with Veronica tempted to pitch herself over the rail and let the sea be done with her. *Was there no power on Earth that could soothe those waves?*

But that night Veronica's pain had subsided, and she was able to hold water down. In the morning, she even ate. Her strength gradually came back, until, spying Dyrrhachium, she'd had a renewed burst of vitality. She'd never in her life been so happy to see a city.

Dyrrhachium, some two and a half centuries ago, had been known by the Greek name, Epidamnus. The Romans who conquered it decided the name too closely resembled the Latin word for *damnation*, and opted for a descriptive Greek phrase for *bad spine*, after the craggy ridge that defined the town. Despite its unflattering titles, Dyrrhachium was a rich and lively port, which many Romans called *The Adriatic Bazaar*. But the goods in the marketplace didn't interest Veronica. She was only interested in firm, dry land. The group walked to a taberna close to the pier, where Veronica ate ravenously and her condition became the topic of discussion. Could they resume the trip by sea, or for her sake, must they trek across the Via Egnatia? There was peril by land or sea, so the group deferred a decision until the morning.

But, fate – or the gods – intervened. That evening, the bad spine had cracked. An earthquake rocked Dyrrhachium and a fire followed, threatening to consume much of the town. Her uncle wouldn't say for certain that he discerned an omen, but he did order the group onto the next merchant vessel south.

They'd landed at Oricum, slightly ahead of schedule, where they rented a villa and waited for the servants to rendezvous. Uneventful, but restful, days passed. Veronica kept house, and Theodosius trained the men in swordplay, archery and rhetoric. Veronica observed her two suitors grow from bitter rivals to something like brothers. Valentius actually became quite encouraging of Sabinus; one evening after a few cups of pure wine, Valentius advised the Senator that he should train the crafty boy for the law instead of wasting his time on a thick-necked mechanic.

One afternoon, Veronica made a trip to the market and found that the servants, or rather what was left of them, had arrived. Only Adrianna and Paenulus had made the crossing from Brindisi. The others had deserted, taking the lion's share of the Senator's fortune. Veronica had expected a glimpse of her uncle's table-shattering wrath; they had hoped to strengthen their numbers, but instead had weakened their group by taking on an old woman and a blind man. But if Theodosius was disappointed, he never showed it. He ordered a celebration of their reunion, made even more joyous when the couple announced they'd gotten married! Paenulus claimed it was a ruse to disguise himself as a wealthy gentleman and Adrianna as his wife. But Adrianna told Veronica not to believe him; he'd been in love with her for years.

The group soon sailed again, uneventfully, except for a skirmish with some pirates off the shore of Crete. Once again, Theodosius acted decisively: taking a longbow from Sabinus, he wrapped one of the arrows in cloth and poured onto it some perfume Veronica had bought in Dyrrhachium. He lit the arrow with a coal from the ship's stove and shot it, spiraling towards the other ship's sail. The sheet burst into flames and the ship floundered helplessly. Theodosius then handed the bow back to Sabinus and reclined on the deck. Watching him calmly fall into a deep sleep, Veronica imagined there was no danger in the world her uncle couldn't defeat.

Recalling that scene, Veronica now wondered if Uncle Theo had demonstrated grace under fire or simple exhaustion. He was now visibly tense, which was not surprising, since the travelers were exposed and vulnerable. Disguised as merchants, they'd have to pass through customs, paying a tariff on the goods they were ostensibly importing for sale. The transaction would take place under the noses of whatever guards the garrison had posted. Their Greek clothing and the men's unshaven faces might fool the average Galilean tax collector or soldier of the Auxilia, but only until one of the party spoke in flawed Greek with a very Roman accent. They'd agreed that Theodosius and Valentius would do the talking, but Veronica wondered how long Sabinus could hold his tongue.

Valentius placed a hand on her shoulder, giving a gentle squeeze with his forefinger and thumb. "Don't worry, Mistress. You know what the name Ptolemy means, don't you?"

Veronica sifted through the fragments of her Greek. "Sa—savior, I think."

"Yes, *savior*." Valentius chuckled. "Wouldn't you say that's a good omen?"

Veronica nodded, but without much conviction.

By the time the boat docked, the sun was beating down with a vengeance. Despite the linen scarf covering her crown, Veronica's head ached. She wished they could retire to a cool taberna, but Theodosius expected this port would be crawling with Roman military, and wanted to exit the city as quickly as possible. As Veronica reclaimed her bag, Theodosius spoke quietly in Greek to the ship's captain.

"We'll need a wagon and some horses."

The captain cocked his head to one side, as if trying to get water out of his ear.

"Do you know where you are?" he asked. "Jews don't ride horses. Only horses here are military. And I doubt you'll be walking into the garrison to inquire." The captain paused as Theodosius bristled. "Oh, don't worry; you saved my ship from those pirates. Now, you go to the bazaar — it's just a stone's throw from the pier — you might find a merchant with a couple of asses for sale. There's a smith and a wheelwright where you might get a cart."

"Thank you," Theodosius scratched under his chin. *Was it the new beard or their predicament that irritated him?* He muttered "donkey cart" under his breath with such disgust, Veronica had to stifle a nervous giggle. The boat brushed the pier and a couple of mates lifted the gangplank into place.

"Oh," the captain grabbed Theodosius' forearm and leaned in to speak confidentially. "I'd hire a few bodyguards. You'll find some burly characters idling at the bazaar. But don't tell 'em the Legion's after you."

Theodosius shook his head. "I don't think I want armed strangers following us around."

"Oh, you'll have 'em. The hills are filled with Zealots. They'd swim through a lake of fire to slit a Roman throat."

Theodosius hoisted his bag over his shoulder. He nudged Veronica forward and they walked briskly onto the wooden pier. A publican sat at a small desk with a moneybox open. Flanking him were two pairs of soldiers, in Roman uniforms, though obviously not Roman. Veronica wondered if these Auxilia could know as much about the fugitives as the actual Legion?

Valentius and Sabinus laid the baggage beside the desk. Theodosius presented the forged passport he'd labored for weeks to produce.

"Your business in Ptolemais?" the publican inquired.

"Trade." Theodosius placed a rolled cloth on the desk, and unrolled it to reveal several sparkling bracelets. The publican's eyes widened.

"How much merchandise...?"

"Very little," Theodosius sighed. "Our intention is to purchase gemstones with which to make additional pieces of jewelry. We also have some fine perfumes to trade." Theodosius gestured for Sabinus to open a wooden chest containing neatly wrapped alabaster jars – most of which contained only water. The guards seemed uninterested, but the publican leered. He lifted a gold link bracelet from the desk and let the sun play across the inlaid rubies.

"It may take some time to give an accurate assessment of the tariff due," he mused. "If you wish to take some time to visit the bazaar..."

"I prefer to stay with my property," Theodosius answered.

"Prudent," the publican smiled, revealing badly stained teeth. "But I regret the inconvenience. The many hours wasted."

"The cost of doing business," Theodosius shrugged.

"Yet," the publican slavered, "to conclude business swiftly is always desired, and for that some merchants are willing to incur extra costs."

Theodosius held his gaze steady, directly into the publican's eyes. The guards had once again focused their attention; it apparently amused them to watch the publican squeeze a captive merchant. They even joined the act, puffing their chests in a blatant display of intimidation. Theodosius reached into his purse, withdrew a stack of gold coins and placed six aureii on the desk. The publican sat back on his stool and crossed his arms, holding the passport between his thumb and index finger. Theodosius added three coins to the stack, winning a smile from the publican who placed the passport flat on the desk and swept the coins toward himself. Theodosius placed the passport in his tunic and rolled the jewelry up in the cloth, except for the ruby link bracelet that had found its way onto the publican's wrist.

Theodosius marched away, ordering Sabinus to close up the baggage. Veronica stepped briskly after her uncle who seemed determined not to look back. Valentius edged her out of the way in a manner even too brusque for him.

"If I may," Valentius interjected, "that wasn't a bad idea the captain had. Coastal towns draw men from all corners. Some rough, but many hard workers looking for honest labor."

"I don't have time to conduct interviews," Theodosius answered. "And I won't expose us to treachery."

Valentius seemed to struggle for words, and finally just held up his maimed hand. "I know we can count on your valor, sir, and your skill with a sword. But as hard as you've trained me, I'm not a soldier anymore. And the boy? He never will be."

If the remark stung Sabinus, he didn't show it.

"Can you find the men? Judge them reliably?" Theodosius asked.

Valentius nodded. "I can look in his eye and know a man from a cutthroat."

"Well," the Senator sighed, "you assess the men and I'll assess the... asses."

This time Veronica laughed aloud at her uncle's tone. Adrianna reacted sourly, hooked an arm around her elbow and led Veronica away, momentarily abandoning poor Paenulus, until Sabinus placed a firm hand on his former mentor and guided him towards the bazaar.

Veronica again felt the intense heat of the sun and craved some refreshment to ease her headache and settle her stomach.

"Grapes, Mistress?" a merchant asked in Greek.

Veronica shook her head slowly, no. But Adrianna intervened.

"Half a bushel," she said. "Nothing better for the body on a warm day." Adrianna continued to order foodstuffs: bread, cheese and dried fish.

Veronica turned away, shielded her eyes from the sun and looked up to the tall parapets. Again, she had the image of arrows raining down from which there'd be no escape. Adrianna nudged her, and Veronica took a couple of loaves, slipping them into a mesh sack slung from her arm. Then a log of cheese, still in the cloth. Through the crowd she spotted Valentius clasping hands with a swarthy, broad-shouldered man. He gripped the upper arms and pounded the chests of two more, before nodding, apparently in approval of their fitness. The men showed Valentius the short swords in their belts. He pursed his lips and shrugged. Then loosening the string of his purse, gave each man a bronze sestertius[63].

"I feel safer already," Sabinus chirped.

"What's that you say?" Paenulus asked. Veronica huffed, then immediately regretted it. She had become impatient with the old man asking to repeat what anyone had said, instead of asking for an explanation. It was as if he was pretending to be deaf instead of blind. But she shouldn't be short with Paenulus; it was Sabinus and his sarcasm that annoyed her.

"We've got bodyguards," Sabinus smirked. "To watch over us."

"Ah," Paenulus grunted. "And who'll watch them?"

Before Sabinus could give a clever retort, a murmur swept through the crowd, followed by the clopping of hoofs on stone. The throng parted, giving way to a large, tented wagon, drawn by two horses, chestnut and grey. Theodosius was at the reins. He halted the team and immediately issued orders.

"Toss in the baggage. Come. Adrianna, get Paenulus aboard."

Valentius flushed. He kept his voice down so as not to alert his hired men. "Sir, I thought we'd said donkeys?"

"The horses were available. Come, Veronica, hop up."

"But they are... conspicuous."

Veronica took her uncle's hand as he lifted her onto the bench beside him. She noticed he didn't look at Valentius and his rambling explanation about a bargain price and the necessity of a larger wagon fell flat. Veronica realized her uncle had no good reason for the purchase other than he was a master horseman and he wouldn't sit behind a shaggy, lop-eared beast no bigger than a calf. Not that the old grey Veronica sat behind was so fine a specimen. Still, for the first time on this journey — perhaps in his career as soldier and Senator

---

[63] A Roman coin worth two and a half times the value of a copper as

— it seemed Theodosius had made a decision based on pride rather than strategy or philosophy.

"Very well," Valentius conceded. He gestured toward the hired men. "I've contracted these men to escort..."

Theodosius acknowledged them with a few hasty nods. "I'll trust your judgment."

Valentius muttered, "And I, yours," then bid the men fall in. They stepped onto sideboards and gripped the wooden frame.

Theodosius cracked the reins, and the wagon started forward with a lurch that knocked Veronica back onto the baggage. With a sweep of his arm, Theodosius lifted her bent knees over her head, so she landed in a fetal position, starring back at Adrianna and Paenulus, bobbing against the side of the tent.

"Might as well stay back there," Theodosius called. "Until we've cleared the city."

*   *   *   *

The boy had run so hard he was completely out of breath when he fell down before the Centurion. Patiently, and rather amused, Longinus held out a shekel and waited for the lad to catch his breath. But before he could gather himself, a second boy arrived, blurting out, "The horses are sold!"

"Who bought them?" Longinus asked.

"Stranger," the second boy declared. "Speaking Greek."

Longinus waved to a liveryman to bring his horse, and tossed the coin to the second boy, who caught it grinning.

"Wait," the first objected, finding his voice. "I got here first!"

Longinus swung up into his saddle, as Juvenal trotted his stallion toward the garrison's gate and half a dozen Auxilia horsemen fell in behind. "Let that be your lesson, son. Better to be second and complete the task than be first and fail."

Longinus cantered Formido to the front of the line. After hearing from the magistrate about the fugitive Senator, Longinus had visited the two stables in town. Their stock consisted of donkeys and mules, but one had a pair of retired military horses. He'd told the stable boys to alert him if anyone bought them. This alarm was probably nothing more than a peddler with heavy wares — bolts of fabric or jars of oil — that wanted the horses' speed should bandits attack. But Longinus would investigate all the same.

The main road leaving Ptolemais was the Via Maris, the Roman name for a trade route along the sea from Egypt to Mesopotamia that had existed for centuries. The Empire had reconstructed the road, but it was still plagued by highwaymen and those pesky Zealots.

The man Longinus was seeking would have thought of that. Though the horses he he'd purchased were long in the tooth and somewhat swayed in the back, they could pull a cart more capably than jackasses, and were broken to the saddle, in case a rider needed a quick escape. They were gentle enough for even a girl to ride, if necessary. Yes, the Senator would want a horse for the girl, should the Zealots attack. Of course, this was probably his imagination running away with him. The chance that the fugitive senator would land at Ptolemais, rather than Tyre, Sidon or Jaffa, or that he'd come to Palestine at all, was very remote.

At the garrison gate, Longinus slowed Formido to a trot. He was in no great hurry. He wanted to confront the purchaser of the horse outside the city walls, on open ground away from passersby who might complicate matters. The eight riders clopped at an easy pace. The streets were mostly empty as the townspeople had retreated indoors from the afternoon heat. After the octet exited the city, Juvenal appeared at the Centurion's right flank.

"What will you do if this is the Senator?"

"Obey my orders," Longinus replied.

"Which version?" Juvenal prodded. When Longinus refused to take the bait, the Princeps probed further. "Macro's orders are to arrest the Senator and his niece and return them to Rome for questioning. But our magistrate says the girl must never return to Rome. It would seem by obeying orders, we might enable a contrary outcome."

Longinus couldn't hide his amusement. "You think we're being duped. Used as pawns by the politicians."

"I'm sure it's something you've considered. Otherwise you'd have ordered me to the back of the line as soon as I broached the subject."

Longinus fixed his gaze at the road ahead. About half a mile on, a horse-drawn wagon led a train of several foot travelers.

"I'm ordering you there now."

"And I obey, Primus." Juvenal reined his horse to the side and waited for the line to pass. Longinus led the octet off the left side of the road, in a circuitous route behind a low hill. He wanted to head off the expedition. He urged Formido on, mindful not to get too far out in front of the men with less powerful horses. As the hill sloped down, Longinus drove Formido over the knoll and onto the hard flagstones, stopping sharply, Formido's breath hot on the snouts of the old carthorses. The Auxilia quickly formed a line across the road.

The carthorses lurched back and hoofed the pavement nervously; the driver held them steady. Longinus glared first at the driver, then quickly scanned the party. The driver looked capable, though past his prime. A soldierly type gripped the hilt of his sword, but with a maimed hand. A thin youth who hadn't filled out yet came forward to hold the bridle of a horse and stroke its nose. What's he up to? Would he foolishly try to unhitch that horse and ride away? Three other men idled about the wagon. Mercenary types. Had they been paid enough to challenge Rome?

Juvenal walked his horse down the right side of the wagon. Another rider took the left.

"Identify yourself," Longinus commanded.

The driver answered in well-spoken Greek, "My name is Herodotus. I am a merchant of Oricum. This party is my family and hired men."

"And?" Longinus prompted.

The driver opened his palms in confusion. "I have my passport. I can show you."

Suddenly the mercenary types raised their arms. "Stay your hand, Centurion," one cried. "We want no quarrel with Rome."

"We were hired to guard against Zealots, not the Auxilia," moaned a second. "We didn't sign on for crucifixion. We beg you, let us go now in peace."

Longinus snorted and waved a hand. In an instant the three mercenaries ran back toward Ptolemais. Now, with a clear advantage in arms and men, Longinus turned his attention back to the driver.

"It is beneath the dignity of a Senator to lie," he challenged. Then with a touch of wry humor, he added, "Though it is to your credit that you do it so poorly."

"Let me show you my passport," the driver calmly offered. *Too calmly,* Longinus thought. *This isn't a merchant. This man has seen combat.* But if he was the Senator, where was the girl? Hidden in the wagon, no doubt. *What would draw her out?*

"I shall give you a choice, Senator Proculus," the Centurion declared. The driver registered no reaction to the name. Yet, Longinus' heart raced; this had to be the man. "Find your sword. I'd wager it's within reach." Longinus tapped his own sword on the planks beside the driver "Most likely under that bench." Longinus swung down from Formido. So heady was his feeling of conquest he could no longer contain himself in the saddle. He gave Formido's reins to one of his horseman and positioned himself a few strides to the driver's right.

"Draw your sword and you may do one of three things. One, hand it to me. In which case I shall accept your surrender and show all due courtesy until I turn you over to the Legion for transport to Rome." Longinus was pacing unconsciously. He found himself eye to eye with the youth soothing the horse. *This one is crafty. He bears watching.* Longinus snapped back toward the driver. "Two, you may fall on your sword. Play Brutus to my Mark Antony. I shall proclaim you a noble Roman and dispose of your body with all due ceremony."

Longinus checked the driver's eyes. The total absence of fear caused Longinus to hesitate for a second. But having started the gambit, he must see it through.

"Three," he barked. "You may draw your sword, climb down from that wagon and challenge me for the right of passage."

A sudden clop of hooves distracted Longinus; Juvenal, a quizzical look on his face, sidled toward the front of the wagon. Longinus stared him down.

"Princeps," he declared, "here are my orders. If this merchant chooses option three, his valor shall not count against him. Should he succeed in dealing me a mortal blow, he shall have won passage for whither he shall go."

Longinus detected importunity in Juvenal that struck his pride. Did his Princeps — his friend and comrade — believe this council elder could match him with a sword?

"Aye, Primus," Juvenal answered.

Longinus smiled and turned back to the driver. "What say you, *merchant*? Do you want once more to offer your passport, or shall you take up the sword?"

The driver stroked his close beard. *Newly grown as a ruse*, Longinus thought. The man reached beneath the bench and withdrew a sword. Not a foot soldier's cudgel; the Centurion's eyes widened slightly, noting the craftsmanship. *This is a nobleman's weapon, but can he wield it?*

The driver stepped gingerly from the wagon. With of flick of his empty hand, he signaled the youth to clear out. The boy bumped the flank of an Auxilia's horse and was swatted towards the rear of the wagon. The driver held the sword at a low angle, like a blind man tapping his way along a street, as if the weapon were too heavy for him. *An obvious ruse.* Longinus chided the driver by lowering his own sword and tapping the driver's at the tip. *This is no novice swordsman: he is too relaxed*. But he wanted Longinus to judge him lightly. He was counting on overconfidence, a moment of hubris that would open the Centurion to a mortal strike. Longinus would not be so foolish; he assessed the posture of the driver, his balance. This man isn't flaccid; he's coiled to strike. *But just how skilled is he?*

The driver's robes exposed little of his physique, but the muscles of his forearm were taut, defined. Had Longinus dismissed a grey beard too readily as a mark of dissipation? The driver scraped the tip of his blade across the flagstones. *All too casual*, Longinus thought. *He's seen something in me. Without a blow being struck, this man has detected a weakness. In my stance? In my grip? In my focus, my bearing?* He's seen something that tells him he can defeat me.

"What say you, merchant," Longinus blurted. "Shall you lay down your sword?"

"I think not," the man shrugged.

"Fall on it, then?"

That only elicited a smile. And Longinus hated the sound of his own voice. What should have been supreme confidence sounded like he was begging out of the fight. *Curse this Senator. And where was the girl?* He should have his men ransack the wagon. Drag her out to watch. That would shake this Senator. To see that immediate consequence, her life in the balance. But he couldn't do that now. He'd laid out the terms already.

"Of course," the Senator chuckled, "this would hardly be a fair fight. You're wearing a breastplate."

Longinus tensed. "The privilege of rank," he spat back.

"Certainly," the grey beard assented. "If you think you'll need it..."

Longinus fumed. Then thought, *this is a ploy. He's goading me. He's found my weakness: passion.* Juvenal evidently agreed; he had crept ever closer. His eyes now seemed to implore*: remember your orders. Capture the man.* Longinus ignored him. He'd set his course. He'd offered terms. Terms rejected, it was time for combat. He only needed an opening and his superior strength and agility would rule the day. *But could anything shake this Senator?*

"Let's get on with this," Longinus snapped. The affair had become tedious. This Senator, or whoever he was, was entirely too coy. There was mockery in his attitude, the haughty sneer of the privileged patrician. Longinus suddenly had hatred in his blood for this man, such that only blood would satisfy. He smacked the tip of the Senator's sword with his own, demanding the man take a defensive stance: *Show some respect for the man who's about to kill you!*

A yelp went up somewhere. Over the patrician's shoulder. He turned instinctively to the wagon. That gave Longinus the opening craved. He raised his sword and swung down with fury.

Chapter 13

Veronica was tired of sitting on the lumpy baggage. It was impossible to get comfortable, especially since she had to crane her neck to see out the flap of the tented wagon. She knew they were well outside the city walls, but Uncle Theo was being so cautious. Finally, she wriggled forward and planted her elbows on the bench beside him.

"Can I come out yet?" she cooed.

Theodosius exhaled loudly, then patted the bench beside him. "There you go. Hop up."

But as Veronica drew her legs underneath her to scramble forward, Uncle Theo suddenly planted a palm on her head and pushed her backwards.

"Sorry, spoke too soon."

That's when the riders came over the hill. Veronica crouched as low as she could. She saw very little through the slit between the tent flaps, but heard the lead soldier taunting her uncle. When Uncle Theo drew his sword from under the bench, Veronica was terrified. He'd been right at every turn, and conquered every threat they'd faced — highwaymen, Legionnaires and pirates — but this soldier had a different bearing. His strength and stature — and his dark countenance with black hair and leathern skin — filled Veronica with dread. Yet, she couldn't look away from him. She became deeply frustrated when he stepped out of view. Her nerves jangled as she heard the tips of the swords scrape the flagstones. She could no longer crouch and wait for the first blow.

Veronica thrust the tent flap aside and — seeing her uncle square off against this adversary — yelped involuntarily. Uncle Theo spun back toward her, showing alarm for her safety and not his own. Then she saw the flash of reflected light as the soldier's sword caught the sun on high and came crashing down.

The clang was painfully loud, and Veronica flinched. The next image she saw was two swords, hilt to hilt, Uncle Theo on his tail, his free hand bracing his fall. The soldier did not withdraw, but met Veronica's gaze and suddenly went slack. Theo grimaced, rolled under the haunches of the nervous grey. The wagon shook as horses tossed their heads and sidestepped the scrambling Senator. Theo passed his sword from his right hand to his left. He opened and attempted to close his dominant hand, grimacing from the pain. No good; he couldn't grip his weapon. He'd have to fight left-handed. Against this brute, that could only mean death. But the brute didn't move. To Veronica, he seemed more interested in the wagon. Uncle Theo crept from behind the horse, raised the sword in his left hand and prepared to thrust.

"Show me your passports," the soldier demanded.

Uncle Theo was baffled. *Passports?* The soldier was calling a halt to the battle just when he had the upper hand. But he recovered enough of his confidence to wink at Veronica as he reached for the leather-bound documents. He turned and handed them over. "I'm sure you'll find everything's in perfect order."

The soldier sheathed his sword and accepted the booklets. He scanned them quickly and slapped them shut. "So, you are Herodotus. A merchant."

Theo nodded his head.

"Show me your wares."

Veronica handed her uncle the rolled cloth of bracelets, which Theo untied and spread open on the bench. The soldier regarded the jewelry briefly, looked again into the wagon, acknowledging Veronica with a curt nod.

"Those men you hired were no good," the soldier said.

Uncle Theo offered a mild rebuttal. "You can't blame simple men for not wanting to be crucified." That was the second time Veronica had heard that odd word. She had no idea what it meant to be *crossed*, but by the tone of the men, she could tell it was something awful.

"They gave up before there was even a fight," the soldier scoffed. "No, what you need are professional soldiers." Veronica recoiled as he glanced at her. He smiled warmly as he continued, "You're carrying things of value."

"Indeed," Theo muttered, agreeing, but not agreeably.

"What you should do, er, what I would recommend, is that you continue along this route, taking the left fork northeast towards Tiberius. It's the city of Herod Antipas. He's a… worldly man. He appreciates finery. He's also prodigal with his resources. If he could see your handiwork, he might loan you soldiers to escort you to your final destination. Which is?"

Veronica studied her uncle's measured reaction. He seemed to suck in his cheeks and bite down on them, before replying, "Oh, undetermined. We'll stop when we've traded all we've brought and find the precious stones we need for more jewelry. So. Herod. Tiberius? How far…?"

"Thirty miles," the soldier pointed east, "although you'll have to leave the Via Maris and travel local roads and cross-country. It is rather due east from the first fork."

"Cross-country?" Theo remarked. "We're told the hills are rife with Zealots."

The soldier flicked his fingers as if dismissing a gnat. "The Zealots," he said, "are highly political. They attack occupying forces. Anything with the stamp of Rome. Since you are not Roman," his dark eyes shone like opals, "there is no danger."

Veronica sensed an element of theatre in that last remark.

Theodosius played the scene, too, nodding. "That's some comfort. Since our hired men have deserted us."

"Cowards," the soldier scoffed. He reclaimed the reins of his horse and swung into the saddle. "But Galilee's villains are no different. Show resolve and they scatter." The soldier raised his right arm high and his men came to attention. He cantered back toward the city, his men falling in line behind him.

For but a second, Theodosius watched the departing horsemen wistfully, then replaced his sword in the scabbard under the bench. "Valentius," he called. "Come take these reins."

"Sir?"

"I could do with a stretch," the Senator declared to no one in particular. He squared his shoulders and began a brisk march in strict military tempo.

Valentius climbed onto the wagon beside Veronica. He brushed the reins across the horses' rumps and they started at a slow walk. The wagon rolled for some time without anyone in the party speaking. Valentius seemed to hold the horses back, allowing Theodosius to increase his distance from them.

"This is all very odd," Veronica muttered.

Valentius raised a reproachful eyebrow, but Veronica would not be cowed into silence.

"We've been given free passage. Uncle should be happy, or at least relieved."

"The Senator's a proud man," Valentius said softly.

Veronica was scandalized. She jumped to her uncle's defense. "Why should his pride be hurt? That soldier caught him off guard. Uncle Theo would have recovered; he'd have beaten him, too."

"Aye, Mistress. Perhaps. But he didn't have to."

"Thank the gods."

Valentius huffed. "It may be a sacrilege, but I doubt the gods had anything to do with it."

Veronica looked closely at Valentius, trying to read something in his facial expression. His jaw was scooped forward and locked. She knew he was hiding something. "You're saying Uncle Theo wanted to fight, but you know he only fights when necessary."

"Aye, Mistress."

Veronica was getting nowhere. "Then what is bothering him?"

Valentius shrugged, as though he were about to state something self-evident. "He cares about nothing more than protecting you, yet it was you who saved him."

"What?" Veronica was stunned. *Was this some kind of a joke?*

"He's not angry at you. Not really. Oh, he might make it about that. That he had ordered you not to poke your head out, and you did."

"Well... I'm sorry, but... I couldn't stand not seeing what was happening."

"Understandable."

"And, it caused us no harm, in the end."

"Not at all. In fact, it saved us."

Veronica's mouth dropped wide. "Now you're making fun of me." She slouched into a deep pout.

"No, Mistress. By all the gods." Valentius was flustered. His cheeks puffed and nostrils flared as he searched for words.

"She doesn't understand you, sir," Adrianna interjected. She had crept from the rear of the wagon and had probably heard everything. "She's a true innocent."

Valentius cocked his head slightly to peek at Veronica's downcast eyes. She glowered at him.

"Mistress, you see no connection between your pretty face appearing and that Centurion lowering his sword?" he asked. His smile widened, and he broke into a hearty laugh.

Veronica turned away, only to see Sabinus walking backwards beside the grey. "You disarmed him, dear Veronica," he called. Then he laced his fingers together, forming a cradle for his chin. He smiled prettily and batted his eyelashes. Valentius roared.

"Oh! Fine," Veronica cried. "Keep walking that way, Sabinus, you give me a third horse's behind to look at." She shot back at Valentius, "You're unbelievable. You think he let us go, because – what? – he thought I was pretty? He's a soldier! A commander!"

Now Paenulus chimed in. He, too, was at the front of the wagon. "Stranger events have transpired," he crowed. "Soldiers have started wars over pretty girls."

Valentius chortled heartily. "That's who you are! Helen of Troy in reverse. Her face launched a thousand ships; yours could make them drop anchor!"

More riotous laughter erupted, and Veronica buried her face between her knees. *Oh, the mockery!* She wouldn't look at them! Then the cart stopped so abruptly that she pitched forward nearly onto the grey. She steadied herself with flat hands on its haunches. Valentius grasped her shoulder and eased Veronica back to retake her seat on the bench. And there was Theodosius, imperiously blocking the road and glaring at them.

"Why did I buy horses," he thundered, "when I've got so many braying jackasses?"

*   *   *   *

All the way back to Ptolemais, Longinus revisited in his unsettled mind the encounter and his decision. Outwardly, holding his shoulders and head erect, he was the image of imperial might, but inside he was crestfallen. An ominous void had opened within him and he seemed to teeter on a dark abyss of confusion, despair, even madness. The girl. That girl had wounded him more deeply than any barbarian weapon could. Alternately, he thought he might weep or laugh like a lunatic. The irony! In all these years abroad, he'd imagined losing his heart to an exotic beauty, some Thusnelda, Pouruchista[64], Roxana[65] or Cleopatra. Yet, it was a Roman girl – and she was unmistakably Roman – who had pierced him with a dagger of desire. Only days ago he'd mused about finding a simple country maid, a homely tender of his hearth. That would never do now; having tasted wine, he would not return to water.

But having found her, he'd let her slip through his fingers. And worse, he may have exposed himself to charges: dereliction of duty. Even treason. The Roman military dealt with such matters swiftly and brutally. The tribune would hastily convene a hearing. Though an officer of Longinus' rank would require a court martial, it would be held in private in the form of an inquisition. He'd have no opportunity to see or confront witnesses against him. Nor would he necessarily be informed of a verdict. Afterwards, the matter might simply be

---

[64] In Persian legend, the virtuous daughter of Zarathustra
[65] A princess of Bactria who married Alexander the Great

forgotten, or on some random day, when the troops were assembled for inspection, he'd feel a tap on the shoulder and turn to see the tribune holding a ceremonial cudgel. That was the signal to commence the dreaded *fustuarium*. The remaining troops would fall on him, beating him mercilessly with clubs until he was dead.

That was not how Longinus wanted his military career to end. Yet, that's what he'd risked in letting this alleged merchant and his alleged daughter go. But what other choice had he? Contrary to the attitude he'd projected to Juvenal, Longinus had been carefully weighing the consequences of following the magistrate's politically motivated instructions. If he turned the Senator and the girl over, Rome's magistrate would follow his tacit instructions. The Senator would shortly "commit suicide" in his cell. The girl would be passed from barracks to barracks until she found the means – poison or a sharp object – to end her suffering. Though he'd reasoned this out, Longinus had still been confirmed in his duty. His last attempt to maneuver around the politicians for justice's sake had failed spectacularly, landed him in Ptolemais and caused a rift with Juvenal. So, he'd convinced himself it was better to pursue Rome's accolades by apprehending Rome's enemies.

But then he'd seen her face. Instantly, he knew why this Senator would raise his sword when he was clearly overmatched. He was protecting this beauty. Longinus had felt a wave of shame wash over him; he was on the wrong side of the fight. The pride he'd felt in taming barbarians to expand civilization came crashing down. In that moment, on that road, Longinus was not an Officer of Rome, he was an assassin. An Iscariot. He was aiding and abetting jackals ready to feast on the Empire's carcass. That he would not do. But could he protect himself against the consequences of his refusal?

The first step would be to reinforce the loyalty of his men, so they would commit to his version of events. So, as they approached Ptolemais, Longinus stopped the line and turned, walking Formido up the road to address them. "Men, I want to commend you for your professionalism on that stop. You performed admirably. It is unfortunate your efforts were spent on a humble merchant rather than an adversary. Let us then extend this patrol down the southerly route of the Via Maris to see what we may encounter. If you continue to display good soldiery, there'll be an extra ration of wine this evening."

So the remaining hours of daylight were spent harassing donkey carts and stripping down heavily laden camels. Longinus was hoping to find as many merchants traveling with teenage girls as possible. There were merchants aplenty, but the women in their company hardly fit the description of a comely maiden. Some, haggard and toothless, were barely discernible as female. Thus, the octet returned to Ptolemais without beholding an image of feminine beauty that might diminish their memory of the first. If anything, the first impression was only reinforced. Because even though half the men, those posted at the side and rear of the wagon, never even saw the girl, by the end of patrol they were speaking as though they'd dined together at leisure.

Well, Longinus knew there were two ways men forgot women, and if immersing oneself in work failed, the alternative was to drink. Back at the commissary, Longinus ordered extra rations of wine for the men of the patrol. He praised their discipline. "It's easy to let your guard down when out on routine patrols. But that's the moment a band of Zealots will attack. Vigilance, more than might itself, is what keeps the peace, and allows us to return to these barracks to celebrate as brothers!"

Longinus lifted a cup to the cheers of his men. The cup was his own, a silver trophy he'd won for heroism in the field. He did not often drink from it, but he toasted with it this evening to further impress his men. Time would tell if he'd succeeded, and whether the men would back his version of the facts should the magistrate inquire.

There was only one last detail to address: his Princeps. The officers left the men to their revelry and exited into the open air under a multitude of stars. Longinus loosed the straps on his lorica so it dangled freely. The night air seeped into his sweat-soaked tunic, cooling him so quickly he almost shuddered. Juvenal seemed to read some symbolism into this gesture that Longinus hadn't intended, as though by opening his breastplate the Centurion was set to reveal his heart. Longinus chose not to correct this impression when he saw Juvenal's visage soften, to the point where he could read sympathy in every faint crease.

"If you're worried about the tap on the shoulder," Juvenal assured him, "it won't come from me." With good humor he averred, "I can safely swear – on my life in the Basilica Julia – we met no enemies of Rome on the road today."

Longinus nodded in appreciation. "So, you're saying I did the right thing?"

Juvenal smirked playfully, "Primus, I believe you can always be counted on to do the right thing. After you've exhausted every other option!"

*　　　　*　　　　*　　　　*

As the sun descended on the western hills, the party pulled onto a narrow road, which turned out to be mere wagon ruts cut out of the grass, exposing clay and stones. Though hilly, this country was green and fertile; they had passed herds of grazing sheep and fields of grain. It would have been a pleasant journey except for their mood. Theodosius had apologized for his outburst, but that had done little to relieve the tension.

When they arrived at a spot suitable for camp, the Senator issued orders in a rapid, clipped tone. It was uncharacteristic and ungracious, Veronica thought. Especially since the Senator did not deign to assist in any of the work, but stood apart and aloof. Veronica did not trust Valentius' explanation: her uncle's pride may have been stung momentarily, but that wouldn't have put this stoic priest into a foul humor for so long. He was not thinking back, he was worried for what lay ahead.

The women built a fire and prepared to serve some of the dried fish, cheese and bread Adrianna had bought at the bazaar. *Was it only that morning?* To Veronica it seemed ages ago. She was already tired of this food which she'd been nibbling since midday and that seemed to be the group's consensus. So, spirits rose when Sabinus came bounding into camp with a plump rabbit he'd shot with his bow. Adrianna dressed the rabbit and placed it on a spit, which Veronica turned dutifully. The liver, kidneys and heart she placed in a pot with wine and vegetables, and boiled it to a thick stew. The aroma was intoxicating! The group hadn't had a hot meal since leaving Oricum, so even though one rabbit couldn't go very far, everyone who got a small taste had something to celebrate. Except, of course, for Theodosius, who refused any food.

As the women performed their post-meal duties, Theodosius convened the men: each would keep watch for three hours before waking his relief. Theodosius insisted on the first watch, and instructed that the last watchman waken him before dawn, when he judged they'd be most vulnerable to attack. Sabinus asked permission to hunt for more rabbits, but Theodosius wanted the watchman to have the bow. Taking it from Sabinus, he muttered under his breath, "That's a weapon I can wield."

With a pass of his hand, Theodosius dismissed the men. Veronica thought perhaps she owed Valentius an apology. Clearly, her uncle was still in a dour mood because of his encounter with that Centurion. Veronica wondered why he gave the man another thought. He was back in Ptolemais. But, in truth, the Centurion had repeatedly crept into Veronica's mind throughout the day. She worried if she might be feeling what Claudia had felt when she'd first glimpsed Pontius. Like Claudia, Veronica marveled at the man's dark countenance, his frame and form that suggested epic poetry. But more impressive were those eyes: portals to another reality. Through them Veronica imagined she could see every hope, pain, victory and defeat this man had recorded. She read in him the confidence of someone who knew he could have anything in this world, except perhaps what his heart truly desired. It was at that point his confidence waned and he measured himself inadequate, or incomplete. Oh, this was her imagination running wild.

Distressed by these thoughts, Veronica lay her head down. She would share the wagon that night with Adrianna; the men – even Paenulus – would sleep under the stars. Would their vigilance keep out intruders? Dreamily, Veronica imagined the Centurion sneaking into camp. He'd wait until Theodosius had left the watch and Sabinus went off chasing a rabbit. Then he'd creep towards the wagon. He'd sense that Veronica was inside. He'd reach between the flaps of the tent and gently touch her shoulder.

"Aaugh!" Veronica bolted upright. She batted away the hand that had nudged her. She grabbed the wrist and scrambled to her knees. The invader lifted the tent flap: Sabinus.

"What are you doing here?" Veronica scolded. Adrianna stirred beside her. The boy stammered.

"I-I-I... I thought you should know."

"What?"

"Your uncle isn't mad at you."

"I know that," she grumbled.

"Then you know why he's despondent?"

Now Veronica was interested. She checked on Adrianna then scooted forward. "What do you know?"

"I heard him talking to Valentius," the boy whispered. "Since the fight with the Centurion, he hasn't been able to grip a sword. He thinks the blow broke his wrist."

Veronica stiffened. She muttered her thanks and closed the tent flap. She settled into a tight ball on the floor of the wagon. Her uncle was injured. Disabled. *A broken wrist would take, what, six weeks to heal?* During that time, their most able defender would be physically useless. They'd have to rely on their wits.

Chapter 14

Longinus was up early, busying himself about the garrison. He wanted the men to see him, actively engaged in the business of the moment. A few of the troops seemed a bit groggy, having indulged too much in last evening's festivities. Their Primus graced them with some inspirational words before they turned out for inspection, giving them a wink of forbearance even as he urged them to optimum performance. When the troops lined up, albeit a quarter hour tardy, they looked every bit exemplars of Roman might. Longinus again swelled with imperial pride as he reviewed the files and columns of his Auxilia. Helmets, breastplates, gauntlets and greaves glowed molten in the morning sun. His men, though only three times eighty, were a radiant force, otherworldly in the barren dust of this frontier. True, his men weren't Romans – they were recruits from these provinces – but still they strode like gods where no god had ever stepped foot.

Longinus watched his men parade in tight formation around the courtyard and dreamed of a glorious campaign. He'd seen much combat early in his enlistment, but those memories receded further with each passing day. He'd been yearning for battle yesterday, hadn't he? There could be no other explanation for his aggression with that... merchant. The charge had gotten his blood up. Feeling black Formido surging under him as he dared his comrades to keep pace, climbing over and down the hill, like a winged raptor dropping talons extended on his prey. He'd complimented his men on their discipline, but in reality, he, their Primus, had been rash. Had his example contradicted his instructions? Had his actions undermined the respect he needed now?

Longinus knew he must reflect scrupulously on the events of yesterday, but now was not the time. Now, he must stand firm before his troops, presenting a model to emulate. Someone she might also... *she?* As his thoughts returned to the girl, his throat tightened. He hadn't been rash on the charge or too hot to attack. He'd gone soft too quickly when he'd seen that face. His flaw was meekness before beauty; the girl would be his undoing.

His men halted abruptly with a uniform stomp. The only motion in the yard was the gentle wafting of dust at their feet. Nearly five hundred eyes fixed straight ahead. They'd played at soldiering; their blood was up. In his rational mind, Longinus knew these were hired men, and having gone through the paces, they wished to be dismissed, back to the restful boredom of the garrison routine. But in his fantasy of grandeur, these were his dogs of war, straining at the leash, salivating for havoc. Would there come a day he could give that terrible order? Could he banish meekness and loose the fury? Take what Rome demanded? Take *her?*

The girl again. He'd had her in his grasp and released her. He'd failed, and each of these five hundred eyes was looking at that failure, writ large across his visage. *Dismiss them now,* he thought. *Their blood is up and they can sense weakness. Dismiss them now and retire to reflect.*

"Troops!" Longinus cried. Then he froze.

He'd been tapped abruptly, three times on the shoulder.

Instinctively his eyes darted to Juvenal. The Princeps, standing expressionless beside his horse, passed the reins to a stable hand. His arms hung at his sides; the cudgel stayed in his belt.

The troops looked past Longinus. Were they awaiting a signal? The fustuarium. Longinus slowly turned toward the figure behind him, to a pair of hands wringing a heavy cudgel held close to a red toga.

"Dismiss your men, Primus," the magistrate almost warbled.

Momentarily struck by this sweet affectation, Longinus gathered himself and turned back to the assembly. He shouted, "Dismissed!" and stood firm as the Magistrate circled him, still caressing the cudgel and slapping it against an open palm. The toga-clad vulture waved Juvenal over.

"I understand you had a busy afternoon yesterday."

"Routine patrols," Longinus answered.

"Do you agree with that assessment, Princeps?"

"I wonder what cause you have to doubt it," Juvenal chuckled.

The Magistrate dropped the pretense and continued grimly, "You might consider, Primus, that when you give your troops wine, you loosen their lips. They speak without duplicity. Because in wine there is truth."

It struck Longinus that he likely had a spy in his ranks. He spoke in measured cadence, matching the Magistrate's intonation. "And what has this truth-talker said?"

"You rode with great urgency to overtake a horse-drawn wagon. The driver was of noble bearing, confident enough in his ability with a sword to accept a challenge from a Roman officer."

A slight smile curled the corners of Longinus' mouth. "His confidence was misplaced."

"The driver had a girl," the Magistrate spat. Recovering his composure, he spoke with a leer in his voice. "I hear she was quite lovely."

"And quite Greek," Longinus attested. "Their passports were in order. Greek merchants, selling baubles. To detain them further would have been a grave injustice."

"That's what you believe?"

"I do," Longinus swore confidently. Juvenal did not speak, but his eyes shone with perfect agreement.

"Suppose I decide to believe something different," the Magistrate frothed. "If I choose to believe you had the fugitives in your clutches and either through incompetence or treachery let them escape. And to test that belief, I convened a tribunal. And having that belief confirmed, I assembled your men to mete out proper punishment, to beat you both to bloody mucous on this very dust! What then, Primus?"

Longinus let the Magistrate stew in his own drool for a second. Then after the petty tyrant wiped the spittle from his lips, the Centurion coolly responded, "That also would be a grave injustice."

"Why argue belief?" Juvenal interjected, quickly adding, "If your honor is so convinced we erred, why not just have us produce the Greeks for your inspection?"

"You know where they are?"

"We know where they were going," Juvenal said, "To Tiberius."

The Magistrate looked stunned. "Impossible."

Longinus strained to keep his eyes from rolling upward. "Not the emperor. The city."

"We could ride there immediately," Juvenal offered. "You could accompany us. On horse. Or by chariot."

"Herod?" the Magistrate muttered. "No, that won't do. I couldn't, under these circumstances. But you go. You two. Take a century of men." He

narrowed his eyes to dark slits, ordering, "Bring back that... Greek merchant.
And the girl."

*   *   *   *

Veronica was stiff from her tailbone to the base of her skull. The wooden
bench was too hard, and the wagon jostled too much, especially on the uneven
stones of this poorly laid road. The city of Tiberius had an unreality to it; like
one of Claudia's dreams it was crammed with dramatic but strangely
incomplete images. Ambitious buildings, if judged by their foundations, simply
stopped above eye level, while their scaffolding sketched the architect's
intentions against the empty sky. It seemed to Veronica those intentions would
never be realized, for nowhere on any of the scaffolding was a worker to be
seen. There were stones in abundance, but no mortar, and no laborers to
assemble them.

Veronica dipped her fingers into the bowl on her lap. Adrianna had
prepared some dates, cheese slices and slivers of rabbit meat for the travelers
to pick at. The rabbit had come courtesy of Sabinus' pre-dawn hunt. Early that
morning, Veronica had been stirring the embers of last evening's fire when the
youth approached and laid the slain animal beside her.

"I can clean it, too, if you like," he offered.

Veronica shook her head. "You've done the man's part," she said.

At that Sabinus stood as straight as she'd ever seen him. "I can. I mean, I
will if necessary. I mean, Mistress Veronica, you shouldn't worry. The Senator
isn't the only man prepared to lay down his life for you."

Veronica picked up the rabbit by the hind legs and reached for Adrianna's
butcher knife.

"May the gods forbid."

With that, Sabinus bowed slightly and left the fire. Veronica's hands
trembled as she coursed the blade around the foreleg, then slit the fur from the
ankle to the thigh. The next thing she felt was Adrianna's hand touching her
wrist. She took the carcass and knife from her, and Veronica had crumpled and
wept.

Now, Veronica stuffed her face. She needed a distraction from such
thoughts, and she found the sweet dates, pungent cheese and chewy rabbit
flesh oddly soothing. She offered the bowl to her uncle, who shrugged her off.
Then, thinking better of it, reached his right hand into the bowl, extracting a
small morsel. Veronica looked at her uncle's hand and wrist. She couldn't see
anything unusual. No bruising or swelling. But it was clear from his sullen
mood that he was in pain. He held the reins in his left hand, as he'd done the
entire day. Veronica wished for something to rouse him from his silence.

"Uncle Theo," she said, "Twice yesterday I heard a word that puzzled me.
Crucified. What does it mean... to *cross* someone?"

"Be grateful you haven't seen it. It's outlawed in Rome. And not allowed anywhere for Roman citizens."

"So," as she had surmised, "it's a punishment."

"Yes," the Senator answered. "It's a slow and painful means of execution."

"Then," she pried further. "You've seen it? In your campaigns? Did you... do it?"

Theodosius stared down the road as if there lay the details of a long ago event. "There are things rough men do," he said softly, "so that gentle women may sleep soundly. You should never inquire as to what they are."

They continued down the road, the falling sun stretching shadows to obscure the path ahead. The only sounds were the grinding wheels and the clop of the horses' hooves.

The Palace of Herod Antipas was an immense, but disappointing, structure. The façade was mismatched in three distinct layers, as if construction had stopped twice, and restarted with cover stones from a different quarry. Problems went beyond discord in the surface hues: ornate colonnades were abandoned halfway across the second-level parapet; upper-level parapets lacked balustrades altogether and uncapped towers reached for the sky like arms lopped off at the wrist.

Valentius summed it up bluntly. "If this edifice were widely known, it would be widely mocked."

"The proprietor seems to have no shame about it," Sabinus observed. True enough, there were several grand chariots and coaches lined up outside the entrance. Theodosius stopped the wagon and handed the reins to Valentius.

"What are your thoughts, sir?"

Theodosius was already rummaging through a pouch of his personal belongings. He placed a gold signet ring on his finger, the symbol of his family and his rank. He handed Veronica two of the jeweled bracelets. "A senator of Rome and his daughter will be attending the Tetrarch's party."

Theodosius had Adrianna pull their Roman dress from the deep recesses of the luggage. He and Sabinus, then Veronica, quickly changed costumes inside the wagon. The old soldier then demonstrated he hadn't forgotten how to breach a compound. Flashing his signet, he identified himself as Senator Commodius on a mission from the Emperor to the Prefect in Judea. He explained to the Captain of the Guard that, having landed at Tiberius, he'd heard of the Tetrarch's feast and thought it would be a horrible breach of protocol if he did not convey Rome's fondest regards. He had therefore deviated from his course in great haste so as not to offend the Tetrarch by his absence. Within seconds, a pair of obsequious servants whisked the Senator's entourage inside.

They entered the main vault of the palace to find a household completely mobilized. Servants dashed about, positioning potted plants, cushions, tables, lamp stands, musical instruments – everything needed for a great feast – but all apparently in the wrong places, according to the hostess organizing the melee. It reminded Veronica of their hasty evacuation from Rome, that is, if they'd been driven out by a shrieking hysteric. The high, arched ceilings reverberated, not with urgency of Uncle Theo's profound baritone, but the shrill desperation of a cat with its tail on fire. Veronica flinched so greatly her shoulders nearly rose to plug her ears.

"Don't place the musicians so close to the throne! The Tetrarch is not deaf!"

Sabinus whispered over Veronica's raised shoulder, "Though he may wish he were"

Veronica laughed nervously, a slight giggle amidst an awful din, yet it brought a hush over the vault. Servants turned to stone in mid-stride, as the hostess twisted to stare daggers at an insolent slave. Veronica gazed into the attack mask of what had probably once been a beautiful woman. But into her appealing features had been etched deep creases, the source of which, judging by their placement, could only have been chronic rage. The servant who'd escorted them scrupulously avoided eye contact; he bowed as he offered introductions.

"My lady, Senator Commodius of Rome, and his daughter, Antonia."

The hostess rearranged her features — with such effort Veronica thought for a moment she heard wood creaking — into a broad, though ghastly, smile. She sang effusively in rustic Greek, "Ave, Senator. Ave, Princess."

"Ave...?" the Senator responded, begging the hostess to introduce herself.

"I am Herodias, the Tetrarch's wife," she said with an odd hint of defensiveness. "Forgive our clamor, we're in the midst of preparations. So kind of you to grace us on the Tetrarch's birthday. My husband should be here to greet you. I apologize, he is... occupied. Salome!"

At the sound of her name, a teenage girl, lounging lazily on some oversized cushions, rolled over to face Herodias and sneered, "What now, Mother?"

"We have guests."

"Yes, that's the point of a party, isn't it?"

Spotting Veronica, Salome uncoiled to her feet. Veronica was taken aback by this girl, probably a year or two younger than she, dressed like a courtesan at the slave market. The fabric covering her extremities was so sheer, one could easily see through to her limbs. She wore no tunic, just something of a sash across her chest, which, though opaque, revealed a distinct coin outline at the tip each breast. Another sash, tied at her waist, sliced from the point of her right hip to the left knee, leaving her right leg completely exposed, but for the ultra-sheer legging. She crossed toward Veronica with a lithe strut Veronica had only witnessed in cats with their tails raised. As Salome stepped in front of her, Veronica saw how heavily painted the girl's face was. She also noted, from the corner of her eye, that Sabinus was under some spell of euphoria.

Salome sighed, utterly bored. "So, what do we do? Give her a bath?"

As it turned out, the baths were the premier attraction of the palace. Deep in the foundation, natural hot springs ran, filling the pools that Herod had constructed. There were two separate chambers, one for men and the other for the women. Bidding good-bye to Uncle Theo and Sabinus at the archway of the men's baths, Veronica followed Salome down a steamy corridor to the women's entrance. The chamber was lit with oil lamps whose radiance played off the surface of the pools and danced across the ornate tile walls. A large mosaic depicted nymphs bathing in a pool at the bottom of a waterfall. From that pool sprang on odd, long fish with a deep, black eye. But what seemed like dark stone was actually a hole.

"Oh, that," Salome yawned. "That's for my degenerate uncle, so he can watch me bathe."

Veronica's mouth dropped open. This girl was awfully casual in revealing such a scandal.

"Not just me," she whispered, "but all of them." Salome gestured towards the women, fully disrobed, getting into or out of the bath, or relaxing comfortably in the roiling water. There was such a variety of women, Veronica imagined they must have come from all over the world. There were dark-haired women whose skin was the color of cinnamon or honey. There were even pitch-black Abyssinians, with small faces and high, wide foreheads, whose close-cropped hair had the texture of moss. Veronica wondered if these women knew their host might be peeping at them through a hole in the wall.

"We'll step in over here," Salome pointed.

Veronica stepped gingerly towards the lip of the pool and removed her sandals. An attendant extended her arms to receive Veronica's palla and stola. Veronica glanced back at the fish eye. She couldn't be seen from this angle, could she? Salome was on to her uncle's tricks, so this had to be the safe spot, right? Slowly, Veronica lifted the garments over her head, until she heard a pitiful moan rumble through the chamber. Frightened, she pulled her clothing back down, poking her head through and furtively searching for an exit.

"Don't worry," Salome laughed. "The palace isn't haunted. We've got a madman in the dungeon."

A second growl shook the walls, and Veronica thought she heard distinct words in an odd language. "What's he saying?" she asked.

"What he always says, 'Baruch atta Adonai Eloheinu. blah, blah, blah.'" Then Salome laughed cruelly, "Maybe he'll come to the party tonight and you can ask him!"

With that, Salome tugged upwards at her palla, but Veronica instinctively crossed her arms against it, glancing suspiciously again at the fish eye.

"Don't worry," Salome assured her, "He's not there. He's in the pit with the lunatic."

So, off came Veronica's garments and in she stepped to the soothing waters. Instantly, every knot in every muscle melted away.

Salome waved the attendant away. "We'll get your clothes washed. I'll send you down something fresh from my wardrobe." Then she laughed loudly; apparently Veronica had revealed abject horror at that suggestion. "You're such a worrier, Antonia. But I know how to dress a princess."

*   *   *   *

It was a long time — about the time it takes a boiling rabbit to turn to stew — before the clothes Salome had promised arrived. As Veronica patted herself dry, she was grateful her flesh didn't fall away from the bone. Salome's clothing was too ornate, but modest at least, and entirely appropriate for a lady. It appeared to have been worn very little, if ever.

The attendant gestured for Veronica to follow her, presumably back to the main vault for the party. But as Veronica stepped from the humid bath chamber into the dank corridor, she heard again the haunting moan of the alleged madman.

"Can I see him?" Veronica asked. The attendant seemed to pick up her meaning, for she wagged her head reproachfully, uttering some apparently negative syllables. Veronica was prepared to concede, when the moan came again, plaintive as before, but now strangely musical, as if a minstrel were exorcising his spiritual pain. Veronica loosened the attendant's fingers from her forearm.

"I-I apologize. I-I hope this doesn't reflect badly on you with the Tetrarch-ess?" she stammered, then dashed toward the downward stairs.

Oh, the stench of that passage! The combination of black mold and human waste caught in Veronica's throat. But the moaning continued, like a siren of Hades, drawing her down into the dark. A faltering torch posted on the wall alerted her to the final mossy step. There, she could make out the phrase that Salome had earlier quoted: "Baruch atta Adonai Eloheinu... Baruch atta Adonai Eloheinu..."

Veronica looked down a short corridor. There were three cells on each side. At five of the six, the barred gate was ajar. But the far cell on the left, lit dimly by a flickering torch on the far wall, was securely locked. Veronica saw slim arms and gnarled hands drooping through the bars. As she stepped towards the cell, the hands retracted. She saw a wild man, one who surpassed the frightening descriptions she'd heard of northern barbarians. The creature was on his knees, or rather all fours, rolling his forehead on the dank stones as if to cool a fever. The hung head was a massive, matted animal mane. His naked shoulders were broad but lean, like tanned hides stretched across a wooden frame. As he continued his chant in muted tones, Veronica crept closer.

Suddenly she heard a clamber on the stairs. Stepping instinctively into the shadows, Veronica found herself in an open cell. She felt at the wall, sticky with spiderwebs. She stifled a shriek as the interloper strode into view. From his gilded crown to a pair of silk slippers, this could only have been the Tetrarch Herod. To Veronica's surprise, he addressed the wild man in Greek.

"Baptist! Welcome to my feast. Ah, yes, we're all speaking Greek upstairs. International event, you know. Must employ the universal language."

The Tetrarch held an ornate silver plate, a salver, laden with rich food. But the man he called Baptist simply ignored him.

"Come, now, Baptist. I know it's not exactly grasshoppers and honey, but it is good. Take the platter."

The Baptist snarled, and muttered some words in his strange language.

The Tetrarch snapped back sharply, "Oh, again with *corruption*." He sampled a morsel from the platter and proceeded to speak over the objections of his prisoner. "You see, it's tasty. Oh, what can I do? What's done is done! What?"

The Tetrarch was in earnest; he wanted an answer from the Baptist, and crouched at eye level to get it. But the Baptist's eyes flicked past his, locking onto Veronica's. With a start, she stepped back into the shadows, just as Herod followed the Baptist's sightline and peered over his shoulder. Seeing nothing, Herod turned back to his prisoner, and Veronica exhaled.

Herod paced back and forth a few strides before trying another tack. "Your law of Moses, now this is interesting. Oh, you don't mind if I continue in Greek? The mood is upon me." After no objection from the Baptist, Herod continued. "Your Moses says, if a man dies, his brother is obligated — *obligated!* — to marry his widow. But..." he spoke stealthily, "if the woman considers her husband dead, as Philip was to Herodias, and prefers his brother, as Herodias did, oh that's corruption! A plague! It is the woman's choice after all; can't we honor that?"

The Baptist boomed, "Repent!" And, showing he had as much ability in Greek as his tormenter, he rambled on, "This day I call heaven and earth as witnesses against you, that I have set before you life and death, blessings and curses. Now choose life, that you and your children may live!"

Herod only chuckled, "But I am living, Baptist. A far sight better than you. And tonight I celebrate my life!" Again he offered the platter to the Baptist, who swatted it out of the Tetrarch's hand. It clanged to the floor, as the Baptist ranted.

"That you may love the Lord your God, listen to his voice, and hold fast to him!"

Herod stooped to retrieve the platter. The food he simply kicked out of his way, leaving a feast for the rats Veronica heard scurrying about.

"As for love, my mad prophet friend, you're not exactly bubbling over with it." Then with what seemed genuine disappointment, the Tetrarch sighed, "Good night, Baptist. I hope our revels do not disturb your sleep."

With something of a slouch, the Tetrarch left the cell. Veronica listened for his feet on the stairs before emerging from her hiding place. The Baptist was back to cooling his brow on the floor.

"Ave," Veronica said quietly.

The Baptist tilted his head up, eyeing the girl. Without acknowledging her, he returned to his chant.

"Baruch atta Adonai Eloheinu..."

"What are you saying?" she asked, speaking Greek.

The Baptist leapt up and grabbed the bars with such fury, Veronica felt for a moment the cage would fly open.

"Repent! Prepare the way. The Lord, your God is coming."

Veronica didn't know how to respond. Why was this barbarian so impassioned, when others who ruminated on the gods — such as her uncle — were detached and philosophical? *My god is coming?* she thought. *Who could that be, and why would he be so angry?*

"My uncle is a priest," Veronica offered. "He says the gods are tired of us."

He only muttered, "Baruch atta Adonai Eloheinu."

"Is that a prayer?" she asked. "Can you say it in Greek?"

The Baptist lifted his eyes toward the fluttering torch and proclaimed, "Hear, O Israel, the Lord your God, the Lord is One."

Veronica was impressed by his devotion. "Who is your god?"

"If you wish to know him," he whispered, "Come closer."

* * * *

It was roughly thirty miles from Ptolemais to Tiberius as the crow flies. But Longinus had to choose between indirect roads veering south and steep country directly east. After climbing an arid slope, Longinus halted his men at a town called Cana. Finding a well with a long trough adjacent, he had the riders water their horses.

"And make sure it's only water!" Juvenal playfully reproached the men. "No trickery!"

Longinus didn't get the joke.

"Oh," the Princeps explained, "Just a story I heard back at Capernaum. I actually stopped here on my transfer west to confirm the tale. Some magician at a wedding party turned six jars of water into wine. No one could figure out how he did it."

"An impressive illusion."

"More impressive was the vintage. Or so they said. That is, they're said to have said. Probably all too drunk by then to judge. Certainly too drunk to see when he made the switch."

"He must have had plenty of accomplices," Longinus suggested.

"All, no doubt, sworn to secrecy."

"Well," Longinus sighed, "You know how these Jews love to conspire. Propaganda begets folklore, folklore begets religion. Religion begets insurrection."

Juvenal smiled, "So much for wine containing truth."

Longinus asked Juvenal his opinion on the best course to take. If they rode cross-country, over the hills, they could reach Tiberius by late afternoon. Of course, there was a chance the travelers had not gone there. They may have kept a southeasterly course bearing towards the King's Highway, which would take them directly south, though to the east of Jerusalem. The most prudent course of pursuit might be the main road southeast to the town of Agrippina. At that point, if they hadn't overtaken the wagon, Longinus would take forty men north to Tiberius, and Juvenal would continue southeast with the remainder towards the region of Decapolis and the intersection of the King's Highway.

"So you'll be attending the Tetrarch's feast?" Juvenal teased.

"What feast?"

Juvenal practically doubled over with mirth. "It's why the Magistrate wouldn't join us! It seems Herod is celebrating his birthday, and has invited all the fashionable patricians from Syria to Abyssinia and east to Persia. But our magistrate was left off the roles. He's insulted, and didn't want to show up in Tiberius looking like he was begging an invitation!"

Longinus enjoyed a deep belly laugh. When he'd finished, he actually had to wipe his eyes. Ah, it was good to have his friend with him! But before they returned to their men, Juvenal had another question.

"What exactly is our mission, Longinus?"

The Centurion looked high at the sun, then back at the horsemen milling about the well.

"We escort the party back to Ptolemais."

"And if they won't come willingly?" Juvenal pressed. "That, um, merchant? He strikes me as one who'd fall on his sword rather than face a show trial and strangulation."

"Keep the girl alive," Longinus said. "As long as she breathes, he has a reason to cooperate."

"What makes you think she wouldn't plunge a dagger or hug an asp to her breast?"

Longinus braced the Princeps by the shoulders, leaning in until their helmets clicked.

"Keep the girl alive."

*   *   *   *

Veronica peered deep into the dungeon cell. The Baptist retreated to the far wall and placed his fingers against the stones. He walked back towards her with cupped hands, and Veronica deduced that there was some rivulet from the hot spring that seeped through his cell wall. He gestured for her to bow her head. Veronica hesitated. She had kept her hair out of the bathwater and certainly didn't want it wetted down now with murky runoff. But the man's plaintive eyes were so insistent, Veronica felt a strange obligation to go along. She tucked her chin and braced herself for the unsettling trickle.

The Baptist muttered his familiar prayer again, then spoke some other words in that same guttural language. Veronica felt the water drip through his fingers onto the top of her head. The flutter of nervousness in her stomach swirled and solidified, like a fist, forcing itself upward. Her throat tightened and her eyes swelled. Suddenly the knot broke. Veronica felt energy surging upward, out her mouth and nose and through her eyes, even through the top of her skull. And then she laughed. An alien feeling came over her, and she realized it was happiness.

"How did you do that?" she panted. "Are you a magician?"

He tossed his great matted head. "I am no one of consequence. The one who matters has come after me. I must decrease, so he may increase."

What does that mean? she thought. But she sensed she'd get no more words from this Baptist tonight. He fell to his knees, then to all fours. Veronica glimpsed a pair of rats nosing at the dropped food. It was time to go.

Returning upstairs, Veronica trotted towards the main vault to find the Tetrarch's party highly animated. Several instruments struck a harsh tune. She made her way across the crowded floor to her uncle and Sabinus, reclining on some cushions and facing Herod's throne. They'd both had their faces shaved. Her uncle once more looked civilized. Sabinus just looked like a child.

"Where have you been?" Theodosius demanded.

"They have a holy man in the dungeon."

"You were in the dungeon?" Sabinus gasped.

Veronica perceived a bit of jealousy in his tone. She took a crust of bread from the platter on the low table and dipped it into a bowl of yellow paste. "You should speak to him," she chirped. "Why did you shave?"

"A Senator should accept the Tetrarch's hospitality. It's the first step in forging a relationship."

So, Veronica concluded, Theodosius had determined he would charm Herod out of a dozen armed men. She started to say a prayer to the gods, but for some reason that seemed childish.

The music concluded to loud applause, but as the applause waned, the chamber reverberated again with tortured groans. The Baptist renewed his lamentation, this time in clear Greek, no doubt calculated to scandalize the guests.

"Repent, Herod! Cast out that woman who corrupts your soul!"

Theodosius rose on one elbow and searched the entrance of the vault. "That's him," Veronica said. "In the dungeon."

Herod, withering under his wife's intense glare, tucked his feet under and boosted himself to sit on the arm of his throne. Clapping his hands over his left shoulder he called, "Music, please! Keep the music playing!" Then he abruptly stopped as he spotted someone in the crowd. Veronica followed his sightline to Salome.

"A special performance," the Tetrarch cried. "A gift to myself, which I am pleased to share with all assembled." He gestured so broadly he nearly toppled off his throne. "My joy, my niece, shall dance."

There was a flutter of applause as Salome stirred, turning herself over on her cushions. She arched her back so her bare midriff rose toward the ceiling and her breasts ebbed toward her chin. Then she collapsed like a rag doll and declared, "No, I don't feel much like dancing."

Stunned, Herod coiled his face into a contrived smile and attempted a laugh, as if this affront was part of a comedic act. Clasping his hands in mock supplication, he urged the audience to laugh with him.

"Here's a woman who knows her value," he declared. "Perhaps we can strike a bargain."

Salome played to her audience, and specifically Veronica, with a face that boldly mocked the sad lecher.

"Dance for us, Salome," Herod continued, "and you may name your price. Anything mine is yours."

"Anything?" Salome raised an eyebrow, dropping the façade of excruciating boredom.

"Up to half my kingdom," Herod declared. A murmur rolled through the crowd and grew to a roar as he extended his arms and bowed slightly at the waist, the very picture of magnanimity. Veronica caught the excitement like a fever. *I'd ask for a horse*, she thought. *A milk-white Arabian fit for a patrician's chariot. And a saddle of hand-tooled leather*. But Salome just sat on her cushions, calmly considering her options. The cat already had its claws buried in the mouse's hindquarters. All that was needed was the deathblow. With a subtle tilt of her chin, she looked at her mother, seated in her cathedra beside the Tetrarch.

"I wouldn't know what to ask for," the cat purred. Veronica wondered if Salome was being coy or genuine. *Is it possible this princess already has everything? Is that why she's so bored?*

The Baptist put an end to her deliberations with a bone-chilling roar, "Herod, repent!"

Decidedly unrepentant, Herod signaled the musicians, who promptly played a discordant tune with an urgent rhythm. Salome, without a hint of acquiescence, nevertheless strode to the center of the floor. Herod, after a spasm of triumph, slinked back to his throne, as Herodias dug her nails into the arm of her cathedra. Salome's dance consisted of stretching and undulating in a manner that subjected her more private parts to lurid, public scrutiny. Theodosius turned away, Sabinus leaned forward and Veronica simply stared transfixed. She was at once repulsed and delighted; she marveled at the audacity of this girl, who for however long had coyly managed her uncle's lascivious intrusions and now seemed determined to expose his covert lust to the world. This girl was brazen in a way that would have earned Veronica, or even Claudia, several stripes in the Proculus home. Salome presented an image of a completely emancipated youth, free from the strictures of adult discipline. Free — if a willful mind were enough — from the moorings of civilization, she proclaimed her animal nature. Veronica didn't know whether to cheer this phantasm, or banish it from her consciousness. What was right in this rebellion deserved laurels, yet what was wrong seemed to violate the natural law that ordered Veronica's life. For his part, Herod seemed to shrink, either from the cold exposure of his private sins or from the seething glare of Herodias.

As the music swelled, the baleful moans of the Baptist thundered, prompting Herod to flail his arms demanding a greater crescendo. The orchestra, magnified by the echoes bouncing off bare stone, built to a deafening cacophony, into which Salome abandoned any restraint, gleefully projecting back to Herod the bestial appetite she knew he was hiding. She leapt, turned and spun herself down to the floor, landing on knees and elbows as the music abruptly stopped.

Silence.

Salome raised her cat's tail towards the Tetrarch's throne, tilting her chin over her shoulder, to look back at her uncle. She flicked her tongue, snakelike, and slithered forward prostrate on the floor.

The befuddled audience offered no applause. But Herod rose, wiped the corners of his mouth and stroked his beard. "What shall I give?" he asked. The chamber said nothing. Even the Baptist was mute. "What could any man give to reward such... art."

Salome rolled to her knees, and regarded Herodias briefly. A smile wormed its way across the bitter queen's face and Salome spoke with grim delight, "Give me... on a silver platter... the head of John the Baptist."

A shudder coursed through the room stirring a bizarre mix of reactions: gasps of horror, laughter, even some applause. Herod seemed to crumble inward. He expelled what seemed true grief, "Oh, Salome, no."

But Herodias leapt to her feet, snuffing out this spark of pity. She scolded the guards. "What is this malingering? The Tetrarch has spoken? Is his word not law in Galilee?"

Veronica pivoted to see the guards run for the exit. *The Baptist? They wouldn't... not on the word of a child. Would they kill an innocent man just so this spoiled, bored girl could laugh in her uncle's face? Didn't the law — didn't the gods — forbid this?*

Theodosius grabbed Veronica's arm, pulling her up.

"Come. We're leaving," he said. "Sabinus, fly to Valentius. Tell him to bring the wagon."

The youth ran from the chamber, hopping over reclining guests. Very few had reacted as the Senator; they anxiously awaited the climax. But Theodosius seemed determined to exit before the crime was committed. As Veronica reached the atrium, she peered down the corridor towards the downward staircase.

"They can't just kill him," she implored. "Uncle? Can't you stop them?"

"We're not in Rome."

"Aren't we? Isn't this our Empire?" Veronica searched her uncle's eyes for the heroism she'd seen so often. Theodosius turned back to the main vault — to Herod, a tiny man slumping on an oversized throne.

Incited once again, the Baptist's voice resounded through the hall, "Repent! Make way a straight path for the Lord!"

"Get your things," Theodosius told Veronica.

She clutched her stola, realizing she wasn't wearing her own clothes.

"Forget it," he said. "Not important."

But Veronica spotted the attendant who had taken her clothes to be washed. She squeezed her uncle's forearm, begging a moment's forbearance and ran to address the slave. In the level below, the Baptist launched a tirade against the guards, his cries invading Veronica's ears as she padded across the hard floor. Reaching the attendant, Veronica froze. There was silence. She snapped toward the dungeon stairway and listened.

Heavy footsteps. Then out of the black void, the guards marched and Veronica dissolved against the wall. Her heart ached and her legs buckled as she saw on the salver the blood-matted head of the wild-eyed prophet.

"No! Gods, no!" Instantly her grief turned to rage, and Veronica ran back to the main vault. The guards cut a path through the assembly, who variously gawked or averted their eyes. An Abyssinian vomited. The guards slowed as they approached Salome, still coiled on the floor. Then, bowing perfunctorily at the waist, the Captain of the Guard handed her the salver. As the guards dispersed, Veronica watched Salome twist a finger in the Baptist's hair, then bend to kiss his cheek. Laughing, she skipped past Herod and deposited the platter in her mother's arms. Herodias cast a jaundiced eye at her cringing husband, then grabbed the Baptist's hair in her tight fist and turned the head over admiring the lifeless eyes, the gaping mouth and the sagging tongue. Content, she passed the salver to one of her slaves.

The spectacle was all too much. A few in the crowd rose to leave; those few dissenters sparked a rebellion. As the bulk of the audience emptied out of the chamber, Herod left his throne. He paced, apparently tormented by his weakness, as his prestige drained faster than the hall. Herod evoked in Veronica a feeling of pity, which, strangely, drew her towards him, so that as the Tetrarch bid the Captain of his guard come forward, Veronica floated in his wake, and overheard the orders.

"When she goes to her bedroom," the Tetrarch whispered, "take her out of the palace and kill her."

A hand clamped Veronica's shoulder, startling her.

"Why are you still here?" Her uncle pulled her toward the exit.

"He's going to kill her. Salome."

Theodosius pressed her onward. "That's some measure of justice."

But Veronica wriggled free. "It's not justice at all. She asked for the head, but she's only a child; children say rash things all the time. He's a king!" Looking into her uncle's eyes, she pleaded. "We've got to warn her. Please, Uncle."

Theodosius released her. "I'll give you two minutes."

Veronica took a breath, then marched along the far wall of the chamber to Salome, still rapt in a strange euphoria, massaging her shoulders against a column. As Veronica approached, she giggled. "I ruined the party!"

Veronica whispered sternly, "You've got to get out. Leave the palace."

"Oh? And go where?"

"Anywhere. Herod's ordered the guards to kill you."

"Him? He wouldn't dare. You're a worrier, Antonia. You. Worry. Too. Much."

Veronica ground her teeth. *This brat was suicidal.* "Suit yourself," she said. "You've been warned." Veronica locked eyes with the Captain, studying them from across the chamber. Salome tilted her head in that direction and Veronica thought she detected a flinch. No matter, her time was up. She spotted Theodosius, and trotted towards him. As they headed toward the gate, the chamber was almost empty; only a few servants and the guards remained.

Valentius was in the atrium, holding a scroll almost as long as his arm. "Senator, I purchased this map."

"Fine, we'll discuss outside."

"And, hired these men." Almost apologetically, Valentius gestured towards a foursome of lean, stolid mechanicals. "Stone masons, sir. From Hippos, across the great lake. Out of work since the Tetrarch stopped construction."

This was too much to foist upon that Senator at that moment. "We're to match swords with hammers?" he muttered. Then, recovering, Theodosius patted Valentius on the shoulder, adding, "You've done more for our chances than I. That is..."

He didn't get to finish. Veronica had taken one last peak inside the chamber, only to spy Salome walking briskly towards her, the guards on her tail. Veronica tugged at her uncle's toga, so that, turning, Theodosius saw, not the frightened girls, but Herod's soldiers closing in. Instinctively, he reached for the dagger in his belt, only to drop his hand when Salome rushed practically into his arms. Brushing the girl aside, Theodosius addressed her pursuers.

"Excuse me, Captain," he called, imposing himself between the guards and their quarry. With Valentius' assistance, he stretched the scroll open, forming a partition. The Captain continued to regard Salome, until she shifted behind the sheep skin curtain.

Theodosius gestured to a point on the map, "A gentleman has offered us lodging at Arimathea. What is the best route to take?"

The Captain took a dagger from his belt and pressed it to the surface of the map. On the reverse side, the dagger tip tented the scroll at the level of Salome's throat. Veronica gripped Salome's hand; only a thin sheet of leather separated the girl from her assassin. The blade traced downward, to Salome's heart then her belly.

"South to Jerusalem. Then west."

Theodosius nodded cordially, then bid the Captain look more closely at the path his dagger had traced. "And if we continue along this road here," the Senator whispered, "Herod will never see the girl again, and you won't have to murder a child."

From behind the scroll, Veronica couldn't see the exchange, and it seemed an eternity before the Captain responded. His voice seemed deliberately loud. "Yes. That would be the best course to take."

Theodosius swept an arm behind the scroll, commanding the girls out the door.

"Thank you." The Senator adjourned their meeting, leaving Valentius to roll up the map.

As she burst from the palace out to the plaza, Veronica nearly tumbled down the uneven stairs. It was dark and the rush to evacuate had created a scene of utter chaos. But she kept a firm grip on Salome and dashed through the tight crowd toward the wagon where Sabinus held the reins. She handed Salome off to the youth, ordering, "Hide her."

Sabinus, thoroughly delighted with his assignment, hefted Salome into the wagon. Veronica scrambled in after them to find Adrianna and Paenulus sitting tightly together. The next second Valentius climbed onto the bench and Theodosius was at the reins. Veronica shrieked as the wagon rocked and menacing shadows played on the surface of the tent. But it was only the hired men climbing onto the sideboards. The Senator cracked a whip and the horses lurched. Still, the route out of the plaza was jammed with carriages; there was nowhere to go.

Peeking through the rear flaps of the tent, Veronica saw horsemen. *Roman troops!* Their lead horses reared, cut off by a hasty chariot. They circled. Found an opening, only to have a carriage roll up and close the gap. The carriage was lit inside by an oil lamp, whose radiance fell upon the lead horseman. Veronica recognized the muscular black stallion, then the rider's face caught the lamplight. It was him: *that Centurion.*

"Uncle Theo," Veronica cried. "Auxilia!"

Theodosius whipped the horses again, forcing the wagon into a breach. Within seconds, they were at a full, bone-jarring gallop, while the Auxilia stood paralyzed on the plaza.

Chapter 15

Veronica lifted her head, releasing a throb that rolled up from the base of her skull and across her left temple, landing heavily on a tender spot behind her eyes. After blinking tightly, she peaked out between the tent flaps. They'd set no fire last night, nor had there been any moon, so the only light came from the misty band of stars that arched towards the distant hills. It intersected one prominent peak at an angle that suggested a bridge from this Earthly realm to the celestial. How Veronica longed for such an escape route. She wondered — or lamented —about the Baptist: vitally, passionately alive one minute, mute and inert the next. All so final, irreversible. How could such a dynamic soul be snuffed out like a candle? Or could he, having shed his corporeal trappings, be somewhere in transit?

Roman lore — and Greek before it — contained tales of an underworld. The dead passed through Pluto's realm either to Tartarus, the place of torment, or to Elysium, the isle of paradise. But Veronica didn't like horror stories. Gazing at the band of stars, she preferred to imagine the mad prophet traversing that lofty arch. Yet she'd never heard of such an ascension; no matter how heroically a mortal had lived, Olympus belonged to the gods alone. She considered the state of her party, and wondered if the reverse were possible, that, considering her uncle's faithful service as a priest, might some god descend the celestial bridge and aid them in their journey? Could that have been what the Baptist had meant when he'd said, "Make straight a path for the Lord"?

The sun was not even threatening to show, but the men were already alert. Apparently, the last watch was over. Veronica recalled the hushed argument of last evening. The wagon had turned off the road and rolled some distance across country to get well out of the path of any Auxilia patrol. They'd tucked themselves into a cavity in the western range, a small alcove where, it seemed to Veronica, every sheep in Galilee had come to do its business. She was never so grateful to sleep in the wagon rather than on the ground.

The men had to make a decision then about how to set up a perimeter. Uncle Theo was not prepared to trust the men Valentius had hired. He insisted that either he or Valentius be paired with one of the new men throughout the night. Though Valentius could not dispute the Senator's rationale, he took it as a personal slight, as though he'd been negligent in recruiting stonecutters as bodyguards.

"If they've never touched a sword, they give us numbers, sir, and that's a deterrent to attack."

"Agreed," Theodosius whispered, "unless they've got treachery on their minds."

"These men aren't Zealots, Senator. I don't think they're even Jews. Assyrian, I make them."

"So," Theodosius asked, "you'll sleep soundly while they've got swords in their hands?"

"They've daggers already."

It went on like that for some time, until Veronica felt she had to intercede or forget about sleeping all night. Over Adrianna's protestations, she hopped out of the wagon and squarely onto a pile of sheep droppings. After rubbing the soles of her feet on a patch of grass, Veronica marched to Theodosius.

"Do you want to know if these men are Jews?" she asked.

"Please, Veronica," her uncle admonished.

But, perhaps exhibiting a tinge of insolence she'd picked up from Salome, she'd waved her uncle off, and strode over to the pack of stonecutters. They had their eyes fixed in the direction of Tiberius. Veronica circled in front of them, lowered her head in deference and whispered, "Baruch atta...?

The one who appeared eldest among them nodded, completing the phrase, "Adonai Eloheinu melech ha'olam."

In Greek she asked, "Did you know the man John, called Baptist?"

The men stirred, mumbling among themselves, before the elder spoke again. "We'd seen him in Tiberius, while we were working. We couldn't tell if he was holy or insane. Herod Antipas, he couldn't tell either. He wanted to silence the man, but he was afraid."

"Tonight he did silence him," Veronica said. Against her efforts, her eyes welled up.

"Yes, we heard. We saw the commotion," the leader said. "It was quite sad."

"He was my friend," Veronica declared. "He gave me his blessing." She looked sternly at each of the men in turn. "If you serve us well, you'll have his blessing, too. But if you betray us, his curse will be upon you."

One of the younger men laughed, but the elder cut him off. They had a testy exchange in their local language before the elder got him under control.

"Forgive him. He is not religious. In truth, none of us... We're simple men who break stones with our hands."

Veronica scanned the men's faces again. Three of the four met her gaze with respect and humility. The youngest continued to scoff. Veronica returned his impudent sneer and hurried back to her men.

"They're Jews," she said. "But not religious, and they seem honest enough."

"I told you, Senator," Valentius entreated. "Simple men. Simple virtues. Not a traitor among them." When Theodosius didn't immediately acquiesce, Valentius launched into a secondary defense. "I know, the men from Ptolemais, but even you said..."

"Yes! I know," Theodosius cut him off. "Nowhere will we find men who'll fight against Rome."

"And that doesn't make them cowards," Valentius insisted. "But those Zealots, with their clubs and short swords? These men will fight. I'll stake my life on it."

Theodosius looked toward Veronica. She knew whose life weighed on him. She felt a twinge of shame at her vulnerability. She curtseyed to the men, uttering, "I'll say goodnight now, Uncle," and returned to the wagon.

There she'd found Sabinus engaged in a rather intimate exchange with Salome. She gave the palace imp the dirtiest look she could muster, which set Sabinus back on his heels, but elicited a giggle from the princess of Galilee. She toyed with his bowstring and cooed: "This young Nimrod[66] has promised me venison."

Veronica scraped her feet on the grass again before hoisting herself into the wagon. "I'm surprised he hasn't offered you half his kingdom."

That line landed like a fist to the solar plexus; Sabinus grunted something inaudible and backed away. Salome seemed not to care. She scooted down onto the wagon bed and turned over to sleep. But after a moment she spoke quietly, "You think it's wrong to make men do what you want. But it's the only real power a woman has."

The remark burned in Veronica's belly. *Like poison,* she thought, *only... what if it were true?* What if the only way a woman could be strong was to become wicked, to wield her outward beauty as a weapon, until, like Herodias, the wickedness shone in every crease of her vain mask? And the only way to satisfy that lurking evil was to force weak men to commit abominations? That thought did more to shake Veronica's hope than all the Legionnaires on all the horses in all the Empire.

A host of unsettling thoughts had led to an unsettled night's sleep and to Veronica's premature rise with a throbbing headache. She crawled past Salome, who slumbered as though she'd no concern in the world, and slipped

---

[66] In bygone days, a compliment, since Genesis names Nimrod as a great hunter

gingerly from the wagon. She found her uncle as she'd left him hours ago, in close consultation with Valentius.

"Can I build a fire, Uncle?" she asked.

"We were just discussing that."

"We'll have sun in half an hour, sir," Valentius offered. "By that time, the wagon will be visible. Anyone who sees it will wonder why there is no fire."

"All right," the Senator acquiesced. "Let's give the party a decent meal before we push on."

So Veronica set off to gather twigs. She met Sabinus, returning from his hunt with a pair of large rabbits.

"That's hardly the stag you promised her, Nimrod."

Sabinus was flustered, but recovered quickly. "I only meant, well, you didn't hear, but I asked if it was true Jews don't eat rabbits. I just wanted... there are others besides her. Those men. They have to be fed."

"Oh, I don't care!" Veronica lied. She snapped twigs angrily off a fallen bough. "You want to play the fool for that kind of a girl, go right ahead. I'm not going to stop you. Go. Give her the rabbits. See if she even knows how to dress them. Or if they'll rot in their skins before she figures it out."

Sabinus took the rabbits to the wagon and tied them up by the hind legs. Veronica had enough twigs to get a fire going, so headed back also. Adrianna was just getting up, and greeted Paenulus, who looked like he'd spent a very uncomfortable night on the grass. Valentius was offering feed to the horses which, though hobbled, had drifted a distance from the wagon. He'd use the sack of oats to lure them back for hitching.

The surrounding hills became more distinct as the eastern skyline took on a softer shade of gray. Veronica dropped the armful of twigs onto a rocky outcropping. Adrianna brought over the kitchen utensils, including the flint for the fire. Veronica went back to the wagon for the rabbits. As she slipped the knots from their tethers, a loud yawn startled her. Salome was rousing herself.

"Good morning," Veronica muttered. She held up the rabbits. "Bad news. Nimrod had a poor night."

Salome just yawned and with the back of her hand fanned Veronica away. Adrianna already had the fire roaring when Veronica got back. She took one of the rabbits and began cutting.

"Don't trouble yourself with that one," the matron advised. "She's full of certainties that just aren't so." She bid Veronica hold the rear feet as she pulled the fur down and off the carcass. As Adrianna cleaned the cavity with a butcher knife, she continued, "The power a woman has? It's to not to make a man do anything, it's to make him do the right thing. Men, they live in their proud heads or by their appetites. The stomach. Other... parts. A good woman brings a man back to his heart." When the carcass was stripped and emptied, she quartered it for the pot. "Even the best ones, like your uncle. He has his cold logic. His practicality. Oh, they chide us for it. Our emotions. But when they are deepest in their thoughts, they need us most. They need our hearts."

As they worked on the second rabbit, Veronica reflected on Adrianna's words. Judging by her life, her power over the opposite sex seemed sorely limited. She'd been a spinster, then, too late in life, a bride to a man she'd known for decades. Yet, there seemed some truth in her words. As a child, Veronica had often imagined that Uncle Theo and Adrianna were secretly married. It had been a game between her and Claudia. Now Veronica wondered if Adrianna hadn't put off marrying Paenulus out of loyalty to Uncle Theo. Veronica had heard of the Senator's grief at the death of Claudia's mother. Perhaps Adrianna felt so strongly that a brooding, introspective man needed a tender woman that she'd dedicated her life to her master, at the expense of her own happiness.

As pieces of the second rabbit went into the pot, Veronica spied her uncle surveying the camp. Theodosius waved toward the top of the ridge behind the wagon. He'd positioned two stonecutters there during the night. They acknowledged his signal, apparently indicating they saw no threat. The Senator turned his attention to the northern terrain, anxiously opening and closing his right hand. Veronica wondered if Adrianna's loyalty had come at a price; if she'd been less solicitous of the Senator, he might have felt the want of a true spouse. He might have remarried, freeing himself and her from that burden of duty.

Veronica found these thoughts ponderous, and too far from the delirious joy Claudia had exhibited in her courtship with Pontius. Of course, by now they too could have settled into a grim routine – her heart, her vivid dreams, counterbalancing his careerist ambitions – but Veronica prayed it weren't so. She wanted to believe that elation could glow forth despite the abrasion of daily life and ritual duties. If Claudia, with her expansive spirit that so feasted on fantasy, could be bridled like a pack horse, what did that foretell for a child of tragedy like Veronica who tilted towards melancholy as a compass needle points north? After such a long journey, during which she'd had to exercise constant forbearance towards the sorely limited men in their troupe, Veronica had started to dream of a romance like Claudia's. In fact, the second glimpse of that Centurion had delivered an intense thrill, even though Veronica knew that his discovery of her could only end in disaster. Still, despite their limited contact, the aspect of the man had so impressed her, Veronica doubted she could be satisfied with anyone less. Certainly not with the likes of Sabinus, a boy so easily tied in knots by a painted brat with naked limbs.

The water started to boil. Adrianna tossed in some wild herbs and green onions she'd picked by the morning light. The meat would be ready in half an hour. It was time to mix flour and water to make the cakes.

Theodosius wandered over to the fire and warmed his hands. He looked weary; he'd probably stood guard all night.

"We'll need more wood," Adrianna said.

Veronica reached to pick up a small hatchet, but her uncle already had it in hand. He surrendered it to her and they walked together toward the fallen bough. Veronica had so many thoughts swirling in her mind, she was grateful for a moment to speak to him. But she feared he couldn't help her with the most immediate thing, which was what to make of the Baptist.

"I wish you'd had a chance to speak to him," Veronica said. "He was angry, maybe even a little crazy, but..."

"Prison will make any man crazy," Theodosius conceded.

"I told him how you said the gods ignore us. He said that's not true. He said..."

"God is coming!" a voice boomed "Make straight a path for the Lord!"

Thus Salome announced that she was awake. She climbed down from the back of the wagon, her shoulders draped with a blanket.

"Oh, Antonia, it's so cold! How can you stand it?"

"I'm fully dressed," Veronica said flatly. "I'm sure you have cold mornings in the palace."

"Yes," Salome groaned. "But we also have chamber pots." She looked around the stony alcove for a place to take her morning relief. Theodosius turned away. She spotted a nearby cluster of small boulders at the base of the sheer cliff, and toddled towards them. "If I were you, Antonia, I wouldn't be so anxious for the Zealot god to arrive. Have you any idea what happens then? The wicked — oh and that's you by the way, the Romans, the oppressors — get thrown into the fire. Well, you saw. His god didn't come for him, and you better hope he doesn't come for you."

"When did he say this god will come?" Theodosius asked.

"He said He's already here."

Salome prepared to crouch, then, betraying uncharacteristic caution, remarked, "You don't think there are any vipers out here, do you, Antonia?"

Veronica spoke with absolute certainty. "Vipers? By all the gods, no. Definitely no vipers." Then as Salome squatted among the stones, added, "Out here there are only cobras! Sssssssstht!"

Salome bolted upright, with a spark of anger, then abruptly ducked as a swooping figure cast its shadow over her and crashed onto her rock pile. Veronica screamed: it was the young stonecutter. A short, curved knife jutted from his back.

"Iscariots!" Salome shrieked.

Theodosius drew his sword. "Girls, get to the wagon! Now!"

A landslide followed. Boulders rained down, just missing Veronica, bouncing and battering the wagon. At the front of the wagon, a horse reared as a wave of rocks broke below its forelegs. The horse escaped; Valentius was not so lucky. A slab of granite shattered and pinned his left foot. Unable to look,

Veronica spun into her uncle's arms. Theodosius shielded Veronica and, dodging falling rubble, deposited her by the rear wagon wheel.

Then the men came. They swept from the hill in two prongs, attacking at the front and the rear of the camp. At the front, the elder stonecutter was trying to pry the slab from Valentius' foot, but the marauders got on him too soon. A club shattered the mason's skull. Sword drawn, Valentius parried several opponents, then hacked his ankle free, and continued to fight while pivoting on a bloody stump.

Salome had defied Theodosius' order. With rocks falling around the young mason's corpse, she had grabbed the knife handle and, bracing one foot on the dead youth's spine, jerked the blade loose. Now armed, Salome leapt from her cluster of rocks, skipped across the stony field and slid under the wagon.

Theodosius defended the rear of the wagon. Employing a double-fisted grip on his sword, he cut through the attackers like a scythe through wheat. But what these marauders couldn't go through, they slipped around, overrunning the camp. One assailant broke through, cocking an arm to bludgeon Veronica, but an arrow sliced past her shoulder, lodging deep in the man's chest, dropping him at her feet. Instantly another cudgel whipped through the air. Veronica ducked the club and, realizing she was as deeply in this fight as any man, she countered, swinging her small hatchet as viciously as she could, catching her attacker cleanly on the chin and severing half his jaw. Then there was a massive hand upon her — pulling away only forced her down onto her knees into the muck. Her attacker pinned her with his weight, then drew a short, curved knife. But a second arrow struck inside his thigh. He cried in pain and rolled just enough so Veronica could scramble free. *That's twice Sabinus has saved me*, she thought, as she crawled on her belly under the wagon.

Salome lay there, cowering, clinging to the bloody knife. "Your men are losing," she spat.

"We're outnumbered."

Paenulus stood by the fire waving a kitchen knife. A brute clubbed him into the pit and his clothes burst into flame. Adrianna cried in horror, but another attacker slit her throat.

"If you haven't figured it out," Salome sneered, "Zealots don't take prisoners."

"Zealots!"

"Old blind men. Women. Girls? I wouldn't stick around if I were you."

With that, Salome broke towards the horses. They were bridled, but still hobbled, though they fought against the leather tethers on their ankles. An enormous Zealot with an iron lance tramped through the carnage. He hurled his lance into the flank of one of the horses, causing it to scream in hellish torment. As that horse went down, the other reared, thrusting its forelegs at Salome, who deftly slashed at the hobbles with the Iscariot knife. Then, grabbing the bridle and the horse's mane, she swung herself onto its bare back, dug her heels into its ribs and rode furiously south.

The giant traipsed over to the fallen horse and planted a cruel boot on its ribs. He pulled the lance free, then stroked the tip along the poor beast's jugular, severing the vein, which spurted crimson rivulets as the animal expired. Veronica watched as this monster walked with his lance shouldered over to the faltering Valentius. As his blood had drained from his severed ankle, he'd become ashen. Sluggish. The attackers taunted him, waiting for the moment he could no longer raise his sword. Veronica prayed for a volley of arrows. Sabinus had saved her twice, couldn't he do something now for Valentius? *Where was he?*

But across the field, their archer was under siege. His perch discovered, he'd been overrun, and now swung his bow in a feeble attempt to beat back the mob. Within seconds he was on his back, a flurry of cudgels produced rapid thumps followed a sharp crack. A Zealot celebrated by tossing his cudgel, spraying the air with pink foam.

Veronica focused again on Valentius. The Equestrian was surrounded. He could no longer have been thinking of self-preservation, only of dispatching as many villains as possible. Veronica had the same thought. If she broke from her hiding place now, could she strike one or two of these fiends with her hatchet before she was struck down? She gathered her legs up and crouched, prepared to attack.

To rally his fading strength, Valentius raised his arms over his head and roared for his attackers to come.

"Cowards!! Assassins!!"

The iron lance pierced under his right arm and emerged above his left hip. Valentius coughed blood, dropped to his knees and fell backwards.

Choking down her grief, instantly fomenting it to rage, Veronica sprang, determined to take at least one life. But a whack across the shins sent her sprawling forward, as a zealot had raked a pike in her path. She scrambled to all fours, but the hatchet was gone, and a huge hand slapped her head, gripping her hair and yanking her upward. She braced herself for the assassin's knife, but it didn't come. Instead, her captor marched her towards the rear of the wagon.

It was clear why. Theodosius was the last combatant standing. He continued to wield his sword against a circle of attackers, lunging and feinting all about him. Veronica had seen her uncle many times spar with a sword in each hand against two opponents. Today, limited to a two-hand hold because of his injury, the Senator was only a shadow of the swordsman he'd been. Still there was no man on this field to match him, nor could this mob in its entirety. Yet, the ultimate outcome was clear, so business could yield to sport, with the giant Zealot determined to make sport of Uncle Theo.

Holding Valentius' sword aloft, the monster signaled his gang to withdraw. He addressed the Senator in barely comprehensible Greek.

"Did you enjoy seeing the Baptist die? Did it amuse you?"

Theodosius was dumbfounded, but the giant had no intention of debating. He swung Valentius' sword high and crashed it down, an artless attack, bolstered by immense force. Theodosius easily deflected the blade, but his *riposte* required a pivot and cross-body swing that the slow-moving ogre thwarted. Then came an overhand blow. And another. The brute meant to win by force what he couldn't claim by skill. Blow followed blow until Theodosius abandoned the two-hand hold and relied on his weaker left hand. Conceding that he lacked strength and facility, Theodosius resorted to speed. He deflected several heavy-handed blows from the giant, and each time delivered a cut: superficial wounds to the thigh, the opposite forearm or the belly, but enough, Veronica hoped, to shake the Zealot champion's confidence and provoke him to a fatal error. Facing a left-handed swordsman had to be disconcerting, yet the giant absorbed the stabs like a boar charging through thistle. Veronica could see her uncle — her hero, her savior — would not win this bout. The brute grew impatient, and delivered a barrage of rapid and forceful blows that drove Theodosius backwards.

"What do you think of us, Roman?" the giant taunted. "Are we weak? Backward?" The giant punctuated each affront with a furious blow. Each time Theodosius parried, he raised his sword more slowly.

"Oh," the giant mocked, "these silly people and their silly God! And the silly looks on their faces when you chop off their heads! How easy they are to master! To master!"

With one last crushing blow, the giant wrenched the sword from Uncle Theo's hand, then planted his massive boot on the hilt. The ogre's sword was at the Senator's throat as he prodded him backwards. With a feint, the giant drove Theo left, where he met him with a blunt fist to the face. Bloodied, the Senator staggered back. The giant discarded the sword in favor of a bare-knuckled assault. One punch after another sent the Senator reeling towards the wagon.

As Theodosius crouched defensively, a spiteful villain took a brand from the fire and torched the tent. Theodosius was trapped between the blaze and the giant. Veronica strained against the Zealot still grasping her hair. She watched the giant reduce her uncle's face to a bloody pulp. Theodosius scrambled blindly away. As he crawled towards her, Veronica's rage drained. She wanted to hold her uncle and console him in his agony. But her mind rebelled, refusing to recognize this desperate creature, this victim, whose piteous, leprous face was so foreign. Veronica knew she should have felt sympathy. Charity. But all she felt was horror.

The Zealot giant drew a curved Iscariot from his belt. "We have a saying in these hills. *No master but God*. Rome may object, but do you know what we say? *Sic semper. No master but God!*"

The Zealot monster plunged his knife between Theodosius' ribs. Veronica watched helplessly as her uncle gasped, drowning in his own blood. Despite the firm hold on her hair, Veronica collapsed in grief, wailing, "No! No! Uncle Theo, no!"

The giant pulled his knife from Theodosius' side and swaggered towards her. He held up the crimson blade, and Veronica welcomed it. *Come, Death,* she thought, and arched her breast forward.

Pulling the blade back, the brute again bellowed, "No master but God!"

But suddenly, without thought or even breath, as though impelled by fate, Veronica exclaimed, "Baruch atta Adonai Eloheinu melech ha'olam."

The Zealot champion froze. He muttered something in the local language, then quickly reverted to Greek. "What did you say?"

Veronica translated the prophet's prayer to Greek. "Hear, O Israel, the Lord your God, the Lord is One."

His massive brow folded into deep creases. "How do you know...?"

"The Baptist taught me," she declared. "Before he gave me his blessing."

The giant rocked back on his heels. He sheathed the Iscariot in his belt. "Release her," he ordered.

The Zealot gripping Veronica's hair snorted, "Release her? We swore a ban.[67]"

The giant waved his hand dismissively, then gestured to the battlefield. Veronica followed his hand and reconnoitered the fallen. There were two masons lying in a heap. A horse had been slaughtered. Valentius, despite his bold defiance, had dropped to his knees, then rolled onto his back. Paenulus was a blackened ember and Adrianna slept beside him. Farther off, Sabinus lay dead. There were two more masons who'd been struck down. And then there was Theodosius. Her beloved uncle, the only father she'd ever known, was facedown in the dirt. The wagon was fully ablaze and crumbling. The only one who'd escaped was Salome, who, if vengeance for the Baptist had been the Zealot's incentive, may well have been the source of all this misery.

Still unsatisfied, the Zealot holding Veronica upbraided his leader, his blade firmly against her throat, "You said *like Joshua*. Joshua observed the ban."

The giant smacked the impudent zealot across the side of the head. Again. Veronica felt her hair slip free. The leader placed a massive hand gently on her shoulder and whisked her to the side.

"Joshua spared Rahab[68]," he boomed. "This one is spared... by Barabbas."

---

[67] The ban goes back to Joshua: the Israelites would not take prisoners or plunder from battle but would destroy all as a holocaust to the Lord.

The giant, the ogre, the brute, ordered his troops to withdraw.

Veronica rushed to her uncle's corpse. But what could she do? His swollen eyes stared, his tongue lolled, just as the Baptist's had. Veronica gripped her hair at the roots and pulled until her tears streamed. She threw herself on the ground a wailed, pounded the earth with tight fists, with all her soul wanting to crack that surface and open a crevasse to the underworld. But no, she had been spared. *Spared? Had mercy ever been more cruel?* Exhausted, Veronica rolled to her side, striking her elbow on cold metal: the hilt of her uncle's sword. Ecstatic, she braced the hilt on the ground and, kneeling upright, touched the tip of the blade below her ribs. In his observance of the ban, Barabbas had left the Roman sword, and so the final chore had passed to her.

Chapter 16

The point of the blade pinched her skin, and Veronica wondered if she'd positioned it properly. She wanted to end her pain, not impale herself and die slowly. What was the angle to best pierce her heart? She had to get this, her final act, right. Smoke from the wagon stung her nose and eyes. She brushed her hair from her face and looked again at her uncle's body. She took a deep breath and leaned forward onto his sword.

The burning wagon collapsed with a crash that startled Veronica and impelled her back onto her tail. The sword toppled and slapped her thigh. She grasped the blade to reset it. But looking again at Uncle Theo's body, inches from the smoldering wreckage, a thought occurred to her. She looked up at the vultures circling. Within moments, those nasty scavengers would descend to feast on her party, her family, herself. Her body was of no consequence. But the others deserved some action on her part, some ritual of closure to countermand the brutality that had declared their lives mattered naught. Of all who'd fought and died, certainly Uncle Theo should not be torn to pieces as carrion. She could save him from that at least.

Rising, Veronica staggered to her uncle's side. She could roll him, she thought. Once, twice over and he'd be lying on the smoldering wreckage. She could add twigs to build the flames. He could have — not the funeral he deserved, but enough of a pyre to consume his flesh. She knelt and grasped his

---

[68] Rahab was a woman of Jericho who protected Joshua's spies. In recognition, Joshua spared her when the Israelites took the city.

toga at the shoulder and hip, then lifted and tossed his body so he turned face up and his right arm landed on the fire. The hair on his arm sizzled and the flesh began to roast. The smell was disgusting. His face — so brutalized — forced tears to her eyes.

The fire made Veronica sweat. She grasped again at Theo's toga and heaved, rolling him facedown into the low flames. His toga ignited. Veronica dashed to the fire pit to retrieve unused wood. There was Adrianna, her body at least, her face contorted and her eyes... astonished. Paenulus had partially burned, but the flames had died out. They'd have to go into the fire. Together, as husband and wife. And Valentius. He'd been heroic. But he'd be difficult to carry. And Sabinus. He was so far away. *And what of the masons? Valentius had said they'd fight; he'd stake his life on it. And they had. Didn't they deserve some ceremony?* All right then, she must keep the fire going. She ran to the wagon and placed the twigs gently around her uncle.

Turning, she scanned the field. A committee of vultures had assembled where Sabinus lay. They hopped and waddled around his corpse and dipped their bald heads.

"Noooo!" Veronica screamed. She grabbed her uncle's sword and chased after the hellish birds, scattering them. But the sight of Sabinus, his head and faced caved in, was too revolting. She lurched forward and vomited. Turning her head away, Veronica saw the vultures had alighted at the fire. They pecked at Adrianna. She had to beat them away. *But what of Sabinus?* Could she lift him? Could she even bear to touch him?

Testing her nerves, she looked at his feet. She let her eyes proceed up his legs to his waist. On his chest, a vulture hopped and indulged himself.

"No!" she cried, and swung the sword. But it was too heavy. She slumped to her knees, and the vulture dined.

There was no saving Sabinus. *Adrianna? Maybe. She wasn't so heavy.* But the scavengers were there *en masse*. She'd have to kill them. She swung again at this vulture. It squawked, fluttered its wings and easily slipped the blow. Went right back to eating.

They were all food for vultures. Veronica's stomach heaved again. She gripped the sword, her path to peace. *But would it be peace? These bodies were mute, inert, but did they feel? Did they know they were being devoured, and were simply paralyzed, unable to stop it? Were they frozen in torment?* Was that her fate if she joined them?

Veronica tossed the sword away. Away. She couldn't watch the scavengers gorge themselves, and she wouldn't serve herself up to them. The day they'd left their burning home, her uncle had sworn that someday they would return to Rome. On this smoky field that promise had died. Veronica swallowed her grief. She prayed her family's souls would forgive her, turned and ran east towards the road.

*   *   *   *

After several miles, Veronica found a road, broad and flat, as sturdy as any Roman had built. Beyond she saw a great lake. Veronica was so hot and thirsty, the water tempted her, but her route was south. That's all she knew. Not how far or what type of terrain. But she must continue to Jerusalem, and avoid the Auxilia at all costs.

After only a short distance on the road, Veronica's feet and legs began to ache. The sun, now high above her, beat down with menace. She should try to find shade from the heat of the day, but couldn't risk discovery this close to Tiberius. The Auxilia had been there. *Looking for them?* She couldn't be sure, but neither could she assume they hadn't been. She was better off continuing down the road.

Her throat was terribly dry. Her stomach growled. She regretted not taking the pot from the fire. The broth and rabbit meat were just what she needed. She had been foolish. She'd given in to her emotions instead of thinking rationally. Adrianna may have been right that a man needs a woman's heart, but there were certainly times when a woman could use a man's practicality. What would Uncle Theo do to stay alive? First, he'd get out of the sun. Then what? Steal a horse? Uncle Theo wasn't a thief, and neither was she, but there was a law of necessity. Veronica would do whatever was necessary.

Another hour passed and Veronica felt herself beaten down. The ache in her lower back and the loud slap of her sandals against the flagstones told her she'd had enough for today. She needed a respite, some water and a meal, and then to find shelter. But this was open country; on this road, she hadn't seen another soul. And — another thing she kicked herself for — she had no money. She could have taken the jewels. The Zealots took nothing; all they'd wanted was to destroy. The bracelets were still there. Now she wondered, should she go back? She could get there before nightfall. But what would await her? Vultures. Gorged. Her loved ones picked to the bone. No, she'd keep going south.

The great lake receded over her left shoulder. The road bent east towards running water. The lake was a source for a river! Veronica had lost her hunger about an hour ago, but her thirst continued to torture her. She practically danced off the road and down the grassy slope to the riverbed. Kneeling at the bank, she splashed her face, cupped water in her hands and guzzled it, then bowed and scooped, dousing the crown of her head. *Such cooling relief!* For a moment she forgot the agony of that morning. She lay on her back on the cool grass and shaded her eyes from the sun.

It occurred to her that she'd been wrong when she'd placed that sword to her breast. Uncle Theo, Valentius, Sabinus. They'd all given their lives so that she might live. Surrendering to despair would have betrayed them; it was her duty to survive. But alone in this wilderness, what were her chances? Perhaps she should return to the wagon. Find the jewels. A knife.

Oh, but suddenly her stomach roared! She hadn't eaten a morsel since last evening. Maybe she could find some fruit trees? Grapes, maybe. She drank another scoop of water then eyed the path south. The road cleaved to the river. Maybe she could catch a fish. Weave a basket of twigs and set the opening against the current. Uncle Theo often set traps like that at the villa. He'd place them in the stream around sundown and by morning they'd have fresh brook trout. Oh, that thought reminded her how hungry she was.

Then, brushing her hair back over her left shoulder, Veronica glanced north. There were people. Not a few drawing water, but a crowd, an actual wall of people. Curious, Veronica climbed a low hill between the river and the road. A wedge of open space, between the river running north to south and the road that veered northwest, was filled with people. There must have been hundreds. Thousands.

Veronica considered her options. Continue south on the road and remain anonymous, but hungry, or venture into the crowd, where she risked exposure, but might beg a mouthful of food. Too tired and hungry to think deeply about anything, Veronica ventured closer.

It struck her that most of the people, at least these on the periphery, weren't engaged in any activity. They were spectators, but, apparently whatever they'd been watching had ended. Like theatregoers between acts, they seemed to discuss the merits of staying versus returning home. Veronica couldn't make out the local language, so she weaved through the crowd, listening for a word of Greek.

Deeper in the crowd, she encountered a young man, not much older than she, imploring people to sit. The people responded, gathering in circles of a dozen or so and sitting on the ground. The man touched Veronica's arm and nudged her towards a circle. Those people regarded her suspiciously. Her dress, from Salome's wardrobe, had a touch of Rome to it. But she did as the man bid her, crouching between a pair of heavily robed and bearded men, crossing her ankles and sitting on the grass.

Now her head started pounding mercilessly, from hunger, or the sun, or the stress of close contact with people who didn't want her around. The young man returned, a cloth sack under his arm. From the sack he withdrew a quarter loaf of bread. He handed it to a man across from Veronica and ordered him to do something. The seated man had a quizzical look on his face, but, begrudgingly it seemed, he tore a piece of bread off and passed the loaf to his left. The young man then took the tail end of a dried fish and gave it to the same seated man with the same instructions. The seated man pulled some flesh from the fish's spine and passed it also. The food went next to a mother who tore some for her two small children. A boy complained, probably that it wasn't enough, and she shushed him, passing the food on. Veronica found this rather irritating. There was hardly food for one person; there certainly wouldn't be anything left for her. She let her throbbing head hang, hoping to relieve the tension.

Then the man beside Veronica nudged her with an elbow. She opened her eyes to see the bread. A quarter of a loaf. The young man must have pulled another from his sack. She took the bread and pulled a piece off. Then the man gave her the tail end of a fish. She peeled some dried flesh away and passed it. As she chewed, Veronica noticed that the people in her circle were somehow amused. At first, she took it personally, but then realized, they were following the bread and the fish as it went around the circle. A loud, choral *"Ah!'* resounded, followed by laughter, as the bread and fish made its way back to the first recipient. He held them both out in wonderment. *Wait,* Veronica, thought. *The young man hadn't handed out more? These were the same? They'd made it all the way around the circle and... there was just as much as when they'd begun!*

The first man tilted his head, acknowledging the peculiarity of the moment, then took pieces from the loaf and the fish and passed them to the mother. She said something motherly to her son, which Veronica imagined had something to do with the virtue and reward of patience, then passed the items again. Veronica watched the food make its way around the circle. She actually started salivating; if this were true, if this were really happening, she could get more than a taste, she could truly eat. The food went around, repeatedly torn, but losing nothing of its mass. Veronica tore into the bread and fish again, passing it like before. She chewed greedily as the food completed the circuit. When it reached the starting point — intact, identical to how the young man had presented it — the circle cheered.

Veronica knew she had to be dreaming. When she'd lain down by the river, she must have fallen asleep. Now she was imagining some miracle so she could be fed. But this was too real: she felt, she tasted. *This had to be happening, and yet it couldn't be.* Veronica was the only one distressed by the apparition. Everyone else was laughing. In fact, it seemed that this was not a singular event; each of the circles in their vicinity displayed the same wonder and amusement. So the camaraderie that had spread from person to person now leapt from circle to circle.

The food made a couple more circuits until the group was sated, if not subdued. The laughter and animated conversation continued until the young man came back with a wicker basket to collect the refuse. Veronica wasn't the only one to notice the next odd occurrence: the group had more scraps to discard than the original volume of bread and fish. The young man shook his head in bewilderment, offered no explanation, but went to the next circle and repeated the task to the same effect.

The sun was dipping now towards the western hills, and people rose from their circles to go. *But go where?* Veronica thought. She had a full belly, which solved her most immediate problem, but she needed shelter. She wondered if she might get assistance from the people in her circle. They'd been suspicious when she first sat down, but breaking bread together seemed to stir warm feelings from which she didn't feel entirely excluded. In fact, some of them had perceptibly softened their attitude towards her. That was natural, she supposed; she must have been a pitiful sight. Her clothes were covered with dirt, ash and blood. Without staring directly back, Veronica tried to acknowledge that yes, she was lost, alone and vulnerable. Unfortunately, Veronica was not a lost puppy; she was obviously a foreigner. She got no takers.

Should she press the issue with this group, or work her way farther into the crowd? She might yet hear a word of Greek. Or maybe she should just go back to the road, find some people walking south and latch onto them. She looked over to the road and gasped, then crouched, ducking her head. The road was lined with Auxilia. Veronica quickly estimated their number. There had to be thirty horsemen, maybe more. Her Centurion wasn't there. *Hers? Where did that thought come from?*

Veronica straightened again and sidled back to her group. The mother was there, her hands resting on the heads of her children. She spoke to a pair of women from a neighboring circle. *They had to be mothers, too,* Veronica thought. They'd respond to a girl like herself, if they knew she were lost and alone? They chattered in that harsh, local tongue. Would they even know Greek? Would they count it against Veronica if she spoke it? There was only one thing proven to work. Veronica stepped up and said, "Hear, O Israel."

The women looked dismissively at her, then tightened their ranks.

"Hear, O Israel, the Lord your God. The Lord is One."

They stopped talking. Now they eyed her with suspicion. One of the women whispered to the mother; she seemed to think Veronica might be crazy.

"Does anyone speak Greek?" Veronica asked, trying her best to appear harmless while intoning the language of global conquerors. "Please, can anyone speak Greek?"

The women warned the mother again. She listened impassively, then shook her head. She crouched and whispered something to her son, dispatching him into the crowd. This brought impassioned protests from the other women, which the mother stifled with a flat statement and an outstretched arm. She was pointing. Veronica followed her gesture north to an elevated area, sort of a grassy mound. A bearded man stood there, common enough in appearance, conversing with a dozen or so other undistinguished men, who had baskets of scraps at their feet. The mother kept pointing at the man or men and gesturing back to her ears. As though accusing her friends of not hearing something the man on the mound had said. Chastened, the other women departed, but not without acknowledging the mother's point and appearing to wish her well.

It was a few minutes later that the son returned, pulling an older man by the hand. Looking at him, Veronica was reminded of the old trader they'd met outside Rome. He had the same bearing, the same expression, as Joseph. In Rome, he'd have been a patrician, not one of the idle schemers, but like her uncle: a man of philosophy and learning.

"I'm told a young lady wants to converse in Greek."

"Thank you," Veronica sighed. "I... I'm going to Jerusalem."

The man stroked his beard. "You're a long way off."

Veronica searched her memory. "Then Ar-in-mathea?"

"Even farther." The man gestured for Veronica to step closer. Then put up a hand for her to stop. "There's blood on your clothes and in your hair."

"My caravan." Tears welled up as images of the slaughter flooded her mind. "We were attacked. Zealots."

The man shook his head sadly, "That is the unfortunate state of Galilee. You must make your complaint to the magistrate." He raised a hand toward the road. "The Auxilia. I'll take you to them."

"No!" Veronica blurted.

The old man scrutinized her closely. "Do you have reason to fear them, young lady?" Veronica didn't answer. "Then perhaps we have reason to fear you."

"No," she practically whimpered. She looked back at the mother. Her face was tense. The man gestured as though dismissing the mother and her children. But she didn't go; she looked away from her elder back to the mound. To that man. The elder took the mother's hand and prepared to lead her away.

"Wait, please," Veronica asked. She was suddenly curious about the mother's seeming fascination. "Can you tell me, why were so many people here today?"

The man pursed his lips, and only answered after the mother nudged him. "We came to hear from a prophet."

"I met a prophet," Veronica offered. "He said, *Prepare the way, The Lord is coming.* What did your prophet say?"

The man answered firmly, "He said, *The Kingdom of Heaven is at hand. Repent and believe the good news.* Good news for Israel, not for Rome. Not for Greeks."

The mother insisted the man translate the exchange and then burst forth with a torrent of objections. After hearing more than he was willing to tolerate, the man cut her off. He waited until the woman bowed her head submissively before turning back to address Veronica.

"He also said, *I was a stranger, and you invited Me in; naked, and you clothed Me.* We live two miles to the northeast. You can spend the night. We'll figure out what to do with you in the morning."

"Thank you, sir," Veronica cried. "Thank you, so much."

He spoke again softly, "Your caravan was attacked?"

Veronica nodded.

"And you're the only survivor?"

She wiped her eyes and nodded again.

"Do you remember where?"

"Roughly. Maybe." Veronica struggled to recall her march. "Up the road to where you first see the big lake, then over west. I had the sun overhead and to my back all the way."

"We'll figure it out," he said. "Then I'll send my sons to bury your dead."

*   *   *   *

"I-I don't know how to explain it, Primus," the Optaio stammered. "They were there and then they weren't. Th-they were out in the open, then the mob closed around, and then... It was like blinking, and... whatever was there, wasn't."

Longinus fumed. "You had one assignment. Watch the Iscariot! You couldn't focus your eyes on one man?"

The Optaio hung his head. "I can't explain it, Primus."

What a day — no, two days — this had turned into! Having divided his forces and taking five octets north, he'd arrived at Herod's palace just when the guests were fleeing as though plague had broken out. After requesting to see the Tetrarch, he'd been escorted to the main vault, where he found the Tetrarch's sardonic wife viciously taunting an unresponsive head.

"Remember him," she cooed, as she lifted the inert mass from the salver. She turned the face to the Centurion, and he nodded. Yes, he recalled seeing the rabble rouser out on the streets, being rousted by the Tetrarch's guards.

"Your husband, please," Longinus pressed.

It took half an hour to locate Herod, who was besotted to the point of incoherence.

"It seems you had quite the party, Tetrarch," Longinus proffered.

"Can you find her for me?" he babbled. "I ordered my Captain of the Guard, but I'm sure he betrayed me. Thinks I'm... intemperate. But really," he looked fearfully at his wife, then back to the Centurion before whispering, "the girl must die."

"What girl is that?" Longinus asked.

"Salome!" he roared. "My niece, my stepdaughter."

"The Auxilia," Longinus stated, "does not discipline children for ineffectual parents."

"No, she's the devil, that one," Herod drooled. "Not an ordinary girl. Evil. To the core. And I'd have had her, except that Senator took her. I'm sure he did."

Longinus' eyebrows shot up, nearly flipping his helmet. "What Senator?" he asked.

"Commodius," Herod groaned. "Senator Commodius and his daughter, Antonia."

So they'd been here. Then, Longinus concluded, when the evening's entertainment had devolved to bloodlust, the Senator had whisked his *daughter* away. And somehow this Salome had gotten involved. Longinus shot off question after question which the drunken despot could not answer. *Was there anything more pathetic,* Longinus lamented, *than a weak man cloaked in the power of office?* He summoned the Captain of the Guard and examined him out of the Tetrarch's hearing. The Captain admitted letting the girl leave in the Senator's custody, for he feared murdering a child and suspected that when the Tetrarch saw the light of day, he'd grieve the girl violently and suffer from his wife's retribution. Longinus pressed him for information he might use. The Captain did reveal the Senator had declared his ultimate destination was Arimathea. They'd be traveling the King's Road.

Longinus regrouped his cavalry and charged south. They swept every town and rousted each taberna. They rode to Agrippina where they met Juvenal's five octets, who had discovered no trace of the fugitives, and so camped for the night. In the morning, they decided to retrace their steps. *Were their minor roads — even goat paths — that the wily Senator could have taken?* They'd find his turnoff with a thorough reconnoiter. But, riding north, they'd encountered something that attracted their intention: a flood of foot travelers converging on a rise of ground between the road and the Jordan River.

They stood their horses to observe the length and breadth of the assembly. There were no merchants. No troupes of minstrels or entertainers. But there did seem to be a central figure, on the crown of a hill, delivering some kind of lecture. And Longinus recognized immediately the Rabbi from the hilltop outside Capernaum. The charlatan who'd pretended to heal a leper, the *healer* before whom the gouty Primus had humbled himself. Longinus was surprised his act had survived the summer: most weeds dry out in the harsh sun.

No doubt indulgence from the old Primus had allowed this fraud to prosper. He probably viewed his orations as innocuous, even edifying for the ignorant masses. But Longinus knew this was just how civil unrest begins: lulling the masses from productive work, encouraging them to idle on the countryside and convincing them that somehow the Empire owed them their sustenance. Then once this swindler, this demagogue, had amassed enough of a following, we'd see just how harmless his intentions were. He'd had perhaps a thousand gather outside Capernaum in the spring: this crowd seemed four times that number. Longinus needed to investigate; the old Primus had technical jurisdiction, but would likely ignore any seditious activities until a full-blown revolt erupted. Then he'd frantically demand the magistrate in

Ptolemais send troops. The burden of restoring Roman supremacy would fall on Longinus, which meant it was his duty to nip rebellion in the bud.

He wanted to know the stated purpose of this event. The locals would never talk openly with the Auxilia, but certain sources, if pressed, might be fruitful. Richly dressed curiosity-seekers had the most to lose in an encounter with Roman authority. And one seemed to be leaving the event in haste.

The Rabbi had descended the hill to mingle with the crowd. There, a wealthy Galilean had thrust himself through the wall of hopefuls to present his supplication. Whatever the Rabbi had said, the rich man seemed to take as a rebuke, retreating immediately to his sedan chair and ordering his servants to port him around the mound, northwest to the road.

"Fetch me that man," Longinus ordered.

The Optaio rode with an octet and arrested the sedan chair. Its occupant turned out to be a spoiled, young fop whose tendency to cower was reminiscent of Herod's. Facts gleaned from Longinus' interrogation were intriguing, but not actionable; the Rabbi had instructed him that he needed to give away all his worldly possessions to the poor. Longinus was no philosopher, but he recognized when a charlatan was playing to the crowd, inciting the mass of *have-nots* against a lone, conspicuous *have*. Rome, of course, was the ultimate *have* and necessarily the final target. Though it would be imprudent, considering the size of the crowd, to seize this Rabbi, he certainly bore watching.

Longinus dismissed the fop and, as the sedan chair trundled away, led a dispatch of half a dozen Auxilia, on foot, from the road to a thicket of cedars a short distance from the base of the mound. Many Jews scattered. But the Rabbi himself continued his tour of hapless supplicants. Such patience with the infirm, the lunatic and the lost could only have an ulterior motive. This Rabbi was courting the affections of the mob.

The Centurion's suspicious were confirmed when he spotted some familiar faces within the Rabbi's retinue: the sly publican and the burly fisherman from that row at the tax table. They weren't fighting over assessments; they held back the crowd and filtered urgent cases forward to their leader. Then Longinus spotted the woman. She didn't mingle with the men; Jews forbade that. The Mad Hag of Magdala simply sat on the slope of the hill, her arms wrapped tightly around her raised knees. She was looking quite well; the skeletal beauty he'd discerned had borne radiant flesh. But what truly alarmed Longinus was the man a few feet removed from her. The Iscariot, Judas, reclined on the periphery, glancing back at the Mad Hag, calling in some manner she chose to ignore. He'd said he'd come north looking for a holy man; he'd been in the crowd when the Primus went searching for the healer, and here he still was in the man's company. With an entourage such as this, trouble was sure to follow.

Longinus marched his men back to the road, deliberately angling towards the Iscariot; he wanted this assassin to know he was watching. Upon reaching the road, he met Juvenal, who had two Galileans in custody. He advised Longinus to speak with them discreetly. So, the Centurion ordered his Optaio, "Keep your eye on that Iscariot."

The Galileans identified themselves as Zev and Eli, then promptly removed their tunics, revealing Legion breastplates.

"Then name Zev is Hebrew for wolf," the first spy chuckled. "And I am, as this Rabbi would attest, a wolf in sheep's clothing."

"You've studied his teachings," Juvenal laughed.

"Oh, this fellow's become quite famous," Zev admitted. "Reports of him and his crowds have attracted Pilate's attention. He ordered us north to investigate."

"You speak Aramaic?" Juvenal asked.

"I'd be a fine spy if I couldn't," he laughed.

"He can follow its meaning," Eli chided, "but don't ask him to repeat it."

"Did you get a sense of his speech?"

Zev shrugged. "Not political. The man's a philosopher. And a storyteller. They also say he heals cripples and lepers."

"And you believe it?" Longinus scoffed.

The men wagged their heads defensively.

"Those things are too easy to stage," Zev groaned. "And these people? Ignorant, superstitious lot. He's got an inner circle, roughly a dozen men. I'm sure some pass the basket while the others pick your purse."

"He has a Zealot close by," Longinus said.

"We count two," Eli amended. "There's Judas. We knew a little of him in Jerusalem, but he disappeared. Now we know where. The other one's Simon. He's a mystery."

Longinus related his encounter with Judas, including his order to leave Galilee.

"Well, don't send him back to us!" Zev laughed.

"Can't you kill him here?" Eli suggested.

Longinus drew a slow, deep breath.

"Not today," Eli chuckled. "We should wait until the numbers are in our favor."

Yes, Longinus conceded, they'd have to wait. He and Juvenal conferred with Pilate's spies into the late afternoon waiting for the crowd to disband. They withered under the sun, sitting in circles and sharing their meager food. Longinus would bide his time, track this band of rebels, find the Iscariot and slit his throat. The Iscariot's death would alert the Rabbi that his little game was over. It was time to take his magic show to another province.

But when the crowd finally dispersed, his Optaio confessed he'd lost their prey. Longinus scanned the thousands of souls walking north and south.

They'd never find the Iscariot now. Such a simple command, and his junior officer had failed. Incensed, Longinus wanted to flog the miscreant, but Juvenal reminded him of more pressing matters, in particular, the Senator.

Longinus assented. "Let's say he fled the Palace during the uproar. He gets out of Tiberius as the sun is setting, his choice is to run south on the road through the night, or find a camp before total darkness."

"If I were seeking security," Juvenal stated, "I'd want the hills to my back, so I'd only have to fight on one front."

"You'd turn off before the road broke east away from the western hills."

Juvenal nodded, "Probably."

Longinus ordered his forces north, fanning out to the east and west to carefully observe the off-road country: any disturbed ground, especially ruts dug by a heavily laden wagon. After an hour at a slow trot, they started to lose the light and soon were forced to make camp. Longinus spent a sleepless night, walking the camp and riding to the several checkpoints. Two thoughts weighed on his mind: the fate of the girl if he found her and the machinations of the magistrate within the garrison while he was away. There was a saying of Thucydides he'd learned early in his enlistment: *The State that separates scholars from warriors will have its thinking done by cowards and its fighting done by fools.* Right now, a coward was weaseling his way into the hearts and minds of the garrison's troops, while Longinus, the warrior, was being made a fool by affections he could not control. He must find the girl. But not so a careerist magistrate could advance his ambitions across her tortured body. *That body...* already he felt she was flesh of his flesh. Surely, this girl would lead him to ruin.

The next morning Longinus had his cavalry saddled before the sun had crept over the eastern hills. They continued north, and soon verified Juvenal's hypothesis. As the road cut west, deep wagon ruts were freshly carved into the soft soil.

Longinus ordered a brisk canter. By now the grass had largely recovered and only an occasional depression reminded them of the course they needed to pursue. But in the distance, the sky was smudged grey, as though a fire, starved of fuel, smoldered in obstinate malice. Longinus ordered a charge and with bold Formido under him, outpaced his riders. He spotted the remnants of a camp in the cleft of the mountain. Vultures burst into flight. Men, raking the coals of a dying pyre dropped their tools. *Raiders*? Longinus thought. *They'd slaughtered the Senator's party and now sifted through the spoils! And where was the girl? Was she a mute mass of earth? Had they drenched the grass with her blood?*

The men raised their hands in supplication; Longinus drew his sword and flexed his arm to strike.

Chapter 17

Veronica walked in silence. The only person she could actually have spoken to was the older man, who was not pleased to have her along. She was just grateful they'd taken a narrow dirt road along the lake rather than the main road where the Auxilia was. Of course, she'd have preferred to be walking south. Instead, from the lake to her right, Veronica knew she was heading back towards Tiberius. The sun was touching the crests of the western hills when they arrived at a cluster of low, mud brick buildings, which reinforced just how tenuous Veronica's position was. The first time she'd been orphaned, she'd been whisked off via chariot to her uncle's palatial townhouse. These people were literally dirt poor.

The older man introduced his sons – three men ranging from around thirteen to thirty – so she could describe the site of the ambush. The oldest son nodded, indicating with certainty that he knew the cleft in the hills with the high cliff behind it. The sons declared that, facing a march six miles there and six back, they'd rather do it in the cool of night. Though they'd have no moon, they'd take lanterns. Veronica thanked them, which they seemed to understand before their father translated. Then, as they turned to go, she remembered and blurted out, "There are jewels!"

The father raised an eyebrow.

"The Zealots took nothing. They just killed and burned. I should have taken them, but I wasn't thinking. They'll be in the wagon. What's left of it. You can have them, for your trouble."

The father seemed deeply suspicious. He spoke again to his sons, but Veronica sensed he was not simply translating. He was instructing them on some kind of precautions. They nodded obediently and departed.

The young mother – Veronica was confused about whether she was the father's daughter, his second wife or the wife of the oldest son – took Veronica down to the lake. She had a frock of coarse fabric, a towel and a pair of bowls. She gestured that Veronica would have to wash off the blood before she could enter their house. The woman recited something as Veronica scrubbed, giving the impression that this washing had to do with the family's religion. After Veronica had washed her hair, face, hands and feet, the mother helped her off with her tunic and gave her the coarse frock. The mother then scrubbed Veronica's tunic, then cleaned her own hands, reciting as she had when Veronica had washed. They returned to the house and the mother hung Veronica's tunic by the fire.

The remaining members of the family gathered and shared a small meal.

The mother implored the older man to translate again, so Veronica learned about their family. The older man's name was Judah, and he was the woman's father and a widower. He'd been a scholar and a priest of some kind, but had fallen out of favor when his religious community split over a new teaching about something called *resurrection of the dead*. A group calling themselves Pharisees rejected this notion, that a person who died could somehow rise again, or, as Veronica understood it, have his same body in the afterlife. Judah was not certain; he had studied his people's scriptures as well as many Greek texts, and he'd debated these Pharisees, who increasingly accused him of dragging pagan beliefs into their Jewish faith.

Then Judah's wife died, and the Pharisees mocked him, demanding to know if she had risen yet, or when he expected it to happen. Then, his daughter – her name was Leah – had lost her husband. He was a fisherman and had been on the big lake when a violent storm came up and capsized his boat. They'd found his body wrapped in his own nets. The Pharisees mocked Judah again for his belief in resurrection.

"Those Pharisees sound like horrible people," Veronica said.

"They are the worst kind of hypocrites," Judah said, "those that claim to know, but are afraid of questions."

So Leah had come back here with her two children to live with Judah, her two younger brothers, her middle brother's wife and their children. Veronica did a quick count: ten people. The home looked to be about three or four small rooms. These people were exceedingly generous, taking Veronica in for the night, but it was pretty clear she'd have to leave in the morning.

After the meal, Veronica volunteered to help clean up, but Leah insisted she rest by the fire, where her father was sipping tea. Judah leaned over the fire and stirred the coals. "We are living in an age of radicalism," he lamented. Suddenly weary, he stared into the smoldering embers. "All demand purity of others, but their hearts are far from pure. The Essenes are radical aesthetics. They mortify their bodies and disparage anyone who takes a moment's pleasure. The Pharisees are radical in their interpretation of the law. They lay on rules like stones then chastise anyone who buckles under the weight. The Zealots are radical nationalists. Insurrection is their religion. Until someone rebels against them! God help us if they ever take power; they'd be worse than the Romans."

Veronica was beginning to understand why four thousand people had gathered around that hill. "What about the prophet you saw today?" she asked. "Is he also a radical?"

Judah nodded. "He preaches a radical love."

Leah tapped Veronica on the shoulder; it was time to retire. The interior of the house was stuffy, almost airless. The room was draped off into separate sleeping quarters. Leah showed Veronica to a small cot; a sack mattress stuffed with straw on a wooden frame, crisscrossed with rope. For comfort it was little better than the floor, but Veronica was so exhausted, she fell immediately into a deep sleep.

After a few hours, Veronica woke with a start, her heart battering her ribs. *What?* She gasped for breath and wrapped her arms around herself, trying to calm down. What had been in her dream? She saw the images again: faces. The horribly brutalized faces of the dead. *They'd come back.* They were looking for her. They were crying for revenge. As she shivered, it occurred to Veronica that maybe resurrection wasn't a very good idea.

She looked through the tiny window high in the mud brick wall. The sky was still dark. She had to get back to sleep. She couldn't afford to be dead on her feet when she left this village tomorrow. She needed to have her wits about her and all her strength at her disposal. But every time she closed her eyes, she saw the faces of the dead: Adrianna, Paenulus, Sabinus, Valentius and Uncle Theo. They were truly gone, and she'd never see them again. Veronica stifled a desperate wail and cried herself back to sleep.

She awakened some hours later. A narrow shaft of light cut through the small window. Something was jabbing at her foot. Sharp, like – *a scorpion!* She sat up, pulling her legs to her chest. The shaft of light turned silver. A breastplate. The point of a sword touched her knee. The Centurion had found her.

*   *   *   *

Longinus had charged the smoking camp hoping to draw Zealot blood. But these men weren't raiders. They carried spades, not swords. And there were only two. *Opportunists? They'd seen the attack then come to pick over the remains?* He'd have struck them down for that, but rather than defend themselves, these cowards fell prostrate on the ground. One dove into a shallow trench he'd been digging. Longinus couldn't have swung at them without falling out of his saddle.

"Identify yourselves," he demanded as the Auxilia formed an arc behind him.

Without picking his face up out of the hole, one cried, "I am Aaron ben Judah of Ammathus. This is my brother, Ephraim."

"What are you doing here?"

"A work of mercy, that's all. Our father commanded us to bury the dead."

Longinus surveyed the area. These men had been busy. He counted the fresh mounds scattered around the field. Seven. Maybe more. The wind changed and he caught the sharp stench of decay. Vultures were picking at the carcass of a horse. Longinus swung down from Formido. He jabbed his sword at the man's backside.

"Get up. Out of that hole or I'll put you there permanently."

"You'll want to see this, Primus," Juvenal called. He was standing at the charred wood pile that had been a wagon. As Longinus approached, Juvenal raked the tip of his sword through the ashes, exposing blackened bones. A shriveled hand bore a signet ring.

"Take the hand," Longinus whispered. "Put it in a sack. It will stand as proof the Senator is dead."

"And that we failed to arrest him on our first encounter."

Longinus disregarded the remark. "Did you bury a girl?" he asked Aaron.

"We found a woman. We couldn't tell her age. The vultures had got at her."

Longinus had to collect himself. Even with all the battle he'd seen, that image was hard to bear.

"What color was her hair?" Juvenal asked, as he scooped the black hand into a pouch.

"It burned off," the other brother blurted. "She was at the camp fire. Her head must have fallen into the fire."

Longinus looked at the mound near the fire pit. "Dig her up."

The men moaned. "Please, sir, don't ask that! Please!"

He grabbed the older brother by the back of the neck and threw him toward the grave. "Dig her up."

The man fumbled with his spade. He trembled. "It's a desecration."

"Desecration?" Longinus roared. "Murder is desecration! And how do I know you weren't in on this? That your Zealot friends didn't leave you behind to clean up?"

"Zealots don't bury their victims," Aaron cried. "They leave them rotting in the sun as trophies. And warnings."

"Yes," Juvenal interjected. "They're quite like Rome in that regard."

Juvenal tied the pouch with the hand in it to his saddled and sidled towards Longinus. He spoke gently, with no irony to his tone. "Let it go, Gaius. You know Zealots don't take prisoners. A young girl against those barbarians? What chance had she?"

"There should be two girls," Longinus rasped. "You're forgetting Salome. Two girls. And we have one female body. And only one horse."

Juvenal nodded. "All right. But let's have our men do the digging. These Jews have a phobia about dead bodies. Wouldn't hurt to show some cultural sensitivity."

Longinus pursed his lips, then assented with a nod. This was why he needed Juvenal: as a moderating force. The Princeps ordered a handful of men off their horses; a pair to dig up the woman and two more to bury the Senator. Longinus surveyed the battle scene. The Senator had put his party in a defensible position, except from above. Apparently there'd been a landslide, which Longinus recognized as a Zealot tactic. They would hide in the hills and dislodge boulders, setting them precariously at the edge. When any perceived enemy came by, they'd rain the rocks down. When others in the party attempted to give aid, the murderers would attack. They'd set these traps months in advance, waiting for just the right moment to spring them.

Longinus walked out of the cleft with its steep walls, around to the side of the hill. He found the path where the attackers must have come. Well worn, but recently disturbed, where heavy feet had torn divots of grass and moss. He needed to send some troops up there now to reconnoiter. That's something he should have done immediately. Once again, he'd been too hot to engage. He didn't think.

Longinus called his Optaio forward to order an octet up the hill, when a small rock came skipping down. The soldiers drew their swords. The octet dismounted and he commanded them forward. Then Longinus heard someone yelling above his orders: the older brother crying out. Juvenal restrained him with an open hand on his chest. *What was he yelling?*

"He's just a boy! The soldiers frightened him!"

Longinus sent the Optaio and octet up the path.

"Micah!" the brother cried. "Micah!"

Within a few seconds the Optaio brought Micah forth by the scruff of the neck. He appeared to be thirteen or fourteen years old.

"What were you doing up there?" Longinus demanded. When he got no answer, he swatted the boy under the chin, clamped his jaw in his hand and flipped his face upward. "What were you doing?"

"Nothing. Hiding."

"Hiding?" Longinus scoffed. "When I was your age I walked eighty miles to enlist in the Roman Legion. But you hide. Worse than a frightened girl."

"You'll want to see this, Primus," the Optaio interjected. "We followed his tracks all the way up. This was under some scrub." The Optaio handed Longinus a scrolled velvet cloth, singed at the edges. He recognized it immediately as the false merchant's wares.

"So while your brothers dig graves, you loot gold and jewels."

The boy turned white with fear.

"I—I—"

"You what?" Longinus roared. He gave the boy the back of his hand, knocking him to the turf and bloodying his nose.

"I didn't hide it for me," he wept. "I saved it for her."

*　　　*　　　*　　　*

It didn't take long to get the full story from the brothers. A mysterious girl in Romanesque dress, smudged with soot and blood, had evoked their sister's sympathy. The father, who spoke some Greek, learned the girl's story and sent his sons on this fool's errand. She'd told them about the jewels, and though she said they could have them, they'd intended to return them so that she could pay her passage wherever she was going.

Longinus asked if any of the brothers could ride. As was typical of their useless race, they could not. So he marched them in earnest back to

Ammathus. Around noon, as they approached a half mile of the town, Longinus conferred with Juvenal on tactics.

"I'd recommend holding the brothers here," the Princeps suggested, "rather than alerting the whole town about whose house we intend to raid."

And then what? Longinus wondered. He finds her. Takes hold of her. He has in his arms the girl who's haunted his mind these long days and nights, and he does *what?*

"How many riders do you want?" Juvenal asked.

"None."

Juvenal almost groaned audibly. "Primus. Gaius. Think this through. Either let the girl go or..."

"It's too late to let her go!" Longinus snapped. "At the camp — if I could have exhumed that body and declared to the men, *this is she* — I could have stopped. But now, they know. And the spy in these ranks is salivating at the malice he can spread. Unless she's found."

"Then commit to taking her," Juvenal relented. "And all that goes with it."

Longinus nodded and braced himself. He brought the eldest brother forward and got a detailed description of the home and directions to it. Then he struck his heels against Formido's ribs and cantered toward Ammathus.

He found the house quite easily. The sister, Leah, was outside at the fire pit, breaking sticks with a light hatchet. She heard Formido's hooves clop on the stony path and looked up. She dropped the hatchet, perhaps thought about running, then simply slouched and wept.

"Where is she?" Longinus asked.

Without raising her head, as if ashamed to witness her betrayal, she extended her right arm and pointed to the door. Longinus stepped inside, pausing as his eyes adjusted to the dim light. Just a few feet away, on a cot beneath a small window, the girl lay on her side. A shaft of light struck her shoulder; her tousled hair was electrum. Though deep in slumber, her aspect was troubled. Longinus yearned to soothe her anxious brow with tender kisses above her eyes. He thought he might kneel beside her, stroke her hair, drape the locks behind her ear and whisper gently that it was time to rise. He'd gather her into his arms, secure. But that was vain hope, contrary to reality. Her right foot protruded from the bed cover. The Centurion unsheathed his sword and pressed the tip against the sole of her foot. He maintained the pressure until she awakened with a start.

The fear in her eyes distressed him, but he consciously set his features so as not to reveal his weakness. After a moment of high tension, she capitulated, slightly bowing her head and shoulders. She was his. Longinus nearly swooned. Not since he'd first seen the horror of battle had his heart so raced and his knees so threatened to buckle. This was fifteen years of questing come to fruition.

"May I have your sword?" she asked.

"Excuse me?"

"After the attack, I knew my duty. I made excuses not to carry it out." She pivoted and planted her feet on the floor. She sat erect at the edge of the cot. "I convinced myself that it would dishonor those who died protecting me. Suicide."

Longinus swayed back on his heels.

"My mother swallowed fire. Like Portia. I resented her; I thought she'd abandoned me. But it was her duty."

The girl was in earnest. Yet unemotional. But this was an assault against reason.

"So you want my sword?" Longinus scoffed.

She turned her face toward him and stated bluntly, "I know what happened to the daughters of Sejanus."

Longinus did not. But, from context, he could imagine.

"I am also a virgin. They cannot execute me until they... alter that fact."

Her tears stained the dirt floor.

Gaius, you are a fool, he said to himself. He'd completely blocked out the inevitable. But she hadn't.

"You're not going to die," he said.

"Tell that to Macro."

Her eyes struck like a stone between his.

"Rome is... constantly issuing orders," he answered. "Then, contradicting itself. Bold proclamations followed by disavowals. My orders are simply to escort you..."

"To an evening of theatre?" She slid from the cot and knelt on the dirt floor. Her face was implacable, but her eyes entreated. "Give me your sword."

"You shall arrive unmolested at Ptolemais. I give my word."

"And from Ptolemais to Rome? Where will you be then?"

His throat had gone dry. *This girl would be his absolute doom.* "Where were you headed?" he asked. "Where would you have gone if I hadn't found you?"

"I don't think I should answer that."

"Oh," he barked, "you'd rather fall on my sword than have a conversation!"

The girl rose from the floor and sat again on the edge of the cot.

"My cousin Claudia is married to the Prefect of Judea."

"Pontius Pilate."

"Yes," the girl nodded. "We were going to Jerusalem."

It was all as the Magistrate had stated. Yet, if Caesar — or *Macro* — knew she'd fly to Pilate, why not simply order Pilate to deal with her? Did they think the Prefect would choose family over duty? It would be simpler to dispatch her in Galilee. Had the Magistrate already planned her *reception*? Jerusalem was her only chance, whether the Pilate welcomed her or not. Longinus sheathed his sword, then pulled the velvet scroll from his belt. He unrolled it on the cot. Three gold pieces caught the sunlight. He turned to the girl. Her eyes were wide.

"One of these will pay your passage to Jerusalem," he explained. "I need to surrender the others or I'll be flogged for looting." He smiled graciously, but the girl remained impassive. He took at gauntlet from the cloth and dangled it before her. After a moment's hesitation, she extended her hand and let him slip the piece from her fingers to her wrist. "If you'll permit me, I must withdraw." He rolled the cloth again, and tucked it into his belt. Then he took her hand and bid her to stand before him.

"You'll tell no one that I found you. Until you reach Jerusalem. Then, if Pilate receives you warmly, tell him of this mercy."

The girl tilted her face upwards into the shaft of sunlight. She was radiant. Her golden brown tresses, her green eyes dashed with hazel flecks and her delicate, trembling lips. He dropped his mouth towards hers until...

A slap rattled his jaw.

"You killed my uncle!" she cried. Her fist beat on his shoulders and chest. "He couldn't fight. He was twice the swordsman, but he..." Longinus grabbed her wrists and stared into her eyes, red with rage. "He couldn't hold a sword. You broke his wrist!"

Longinus pushed her onto the cot. *What was this insanity? Didn't she understand, he'd given her life back!*

"You had no reason to fight him. It was all a game to you. The Zealots didn't kill him, *you* did!"

This was not how he wanted to part. *She needed to be calm. Quickly, compose herself. How long must he endure her angry rants?*

"I hate you!" she screeched, and Longinus gave her the back of his hand, knocking her from the cot to the floor. This princess of Rome had the heart of a barbarian. She belonged among the Mad Hags of Galilee. He wanted to grab a fist of her hair, crush her into the dirt floor and prove himself her conqueror. Then he watched her crumple and sob. Such weakness was infectious; he had to withdraw.

Chapter 18

After the Centurion left, Leah appeared at the door. Veronica was immobile; she lay on the floor and cried herself out. Leah knelt beside her, a gesture of comfort, which said volumes despite their inability to communicate. They went out to the fire and Leah gave Veronica some food. Veronica dipped a piece of coarse bread into a bowl and scooped up a mouthful of lentil stew. It was a bland, meager breakfast, but her stomach welcomed it. Looking at the sky, Veronica realized half the day was gone, and she still had no plan.

As she ate, the brothers returned, looking much worse for whatever ordeal the Auxilia had put them through. The oldest made no secret of his displeasure. He exchanged brusque words with Leah, who nodded grudgingly and seemed to sue for patience. He walked away, visibly disgusted, to a house farther up the street where a woman with young children greeted him.

The middle and younger brother were no friendlier. They went into the house, no doubt to sleep. Veronica feared they might reemerge and chase her away with sticks and stones, but the afternoon faded into dusk without further incident. Veronica assisted Leah with her chores; she plucked and quartered a small game bird for the crock. Leah seemed determined to drill her native language into Veronica's brain. She made her repeat the words for *bird, feather, knife, pot.* For *fire, cut, hand, stone.*

As the sky darkened, Judah returned home. Veronica thought the warring siblings would ambush him, but without the eldest to lead them, the other brothers seemed no match from Leah. Thus, the evening meal began in earnest. The men washed their hands, muttering what Veronica took for a prayer. Then the family stepped inside the house to the small common area, sitting on the floor around a low table. Each person got a bowl with lentils and warm broth. There were no implements; bread was broken and passed around the circle, reminiscent of the previous day, and each person used the bread to pick up pieces of fish and vegetables from a platter in the center. There was not an abundance of food, but it seemed that each ate a sufficient amount.

After the meal, Leah and Veronica brought the dishes out to the fire for cleaning. Judah reclined and talked with his sons, most likely about their adventures of last night. After what seemed a very long time, Judah emerged from the home. Leah went to work on him, pleading her case, but Judah listened only briefly, then raised his hand to stifle the discussion. He sat by the fire and gestured for Veronica.

"You are not the daughter of a Greek merchant," he said.

"No."

"You are, in fact, the daughter of a Roman Senator."

"No," Veronica said. "I'm actually the daughter of a Roman soldier. The Senator I was traveling with was my uncle."

Judah tipped his head to one side, conceding the distinction while questioning whether it made any difference. "And the Romans are hunting you."

"Yes," she admitted, "but not for anything we did. Caesar is... I don't know, insane? Evil?"

"Perhaps both," Judah said. "But what I must ask, for my family's safety, is whether Caesar is determined. Myself, I see little to be gained in chasing teenage girls across continents. But I am not Caesar."

Veronica had no answer. Caesar had taken everything. He'd destroyed their home. And still that wasn't enough. She wondered if Caesar's wrath had reached as far as Judea, if Claudia had been implicated or if anything had happened to Pontius. What if Macro had recalled him to Rome? Would she arrive in Jerusalem to find Claudia gone? What would she do then, a Roman girl alone in a barbarous country?

Judah stirred the coals with a stick, uncovering bright, orange embers. Tendrils of smoke rose, wafting into the grey fibers of his beard. His heavy brow loomed above his eyes like storm clouds on the sea. Veronica imagined her fate was preordained; whether by political scheming, the forces of nature, the cynical manipulations of uncaring gods, or some combination of the three didn't much matter.

She remembered many talks she'd had with Uncle Theo about people's relationships to the gods. Some thought men were simply pawns in a great game for the gods' amusement. Uncle Theo rejected that notion and felt that any trials men endured presented them with a choice: to respond with virtue or vice. Those who consistently chose virtue became good people, those who chose vice became evil. Uncle Theo had said his girls should never shrink from life's challenges, because without them, without the choice of doing good or evil, they could never become truly good. He'd told them the story of Pandora, the first woman the gods created, whom they lavished with wonderful gifts. They'd also given her a jar containing all the ills of the world, which, foolishly, she opened. Seeing the horrors of war and disease she'd unleashed, Pandora fell into deep despair. But her jar wasn't yet empty; it contained a faint flicker of light, which announced itself as hope.

Veronica knew that even if her journey were all for Olympian sport, if she were a pawn in a game that was already lost, she still had some obligation to keep playing. As long as she could move, breathe, run, reason... she had to embrace hope. It might only be Pandora's faint consolation, or a frightened girl convincing herself she had a chance, but she needed to respond to that flicker of light and, like Judah stirring the coals, make it glow brighter.

Veronica reached her right arm up her left sleeve to the point between her triceps and shoulder. She pulled the gauntlet down her arm and held it tightly in her fist.

"I need to get to Jerusalem," she said. "If you can sell this, you can help your family, and I can pay my passage." Veronica reached across the fire and slipped the gauntlet from her fingers to his. The old man looked at the gold, the inlaid rubies and sapphires.

"There is no one in this village who could buy such a prize," he said. Then he raised his index finger as if to point to an idea that had just materialized.

"My brother Jacob is a merchant; he travels from Alexandria to Persia. Well, not so far anymore, because like me, he's gotten old. But he has traveled the world, he's seen wonders and he always has in his stores the most fabulous items. We see him twice a year, very regularly. He is due in three or four months."

Three months? Veronica's heart sank.

"Now," The elder continued. "Leah is afraid to send you away. Terrible things can happen to a girl alone. But Leah says you're a good student; she can teach you to speak Aramaic. I think she just wants another woman around. She is mourning her husband. And frankly," he whispered, "she does not care for Aaron's wife."

"And he doesn't want me here," Veronica sighed.

Judah smiled, "You let me handle him! My sons are good men, but presently without occupation. Being idle is not good for men. Remember I told you Leah's husband drowned? That boat belonged to Aaron; he fished with Ephraim and sometimes Micah. It was heavily damaged in the storm. For months, Aaron has hoped to get the money to repair it, but what little work he gets is just enough to feed his wife and children."

Judah took a small knife from his belt and leaned into the light. He used the tip of the knife to delicately pry back the tines that held a ruby in place. He popped the stone out and held it in the light. "I shall take this stone to a man in town, and secure a loan against it. Aaron will repair his boat. He'll be happy and leave you alone. When Jacob comes, he will redeem the stone, we'll put it back in the gauntlet and you can be on your way."

"On my way?" Veronica asked.

"With Jacob!' he smiled. "Oh, he's an old crank — even grumpier than I am! Because he is sophisticated — speaks ten different languages — he thinks he has license to be rude. But he's a good man. He won't cheat you. And you can help him. Pretty girls attract customers. And see that he eats well. He's never had a woman to look after him."

Veronica felt like she was back with Uncle Theo, arranging her marriage! She tried to interrupt Judah, but he was rolling like a boulder down a steep hill. "And he'll be going to Jerusalem. Goes every year for Passover. Not that he's religious, but he does a great deal of business."

"I-I'm not sure..." Veronica sputtered.

"But let me say one thing." Judah's tone became very grave. "I'm not putting my family at risk for you," he said firmly. "If the Romans inquire, we will not hide you. I sent my sons to bury your dead, because they've been idle and men need work to make them feel like men. But they met with humiliation. Your soldiers made them feel less than men."

"Not my soldiers," Veronica insisted.

"Still, humiliation is not death. Tomorrow they will wake up and the sun will shine and they will forget their embarrassment. But I won't have them crucified. No one wakes up from that."

Veronica nodded, even though — that word again — she didn't understand. And she was not convinced that her best route to Jerusalem was to play nursemaid to his aging brother. "Judah," she started tactfully, "how can you be certain Jacob will want me with him?"

"Oh, don't be silly, young lady," he chuckled. "I know my brother," he averred confidently. "I know he'll agree this is the best plan for all involved!"

*   *   *   *

"That's the most idiotic idea I've ever heard!" Jacob shrieked.

Veronica's heart sank. All these months, everything had gone according to Judah's plan: he'd gotten the loan against the ruby, Aaron had repaired his boat and was catching more fish than ever. Consequently they all ate better, and were much merrier. Aaron even took to calling her *Bracha*, a girl's name that meant *blessing*, which she knew because she'd made great progress in learning their language. Leah taught her Aramaic, their spoken language, and some Hebrew, the language of their formal prayers. Veronica had joined in their prayers before and after meals, and had gone with the family to their place of worship on the day they called Sabbath.

She found their religion intriguing, because it was so connected to their history. In the Roman religion, the gods were in their place and the people in theirs, and the stories were usually about what happened among the gods before there were any people. Occasionally, someone like Homer or Virgil would make up a story about gods interacting with humans, but everyone took it for what it was: fanciful adventure. These people believed their god was active in their history, and was on their side. He had freed them from slavery, helped them in wars and given them specific laws to live by. Veronica wasn't sure those laws were much different from the rules her uncle had taught her, but if they'd really come from a god, that seemed more impressive than being thought up by some Stoic philosophers. *Still*, she wondered, *if the god that created the world favored these people, why had they been conquered, and why were they so poor?*

There'd been difficult days and nights, too. Veronica was still troubled in her sleep. She'd wake up screaming, but not remember what had frightened her. Leah would emerge through the curtains and kneel at Veronica's cot. She spoke soothingly and stroked her hair. And it wasn't just bad dreams that plagued Veronica. Fits of anger would come over her. She was cleaning a fish one day, scraping the scales off, when a wave of anger came over her and she just started smacking the fish with the side of the knife. Slapping turned to stabbing, until she shredded the flesh. She was about to plunge the blade into her thigh when Leah grabbed her wrist.

Veronica hoped her rage was finite, like firewood that would burn itself out, but feared it was more like the sea beyond Ammathus that drained into the river, but kept replenishing itself. Leah promised that things would get better with time, but Veronica sensed that was her hope for her own future.

As the third new moon started to wax, the household began to anticipate Jacob's arrival. Leah worked Veronica harder on vocabulary and numbers, and drilled her intensely about money. Leah had very few actual coins: copper ases, bronze semis and bronze quadrans from Rome and bronze prutahs and lepta from Galilee. But they used stones to represent more valuable coins like the Roman denarius and the Jewish shekel. Leah would tell Veronica she was buying an item for such and such a price, give Veronica a coin and challenge her to make change. It was frustrating and mentally fatiguing, but Leah insisted that Jacob was a very precise merchant and wouldn't tolerate a slow assistant.

Veronica applied herself, but she doubted intricate counting would be necessary. She imagined working for the merchant Joseph. She wouldn't be selling wares and handling money; she'd be feeding the mules and brushing them down at night, preparing the fire and cooking meals.

Excitement built as Jacob's arrival grew imminent. Leah chattered so rapidly that Veronica couldn't keep up. The treasures, the clothes, the spices, the perfumes. Veronica wondered where his caravan would camp. Would a servant come to announce his arrival? *On a camel?* Veronica had never even seen a camel. But she'd heard they were almost twice as tall as horses. *What would it be like to sit atop one of those beasts and gallop over the open country?*

Now Veronica was bubbling with excitement. Not only to travel comfortably, well protected, in a merchant's caravan, but to finally go to Jerusalem. And to see Claudia! *Finally!* That is, unless something terrible had happened. But Veronica wouldn't allow herself to think that. She'd had enough suffering for the two of them. There had to be some balance of good and evil in the world, so Veronica figured fortune must be favoring Claudia and Pontius. There were only two things that truly troubled Veronica's mind: having to tell Claudia about Uncle Theo and having to leave Leah and her family. Still, when Micah came running into the yard announcing that Jacob was on his way, Veronica's heart soared. The good fortune that had begun when she'd sat down in that circle on the plain to break bread had reached its fruition. The gods had truly blessed her.

Veronica ran to the road with the rest of the family and looked up the hill toward the center of town. There were no camels. No mules. No wagons. There was a small man crouched on a two-wheeled cart, tapping a short stick on the rump of a tired ox. A small tethered donkey trailed behind. Veronica caught her heart in her mouth. *Jacob? He wasn't a merchant. This man was a peddler!*

*   *   *   *

The immediate disappointment Veronica felt swelled to grief when Jacob rebuked Judah after dinner. He spun the gauntlet, still missing the one ruby, around on his finger like a child's toy.

"Yes, it's beautiful, but what would I do with it?" his voice creaked. "I sell trinkets, not treasures. That's why the bandits leave me alone. And what would I do with a girl?"

"Think of what she could do for you," Judah suggested. "She's young, she has energy. She's very smart for a girl."

"I'm too old..."

"It's because you're old that you should have an assistant."

"Assistant?" he squealed. "Have you looked at her? Or are your eyes gone from copying scrolls all day? The bandits would come out of the hills for that one. Slit my throat and carry her off. You want I should have an assistant? Give me a boy. Give me Micah with a sword."

Judah sighed audibly. He stirred the fire. "You're tired. We'll revisit this in the morning."

"And she's a pagan," Jacob hissed. "Let's not forget that."

"She's an orphan," Judah corrected. "What does the Torah command about orphans?"

Jacob smirked. His silence wasn't exactly surrender, but was at least a grudging admission that his brother had a point.

Morning came, and as promised, Judah revisited the subject of Veronica. Aaron, after a long night of fishing, interrupted them with a gift of a large tilapia. "I tell you, Uncle Jacob, Bracha is good luck. She brings wealth to those who show her kindness." He cradled the fish in his arms below Jacob's nose. "She may not seem like good luck at first; in fact," — he pretended to prick his finger on the spiny dorsal fin — "she may invite some peril. But in the end? A blessing! And look, she can clean the fish, cook the fish!"

Aaron placed the tilapia on a large platter. Leah handed a knife to Veronica and prompted her to cut along the belly. Jacob was unimpressed. "Who'd have thought a pagan could wield a knife?" he snarled. And so another day passed, with Veronica no closer to Jerusalem.

The next morning, after a breakfast of bread and lentil stew, Jacob announced that he was leaving. He'd done enough business in this small town; he wanted to get to Jerusalem in time for Passover. Judah tried one more time to convince his brother to take Veronica along, but the peddler refused.

"I did, however, redeem this for you," he said, holding up the loose ruby. "I'm glad to be of assistance when and where I can. You can repay me the next time I come."

He handed the stone to Judah and turned to take his leave. A shout from Leah stopped him in his tracks.

"No!" she roared. "If you don't do this, you will not come back! This girl is alone in the world. If you cannot find it in your heart to help her, you're not welcome here."

Jacob was dumbfounded. He tried to laugh off the admonition. "I...? Not welcome?"

Leah crossed her arms tightly over her chest. Jacob stared at his niece, then turned, raising a petulant brow to his brother.

"I don't care what father says," Leah insisted. "I keep this house; if I say you're not welcome, you're not."

Judah tipped his head to the side and hunched one of his shoulders, conceding defeat.

Jacob tossed his hands and turned his back. But he did not walk away. Instead, he glared sharply at Veronica. "When we sell the gauntlet, I get half."

Veronica's heart leapt. She nodded, speechless.

Jacob stuck out his hand and reclaimed the ruby from Judah. He held out his palm for Veronica to hand over the gauntlet. After pressing the ruby back into place, he hiked his thumb over his shoulder toward the cart. "Hitch the ox, Jezebel."

She skipped past happily, practically singing back to him, "It's *Veronica*."

Jacob mimicked her, "It's *Delilah*."

Leah helped Veronica get the ox in place, then with tears in her eyes, hugged her tight.

"You've been so kind," Veronica said. "I don't even know why."

"That day on the plain," Leah whispered, "the Master said, *Blessed are they who mourn, for they shall be comforted.* I was mourning. You were. Comforting you has given me comfort." Leah placed a sheathed knife in Veronica's hand. "Keep this with you. Just in case."

Jacob trudged to the cart and took his seat on the bench in front. He waved his bony fingers towards the other end. "You can sit in the back, or on the ass, Bathsheba."

Leah shook her head and laughed silently. "Pay him no mind." She kissed Veronica's cheek once again, and the cart rumbled.

*   *   *   *

The journey by ox cart was no faster than on foot. Veronica walked most of the time, because the cart was so cramped and uncomfortable, and the donkey seemed so old it would be cruel to sit upon him. She tried conversing with Jacob, but he wasn't eager to chat. She discovered his linguistic skills were just another thing his relatives had inflated. For all his travel, Jacob's Greek was not as fluent as his rustic brother's. Plus, he was used to being alone on the trail, so communication did not come naturally.

They spent the night in the open country, setting up camp near the river. Jacob's tent was small and Veronica was unsettled at the thought of sharing it with him. The prospect seemed to make him equally nervous; as they ate, he pointed to the sky and said, "I love to sleep under a canopy of stars. But, you, girl, you shouldn't be out in the night air." So, Veronica had the tent to herself.

Jacob was up before dawn and woke Veronica. "I can cook for myself. Always have. But since you're along, I suppose you should do something."

So, as Jacob brought down the tent, Veronica built up the fire. She boiled some water, adding grain, dates and olive oil to make a thick porridge. Jacob snarled before tasting it, grunted throughout, but finished his bowl. They loaded the cart and headed back toward the road.

They traveled another day before reaching their first town, Agrippina, named a few years ago when everyone expected she'd be an Empress. Like Tiberius to the north, it was not a town fit for royalty. Veronica attempted to set up Jacob's wares as she'd seen baubles displayed in countless bazaars, but he disapproved and insisted she watch him rather than damaging his trade. They did very little business and by mid-afternoon had reloaded the cart and left the town.

They continued south on The King's Road — another highly exaggerated title — and camped close to the river. Around noon on the next day, they came to their second town, which Jacob called Salim. It opened into a large plaza around a community well. Jacob commanded Veronica to draw water for the ox as he unloaded his wares. Veronica wondered whom they might sell to. The place was deserted.

"Where is everyone?" she asked.

Jacob pulled a flat board from the cart and began attaching legs to construct a table.

"What draws the yokels from their homes?" he groaned. "Perhaps someone's given birth to a two-headed goat."

He stood the table up and covered it with a ragged cloth. Veronica started arranging the trinkets according to Jacob's practice. Jacob held his criticism and opened his cache of oils. He pulled a finely crafted bottle out of his stores and waved Veronica over.

"Here, this perfume," he said, "A little on your hands, just a little, then run them through your hair. Let the people smell the fragrance."

Veronica did as requested and found the scent very appealing. Like lilac trees in bloom. But she was afraid it would be wasted, since there still wasn't a soul on the street. It had to have been half an hour before someone came their way, a distinguished man, finely dressed by the standards of the area.

"Have you any medicines?" the man asked.

"No, no," Jacob answered, "That's not something I dabble in."

"Any jars?"

Jacob raised an eyebrow quizzically. "Jars of what?"

"Anything," the man stated flatly. "Anything imported."

Jacob reached back toward the table and grabbed the bottle of perfume.

"I have this," he said. "It's fragrance." Jacob took Veronica's hand and held it out towards the man, who waved her away dismissively.

"How much?" he asked.

Jacob hesitated. "Twenty... five? Shekels."

"Done," the man declared. He took coins from his purse and dropped them into Jacob's palm. He then placed the bottle inside his tunic and walked straight away.

Veronica was suddenly agitated. "What's he going to do?" she wondered aloud. "He wanted medicine."

"He paid. What he does with it is his affair."

That didn't satisfy Veronica. *The man was up to something.* She watched him walk toward a large house with a stone foundation, at three stories tall a palace by local standards. *What was he up to?* Veronica dashed from the cart down the street. She could hear Jacob calling behind her, "Hey... you... *girl*, come back! Bracha! Whatever your name is!"

As Veronica approached the house she slowed her pace. The home had once been splendid but had fallen into disrepair. She paused to let the man enter, then ran to the door. She listened for a moment, then tested the latch. The door opened easily, and Veronica slipped inside.

She felt her heart flutter in her chest. She knew this was wrong — she was, after all, acting like a burglar — but her senses told her — *Oh if only she had such keen senses months ago!* — that something was wrong. She crept to the foot of the stairs where she could hear voices from the next floor. She placed a foot lightly on the first step and climbed.

She heard the man speak distinctly and dramatically, like a trained orator. "Now, I questioned this merchant very thoroughly and he assured me his clients have had great results with this elixir. Wounds that would not heal, mysterious bruises, and conditions like yours. All cured."

Soft whispers followed which Veronica couldn't make out. She reached the second floor landing, separated from the room by a sheer veil. Veronica peered through the cloth to see a woman, ghastly pale with ashen grey hair, reclining on a couch, apparently too weak to stand. The man stood beside her, holding the jar of perfume.

The woman tipped her head forward to speak. "What about the man from Nazareth?"

"Please, don't trouble your mind with him."

"But I've heard stories. Miracles in Capernaum. That's not so far away. If I could... find him."

"Tales told by washwomen," he scoffed. "To entertain and confuse the gullible. You'd risk what remains of your health and for nothing. Listen to what I'm saying." His voice was rich with feigned sentiment. "This may finally be the answer to your bleeding. You can have your strength back. Your vigor. Perhaps even conceive a child."

The woman's face brightened. Veronica recognized the flicker of hope.

"And," the man continued, "in light of our long relationship, I'm happy to give this to you for the very price I paid. Only two hundred shekels."

So that was it, Veronica fumed. *Pretending to be a doctor, offering phony medicine to rob a sick woman!*

The woman seemed to weep, "So this is finally the cure?"

The man smiled unctuously. Reaching down to caress her shoulder, he vowed, "I'm so pleased to say, finally, yes."

That was all she could take. Veronica threw aside the curtain and sprang forward.

"He's lying!" she declared.

The man turned crimson. "What are you doing here?"

Veronica knelt at the bed. "It's perfume," she said. "He bought it from us. Look, I have it on my hands."

The false doctor grabbed Veronica by the wrists and whipped her against the wall. He fastened his hands around her throat.

"I should strangle you right here," he spat.

But Veronica was ready. She didn't even try to pry his fingers off; she unsheathed the knife Leah had given her and slashed the back of the doctor's hand. He screamed and released her. Veronica held the blood-stained knife out ready to jab. Defeated, the doctor fled, and Veronica turned to the wasted figure on the bed. Veronica sheathed her knife and knelt beside her. The woman's lips were trembling.

"I always suspected. But I wanted to believe."

"I'm sorry," Veronica whispered.

*　　　　　　*　　　　　　*　　　　　　*

Veronica returned to the cart, convinced she had done the right thing, but no happier for having done it. Now she trembled, worrying the phony doctor might return. Would he bring men with him? Jacob groused about her abandoning him, but since no townspeople had gathered, she felt not a shred of guilt. Just irritation that this old peddler would be no good in a fight. Suddenly there was a commotion: a large mob approaching. A pair of boys ran ahead of the crowd, and Jacob hailed them for news.

"Boys. Boys! What's all this?" he demanded.

"The prophet's coming," the taller called back. "To cure Jairus' daughter."

"What prophet?" Jacob scoffed.

"The healer from Nazareth. He works miracles."

Again, Veronica's senses sounded an alarm. *That's the man she's been waiting for!* If Jacob turned to Veronica to mock the boys' gullibility, she didn't see it. She ran as fast as she could back to the stricken woman. Reaching her bedside, Veronica was completely out of breath. She took the woman's cold hand and squeezed, asking, "Can you walk at all?"

By the time Veronica got the woman out of bed, down the flight of stairs and to the opened front door, a huge crowd was clogging the street. Veronica propped the woman against the door jamb and scanned the throng for anyone who looked like a prophet. Not that she knew exactly what to look for; she'd only met one, and he couldn't have been typical. *But who was the center of attention?* Veronica saw someone familiar: a young man. At least, he *looked like* the young man who'd handed out the fish and bread that day on the plain. *Was this prophet from Nazareth the same one Leah had heard speak?* There was a finely dressed man in the center of the crowd. He might be the one, but he looked distraught. Veronica turned back to assist the ill woman, but she was walking into the mob.

Weak as she was, the woman dodged and sidestepped the passing men, until she was almost upon the distinguished man. Veronica was less lucky; she was jostled, then knocked sideways. But she saw the ill woman drop to her knees and extend a hand. Not to the finely dressed man: she swept her fingers along the fringe of another man's robe.

The entire procession stopped abruptly. The man whose garment she'd touched, an unassuming man with a gentle countenance, seemed confused for a moment. The crowd grew silent as everyone strained to listen, confirming for Veronica that this was the prophet.

"Someone touched me," he said.

A companion answered, "Of course. Everyone touched you."

But the prophet insisted, "No, no. I felt power leave me."

A second companion simply muttered, "Lord...?" and pointed to the distinguished man, who seemed anxious to keep moving. The prophet acknowledged the fine man's concern, but still turned to peruse the crowd. His eyes fell upon the stricken woman crouching, trying to hide. Far from offended, he smiled at her.

"Daughter," he said softly. "Go in peace. Your faith has healed you."

The woman looked at her hands, then touched them to her face. Veronica was amazed; the color had returned to the woman's cheeks. Her face was fuller and her eyes radiated energy. She looked years younger. She stood without effort and brushed the road dust from her knees.

The prophet's companion urged him again, "Lord?"

The prophet nodded, "Yes. Of course." He gestured for the distinguished man to lead the way, but someone cut through the crowd, interrupting them. A lean man, out of breath, trembling, addressed the distinguished man.

"Master," he almost wept, "don't trouble the Rabbi. Your daughter, she's dead."

The distinguished man quaked. His face contorted with grief. The prophet placed a hand on his shoulder to steady him.

"Don't be afraid," he told him. "Just have faith." Then he turned to the crowd and announced, "The child is only sleeping. And I intend to wake her."

He marched briskly past the dumbstruck servant, and the reinvigorated crowd fell in behind him.

"Sleeping?" the servant cried. "She's dead! I saw her!"

The stricken woman approached to comfort him, but he broke away angrily.

Veronica burned with curiosity, and sprinted through the crowd, which flowed just a short distance farther to a fine house, surrounded by a low wall with a gate, where women clothed in black were on their knees, wailing. A servant opened the gate and the distinguished man gestured for the prophet to enter, then followed him in. The crowd pressed so tightly towards the house, Veronica thought she'd be crushed. The lean servant who'd brought the news extended his arms to keep the mob back. They settled, but shifted from foot to foot, craning their necks to catch some glimpse through the gate, over the wall or through a window.

Some moments passed, then the distinguished man stepped out through the gate. He smiled joyously, holding up the hand of a happy, young girl.

Veronica heard a man jeer, "And you said she was dead!"

The lean servant shook his head in disbelief. "She was."

Veronica was also fairly stunned. The crowd started to disperse and she realized she needed to get back to Jacob. He'd probably have some harsh words for her — willful, *defiant* — and she'd have to submit to them, if she wanted to keep traveling to Jerusalem. The best she could do was run back as fast as she could, so she would be ready as the crowd wandered back. She hiked up her tunic and sprinted until her legs ached and her chest was about to burst. She braced herself on the cart to catch her breath, but Jacob just grunted.

"You're back?" he sighed. "I thought I'd lost you forever."

"You... you don't understand," she heaved. "There was a miracle. Two."

"Two miracles? My, that's a full day for any showman. Now why don't you perform a miracle and sell something?"

Fine. Veronica scooped a few of Jacob's brass bracelets up off the table and onto her wrist. She held her forearm out to the passing townspeople, but it might just as well have been bare and she invisible. After what these people had seen, glitter held no attraction.

Chapter 19

That night, camping outside the town, Veronica was torn. On the one hand, she wanted to get going before the phony might doctor reappear. On the other, she wanted another glimpse of this prophet. His miracles — if that's what they were — inspired awe, but why was he doing these things? If it was all for attention, well, he had hers and most of Galilee's — so now what? Veronica recalled his speech had had a profound effect on Leah, and Judah had called his philosophy *radical love*. But what did he mean by that?

Despite her active mind, Veronica fell into a deep sleep and awoke reinvigorated. So, she wasn't disappointed when Jacob roused her before sunrise to go back to the well and see if they could do some business before heading south in the afternoon.

At the plaza, several women were drawing water and, from what Veronica could make out, still marveling at the previous day's events. Apparently, many sick people had come to Jairus' house — that was the distinguished man's name — and were waiting for the prophet to heal them. Veronica didn't want to miss another miracle, so she broached the subject to Jacob as craftily as she could.

"If there's a crowd, I could bring some merchandise down there."

"Oh, because crippled beggars always have money to spend?"

"It won't just be them," Veronica insisted. "It's the people who carry them. And others will be curious, too. In fact, if you were smart, you'd take the whole cart down there."

Jacob erupted in mock jubilation. "How fortunate I am! I finally have someone to tell me how to run my business!" The two glared at each other for an overly long time, until Jacob relented. "If you must test your theory, take a few items. We'll see how much money your *smart* approach brings us."

So Veronica took a few scarves and trinkets and walked down to Jairus' house. There were perhaps a dozen visibly infirm people. Some — afflicted with palsy or paralysis — lay on their litters as their bearers milled about. A couple of blind men had guides with them. Behind these, there were rows of onlookers. Veronica passed through their ranks, displaying Jacob's wares on her arms, trying not to appear too crass. After she made a few passes through the crowd, the gate to Jairus' house opened and the slender servant, who'd been criticized for announcing the daughter's death, stepped outside.

"The Rabbi is not here," he declared. "I'm sorry, but his party left before sunrise."

"I don't believe you!" a man shouted. "We've been here all night, we'd have seen him!"

"You lied yesterday," a woman shouted. "You said the girl was dead!"

"We all believed she was," the servant asserted.

"I bet she wasn't even sick!" another man cried. This met with a roar of approval from the crowd, which the servant frantically tried to silence.

"Then why are you here?" he squawked. "You make yourself ridiculous. If the girl wasn't sick, the Rabbi couldn't have healed her. If she wasn't dead, he couldn't have brought her back. So what are you even doing here? Now go, all of you!"

He then retreated within the walls, slamming the gate and throwing the bolt loudly. Disappointed, Veronica trudged back to the cart dreading the reaction she'd get from Jacob.

"He's gone," she admitted. "Slipped out before sunrise."

Jacob was incredibly smug. "One step ahead of the mob."

"What's that supposed to mean?" she demanded. But Jacob shooed her towards the well where more women had gathered. "You don't understand," she insisted. "That prophet really is a healer. Do I have to say it again? He brought a dead girl back to life."

"Oh. Please," Jacob winced. "I've traveled from Athens to Alexandria, miracle workers everywhere. They enter to fanfare, perform their sleight of hand, then the whole town finds their purses cut from their belts. Did you see the girl?"

"Yes!" she declared.

"I mean *before*," Jacob groaned. "To see she was dead. How do you know she was even sick?"

"I saw her father."

"In on it," he sang.

"No," Veronica objected. "He was grief-stricken."

"Trust me," Jacob snarled, in a manner that did not inspire trust. "The man runs a synagogue. He will do anything to fill the pews."

"And that lady," Veronica asserted. "She was near death. She didn't get better drinking your perfume."

But Jacob was utterly dismissive. "The excitement of the moment," he stated confidently. "Trust me, when this all dies down, she'll take to her bed all over again."

"I didn't," a voice declared. Veronica turned to see a man at the display table, sifting through Jacob's wares.

"Pardon?" Jacob said.

The man pushed the sleeves of his robe up his arms.

"The Prophet cleansed me," he said. "It hasn't come back."

"What hasn't?" Veronica asked. She eyed his white skin. There wasn't a blemish. Not even a freckle. It looked like the flesh of a baby.

"My leprosy." The man pulled his cowl down and bared his neck. Then he lifted the hem of his tunic to show his shins and feet.

"You had leprosy?" Veronica gasped.

"And now I don't," the man declared. "That's why I follow him. This man has the words of eternal life."

Jacob snarled again. "I'm sure you drum up a lot of business for him."

With that Veronica tossed the trinkets she was holding onto the table and grasped the corners of the cloth. She deftly bundled the wares into a single heap that she tossed into the cart. As Jacob blustered, she tipped the table on its side and started pulling the legs out.

"Wait, Bra—what is your name? And what are you doing?"

"He had leprosy," she exclaimed. "Leprosy!"

"So he says."

"Well," she stated as though it were patently obvious, "we've got to get to Jerusalem."

"It's a hundred miles away. What's the sudden hurry?"

Veronica tossed the table legs into the cart. "Because what's good for Galilee is good for Rome."

"Oh," Jacob scoffed, "and if only that worked the other way around."

But Veronica didn't mind him; she hopped onto the back of the donkey and gripped the bridle. She dug her heels into the old beast's ribs and forced it into a trot. Perhaps out of filial devotion, the ox followed, dragging the cart and a furious Jacob behind.

*   *   *   *

Veronica had gotten Jacob to leave one speck on the map, but he was obstinate about visiting every other. That night they stopped at nearby Aenon, which in the local language meant *The Spring*, referring not to the season but to rushing water. They camped near several falls, and the cascades kept Veronica awake most of the night.

In the light of day, Veronica explored the landscape. There was a promontory from which gushed several rivulets of fresh water that had carved out a narrow valley. The stream fed into the river. Over breakfast, Veronica remarked on the beauty of the springs as they caught the morning sun and threw rainbows into the air.

"Yes, quite dramatic," Jacob muttered. "Showmen put them to good use."

"What do you mean?"

"Oh, a couple of years back there was a fanatic. Preacher. He was dousing his followers under those torrents."

"You mean *baptizing*?"

"Yes, I suppose."

Veronica rose and stared transfixed at the falls. "So it was here."

"Hmm?"

"John the Baptist was here?"

Jacob finished his porridge and licked his fingers. "How do you know him?"

Veronica shrugged. "He baptized me."

Jacob coughed, shook his head, and muttered something like *fanatic*.

Jacob insisted on traveling west after Aenon. Veronica wondered why they would leave the river — Jacob called it *Jordan*. She imagined it would take them into the heart of Judea's major city, but Jacob claimed it led to a wilderness farther south, and that they needed to turn west, because all the prosperous cities were on the mountains. This struck Veronica as entirely backward. *Doesn't a city need a river to supply water? Why build a city on a mountain top when you'd have to drag everything you need up the side of a cliff?* It might be true that Rome had seven hills, but it also had the Tiber — almost three hundred feet wide — flowing through it to Mare Nostra. Veronica objected to the western lurch, despite Jacob showing her a map clearly indicating Jerusalem was southwest. Traveling west would bring her closer to Ptolemais. And closer to *him*.

She still couldn't believe how she'd erupted at him. When he got close, it affected her in a way she didn't understand. And he'd struck her. She should have expected that. She hated him for it, but he'd have been a perfect coward not to, wouldn't he? She wondered how Uncle Theo would have reacted if a woman had ever spoken to him that way. None ever had. Perhaps because he was a man worthy of respect. But maybe because they were ladies. *Oh, she had been awful!* Ill-mannered. *Willful. Of course, he'd had to strike her.* That was the punishment for willful behavior.

Every time they rolled into a new town, Veronica consoled herself that they were probably out of his jurisdiction. At least she hoped; she couldn't tell where Galilee ended and Judea began. With the way the road bent, they might have crossed back and forth half a dozen times. At any time, they might see an Auxilia patrol. He'd be at the head on that powerful black charger. He must be a masterful horseman to keep such an animal under control. Not just a stallion, but a coveted breeder. In Rome, a horse like that could command a handsome fee.

Well, she wasn't in Rome now, and she wasn't going back any time soon. That is, unless her plan could work. Her plan for the holy man. *Oh, it had to work, and Pontius would have to agree to it. After all, Claudia was his wife. She'd lost everything. If he had any manhood in him, Pontius would be appalled. He'd be ready to take on the whole Legion to restore his wife's honor. But that wouldn't be necessary. The prophet could do it.* Veronica was certain that if she could get this man from Nazareth together with Pontius Pilate, she could change the world's destiny. That was rather ambitious — one might even say willful — but she was confident it could happen.

Days turned into weeks as the ox cart ambled from one ant hill of a town to another. Each time they entered a new hamlet, Veronica dreaded stumbling across an Auxilia patrol. Then after hours of tedious, pointless bartering around the well, they'd trudge south again, and Veronica would feel a pang of disappointment that no patrol had harassed them. She hated...*him*, but she yearned to see him so she could demonstrate how much. To his face. Instead of carrying the hatred around inside.

By Veronica's reckoning they were already into spring. The fervor with which she'd left Jairus' village had long since dissolved, and Jerusalem still seemed a continent away. But they were rising into higher country. They'd viewed some majestic peaks, which Jacob pointed out: Mount Ebal and Mount Gerizim. If Jacob was correct, they could reach Jerusalem in a couple of weeks. That's as the ox cart travels. A good horse could get her there in a day. Veronica would have given anything for a muscular, black stallion like that Centurion's. But what they had was an old ox and an older donkey, which meant that much of the time, Veronica and Jacob had to push the cart from the rear rather than ride in it. It was during one of those periods, ascending a steep, stony incline with Veronica pressing her shoulder to one wheel and Jacob to the other, that Veronica saw the apparition, the spectre that answered a nagging question.

"What is that?" she wondered.

Perhaps a tree, scorched by lightning, and on it hung a leathern effigy. It was a figure like a man, similar to the effigies of great men Veronica had seen in tribute parades or the straw men farmers in Tuscany posted in the fields to keep the crows away. *But what was the point of such an effigy here?* This was no parade route and no grain sprouted from these rocks. The effigy also seemed to attract crows rather than discourage them. The birds alighted on the beam and pecked at the figure.

The ground leveled out and Veronica eased up on the pushing. She looked directly at the figure. Her stomach convulsed. She was looking at *an actual corpse!*

Veronica groaned, then doubled over and vomited. She stood up and wiped her mouth. "What happened here?"

"Apparently," Jacob growled, "a man's been crucified."

The word with all its unimagined horror hit Veronica like a mule kick to the chest. She staggered toward the pole, standing like a mast with a sail of human leather. The crows scattered with a burst that forced Veronica to shield her face with her hands. As she pitched forward, she spotted another horror: the body wasn't lashed to the pole, it was nailed at the feet. The post from there down was stained with blood. She eyed the crossbeam. His hands were pierced, nailed into the wood.

"Who did this?"

Jacob answered matter-of-factly, "The Romans. He's probably a Zealot. Part of an ambush or assassination attempt. They captured and executed him. Left him up as a sign to his cohorts."

"Can't anyone bury him?"

Jacob shook his head, "Rome doesn't allow it."

Veronica dashed back to the cart. She prodded the ox forward to with a crop until the cart stood at the base of the cross. Then she hopped into the cart and dug through the top layer of wares and pulled out a bolt of cloth.

"What are you doing?" Jacob demanded.

"I'm going to cover him."

Jacob was flabbergasted. He sputtered, "B-b-but! That's Egyptian cotton!"

Veronica ignored him. Standing up on the cart, she stretched and strained attempting to drape the cloth over the beam of the cross.

Frustrated, she called down to Jacob. "Come on. Help me. You know this is indecent."

Jacob sighed audibly, but grudgingly reined the donkey over to the cross. Crawling up onto its back, he wobbled to his feet and braced himself against the post. From her position on the cart Veronica reached to pass the bolt of cloth. Jacob wrapped the arm on his side, looping the fabric three times over the crossbeam, and held the bolt out for Veronica.

Suddenly, a thunder of hooves frightened the donkey, whose abrupt bucking knocked Jacob off balance. Rather than crash to the rocks, Jacob grabbed the crossbeam and held himself aloft, kicking uselessly at the air. As he dangled, three octets of the Auxilia surrounded him. Veronica pulled her headscarf tightly over her hair. *Was he among them?*

"Hold still," their leader barked, "I'll get you."

It was him. Veronica felt dizzy. She peered out from under the sloping brim of her headscarf. He sat straight as a pillar upon his storm cloud of a stallion. He pulled a lance from his scabbard, hoisted it onto his shoulder and thrust it toward the cross. One of Jacob's hands slipped at the precise moment the lance stuck the beam with a loud *thunk.*

The Auxilia laughed heartily.

"Now, how am I going to skewer you, old man, if you move like that?"

Jacob fell from the cross, landing in a heap. As the cavalry laughed, the Centurion trotted his horse towards the cross and plucked his lance from the beam. Looking down, he spotted Jacob scrambling to his feet, and prodded him cruelly with the butt end of the lance.

"Come on, get up," he chided. "You don't need this cross. We'll find you one of your own."

"Don't you dare!" Veronica yelled. "He's a decent man. It's this... This is what's criminal. This is obscene!"

The Centurion whirled in the saddle, locking his dark eyes onto hers. He recognized her, of course, but stared at her coolly, with complete detachment.

"We meet again," he said. "The Greek merchant's daughter. I'm pleased you've found new employment."

He smiled boldly, so smug in his playacting Veronica was compelled to expose the fraud, whatever the price.

"You know who I am," she declared. "I'm Veronica Procula, daughter of Legion Legate, Maximus Proculus. Niece of Senator Theodosius Proculus. Cousin of Claudia Procula, the wife of Prefect Pontius Pilate, who, if he were informed of your insolence, would prepare a cross for you!"

Jacob was horrified. But the Centurion only chuckled coldly. "Fortunately, citizens of Rome can't be crucified."

"Lucky you," Veronica snorted.

The Centurion raised the thick brow above his right eye. He discarded his attempt at humor and spoke in feigned graciousness. "The Auxilia is here, because we've been dispatched to Jerusalem. Prefect Pilate desires additional forces for the Passover. Once again, I'm sorry for your uncle. If you are traveling to Jerusalem, I can offer some of my men to escort you."

"Thank you, but no," she said dryly.

"These roads are dangerous; obviously you know."

"And Roman soldiers are prime targets," Veronica reasoned. "Either leave me twenty or none at all."

The Centurion replied testily; Veronica had gotten under his skin. "I could force you to come with me."

"But you won't," she countered. "You've already made a bad enough impression. You wouldn't want me to further inflame the Prefect against you."

The Centurion had no rejoinder. He reached his lance under the loops of cotton and sliced the shroud off the cross.

"I'd be more concerned with the impression this will make on the Prefect," he dissembled. "Let us pray no one informs him you were tampering with a cross." Sternly, he punctuated the exchange, "Vale, Mistress Procula."

"Vale, Centurion," she replied.

But as the cavalry galloped off, fury seized Veronica just as when she'd struck the man across the jaw. "And I'll tamper with any crosses I want!" she yelled.

"No, no, no, no!" Jacob shrieked. "No more —"

"Relax," Veronica sighed.

But Jacob was not assuaged. "I will not relax. If anyone must relax, it's you who has to relax. We're going to see a lot more of these corpse trees going south." Then with churlish disgust, he added, "Courtesy of your brother-in-law."

Chapter 20

Longinus rode Formido hard. He needed to feel those hooves pound the earth, the massive barrel expand and contract, the muscular neck strain, and know that he controlled the beast. Again he'd been humiliated. The girl had defied him in front of his men, then mocked his solicitude. Yet she'd been right. Had he taken her into custody, he'd have delivered her — and all the trouble attached — to Pontius Pilate, who was not a man to trifle with.

An earnest butcher the governor in Syria had called him, some six or seven years ago when the Prefect was newly arrived from Rome. Longinus had first met him five years ago as Optaio to a century of Legionnaires dispatched from Syria to reinforce Jerusalem during the Jewish Passover. Pilate, at first, was aloof. Longinus suspected the Prefect was deliberately cultivating a coolness between them because of their shared ethnicity. Samnites struggled for acceptance from the patrician class. It mattered little to Longinus, who'd risen as high as he had reason to hope, but Pilate was a creature of ambition, and might well attempt to ingratiate himself with pure Roman nobility by disciplining an officer they'd regard as *one of his own*. Yet, three times in successive years, Longinus had repeated that duty — acquitting himself favorably — and so, gradually, he'd become familiar with the man.

Pilate no longer ruled with an iron fist, but he didn't have to; he'd broken the Jews to his saddle. They trotted to his crop. During a couple of festivals, as Jerusalem flooded with young men itching to rebel against Roman authority, Longinus had been charged with rounding up Zealots. This preempted rebellion and helped Pilate curry favor with the Jews by releasing a prisoner in honor of their feast. As one lucky malcontent walked free, the Passover crowd cheered Pilate's munificence, oblivious or willfully ignorant that two dozen more wretches, beaten senseless by Legionnaires, lay rotting in the Prefect's dungeon.

Longinus wanted no reason for that cunning man to focus a jaundiced eye upon him. So, rather than drag the girl kicking and screaming one hundred miles to Jerusalem — and inflaming her to more vile slander about how he had "killed" her uncle — he'd left her to her own devices. Not that he wished the Zealots better luck next time. If she did make it to Jerusalem, she'd have more immediate worries than slander against a Centurion. And even so, Pilate wouldn't take her seriously. *A mere girl?* Even if she was his wife's cousin. So much the better. Longinus had never met the Prefect's wife, but he'd heard rumors. Lovely to behold, but... the charitable term was *eccentric*. She apparently thought of herself as some kind of oracle. Pilate would recognize a common thread. He'd invite Longinus to dine and drink and commiserate. But commiseration was solace to the vanquished. Longinus mustn't let his mind travel a path of defeatism. The girl would not ruin him.

Longinus reined Formido to a trot. "Sorry, my friend," he whispered, then reached down and patted the good brute's neck, wiping away a swath of white foam.

"That was a merry chase, Primus," Juvenal chuckled. He clopped forward as the rest of the winded cavalry fell in behind them.

"How did our riders perform?"

"You don't expect them to keep up with Formido?"

Of course he didn't. Had that been the point of his outburst? To reestablish himself as their superior after being unable to command a maiden? He longed again for combat. *How much simpler it was to slay barbarians than to fathom how to speak to a girl.*

Longinus thought he'd put this issue to rest when he'd returned to the garrison with the Senator's charred hand. *Where is the girl?* The magistrate demanded. *Vanished. Lost,* he'd sworn.

"Where could she possibly have gone?"

"We traced her steps to a home in Ammathus, south of Tiberius. The family told me she'd sneaked out during the night."

"And you believed that!" he squawked.

"We searched the area completely," Juvenal calmly averred.

"Your mission was to find her!"

"And we came across a greater threat," Longinus had declared. "A band of Zealots brazenly attacking travelers. I propose we strengthen our patrol and track those rebels down."

The magistrate flushed crimson. "Isn't there a garrison at Capernaum?" he hissed.

"We're rather familiar with it, Excellency," Juvenal chirped.

"Anything east of the hills to the Sea of Galilee is their concern."

"Then, as I understand you," Longinus pondered, "unless the girl returns westward, she's no concern of ours?"

The sputtering magistrate had stomped off, but that had not ended the issue for Longinus. The girl trespassed on his every thought. Intruded on his dreams. She became such an obsession, Longinus could not bear the confines of the garrison. He went on patrol every day, riding in circles for fifty miles or more, sweeping through town after town, and returning each evening in despair, forced to acknowledge that she was beyond his grasp. Her destination had been south. Not Arimathea, but Jerusalem. She could have reached there by now, and there was no way, short of desertion, that Longinus could follow.

When he'd received his orders to reinforce Jerusalem for the Passover, his first thought had been, *South, towards her.* It was an idle hope, completely unrealistic, but even now, she might be living in the Prefect's Palace. *And wouldn't that be splendid agony?* Him, relegated to the officer's barracks, and her, sealed away in the Prefect's quarters. An easy toss of a lance could cover the distance between them, yet they'd be doomed never to meet. Unless... unless it was fated.

Fate had allowed Pilate — a mere Samnite — to win the heart of a patrician, and rise to his current office. What had that taken? One or two chance encounters under favorable circumstances? Longinus had only met the girl under adverse conditions. That accounted for her hostility. She only had to glimpse him at the right moment: as he rode at the head of his file. He would parade his cavalry across the bridge from the Temple, circle the forum outside the Prefect's Palace to the portico. After dismounting, Longinus would stride up the broad stairs to the landing where Pilate and his court waited. The crowd on the ramparts would marvel at his troops, their bright breastplates, their powerful horses. He'd glance into that crowd and see her. Still lovely, she'd be worn and frail from the hardships of her journey. She'd look into his eyes and see not an enemy to be feared, but a protector. He'd extend his hand, palm open toward her. Pilate's court would part and she'd step forward. She'd place her small hand in his.

"Not quite what you'd expected?" Juvenal remarked.

Longinus snapped out of his reverie. Was his friend now reading his mind?

"Finding the girl like that. At the foot of a cross, no less."

Longinus tipped his head towards the men. "Did they recognize her?"

"No, nor did I," he said. "Until she declared herself. *Niece of this, daughter of that.* And I thought you rode a high horse," he quipped.

"Should I have taken her?"

Juvenal rolled his eyes. "By all the gods, no! Talk about unmanageable. And as far as Pilate's concerned, you're damned either way. You take her to Pilate and say, *Here, Prefect, is your lovely sister-in-law, whom the Emperor would like tortured and killed. Good day.* He'll flay you for leaving him that little chore. Or you report to him immediately upon arrival. *Prefect, I met your dear sister-in-law out on the road frequented by cut-throat Zealots. She declined my offer of assistance, so I rode off.* He'll sell you as a gladiator for that one."

Longinus grimaced and shook his head. "You've aptly captured my predicament."

"Aptly, but not entirely," he said. "The greater dilemma is that you're in love with her."

Longinus wanted to scoff. To obfuscate and deny. He went mute.

"That would be difficult if she weren't a fugitive," his friend warned. "There's a matter of station."

"A patrician girl," he nodded.

"And you still five years from being elevated to an equestrian."

Longinus tipped the visor of his helmet up, letting a breeze flow over his sweat-soaked hair. "I'll have acreage in Lombardy," he shrugged.

THE LANCE AND THE VEIL

"That's hardly a townhouse in Rome or a villa in Capri," Juvenal proffered.

Longinus adjusted his helmet and scanned the road ahead. The road diverted from the crest of the craggy hills and ran along a middle tier between the summit on the right and the canyon floor on the left, making his cavalry vulnerable to an attack from above. He dispatched his Optaio with a squad to scout the ridge for Zealots. He and Juvenal sat their horses until the Optaio reported the crest was clear. Longinus raised his right arm and signaled his riders forward at a moderate trot. On his left side, Juvenal paced him, and revisited the Roman caste system as it pertained to marriage.

"Women can marry up in status," he opined. "Provided they have beauty and cultivate some bearing. Men, even if they have great wealth, cannot marry into a higher station."

The shade of the canyon was a welcome relief from the heat, but Longinus strained to make his eyes adjust.

"Men of our rank will always be peasants," Juvenal insisted. "It's hard to wash off the manure."

"Perhaps if you'd bathe occasionally..."

"Ha, ha."

Longinus thought he saw — perhaps sensed — movement. His eyes were not responding.

"And your beloved?" Juvenal goaded. "You've seen how willful she is. Taking a girl like that — assuming anyone would grant permission — and unable to maintain her as she's accustomed? Might as well fall on your sword right now."

Formido bucked as a cable sprang from the dust and snapped taut diagonally to the crest. The line cut like a bolt past Longinus' eyes, bringing down a wedge of wood. The rockslide followed. Boulders rumbled, smashing horses and riders. Longinus pitched forward as a slab shattered Formido's foreleg. He rolled from his shoulder to his knees, and crouched before the Zealot wave.

Drawing his sword, Longinus responded to the pitiful cries of his stallion. He deftly slit the beast's jugular, then drove his red blade into a rebel's chest. He pivoted, putting the canyon wall to his back, and sliced a second Zealot below the ribs. Beating back attackers, Longinus glimpsed a brute the size of Athos[69], passing towards Juvenal. He watched in horror as his friend, with leg and sword pinned beneath his fallen mount, gripped the giant's spear below the tip. He strained to hold off the point that slowly plunged into his throat.

Longinus roared. At crossed swords with a pair of foes, he tossed them aside like straw men and leapt towards Formido. Retrieving his shield, he charged the giant who lunged, thrusting the iron lance towards his face.

[69] In Greek mythology, one of the Gigantes who threw a mountain at Zeus

Longinus deflected the spear point with his shield and jabbed his sword at the giant's wrist. But in a remarkable show of dexterity, the giant spun, slipping the blow and returning from the other side to rake the ground with his spear. Knocked off his feet, the Centurion landed on his right hip and elbow. Before he could gather his legs under him, the brutish Zealot kicked gravel into his face. The grit stung, forcing his eyes shut. Longinus had no choice but to roll to his left and scramble up to his feet. Blinking his tearing eyes madly, he tried to clear his vision. Effectively blind, he swung his sword madly. After a few useless strokes, the giant clamped his wrist with an enormous hand. A second paw covered the Centurion's face, grinding sharp gravel into the misty pulp. In agony, Longinus thrust his shield forward, smashing the giant's face. The brute was stunned; he stepped back but didn't loosen his grip. Longinus pounded away. Again. Again, the giant staggered backwards.

Longinus sensed a turn in the battle. The Zealots — as always when fighting got thick — retreated. He tried to wrest his arm from the giant, but his was a death grip. He slammed the shield to the brute's head again, and heard the ground scrape away beneath him. Then Longinus himself pitched forward. The road was gone. The world fell away and left him in the air.

Chapter 21

Veronica was thoroughly confused. She'd done everything to chase the hated Centurion away and she'd won. She'd stood her ground and given him no good options, so he had to retreat. And when he reined his horse back to the road and signaled his troops to follow, she felt a tremendous rush of... loneliness. Desolation. She was miserable. And naturally, she took it out on Jacob.

"Oh, I'll pay for the cotton!" she snapped, and resumed draping the corpse in earnest.

"Pay with what?" he barked. "We may never sell that bracelet of yours."

"Ooooh! All you ever think about are the pennies you can scrounge. While you let *this* go on!"

"Sit down," Jacob ordered. When she ignored him, he declared, "I'm moving the cart." He switched the ox across its hind and the cart rocked. Veronica lost her balance and tumbled onto the bed of the cart.

"Don't break anything!" Jacob barked.

"I almost broke my elbow."

"Would serve you right," he huffed. Jacob climbed down from his seat and retraced their path to collect the donkey. "Don't need you stirring up more problems with the Romans."

"Me? I got rid of them," she grumbled. "You should be grateful."

"Grateful?" Jacob cried. "They only stopped because of you!" He tethered the donkey to the rear of the cart. "If it wasn't for you, I never would have touched that cross."

"No, you'd just ride past. Without even caring. He's one of your own people hanging there!"

"And your people did the hanging!" Jacob shouted. He stomped to the front of the cart and climbed onto the bench. He turned back and brandished the crop. "Don't you play high and mighty. Sure, you confront the Romans; you're one of them. Even as a wanted criminal, you've got more rights than any Jew. But they'd have killed me just for sport." He faced front and struck the ox with his crop. The cart lurched forward. "They'll kill any of us." He jabbed his crop at the cross. "You want *us* to stop this? Clubs against swords? You fine patricians could stop this tomorrow. But I don't hear of anyone in Rome standing up to Caesar. You want to think I'm a coward, fine. Maybe we're all cowards for not rebelling. But you didn't like that very much either, did you? When you ran into those Zealots? That's what war with Rome would be. Random slaughter."

"So you put up with it?" Veronica scoffed.

"I'm an old man," Jacob abjured. "I'd like to finish my years in peace. Doing what I enjoy."

"Making money."

"So now that's a sin?" Jacob protested. "I should be a princess in Rome and never work a day? How did your family get their money? Waging war. Pillaging? No, they'd get their hands dirty. You patricians sit back and manage the plundering, so you can live idle lives and look down on anyone who soils himself with honest labor. I should be ashamed? Why? Do I rob and extort? I sell colorful, shiny objects to people who live grey lives on a grey landscape. Perfume to people who sweat in the fields or over a cooking fire. And soft cotton for coarse, callused bodies. Oh, but that makes me trivial. Small and petty. How grand I would be if I could wield a sword and cut people down!"

"All right!" Veronica conceded. "I guess there's nothing either of us can do." She thought of her helplessness when Macro started his purge and when the Zealots attacked. Again, she saw her outnumbered comrades, falling all around her. "But just so you know, not all Romans are like that. We don't approve, I mean."

Jacob harrumphed.

"Most people don't know what goes on here. I didn't. And lots of people want to make things better." She thought fondly of Theodosius, of stories he'd told that had made her proud of Rome. She crawled to the front of the cart and perched herself over Jacob's shoulder. "That's what the Pax Romana was about." He let the remark pass without any acknowledgement. "Do you know about Pax Romana?"

"Never heard of it."

Veronica paused, thinking how she might explain. "When I was little, I asked my Uncle Theo what war was, because they told me my father died in war. He said, from time to time there would be wars, but if we had wise leaders there would be fewer wars. He said that's how it was when Emperor Augustus ruled. Because he was tired of war. He thought it was bad for the nation."

"Which nation?"

"All of them, I guess. Augustus thought it wasn't good to spend so much of our treasure on conquests and have so many young people killed."

"So Augustus was Emperor of the Obvious?"

"But it wasn't obvious," Veronica protested. "My uncle said, like you were saying, the people deciding for war weren't the ones fighting, so they had no idea, or didn't care how bad it was. They were safe in Rome and only saw the good things, like when the generals returned in triumph with tribute from the countries they conquered. But Augustus said we should have no more wars of conquest, and only use our armies to keep order in the land we already had. So, the empire built roads and aqueducts and ports, so that people could trade. And the trade created more wealth than all the wars."

"So what changed?" Jacob asked. "What happened to this Pax Romana?"

"Well," Veronica paused, she felt her emotions roiling again. "When Augustus died, his son Tiberius became emperor."

"From your tone," Jacob drawled, "I take it you disapprove."

"Of Tiberius?" Veronica lamented. "Well, he's evil. Or crazy. He thinks everyone's his enemy. Even people like my uncle who would never dream of breaking the law. His soldiers dragged all these good Romans out of their homes and killed them."

"Sounds as bad there as here," Jacob conceded.

"My uncle said it was our fault. People get the leaders they deserve. And we put faith in men instead of the law. My uncle said if you write good laws, they remain forever, but if you trust a man to do good, you never know what you're going to get."

"Your uncle sounds very wise," Jacob mused.

"He was. I never knew how wise until..." Veronica's voice failed her and she sat back down. Her eyes scanned the countryside. Not grey as Jacob had described it, but definitely beige. The sky, too, seemed faded and colorless. The only contrast came from black specks where carrion birds hovered and dipped.

The cart crept forward, its solid wooden wheels creaking over the stony path. Veronica wondered if she should tell Jacob her plan. She'd kept it to herself, because she thought she'd mock her for it. But in talking about Emperor Tiberius, she remembered his sickness, his deformity. Perhaps he only acted as a horror, because that's how the world saw him. If he could be cleansed, as that villager had claimed, what that would mean for the world!

The cart slowed to a dead halt. Veronica rolled to her knees and looked past Jacob at the road ahead. Vultures and crows gorged themselves, stripping red flesh from brown carcasses.

"Horses?" Veronica gasped.

"And men," Jacob said.

Veronica spotted several boulders in the middle of the road.

"Zealots!" She sprang from the cart and ran forward.

"Bracha!" Jacob warned. "Come back!"

The Auxilia must have been ambushed. Horses — Veronica covered her nose and mouth with her headscarf against the stench —were strewn about, littering the road and the ditch below. There were men — Jews — chopped in pieces. But — was *he* here? A burst of black wings and an angry squawk startled her, as a vulture's bloody beak protested her presence. Veronica skipped back, then eyed the bird's perch. It was *his* stallion. A foreleg was shattered. Flies swarmed about its head, lifeless in a congealing pool of blood that had drained from its powerful neck. That pool had been tracked through by hooves and boots as the Auxilia had pushed on.

"Bracha!" Jacob called. "Come back."

Veronica knew Jacob was worried he'd never get the cart through. All this carnage would terrify his animals. She retraced her steps, measuring the distance between obstacles.

"We can fit," she said. She tied her headscarf over the donkey's eyes and untethered it from the cart. Taking the bridal, she led the beast to the front of the cart. A thought occurred to her and she reached into the cart, sifting through the pile for a small jar of fragrance. She broke the seal and wet the outside of the beast's nostrils. Then Veronica handed the jar to Jacob.

"Do the same with the ox," she said.

"Oh, he won't budge."

"What's our choice, Jacob?" Veronica insisted. "We've got to get through."

Jacob huffed, but he got up from his seat and prepared the ox to move forward. The donkey brayed in protest, but Veronica spoke soothingly, caressed its neck and stroked its ears. Cajoling it forward, she led the donkey through the battlefield. On the other side, she tied the bridle to some scrub brush and ran back to help Jacob weave the cart through. She had to sweep a couple of arms and legs — and even roll one Zealot's body — out of the cart's path, but they were able to inch their way past.

"No Romans," Jacob observed. "I guess your side won."

Veronica pulled her headscarf from the donkey's eyes. "I have no side," she said. "I hate all of this... death."

They resumed their slow pace. Eventually the bloody tracks disappeared. The road returned to the crest of the hills, which Jacob called The Spine of

Judea. Veronica swore she could see as far west as Mare Nostra, and it looked as though the reddening sun would cool itself in those very waters.

"How much farther to Jerusalem?" Veronica asked. She was shocked at Jacob's answer.

"We'll get there tomorrow."

"Tomorrow! Why didn't you tell me we were so close?"

"Well, let me see," Jacob snarled. "The day started with a Centurion threatening to crucify me..."

"All right, all right," Veronica groaned. "Let's not drag that up again. Where are we sleeping tonight?"

"I know a sleepy town," Jacob mused. "At the foot of the hills that rise to Jerusalem. A sleepy little town called Bethany."

But when they rolled into Bethany well after sunset the town square was thoroughly alive. Musicians played. Men danced around a huge bonfire. Women passed trays of food through a large crowd of revelers. Veronica climbed from the cart to investigate the celebration.

"What did I say?" Jacob asked dryly. "No one ever sleeps in Bethany."

"Is this a king's feast?" Veronica wondered aloud.

She spotted the town's well and grabbed a bucket from the cart to water the animals. She took her place behind a few women waiting to draw water. One woman mimicked a drunken man. She staggered, then planted her feet firmly, shoulder width apart.

"So, my husband says *Water into wine? That's nothing.*" She thrust her hips forward to ape a man relieving himself. *I can turn wine... into water!*"

The women burst with laughter. Veronica concluded they were all practicing the husband's alchemy. But what was the occasion?

"Excuse me," Veronica interrupted. "We just arrived. We're wondering what all the excitement is about?"

The women regarded her with suspicion. Perhaps it was her accent. In the low light they couldn't have noticed her fair hair and eyes.

The woman who told the joke answered. "The Prophet from Nazareth, Jesus," she said. She tipped her head towards the bonfire. "He worked a miracle today."

Veronica looked over to the fire. The prophet from Galilee was kneeling, talking to a circle of children. Jacob had overheard. He moaned as if crushingly bored, "Oh, what's he done now? Turned olives into oil?"

But the joking woman was deadly serious. "He raised a dead man from the grave." She pointed to the dancing men, to a slim, smiling man with a short beard at the end of the line. "That one there, Lazarus." Veronica was incredulous, but the woman insisted. "We buried him four days ago. He was sick and his sisters sent for the Prophet, but he didn't come until today."

"Oh, the sisters tore into him!" another woman remarked.

"No," a third countered, "Mary was nice." She pointed toward a lady seated in the circle of children listening to the prophet. "She was gentle, but Martha!" She nodded cautiously towards a kitchen maid collecting empty bowls from the crowd. "Martha was livid!"

"So," the serious, formerly joking, woman continued, "He went — with all of us, the whole town trailing behind — and they opened the tomb, and out comes Lazarus."

"If I hadn't seen it with my own eyes...!" the second woman marveled. "I still can't believe it."

The woman chattered on, filling in more details, but Veronica wandered away, drawn towards the prophet. Did she dare speak to him? He seemed so at ease, enjoying his moment with the children. It struck her as odd that a man of such importance would dawdle with children, though it did make him seem more approachable. *But could he really have done what these women claimed? Then again, if he hadn't, why would all these people — witnesses — be out in the plaza celebrating? He had to be genuine.* He *couldn't* be, but he *had* to be. Veronica made up her mind to tell him her plan: He would come back to Rome with her; he would cure the Emperor. And then, there would be peace. The world would be made right. And she could go home.

Then one of the sisters, the erstwhile livid kitchen maid, crouched beside the prophet and whispered in his ear. He nodded, then reached around the circle, touching each of the children on the head, in sort of a blessing. He rose and walked towards a small, clay brick house. Veronica skipped after him, hoping to catch him before he reached the door. But two men stepped in front of her, hands across their chests, barring her way. She recalled seeing them before, in the crowd around the prophet.

The more rugged of the two glowered and said flatly, "Ave."

"Ave," she replied without thinking.

The men turned to each other with smug grins. Veronica understood: they were proud to have spotted a Roman, even in Galilean dress.

"The Master has retired for the night," the rugged man scoffed. "Tell Caesar to send more spies in the morning."

"I'm not a spy," Veronica objected. But the men just laughed at her and strode into the house. The door slammed shut, and she heard the bolt thrown.

Chapter 22

"Primus," the Optaio sounded, "we're approaching the city gates."

Longinus tightened his grip on the reins as his mount, perhaps sensing the end of the journey, tried to trot ahead.

"Which gate?" he asked.

"The northern, sir."

"No," he demurred. "Circle the wall to the west and enter at the Praetorium. See that the prisoners are secured. Send a rider ahead to request an escort."

"At once, Primus!" the Optaio responded and cantered off.

All too officious, Longinus thought. *Now, after the ambush, this derelict played at being a soldier.* Yet the dullard was still ready to march the tattered Auxilia, with rebel Zealots in tow, past the Temple and through the hostile confines of the packed city already seething with malcontents. *Whose side was he on?*

Longinus had started to wonder about this Optaio back in Ptolemais, when the magistrate had known too much, too soon about their encounter with the Senator. He'd said his information had come from lips made loose with wine, but Longinus knew the cunning martinet had a spy in his ranks. The spy's identity became clear after the second encounter with the girl. Upon returning to the garrison, Longinus had reported his version of events, and surrendered the jewelry found at the scene — all except the gauntlet he'd given the girl. As the magistrate rolled the cloth open, he paused. After a ponderous second he asked, "Anything else?"

When Longinus indicated that was all, another awkward silence commenced. It lasted until Longinus removed his helmet, belt and lorica, and welcomed the magistrate to search his person, his quarters and his horse.

"That won't be necessary, Primus," he chortled. "I know you as a man of honor." But Longinus also read in his face that he had known the number of bracelets, and could only have gotten that number from a man who had pursued the Galilean boy up the mountain and had recovered the treasure. Longinus was then certain the Optaio was his spy.

But though the man was a traitor, Longinus had not judged him a complete fool. When he'd sent him to the ridge to scout for Zealots, he thought the man capable of observing the landscape, of having the capacity to ferret out the sort of trap he'd allowed them to wander blindly into. *Blindly!* Was that his fate now? His best friend dead, his command disgraced, was he now to put out a bowl and beg for his sustenance? *All because this imbecile could not see a stockpile of boulders rigged to crash at the tug of a leash!*

The Optaio returned. "We're at the gates now, Primus. We have the Legion to escort the prisoners."

Longinus raised his right hand to halt his column. "Bring the prisoners forward." The Centurion shifted in his saddle and listened. Heavy feet shuffled across the hard earth. He smelled the giant approach like a boar rising from a swamp. The stench recalled to him the tight combat. They'd tumbled from the brink of the road headlong to the next level. They'd landed hard; Longinus was fortunate that the brute cushioned his fall. They bounced, rolling down a slope with the Zealot's hand still firmly clasped on the Centurion's wrist. When they came to rest, the Zealot was on top, pinning the Centurion's shield and his left arm to his chest. Having the advantage, but witless, the Zealot writhed and groped as Longinus struggled to free his arm. The pain in his eyes was still excruciating, literally madding. Then the Zealot planted his right hand on the Centurion's throat, digging his fingers in to crush the windpipe. Desperate, Longinus thrust his knee upward, jamming it into the Zealot's groin. The giant moaned, listing sideways just enough for Longinus to jerk the shield free, knocking the Zealot's arm at the elbow so his hand went limp. He pushed the shield up under the Zealot's chin and pried the giant off towards his right side. How the Gorgon kept his grip on his sword hand, Longinus could not fathom! But the Centurion rolled on top and shoved his left forearm under the brute's matted beard, grinding his laryngeal cartilage to pulp. When his breath stopped, the grip loosened, and Longinus placed his sword at the Zealot's throat. Thinking the still brute dead, the Centurion clawed at his inflamed eyes, lifting the lids to allow the grit to flow forth with tears and blood.

Shortly thereafter, his comrades descended the slope to aid him. They'd rallied and repulsed the attackers, slaying a dozen and capturing a few more. When they realized the giant was alive, they rousted him and put him in chains. A medic rinsed and bandaged the Centurion's eyes, and one of his riders offered a horse. Longinus climbed into the saddle sightless and helpless. He tapped his heels against the horse's flanks and began the morbid march now ending at Jerusalem.

Military boots striking the flagstones caught the Centurion's attention.

"If it isn't Barabbas!" a voice laughed. "Welcome, old viper. Allow us to show you true Legion hospitality."

"You won't feel so big and mighty after a morning with us!"

"You think you're bruised now---"

"Enough!" Longinus cried. "This man is my prisoner. No one is to lay a hand on him until I see the Prefect." The Legionnaires fell silent as the prisoner cackled.

"You hear that Legion!" Barabbas scoffed. "I have a benefactor. I am under the Centurion's protection."

"True," Longinus said. "But only because I'm selfish: I'm the one who's going to crucify you."

*　　　　　*　　　　　*　　　　　*

When Veronica awoke her body was a mass of knots. She couldn't recall her dreams —she was no Claudia — but she knew her mind had been active and her spirit apprehensive throughout the night. She was so anxious to finally see Claudia and to tell Pontius about the miracle worker. And she was worried that if she didn't act fast, he might slip away as he'd done in Salim. If it had been up to her, she'd have left Bethany last night and traveled by lamp to Jerusalem. She'd have gotten Pontius out of bed, and he'd have ordered a century of cavalry here by daybreak. But Jacob wouldn't have shared Veronica's enthusiasm for her plan, and his animals were old and needed their rest. So Veronica settled for camping outside Bethany, so she could try to speak to the prophet this morning. He'd probably prefer to speak to her anyway, rather than find himself surrounded by Legionnaires. She fixed Jacob breakfast, but took none for herself. After stirring the last burning twigs of their campfire into the dust, Veronica wrapped her headscarf tightly around her hair and let Jacob know her intentions.

"One last look at your hero?"

"I hope it won't be my last," she said. "I think he can help me."

"And why would he help a Roman?"

"He'd be helping the world," she protested. "Why did you help a Roman?"

Jacob sighed. "You may recall I was threatened with familial exile."

Veronica gave him a squinty stare. Jacob shook his head. He lifted a steaming pot off the bed of coals and poured tea into two cups.

"You know nothing about these people. How simple they are." Jacob handed Veronica a cup of tea. "I shouldn't complain, because their simplicity is good for my business." The tea was bitter, but the warmth of the liquid was soothing. Jacob continued earnestly, "But what they claimed happened is not all that uncommon. Not because people tend to rise from the dead. But because these backward hicks are prone to bury the living."

Veronica coughed the tea back into the cup. "What? Why?"

"Oh, many reasons," Jacob sermonized. "They're afraid of epidemics, so they bury them quickly. They can't work on the Sabbath, so they hurry and bury them before sundown. Why do you think they place them in caves instead of in the ground or on a pyre? So, if they've made a mistake..."

"And you think that's what happened with Lazarus?"

"I'm sure of it," he declared with finality.

"Four days in the tomb without food or water. If not dead, at the point of death from sickness. But he can just walk out when they roll the stone away?"

"Things get exaggerated. People want heroes. People want hope."

Veronica swallowed the bitter tea. "And I hope you're wrong."

*   *   *   *

The Legate on duty had refused to awaken the Prefect. "It's the dead of night and this is no emergency. Your forces were victorious. You captured the Zealot leader. You should have the doctor look at your eyes, then go to sleep, Centurion."

But how could he sleep? He'd lost too much. His friend — no, more than a friend, his kindred spirit, his conscience — and what of his eyes? If they were gone, his career was over. Even if he were paroled with his full grant of land, he'd never be able to work those acres, never be able to make a life. And what of the opprobrium this ambush would bring? He'd be branded a dilettante, have his rank and pay reduced, even forfeit his pension. He couldn't go to sleep without settling his mind, and the only balm for his pain was the certainty, here and now at this moment, that he would have his revenge. He searched for words, some eloquence to plead his case, but all he could manage was to mumble, "Don't dismiss me."

"Centurion," the Legate said, "take no offense that I send you away. I shall present your concerns to the Prefect when he awakens. And, having rested, you shall have your audience in the morning."

"I shall sleep here," Longinus stated.

The Legate did not respond.

"Let me show you to the barracks, Primus," the Optaio said. His manner had become cloying. He touched Longinus' arm, but the Centurion snatched it away. "Please, Primus," he spoke softly. "You'd be a spectacle out here. Think of your rank."

Longinus would not be led by this man. But what other choice had he? His declaration that he'd sleep on the stones of the forum —like a supplicant, a beggar — had been rash. Whatever credit his wounds had earned would vanish overnight; the Prefect would think him a madman. He dropped his head. "Take me to the doctor."

The doctor complained that lamplight was inadequate for probing the Centurion's eyes. He flushed them with cool water, picked out some grit, applied a salve and bandaged them. "There is damage to the orbs," he said. "How much they will heal in time, I cannot say. Keep the bandages on for a couple of days, then visit me again."

From there a sentinel escorted them to an unoccupied cell in the officers' barracks. It had two bunks. Longinus made it clear he wanted to be alone.

"Are you sure, Primus?" the Optaio inquired. "You mustn't be rash —"

Longinus lunged at the junior and threw him up against the wall. "You do not give me orders," he spat through clenched teeth.

"I'm sorry, Primus," he bleated. "Of course not."

Longinus released him and felt his way to the bunk. He loosened his armor and untied his cloak. "Wake me at first light," he said.

Sometime later a rap at his cell door awakened him. Pain surged as he lifted his head, stabbing his eyes. The Optaio helped him dress and they headed to the Prefect's hall.

"It is still early, Primus," the Optaio said. "Perhaps we should wait for the Prefect to summon us."

"There is no *we*," Longinus replied. "*I* have an audience with the Prefect." At least he hoped; Longinus would not wait to be called because he feared the call would not come. Pilate was a stern man. The Centurion's previous service may have earned him some credit, but if now the Prefect thought Longinus was through, he'd just as soon crush him to strike fear into his own troops. How Pilate viewed the ambush would be key. If Longinus could mitigate blame for falling into the trap, he might curry favor for having captured the Zealot leader.

At the hall, Pilate had not yet arrived. A sentinel offered Longinus a chair; he chose to stand as a soldier rather than squat as an invalid. Perhaps an hour passed before the door opened and a Legate ushered Longinus in. He strode and was inside the chamber before he realized the Optaio had snuck in behind him. To the Centurion's surprise, Pilate greeted him warmly. He chatted in a relaxed manner, recalling the Centurion's previous visits. He complimented his contributions in suppressing the Zealots during those Passover seasons.

"And now you've captured Barabbas!" he cheered. "That's quite a prize."

"It came at a dear cost, Prefect," Longinus admitted.

"True," Pilate agreed. He adopted a somber tone. "You lost some good men. And you've been wounded. What did the doctor say about your eyes?"

"Too soon to tell."

"But, by the gods, we hope for the best." He returned to his earlier cheerful tone, "Back to Barabbas."

"Prefect," Longinus interrupted, "I should like to make my report on the attack."

"And I —" the Optaio exclaimed, "I, Prefect, can attest to the heroism I witnessed. You've seen the size of the one called Barabbas. It was the Primus alone who subdued him."

"Impressive," Pilate said. Longinus heard Pilate, in his excitement, rise from his cathedra.

"He killed my... my Princeps," Longinus said. He had to force his throat open to continue. "He was a good officer. An honorable Roman. And my friend."

"A loss to the Empire, no doubt," Pilate said.

"His loss cannot be counted," Longinus said. "But it must exact a price."

"And what would that be?" Pilate asked.

"I would ask your permission, Prefect, to personally crucify the leader Barabbas."

"Done!" Pilate declared. "You've earned the honor. But we must wait. As much as the average Judean fears and despises this Barabbas, a crucifixion during the Passover would enflame the mob. We'd make every one of them a Zealot. You don't mind waiting?"

"Not at all, Prefect."

"If the gods are kind, by then you'll be able to see him suffer." Pilate returned to his cathedra. Longinus sensed the audience was drawing to a close. "Anything else?"

"I should like," Longinus declared, "to make my report on the battle. Privately."

An uneasy silence fell over the room. Longinus could feel the Optaio wilting. Longinus may have imagined it, but a pungent odor — one he'd associated with fear in the ranks — reached his nostrils. No words were said, but Longinus heard footsteps heading for the door. A mere gesture had dismissed the Optaio.

*   *   *   *

It was no surprise that the streets of Bethany were deserted. Veronica had expected the town would be slow to rise. But she was surprised to find no one guarding the prophet's house. The fire outside had been fed, but no one was tending it. She approached the entrance and knocked at the wooden door.

A woman answered, the sister who'd served the revelers. Her puffy eyes were barely open, but she narrowed them more still, asking, "Can I help you?" Veronica took it as more warning than greeting, but managed a weak reply.

"Good morning."

A voice cried from within, childlike in its innocence, "Martha, who is it?"

Martha kept her eyes fixed on Veronica. "No one," she replied.

No one pressed her petition, "I was hoping..."

But Martha cut her off, "He's gone."

She seemed about to slam the door, but the voice within chimed again. "Does she want Jesus?"

Martha censured her sister. "I'm handling it!" she declared, then told Veronica, "He left before daylight."

Veronica entreated again, as politely as she could, "Did he say...?"

"Yes," Martha stated coldly. "He did say."

"I understand," Veronica nodded. "You don't like Romans. Sometimes I don't like Romans either. But I haven't found much to like about rude Judeans." She pivoted and marched from the house. She heard the door slam shut behind her, then the latch rattled several times, and a voice cried out behind her.

"Wait. Wait, please," the other sister called. Veronica stopped as the woman, actually a girl not much older than herself, ran up to her. "Sorry," she said. "Martha, she gets," she shrugged and laughed breathily. "That's how she gets. Big party, so she's got to clean up."

"Mary!" her sister called from the house.

Mary looked over her shoulder and gestured palm out for her sister to back away. She turned to Veronica and pointed west toward the steep hills. "But, Jesus went up to Jerusalem. He'll be up there, then back here, back and forth, through the Passover."

"Mary!"

Mary tipped her head at the house and winced. She held both her palms up apologetically as she took a step backwards. "Hope you find him. Shouldn't be hard, he's always got a crowd wherever he goes." Then Mary ran back to the house where Martha stood, fuming beside the fire.

*   *   *   *

Longinus listened as the boots struck the flagstones. Even in the open forum, the parade created an echo, as sound bounced off the surrounding pillars and the not-so-distant fortifications of the city. His Auxilia had been ordered to review for the Prefect, but the Prefect was not in attendance. Instead, his Legate stood beside Longinus watching the files and columns pass in formation.

"I shall indicate when to call a halt," the Legate said. "Then I shall begin the inspection. Stay at my side. I'll walk you into position. You'll merely have to extend your right arm."

The troops circled the forum. Longinus heard the Optaio command abrupt changes in direction and formation. The men progressed through a number of compliments to the march.

"Impressive," the legate said. "For provincials."

"Is it time?" Longinus asked.

"Yes."

Longinus raised his right hand and shouted, "Halt! Attention!"

The troops stomped in virtual unison, but the reverberation gave the illusion of a cascade, of one blunt impact begetting another and another on to infinity. Longinus gripped the cudgel at his belt. As the Legate stepped forward, Longinus sensed a gulf between them open and moved to close it. The Legate steadied the Centurion by placing a baton lightly on his forearm. Longinus stayed abreast of the Legate for several paces.

The Legate stopped, bracing Longinus with his baton. He tapped the Centurion's lorica on the left breast, prompting him to pivot a quarter circle. Longinus felt the pressure of the baton on his breastplate lift. He took the cudgel at his belt into his right hand and reached upward, then struck down on the Optaio's shoulder. Longinus stepped back and the carnage began.

*   *   *   *

The climb up to Jerusalem was steep, despite the many switchbacks that had been carved into the hillside. The going was slow, and though Jacob made several stops along the way to rest his animals, he didn't tolerate their decision to take a break. A couple of times, when the animals would not respond to the crop, Jacob plucked dried brush from along the path, laid it under the breast of the ox or donkey and lit it with coals he'd saved from their campfire. The twigs smoldered, making the beast nervous, then burst into flame, causing it to scurry forward. It was a sure cure for stubbornness, and ultimately less cruel than flailing away with the crop.

They ascended the eastern slope, so there was no hiding from the intense heat of the sun. They walked most of the way, so as not to burden the animals, and Veronica was tempted to march at her own pace, leaving the peddler and his train behind. But they'd been companions this long, it seemed fitting to enter the gates of Jerusalem together.

There was one small thrill on the road. As they reached the crest of the hill, the road branched off down the western slope, and up that path marched a train of camels! Veronica had never seen a camel. She'd heard boys who had been to the Circus in Rome describe them, as though they were part horse and part dragon, but her uncle had never regarded the Circus as a place for young ladies, so she'd had to imagine them. Now there were three coming up right behind her! They seemed to walk in a lazy lope, yet covered ground quickly thanks to their extraordinarily long legs. They towered over the low cart. Unlike horses, they were shaggy and their backs were rounded — or perhaps that was just the way the saddle was constructed, though Veronica couldn't understand why anyone would build a higher seat atop these beasts. Unless it was to see over the head, which sat high atop a long, swooping neck. The lead camel leered lazy-eyed at Veronica as it passed and a long, pink tongue jutted suddenly out, then retracted. *No wonder the boys had compared them to dragons!* They carried what looked like a tremendous amount of cargo, and Veronica didn't understand how they could manage on such gangly legs.

"Have you ever used camels?" she asked Jacob.

He grunted, adding "Dreadful beasts. Unless you're crossing a desert, they're much more trouble than they're worth."

Oh, Jacob! Veronica lamented. *Such a curmudgeon, he can't appreciate any wonder of nature.*

When they finally reach the walls of the city, Veronica was shocked at how small it seemed. The parapets were not terribly high, and the gates were rather narrow. In fact, the portal was so slight, that the merchant with the camels had to order his servants to unpack the beasts so they could fit through. Veronica marveled as the camels knelt on command, then curled their back legs under and descended to four knees.

"More trouble than they're worth, Jacob?" she teased. "They're as gentle as —"

A loud *ffwoosh* and *splaaaat* interrupted Veronica as the lead camel spat at its handler, dousing him in saliva from crown to chest.

"And there it is," Jacob chortled as the ox cart rumbled past.

As diminutive as Jerusalem seemed from the outside, it did have one majestic structure that dominated the inside. The Temple, the center of worship for all Jews worldwide, was stunning. An enormous and ornate structure, it rose like a city unto itself.

"This could rival any building in Rome," Veronica marveled.

"Not surprising," Jacob shrugged. "The Romans built it. Oh, they say it's Herod the Great's Temple, but he got all the funds from Roman taxes. Building this helped him calm the rabble."

"See," Veronica chirped, "that's Pax Romana!"

"More like old-fashioned corruption," he snarled. "Government extorts half of what the people make, then gives ten percent back. And we're supposed to marvel, *Aren't our overlords kind and generous?*"

"But they'd never have been able to build this on their own," Veronica maintained.

"And what of it?" Jacob replied. "Rome steals half a man's wages, then points to this monstrosity and says, *But we're doing God's work*. So I can't complain about being robbed? If I do, I'm against God? Tell you one thing, if God does exist, He doesn't need to live in a vault, and He can't think kindly of the slave labor it took to build it."

"*If* god exists?"

Jacob contorted his mouth, conceding, "I don't claim to know everything." Then he resumed his sarcasm, "He made every mountain on Earth for us, so maybe He wanted us to build one for him. Who knows? People come from all over the world to see it. They spend their money. So, the Temple's good for business, if nothing else."

Jacob turned the cart right, westward, over a bridge to what he called the Upper City. The bridge gave Veronica an expansive view of the tightly constructed metropolis, a narrow labyrinth of piled stone. Descending the bridge, Veronica felt completely walled in, like a cricket in a tiny maze. The street grew broader as they turned left approaching another impressive edifice. Built on a lesser scale, it had an elegant Romanesque design, including an open forum defined by rows of columns slightly higher than a man on horseback. It also had Roman soldiers, hundreds of them, visible on every level. Veronica gawked as even more paraded across the interior forum.

"They've got more soldiers here than in Rome."

"For Passover," Jacob said. "Most of the men in Judea will flood the city. They'll come down from Galilee. From Decapolis, Perea and Idumea. They'll outnumber the soldiers five to one."

"You think there'll be trouble?" Veronica wondered.

Jacob chortled. "A hundred thousand men, young and old, toasting their liberation under the eyes of their oppressors? How could that lead to trouble?" He pointed to the elegant building. "By the way, that's the former Palace of Herod the Great, Herod Antipas' father. Its current resident is that brother-in-law of yours."

Veronica's heart threatened to burst. *Claudia!* After so many years and thousands of miles, she was less than a stadium[70] away. Jacob stopped the cart. He stared sadly at the palace.

"This is as far as I take you," he said. He reached into the cart and pulled out a small pouch. He loosened the strings and reached inside, pulling out Veronica's ruby bracelet. "We never got to sell this, Bracha." He held it out to her, but Veronica waved his hand away.

"No, Jacob, you keep it."

The old man chuckled. "Me? No, I sell trinkets. The publicans find me with this, they'll raise my tax assessment." He placed it in her hand and folded her fingers around it.

"At least, come up with me," Veronica suggested. "Let my cousin reward you."

"Oh, no," Jacob shuddered. "I so much as speak to the Romans, I'll have an Iscariot's knife through my ribs."

"Will I see you again?" Veronica asked.

Jacob pursed his lips. Regret showed in the deep lines of his face. Veronica was suddenly conscious of where they stood. He, a Jewish man with the Temple rising behind him. And she, a Roman girl with the forces of occupation drilling at her back.

"In a dangerous world," her friend said, "it's best we keep to our own side."

Veronica nodded sadly.

"Good-bye, Bracha," he said.

"Good-bye, Jacob."

Veronica's eyes misted over. She turned and ran to the edge of the forum, intending to slip between a pair of pillars, skirt the area where the troops had come to attention, and dash up the stairs to the Prefect's quarters.

"Halt! What do you want?"

Veronica recoiled before a pair of sentinels. She felt a pillar at her back. "I wish to see Claudia Procula," she said, "the wife of Prefect Pilate."

"And just who are you?"

Veronica removed her veil, revealing her chestnut hair. She lifted her green and hazel eyes and declared, "I am Veronica Procula, her... sister."

The sentinel raised an incredulous eyebrow, but yielded, waving her forward. "Come with me, Mistress."

---

[70] A distance of about 600 feet

Veronica followed the sentinel into the forum. They were almost to the palace stairs when she heard a man scream in terror.

"Mercy, Primus!"

Veronica spun her head towards the troops. They'd broken ranks into a thrashing mass. They seemed to be beating — clubbing — a man in the center. Cudgels, tinged in scarlet, rose and fell ferociously. Blood spattered and pooled about their feet.

"This way, Mistress," the sentinel urged.

Veronica turned away from the horror. She'd had enough.

Chapter 23

At the top of the stairs, Veronica encountered a second line of security. The Sentinel announced her to a Captain of the Guard, who asked her to wait on the portico as he dispatched a messenger inside. The delay was agonizing; Veronica knew how close she was to finally embracing her cousin, to feeling Claudia's arms around her, Claudia's cheek against her own, everything that would remind Veronica of home and safety. Yet she had to stand at the archway, just one level above one more episode of the bloodshed she'd been dodging since Tiberius Caesar had purged the Senate.

Veronica wanted to keep her back to the forum, to firmly declare that she was above the violence and depravity. But that crucifixion had taught her otherwise. She was a participant; she had a stake in every atrocity Rome committed. So she peeked over her shoulder at the Auxilia. Having thoroughly broken their victim, the assailants were stepping away. The troops who'd come late to the melee stooped and dabbed their cudgels in the blood, symbolically sharing in the massacre. A pair of soldiers brought a litter; they'd carry the body outside the city walls to be burned. And what of the gore? Veronica imagined soldiers on punishment duty would scour the stones to remove any trace.

"Veronica!"

She jumped and rushed into Claudia's embrace. Their tears streamed, commingling and smearing Claudia's makeup and Veronica's road dust patina.

"How, by all the gods...?" Claudia wondered. She stepped back, bracing Veronica with her hands tightly on her shoulders. "How?"

Veronica shrugged; the flood of words dammed up insider her.

"Well, look at you!" Claudia continued. "You've grown so beautiful!"

Veronica shivered: *How absurd! She must look frightful!* Then she wished she could return the compliment, but in truth, Claudia looked awful. Thin and careworn, she seemed so much older, her golden hair already threaded with grey. *Had they already lost a lifetime between them?* Veronica read in Claudia's face her regret and her fear of losses to come.

"And father?" Claudia asked.

Veronica twisted away, spurting tears as she faltered. Claudia placed a hand gently on her back, petting her as she cried.

"They're all gone," Veronica rasped. "Everyone."

"It's all right, Love," Claudia whispered. "We're together again. We've a chance to make a home."

*   *   *   *

Claudia took Veronica to the family quarters and had servants prepare a hot bath. Once Veronica was in the tub, Claudia snatched her Galilean clothes and told a servant to "Burn them!"

"No!" Veronica cried. She grabbed hold of her headscarf. "Don't you dare!"

"Please," Claudia groaned. "What could you possibly want with these rags?"

Veronica splashed bathwater at Claudia who shrieked and dropped the clothes. Veronica gathered the headscarf and folded it gently. "A very kind woman gave me these clothes. I'd like to remember her." Veronica spoke directly to the servant in Aramaic as she handed the folded scarf to her. "Have them washed, please, and bring them back to me."

The servant nodded and withdrew.

Claudia's mouth curled in a wry smile. "Well, listen to our little barbarian!" Veronica splashed her again and Claudia withdrew, laughing.

After her bath, Veronica donned a borrowed palla and stola and joined Claudia in her chamber. Sitting by the fire — as her cousin, perched behind her, brushed her tangled hair — brought back a flood of childhood memories. But Claudia grew tense; she stopped brushing as her hand began to tremble. Veronica wondered how her cousin's life had gone in Judea. "We've a chance to make a home," she'd said on the portico. What an odd remark from a married woman.

"Have you been well, Claudia?"

"In what sense?" she replied. "Oh, that's silly. Obviously, I'm too thin. It's this beastly heat. I don't sleep. And I'm like a child with my nightmares."

"And how is Pontius?"

"As to be expected," she said. "I don't have to tell you these are stiff-necked, backward people." Claudia leaned forward onto her elbows and clutched the brush tightly. "I suppose you've heard stories."

Veronica glanced over her shoulder. Claudia's head hung low from rounded shoulders. "He hasn't been cruel to you?"

Claudia rose abruptly and straightened her back. "No. Of course not," she averred. "It's his frustration with these barbarians. We bring them civilization; they cling to tribalism. We're building roads and aqueducts. All they care about is this god who supposedly led them out of Egypt. And will answer their cries and send us flying back to Rome. As if gods could care, as if we're anything more than toys to them."

Veronica placed her hand on the chair beside her, inviting Claudia to sit again. Taking Claudia's hand, she asked, "What if a god could care?"

"Oh, Veronica," she groaned. "You of all people? Father did nothing but reverence the gods, and what happened? Did they protect him?"

Veronica didn't want to argue, but she couldn't restrain herself. "It's just, I met this prophet. He said *The Lord* was coming, was *here*. Then I saw this man heal a dying woman, when she just touched his clothes. And a leper. Even a man he raised from the dead."

Claudia sprang from her chair. "Veronica! Do you know how ignorant these people are?" She paced from the fire to the bed and back. "They can't read. They make up stories to entertain themselves. Miracles? Raised from the dead?"

Veronica threw up her hands. "Forget that. Forget the dead. But, *leprosy*. I talked to a man who said he was cured of leprosy."

"These people will say anything!"

"All right!" Veronica conceded. She stood calmly and stroked Claudia's arms with her open palms to soothe her. "But, Tiberius is terrorizing Rome. Because he's a sick, angry man. The world looks at him with horror and he responds with terror. If this healer could cure Tiberius...?"

"Why should we care!" Claudia shouted. "Tiberius killed your father! And mine? Just as well!" She sat on the edge of her bed, sinking again with her elbows on her knees.

"But," Veronica implored, "we could go home."

Claudia tossed the brush aside and rose from the bed. She smoothed her palla. "Come," she said, offering Veronica a smile. "Time to see the Prefect."

*   *   *   *

They walked from the family quarters to the door outside the Prefect's chamber. A sentinel announced them and promptly ushered them in. Pontius sat in an elaborately carved cathedra, elevated two steps from the floor on a wooden platform. On either side stood his Legates, attending to secretarial duties. Claudia walked to the center of the room and curtsied before her husband. She gestured to Veronica, declaring in all formality, "Prefect Pilate, I present my cousin, Mistress Veronica Procula." Veronica likewise curtsied, remaining low to the floor until the Prefect might permit her to rise. Instead, she heard wooden boards creak, as Pilate descended the platform and crossed the floor. He took her hand, urging her to rise, then bowed to kiss her forehead.

"I'm pleased that you're safe," he said.

Veronica saw no warmth in this man's eyes, yet she managed to say, "Thank you, Pontius." He walked to a small table, poured pure wine into a metal cup, then drank without savoring. Like Claudia, he'd aged beyond the years of his tenure in Judea. But he'd grown fatter; his frame had settled and his temples had greyed.

"Claudia has reported that the Senator, and the remaining members of your household were lost in a Zealot attack. You must give my legate a description of the men," Pilate said.

"It happened many months ago" Veronica said. "In Galilee."

Pilate poured more wine. He spoke without looking at either of the women. "Those hills are full of traitors. And Herod is too weak to deal with them."

The doors opened again, and a Judean woman entered, holding the hand of a young boy, not more than three years old. Roman by appearance and dress, the boy toddled on a withered foot.

"Forgive the intrusion, Prefect, and pardon me, Mistress, but..."

Claudia stooped and picked up the boy. Veronica's eyes widened, as she realized Claudia had a son. "Oh, who is this?" she called.

Claudia beamed. "This is Pontius Tiberius Pilate."

Veronica cringed. Was Pontius so solicitous of Rome he must name his son after that butcher? The child had been born before Caesar's rampage against the Senate. But how awful for Claudia to live with that name, knowing what Tiberius had done to her father. Nevertheless, the mother presented her child proudly, "This is your Aunt Veronica."

Veronica shook his tiny hand. From the corner of her eye, she could see that Pilate was not pleased.

"That will conclude business for today," the Prefect declared, dismissing his men. One Legate plucked the Prefect's mantle from the post of his cathedra and placed it over Pilate's shoulders. Tying the cape below his chin, Pilate crossed to Claudia and spoke lowly, but sternly.

"I told you not to carry him."

"I'm just holding..."

"If you're weak with him," Pilate seethed, "he will grow up weak."

Pilate turned with a flourish and marched out grandly with his Legates trailing.

Still holding little Pontius, Claudia lifted a twisted and withered foot to show Veronica. "A scorpion stung him," she said. "This is an accursed place."

Veronica saw an opportunity. "Claudia, let's take him to Jesus."

"Who?"

"That's the man I spoke about. Believe me, he is a healer!"

Claudia spun away, holding Pontius close to her breast. "This is insane! You're not taking my son to some barbarian magician."

"He's not a magician," Veronica protested. "He's a rabbi."

"I don't care if he's Apollo[71]. I'm the Prefect's wife; I'm not traipsing all over Judea…"

"He's in Jerusalem," Veronica said. "At least, I think…"

"I said, *No!*" Claudia declared with stern finality.

"Pardon," the Judean nurse interjected, "but if you mean the Nazarene, the prophet, he is here."

"How do you know?" Veronica asked.

The servant hesitated.

"Yes, Miriam," Claudia insisted. "How do you know?"

"There's been a great deal of talk, in the synagogues, about this man. Some believe, some don't."

"Believe what?" Claudia asked.

"That he's a prophet," Miriam said. "That he has the authority to work miracles. So there has been much anticipation that he would come for the Passover."

"Have you seen him?" Veronica asked.

Many went to greet him today. He rode into the city on a donkey."

"How impressive," Claudia scoffed.

"From the gates he went to the Temple. But he just looked around and left. They say he might be back tomorrow."

Veronica tipped her head to the side, and scanned Claudia's face for signs of a weakened resolve. There was none at the present, but who could say about tomorrow?

* * * *

That evening, Veronica dined with Claudia and Pontius. Miriam tasted the food in their presence and was dismissed to care for the boy. The necessity of a food taster made Veronica anxious. But it turned out to be the most delicious meal she'd eaten since the feast at Oricum. Tender lamb chunks with savory spices and chopped dates served on a bed of crushed wheat grain. The women drank sage tea while Pontius had several cups of pure wine. But, aside from Veronica complimenting the meal and Claudia remarking that the cook had become predictable, there was no conversation. Finally, Claudia announced that she would look in on young Pontius. With Pilate's leave, the ladies rose, curtseyed slightly and exited.

---

[71] The Roman god associated with medicine and cures

Veronica debated mentioning the healer, but decided both of them were too tired to discuss it rationally. So she made her goodnight, hugged Claudia tightly and went to her bed. Veronica fell into a deep slumber almost before her head hit the pillow. She slept comfortably for the first time since leaving Leah's home, but awoke after several hours. At first, she thought she was still dreaming; the apparition at the foot of her bed seemed unreal. Then she realized she was awake, and Claudia was sitting there, watching her.

"Did I wake you?"

"No, but... why are you here?"

Claudia looked at the fire, then rubbed her tired eyes. "I often sit here. After I've had a dream. So I don't disturb the Prefect."

Veronica rose to an elbow and tucked her legs under her. She felt a flutter of hope: perhaps Claudia had had a vision of the healer. "What was your dream?" she asked.

"It's become an obsession," she moaned. "Tombs. Death."

So much for hope, Veronica thought. "Is it always the same?"

"It seems to progress," she said. "Becoming more vivid." She brushed her hair from her face and gathered it in a knot behind her head before letting the tresses fall on her shoulders. "Last night, I felt I was lying on a cold slab, with something weighing on my eyes. I reached and felt coins. I rose and pried the coins off. I realized then I was trapped in a sealed tomb. I tried to scream, but no sound would come out. I panicked, pushing against the entrance stone. Then I heard grinding, stone on stone, and was blinded by a shaft of bright light. The light was not the dawn: it emanated from a being, a winged goddess who'd pushed the stone aside. I tried to thank the goddess, but couldn't speak. The goddess pointed to the ground outside the tomb, at the torn body of a man. I wanted to help him, but I couldn't move. I looked for help, and saw only a barren landscape. Far away on a jagged cliff, a man in a toga stood with a scourge in his hand, dripping blood. I crouched over the man, shielding his body with mine, but a voice commanded me to stop. *Claudia!* The man in the toga hovered over me, cracking the blood scourge. The wounded man grabbed my wrist; his hand had been pierced. He pleaded, *Stop him!* That's when I awoke."

"That was last night?" Veronica asked. Claudia nodded. "And tonight, it was the same?"

"Similar," she nodded. "As I said, it seems to progress. Tonight, the wounded man — only he wasn't wounded — was standing, with his torso bare. A shaft of light illuminated him in total darkness. His skin was pale ivory, unblemished. Then blood started streaming from thousands of wounds. He seemed to rise up toward the source of the light. I stepped backward and my shoulder struck something hard: the breast plate of a Roman soldier... but no, it was Pontius. His face was a mask of death, his eyes hollow. Then the earth opened, and we sank into a ring of fire. Terrified, I grabbed Pontius, begging him to save me. I pleaded with those hollow eyes. And he laughed, revealing bloody teeth."

"Claudia, that's awful."

"It's always the same man. It's always Pontius torturing him."

"Do you have any idea who this man is?"

Claudia shook her head. "I'm certain I've never seen him."

Veronica hugged Claudia. They sat for several minutes without speaking.

"Pontius is not happy you're here," Claudia said. "Oh, he's happy for me — he says — that I'll have someone here to pass the days. But he's concerned about Macro."

"What's he going to do?" Veronica asked.

"He must file a report."

Veronica felt a burning pit open in her stomach.

"He has no choice," Claudia insisted. "This post was supposed to be four years; Sejanus promised to have us recalled. But we know what happened to Sejanus. And after Caesar attacked the Senate — when father fled — Pontius lost favor with Macro. Now it's been seven long years. We can't go on here."

Veronica couldn't believe what she was hearing. "Claudia, Macro has sought my life."

"Father's life!" Claudia corrected. "This is a man's world. You and I don't matter. No one has come after me."

"They just haven't let you come back to Rome."

"And they never will... if we show disloyalty." Claudia took Veronica's hands in her own. "Pontius will write Macro asking to be appointed your guardian. There's no reason not to grant the request."

"There was no reason to suspect us in the first place," Veronica cried. "But they still burned our house and tried to kill us."

"There's nothing else we can do."

Veronica had to shake her head. She rose and paced over to the fire. Facing Claudia again, she said, "You're dreaming of a man who begs you to protect him. From Pontius. Here I am. Do I have to beg you, too?"

Claudia's mouth dropped open as she struggled for words. "You have nothing to fear from Pontius."

"All right," Veronica said, "I'll do as you say. But I need a favor from you."

*   *   *   *

"I can't believe I'm doing this," Claudia groused. "It's the desert sun. Dogs go mad, men become prophets and women chase mirages."

They were following Miriam up the front steps of the Temple to the main courtyard, called The Court of the Gentiles. It was as far as they were permitted to go. Beyond that, Miriam had explained, lay The Court of Women, where

Jewish women could gather for prayer. Though they were dressed to blend in — Veronica in her Galilean garb and Claudia in an outfit Miriam had supplied — they dare not violate the laws of the Temple; if they were caught, it would present the Prefect with a terrible dilemma. Next to the women's area lay The Court of Israel, where circumcised men who were not priests prayed. Chambers beyond that were reserved for priests, including the altar area where they performed animal sacrifices and The Holy of Holies, a mysterious, closed vault that only the High Priest could enter, and only once a year.

The Court of the Gentiles was the largest common area of the entire structure, and, according to Miriam's sources, that was as far as the prophet Jesus had entered yesterday. It was a busy area, where pilgrims from all over the world stopped to change their foreign coins into Jewish shekels, because coins with graven images, such as Caesar's profile, were not permitted to go into the Temple treasury. Once a pilgrim changed his denarii for shekels, he could purchase an animal for sacrifice. These ranged from small doves or pigeons that paupers bought to unblemished lambs and oxen for the very rich. Veronica looked at young Pontius, cradled tightly in Claudia's arms. If they were going to present the boy to Jesus for healing, they would have to catch him in The Court of the Gentiles.

But Veronica worried they'd never get near him. Already, before the sun had topped the city walls, people were flooding into the Temple. Many were infirm, crippled or blind. There would be such a crush around Jesus, how would they get through? And if his goons saw through their disguises, taking them for Roman spies, they'd be in serious danger from the mob.

At the top of the stairs, the crowd compressed as it funneled towards two narrow gates. Veronica grabbed hold of Miriam and Claudia so they wouldn't be separated. Claudia held Pontius with one arm and extended the other forward, so the boy wouldn't be crushed. Bobbing amidst this river of people, Veronica felt the futility of their quest. How could she hope to find anyone? As they squeezed through the gate, she was bumped from behind. Turning, she saw a wooden cage, a veritable aviary of desperate, flapping fowl, held aloft by a stooped, old man.

"Jacob!"

His eyes widened, but what started as a smile contorted into a mask of horror. "I don't know you," he whispered.

"Who's this?" Claudia demanded.

Jacob stared directly into his cage, and mumbled, "Please, I don't want any trouble. I just want to make enough money to get out of here before the Passover."

As they emerged from the gate, the crowd dispersed in the open space, forming several streams toward the merchant tables and the portals to the interior chambers.

"Praise the gods, I can breathe," Claudia said.

Veronica, mindful of maintaining their disguise, reminded her, "This is not the place to use that expression."

They both turned to Miriam for direction, but before she could speak, there came a loud crash from the far end of the courtyard. Through the crowd, Veronica saw tables overturning and coins flying through the air. The crowd roared, seemingly in approval.

"What in the world?" Claudia cried.

A whip cracked. A pen of goats burst open and the animals stampeded. They charged toward the gate, jostling poor Jacob, who tossed his aviary aside as he fell. The cage split upon impact and the doves took flight. Another crack of the whip, and more doves burst into the air. Lambs bleated and leapt. Now men were running for the exit, a whip cracking at their tails. The man with the whip circled the courtyard.

"Jesus!" Veronica gasped.

Claudia, huddled with Pontius against the wall, raised her head. She grabbed at Veronica's sleeve. "Is this your healer?"

His back was to them now. Neither she nor Claudia could see his face, but Veronica knew his form and bearing. She also recognized his voice.

"Is it not written," he scolded, "*My house will be called a house of prayer for all nations*?"

"Answer me," Claudia demanded. "Is it he?"

"You've made it a den of thieves!"

Veronica nodded.

"He's crazy," Claudia said.

"I don't understand," was all Veronica could mutter.

Soldiers — not Roman —responded now, filing onto the upper parapet. Veronica imagined this must be the Temple's own guard. Among them was a bearded man, dressed ceremoniously. Several more men, similarly outfitted, assembled beside him, most likely the Temple priests.

"Come on. Miriam!" Claudia ordered. She grabbed her servant and bolted toward the gate. Veronica tried to follow, but a wall of men formed, apparently to block the Temple Guard from descending the stairs. Veronica saw Claudia slip through the gate, but she was cut off and pinned against the wall.

The ceremoniously dressed man — perhaps the High Priest whom Miriam had mentioned —shouted down from the parapet, "Who gave you authority to do this? Answer me!"

Jesus replied calmly, "Answer me! And I'll answer you."

There was some chittering amongst the crowd. It seemed they were mostly on the prophet's side. This seemed to anger the High Priest. His cohorts also looked uneasy, and regarded the mob with suspicion. When the noise died down, the prophet spoke first.

"John," he said, eyeing the parapet. "Surely, you remember John? Did the authority for his baptism come from heaven, or from men? Tell us, Caiaphas!"

The crowd shouted their enthusiasm, and began chanting, "Tell us, tell us!"

Caiaphas, the High Priest, glowered. "We're not talking about John," he said.

"Because you can't talk about John!" Jesus answered.

The High Priest shouted back, "We're talking about you! Here! Now!"

But Jesus was unperturbed. "If you cannot say anything about John, and his authority, how can you say anything about me or my authority?"

The crowd laughed and applauded. After a moment Jesus held up his hand for silence. He looked up at the parapet again.

"I'll give you another chance," he told the priests. "Tell me what you think. A man had two sons. He said to the first, *Son, go and work today in the vineyard*. The son answered, *I will not*, but changed his mind and went. The father went to the other son, *Son, go and work today in the vineyard*. The second answered, *I will, sir*, but he didn't. Which of the sons did as his father wanted?"

Caiaphas was losing patience. "The first," he snapped.

Jesus smiled and nodded to the parapet. "And that is why," he said gently, and with some sympathy, "tax collectors and prostitutes are entering the kingdom of God ahead of you." The priests on the parapet scoffed, but Jesus raised a hand to quiet them, explaining, "John came to show righteousness, and you didn't believe him, but tax collectors and prostitutes did." He strolled in a tight circle around the yard, before directing his attention back to the priest.

"This is how the kingdom of heaven works," he said. "Like a wedding banquet. The Lord invites. You turn him down, so he says to his servant, *Go to the street corners and invite anyone you find*. And the servant goes out into the streets and gathers all the good and the bad, to fill the wedding hall with guests."

He turned away from the priests, in all their finery standing above the crowd, and he crouched beside some poor beggars, sitting on pallets. He smiled warmly "So come in." He stood and gestured broadly to the crowd on the lower level. "All of you, guests of the Lord. This is your house!"

Jesus turned with arms still outstretched, sweeping the crowd forward and leading them into The Court of Women. Veronica still clung to the wall, wondering if she dare follow. Merchants crept back to their tables and stood them upright. They stooped and picked up coins from the floor. On the parapet, Caiaphas huddled with the other priests, speaking in hushed tones.

Veronica moved with the flow of the crowd. The prophet was almost through the gate to the next chamber. His entourage gathered closely about him. Veronica recognized the burly man who'd called her a spy and the young man who'd passed out loaves and fish. But there, on the fringes of his circle, glaring back at her, was someone she'd never expected to see again, and certainly not in a holy place. With a bored sneer, Salome vanished into the crowd.

Chapter 24

Veronica listened intently as Jesus taught and started to get a sense of what made his religion different from what she'd learned in Rome and observed in the synagogue of Ammathus. The Roman gods were powerful and their actions had great or grave consequences for human beings. But their motivations were all too human. At times they acted from reason and compassion, to be sure, but often they were jealous, greedy, angry or lustful. So they lived in eternal conflict, among themselves and with humans. The god Jesus spoke about — whom he called *Father* — was all-powerful, but restrained. He would act only when asked, because he respected people's free will. When he did intervene in people's lives, he had a singular reason: *love*. Jesus spoke of a generous, loving father who wanted his children to be happy. It was true, he said, occasionally the Father had to punish his children, but only when refraining from punishment would be unjust. Veronica compared this to stories of Roman gods, who only helped a human when they had some perverse attraction to him, or when they'd made a wager with another god. Jesus told a story of a father so generous that, even after his son had wasted everything he'd given him, the father celebrated his return and lavished more wealth upon him.

Veronica could not see Jupiter acting in this manner. Any Roman god would demand revenge. But Jesus spoke against the notion of revenge; he taught his followers to pray for those who persecuted them. *Yes*, he replied to a shout from the crowd, *even the Romans*. Veronica began to understand what Judah had meant when he called the prophet's teaching "a radical love."

The sun started dipping towards the west, and Jesus prepared to take his leave. Veronica couldn't help but wonder how someone like Salome, so selfish and worldly and bored with everything, could be attracted to Jesus. Perhaps she sensed he had power. He'd certainly held sway over the mob. Veronica felt a twinge of jealousy that Salome had wormed her way inside his entourage, while she had been tramping all over Judea and would now be walled up in the Prefect's Palace. But she remembered what the girl Mary had said: Jesus would be back and forth between Jerusalem and Bethany throughout the Passover. With any luck, Veronica could track him down again.

A sudden pang reminded Veronica that she hadn't eaten since early morning — *no loaves and fishes today!* — so she made her way towards the gate, hoping to beat the crowd out of the Temple.

Claudia would be upset that she'd stayed. And worried. But Veronica was sure she wouldn't tell Pontius. As long as she made it back to the Palace by supper time, she'd be fine. She'd explain to Claudia about the riot, which, as she understood it, was a protest against corrupt practices in the Temple. She'd tell her how Jesus had calmed down, and how he'd spoken only of love.

          *   *   *   *

Longinus stood on the portico facing east. As a horse soldier, there was nothing he hated more than confinement, so he'd requested some duty from the Prefect, even as he convalesced. Standing watch here was largely ceremonial; any real threat to the Prefect would be met by sentinels below in the forum. But it allowed him to be out in the open air, which did lift his spirits, but prevented them from descending further. Nominally, he was the ranking officer on the portico, but effectively, he did not exist. Visitors to the Prefect came and went, processed by Sentinels framing the portal, while he stood like a statue, an ornament, no more functional than the pilaster at his back.

His eyes were still bandaged — he'd visit the doctor again tomorrow — so he couldn't help worrying that this was his fate: to feel his way through perpetual darkness. To stand mute and useless on the periphery of life. Dwelling on his condition made him increasingly bitter; his only solace was to contemplate revenge. In his mind, he pictured the Zealot Barabbas, chained to a pillar and scourged until the flesh hung in strips from his back. Longinus had only witnessed that gruesome punishment on a couple of occasions. Each time he'd had no interest in the prisoner, so the spectacle had little appeal, other than satisfying a soldier's curiosity about the limits of human endurance. The few crucifixions he'd overseen were perfunctory: stretch a man out, place the nails and drive them through, then stand the cross in the sun. After that came the long, dull stretch while the soldiers waited for the unfortunate wretch to die. Some placed bets on how long it would take. Longinus found that morbid, but as an officer, he had to make allowances; in every barracks there were men who would gamble on virtually anything.

Yes, as a soldier, Longinus had found combat thrilling and executions tedious. But this was one execution he was going to relish. He'd picked up a few tricks for prolonging the victim's life to extend his torment. Most crucified prisoners died of asphyxia; hanging as they did, they could only expand their lungs by pulling themselves up by their arms and pushing with their legs. The pain, exhaustion and blood loss soon made that impossible. Their lungs filled with fluid, and they effectively drowned. But by outfitting the cross with a peg, jutting out between the victim's legs, the executioners made sure the body was supported, so the victim could breathe. He would last until he bled to death, which could take days, since the wounds to the hands were elevated. If the arms were lashed to the crossbeam, the ropes acted as a tourniquet preventing blood loss. Giving the victim water periodically caused him to linger further. Longinus intended to use all those methods on Barabbas. A man his size might last for more than a week.

The sun was behind the Palace now and Longinus felt himself enveloped in cool shade. Another day almost over. Soon the Passover would conclude, and Longinus would be free to fulfill his fantasy. At this point, what more did he have to live for?

He heard a light patter of footsteps climbing the stairs to the portico. He instinctively came to attention. The visitor did not speak to the guards. But the footsteps did not continue into the Palace. Longinus sensed that whoever was there was focusing attention on him.

"Centurion?"

A woman. *Was it possible?* His chest swelled. He had to consciously counter the pressure, tamping down on his heart.

"Mistress," he greeted her calmly. "You've arrived safely. Praise the gods."

"You've been injured."

"Superficially," Longinus declared.

A breeze wafted across the portico, and Longinus caught the scent of lavender, which he imagined came from her hair. He tried to picture her face. He remembered her vividly, peeking from curtains of the wagon, asleep in that dark room with a shaft of sun illuminating her skin, her mouth coming close enough to kiss, then her fiery defiance. *Was she even now standing close enough to kiss?* Could he abandon all decorum, sweep her up in his arms and take her? What did he have to lose? Even if the guards overreacted, dealing him a mortal blow, he'd still be better off for that one sweet moment. Standing so close to the object of his love, but shut off by a veil of darkness, Longinus was utterly desolate.

"Mistress," he said. "If it please you, it's time that I returned to the barracks."

"Should it please a lady when an officer requests permission to go?"

Longinus cleared his throat. "I serve at the lady's pleasure."

"I only meant," she spoke lowly, "that you should not feel, given our past encounters, you should not feel, that is, I hold no resentment."

"Nor I, Mistress."

"You are a devoted servant of the Empire. No one shall ever hear differently from me."

"Thank you, Mistress."

This was more than Longinus could stand. Either she was in earnest, meaning he had somehow found favor with her, or she was taking pity on him for his affliction. If the former, this was as near to a declaration of love as a woman of her station could issue. It was exhilarating and excruciating, since any chance he'd had at winning her love was doomed now by his infirmity. And if her words were pity, his utility as a soldier, indeed his fitness as a man, was over.

Longinus heard guards in the hallway, followed by those on the portico, snap to attention. It could only be the Prefect coming. He prayed the girl would step away, so Pilate would not suspect they'd been speaking.

"Soldiers, at ease," a Legate sounded.

"Veronica," the Prefect called. "Attend me here."

Longinus remained at attention, straining to hear their conversation, but a voice beside him broke in. "Primus, our watch is ended. Allow me to escort you to the officer's commissary."

"Thank you," Longinus answered. He extended his hand to touch the soldier's forearm. They walked to the edge of the portico and down the steps.

*   *   *   *

Pontius was visibly annoyed at Veronica. "Why aren't you with Claudia?"

"I was just taking some air, Pontius."

"Prefect," he remanded.

"I'm sorry, *Prefect*. I was just taking some air."

"You can do that on the verandas with the Lady of the Palace."

"I understand, Prefect."

"What's that on your arm?"

"Oh," Veronica started. She held the Galilean robe and headscarf draped over her arm; she'd peeled them off as she'd entered the forum. "It's the costume I wore on my journey. I'd ask the servants to wash it, so I..."

"You went to reclaim it?" Pilate's eyes burned into her. "Would you have run such an errand in Rome? Or would you have sent a slave? Understand that when you behave in a manner beneath your station, you insult the dignity of this house."

"My apologies, Prefect." Veronica lowered her eyes, hoping a show of submission would persuade him to truncate his lecture.

"I had hoped that having you here would be good for Claudia." Pilate stepped to the edge of the portico, gesturing for Veronica to cleave to his side. "Vale, Primus," Pilate called. "I'm sure the doctor will delight us with news on the morrow."

Veronica hadn't noticed the Centurion leaving. He stiffened his spine and responded, "If the gods be willing. Vale, Prefect." He stepped gingerly down the stairs with the assistance of another soldier.

Pilate gazed out at the city. "I have my work," he said. "But Claudia is isolated. In other outposts, she'd busy herself entertaining dignitaries. But these barbarians won't enter our grounds. We're unclean to them. Imagine!"

"Perhaps she might go outside the grounds."

"They'd slit her throat within minutes. You know what these Zealots are like." Pilate lifted his chin towards the Centurion. "See there? His eyes were nearly gouged from his head. Pity; he was a good man, Longinus. We got them though. They're rotting in the dungeon as we speak."

Veronica thought of the Baptist. Herod's dungeon was awful; she could only imagine what Pilate's was like. "What will you do?" she asked.

Pilate shrugged. "What would Caesar have me do?"

"You'll crucify them," Veronica said. She meant it simply as a statement of fact, but something must have crept into her tone, making Pilate defensive.

"They killed two of my officers. And six other men."

Veronica watched Longinus cross the area of yesterday's attack. The blood had been scrubbed from the stones, but a reddish tinge remained, spread over a wider area.

"Yesterday, when I came in," Veronica said, "Your men were killing each other."

Pilate blanched. "That was a matter of discipline," he said. "I'm sorry you had to witness it, but these things are sometimes necessary."

Veronica lifted her eyes from the forum over the compact maze of stone walls and terracotta roofs to the Temple, high on the eastern hill. Its gold adornments shimmered in the fading light. She recalled the words she'd heard there, but regretted the simplicity of the audience: farmers and mechanicals, shepherds and stone masons. This cold man, who held the power of life and death, had not heard the teachings. Veronica lamented that irony; if radical love were ever to take hold, there'd have to be a meeting between Pontius Pilate and Jesus of Nazareth.

Chapter 25

"What's in the basket?"

That was the question Veronica had feared. She kept her head down and reached into the wicker sack. *Keep sleeping, baby*, she thought, as she gently pulled a loaf of flat bread out to show the guard.

"Bread, sir," she said. "The Lady of the Palace allowed us to bake Passover bread for our family. That's why I'm leaving so late."

"I guess it's all right," the Guard said. "The Prefect certainly won't eat it."

With that, the guard let Veronica pass. She walked quickly, trying not to jostle the basket. The last thing she needed was for Pontius to start crying before she was off the Palace grounds.

As Veronica had expected, Claudia had been livid with her and nearly hysterical with worry. The riot in the Temple had frightened her, not simply for the immediate threat to their safety, but for the repercussions if they'd been injured. The Prefect could not have tolerated an attack on his wife, and would have demanded the High Priest hand over the guilty parties. That would have been a diplomatic nightmare. Claudia wasn't exaggerating when she suggested it could lead to rebellion. Clearly, Veronica was not going to convince Claudia to leave the Palace again anytime soon. And since the Palace was unclean in the minds of most Jews, they couldn't expect Jesus to wander in either. Veronica had to find another way.

Fortunately for Veronica's plan, if not for Claudia herself, the Lady's hysteria led to a crushing headache and an early retirement. Veronica volunteered to mind young Pontius. She then made her way to the servants' area, scrounged a basket, pilfered some of the unleavened bread Miriam had baked and brewed some strong valerian tea to make Pontius drowsy. She donned her Galilean disguise, placed the child in the basket with a few loaves of bread and exited through the servant's gate. She knew she was taking a great risk — kidnapping the Prefect's son! — but it seemed the only chance he'd be healed. Veronica left a note for Claudia, and hoped she wouldn't awaken prematurely and discover them gone.

As good fortune and potent herbs would have it, little Pontius slept like Endymion[72] from the moment Veronica placed him in the basket until they crossed the bridge to the Temple. At the gate she hired a mule and, to the jaw-dropping bewilderment of the stable hand, proceeded to ride it bareback, the reins in one hand and balancing Pontius on the saddle with the other. Since the moon was nearly full, she had enough light on the trail to follow the switchbacks. She hoped she'd remembered the path correctly and that the flickering lights below were the home fires of Bethany.

*   *   *   *

The streets of Bethany were even more crowded than on the night Veronica and Jacob had arrived. But the mood of the people was not celebratory; a somber tone hung over the travelers and townspeople, huddled around the outdoor kitchen fires. Veronica tied the mule's reins to a tree near the well, gathered Pontius in both arms and walked towards the home of the two sisters.

---

[72] In Greek mythology, the king of Elis whom Zeus granted immortality, but also eternal slumber

The outdoor kitchen fire was blazing and the light from a dozen lamps leaked from the open door and windows. Veronica braced herself for rude treatment, but she didn't see the rugged man or his associate who'd accused her of spying. Monitoring the door was a sly-looking man, whose trimmed beard and curled hair bespoke of feminine vanity. He wore a long, sheathed knife on his belt, from which also hung a full coin purse, which he cradled in his palm and kneaded with supple fingers. Veronica thought his mannerisms reminiscent of Sejanus. It didn't surprise her to see Salome at his side, and the two of them whispering conspiratorially.

Suddenly Veronica realized her blood was up; she wanted to confront Salome. The Baptist's death was on her hands, and Veronica's loved ones had died for her vindictive, cynical joke. Veronica wished they were men, so she could take revenge. Then she felt ashamed, even contemplating vengeance on her way to see Jesus, who'd talked about praying for enemies. She wondered what Jesus knew about this girl. Would he allow her to remain in his company if the truth were revealed? Or would he expel her, forcing her to wander unprotected through Zealot territory? That might be the best revenge. At least the best a woman could hope for. Veronica considered how she might poison Jesus against Salome, but immediately felt a crushing weight of shame. To consider doing harm, then asking for help? Jesus had spoken against this very thing; he'd said, *First make peace with your brother, then approach the altar.* Veronica took a breath. Her mission was Pontius; it had nothing to do with Salome.

Before Veronica could step towards the door, a woman emerged, holding a fistful of coins. She was handsome, but weathered, as though she'd had a hard life. But unlike Herodias, whose turmoil had ruined her, this woman seemed more beautiful for wear, as though her hardships had elicited some inward grace and drawn it to the surface where it shimmered. Eyeing the coins, the sly man extended an open palm, squinting at her to hand the money over.

"Don't even try, Judas."

"Magdalene —"

She pushed his hand away with her elbow and trotted past, clutching the coins, hand over fist. The sly man, Judas, sneered at her, then caught Veronica's eye.

"What?" he demanded.

Veronica lifted the boy and showed Judas his withered foot. Judas pursed his lips, then tipped his head towards the interior of the house. Veronica squeezed past him, choosing to ignore Salome perched over his right shoulder.

"Her?" the palace brat whispered. "She's Roman. She better not talk to him before me."

The interior had been emptied of furniture and was packed with people standing against the walls or seated on blankets and cushions. Lamps, hung from the ceiling, lighted the white plaster vault. Veronica saw Jesus, seated at the far end of the room. He had his eyes closed, and was listening to a recitation. The young man who'd passed out the loaves and fishes sat with an open scroll on his knees. Veronica tried to make out what he was saying. It wasn't Aramaic; it was the more formal language the Jews used for their prayers.

"My God, my God, why have You forsaken me? Why are You so far from helping me, and from the words of my groaning? My God, I cry in the daytime, but You answer not; and by night I am not silent or find no rest."

Veronica felt a tug at her robe. The younger sister, Mary, had sprawled across the floor to get her attention. She retreated to her spot against the wall, and gestured for Veronica to join her. Veronica stepped over a couple of squatting bodies, and settled in next to Mary.

The young man continued, "All the mighty ones upon earth shall eat and worship," but a commotion at the door interrupted him. The handsome woman was back. Clutching something, she barged past the sly gatekeeper and practically trampled half a dozen people on the floor. But she reached Jesus and knelt beside him. Veronica saw what she was holding: an alabaster jar. She broke the clay seal and the room was filled with sweet fragrance.

"Keep reading," she commanded. She poured oil on her hands and stroked Jesus' head, from the part of his hair to his neck and shoulders. At the door, Judas seethed as the young man read:

"All they that go down to the dust shall bow before Him, even he who cannot keep himself alive. Posterity shall serve Him; they shall tell of the Lord to the next generation. They shall come and shall declare His righteousness to a people yet to be born —"

"Woman, what have you done?" Judas barked. "That's expensive oil. You've squandered money that should have gone to the poor."

Jesus opened his eyes and spoke lowly, but firmly. "Judas. You will always have the poor to tend to. You won't always have me." He rose, then placed his hand on the woman's head. He spoke warmly, "Thank you for your kindness, Mary." Then he strode toward the door, the guests on the floor parting for him.

But Judas wasn't done protesting. "Kindness? What has she done?"

Jesus answered, "She's prepared my body for burial."

A gasp went up from the crowd and murmurs of protest followed. But Jesus just looked back at the woman who'd anointed him and said softly, "Every age will remember what she has done." Then, without looking at Veronica, Jesus hooked a finger toward her. "Bring the child," he said and exited abruptly. Veronica scrambled to her feet, hoisted Pontius in her arms and dashed after Jesus.

The crowds at the fires sprang to life as Jesus walked past, but he extended his arms, commanding them to remain where they were. He walked with such determination that Veronica had to jog to catch up. They reached an open area away from the houses near a small pen. Lambs bleated and a small dog yapped. Jesus rested his hands on the top rail of the pen and peered in. Veronica couldn't help feeling that she was intruding. This good man seemed to be laboring under an emotional weight, and she was adding another demand. But if Jesus helped her, she could help him. If he was apprehensive over the powerful enemies he'd made, she could introduce him to a powerful friend. He wouldn't rot in a dungeon like the Baptist until it pleased someone's whim that he should die. Not if he healed —

"Pilate's son?" Jesus asked.

"How...?" Veronica marveled. "You are a prophet." She held the boy up to him and Jesus reached for the crippled foot. "He'll be very grateful," Veronica proffered. "I mean the Prefect. Pilate."

Jesus shook his head. "You mustn't tell him."

"Oh, but I must," Veronica entreated. "The Prefect can help you."

But Jesus stared intently, instructing her, "You must hide the child from him until all things have been fulfilled."

"What... things?" Veronica asked.

But Jesus didn't explain. He simply took the boy's foot between his hands and rubbed it. The twisted sinews straightened and the flesh filled out. The foot looked completely healthy.

"Thank you," Veronica cried. "Oh, thank you.[73]"

Jesus smiled modestly. "Go now. It's your faith that healed him."

Was that possible? She'd imagined it. But it certainly wasn't any power within her that had worked the cure. Still, Veronica didn't want to contradict a miracle worker. She had an urge to simply curtsey and slip away, but realized she might never have another chance to discuss her plan. The sheep started bleating again, and Veronica turned to see if someone were approaching. She feared the prophet's goons might have heard him dismiss her. But looking back, she saw only shadows.

"Master," she said. "Obviously, your power is great." Jesus turned away, resting his elbows on the rail of the pen.

"What power I have has been granted me by the Father."

Veronica knew he meant the Jewish god. "Forgive me," she continued, "but you must want to do the most with it." Jesus nodded sadly. "The Emperor has leprosy," she said. "If you heal him, you will heal the whole Empire. All the misery and suffering that he inflicts, he'd forbear. He'd learn mercy."

Jesus reached into the pen. He pulled out a bleating lamb and held it to his breast. He looked past Veronica and called, almost cheerfully, "Come out of the shadows; we are people of the light."

Veronica followed his line of sight and saw the person he'd called: Salome. She crept forward until she stood at Veronica's side. Jesus spoke.

[73] The story of the healing of Pilate's son comes from The Golden Legend

"There was a landlord who had acres of fine grass and he hired a man to take his flock from the pen to the pasture daily. But the hired man was crafty. He kept the sheep in the pen and leased the acres to other shepherds and grew rich as the landlord's flock waned. The sheep wondered what they should do." He eyed Salome. "Some said, *Let us rise up against him. When he comes into the pen to feed us the meager cuttings, let us attack and kill him.*" Then looking at Veronica, he continued, "Others said, *No, for we would still be in this pen. Rather let us kiss his hand when he feeds us and therefore turn his heart, so he will let us out.*" He scratched the lamb's belly gently; it seemed so content, almost asleep in his arms. "But the landlord learned what the hired man had done and said, *Let me send my Son, who will be a good shepherd to my flock. He shall open the pen and lead them to my green pastures.*" Jesus placed the lamb back in the pen.

Salome fumed. "So you'll do nothing about Herod. You have the power to overthrow him, but you'll do nothing!" She stomped and ran off, back into the shadows.

Veronica paused for a second. She read the strain on Jesus' face. Pontius fussed and she shifted him in her arms and soothed him. She just had one more question.

"What did the hired man do when the Son came?" When Jesus said nothing, she answered for him. "He killed him, didn't he?"

Jesus smiled and touched Veronica's head. "But the lambs were fed."

Chapter 26

On the ride back to Jerusalem, Veronica's spirits were buoyant. The rented mule was her Pegasus as she glided on air towards her mansion in the sky. Of course, she was still apprehensive about being caught sneaking into the Palace. Her plan had not entailed keeping the healing a secret. She'd hoped that once the boy's foot was restored, the Prefect would grant her clemency for her infractions. But Jesus had given her strict instructions not to reveal the miracle "until all things have been fulfilled." What that meant was anyone's guess, but she assumed she'd recognize it when it happened.

Veronica wasn't the only one who'd have trouble keeping the secret. Pontius was wide awake and fascinated with his healthy foot. He flexed it, he kicked, he reached down and grabbed his toes. He was so fidgety, Veronica struggled to keep him centered on the mule. "Yes, it's wonderful," she told him.

"You're going to be able to run and jump like all the other boys." *And your mother won't worry so much*, she thought, *and your father will be proud of you.*

The moon was setting when she entered the city and returned the mule. Pontius was so happy to stand on his new foot. He jumped excitedly and ran in tight circles. There was no way Veronica was going to get him back into the basket. So she let the boy walk — down past the Temple, across the bridge and through the narrow streets to the forum. By then he was tired enough to ask to be carried. So she hoisted the boy in her arms and trundled towards the servants' entrance.

But how to get past the guards? She really had not thought this through! If she could wait a couple of hours, some of the workers would arrive and she could take a chance of slipping past within a group. But by then Claudia would surely have discovered that Pontius was missing, and even if she'd read Veronica's note, she'd dissolve into hysterics. Veronica had to get into the Palace while Claudia was still in some tenuous control of her emotions.

Veronica concluded that since she couldn't escape detection, she should allow herself to be caught. She hid behind a pillar and removed her Galilean robe and headscarf. She placed them in the basket, then strolled onto the forum. Holding Pontius in her arms and singing to him, she walked back and forth in the open area in full view of the Sentinels. After a few minutes, a Captain of the Guard descended from the portico and approached her.

"Mistress, may I ask what you are doing out here at this hour?"

"Oh," Veronica smiled, "the Prefect's son wouldn't sleep. He was so fussy, I was afraid he'd wake his mother — my sister? — and the Prefect, too, of course. He's a busy man, he needs his sleep. So I thought the night air might tire him out."

"But, Mistress," he asked, "the forum? It's not safe for you out here."

"No?" Veronica feigned surprise. "Why is that? I can walk down any street in Rome at any hour and not fear being molested," she lied. "And this forum? Surrounded by soldiers of Rome? Oh, I don't think you want the Prefect to hear his family is not safe."

"I-I," the Captain stammered. "I only meant... how did you get out here anyway?"

"Oh," Veronica's eyes widened. "You didn't see me walk past? When I strolled right out the front door and down the steps from the portico?"

"That's impossible."

"Oh, the Prefect would not be happy to hear that. No wonder you claim I'm not safe."

The Captain blanched. "Mistress, it would please me greatly if you would return to the Palace."

"Captain, you have convinced me." Veronica started immediately towards the stairs. She called back over his shoulder, "I'll put in a kind word for you with the Prefect."

"Mistress," the Captain called, "that won't be necessary!"

Veronica dashed up the stairs and headed directly for her quarters. She'd keep Pontius in her bed tonight and present him to Claudia when she awoke. She tossed the basket on the floor and turned down the covers of her bed. She laid Pontius down and sat on the edge beside him. She'd done it! But now she was thoroughly exhausted and needed —

"I really think you've gone insane."

Veronica's head spun: Claudia sat on a stool by the fire.

"If Pontius had found your note, he'd have sent a legion after you."

"He would have regretted that," Veronica said. She waved Claudia over. "Come. Look."

Claudia rose listlessly and padded over to the bed. Veronica lifted the blanket, revealing the healed foot.

"Oh, gods," Claudia gasped. "It's healed!"

"We have to hide it from Pontius," Veronica said. "Just for a few days."

"Why? Your prophet?"

Veronica's mind swam just thinking about him. How could she explain him to someone who hadn't met him? "He's a great, great man, Claudia. If ever a god walked on earth."

"Please, don't talk of gods," Claudia groaned. "Not while they've all conspired to haunt my dreams."

"You're still not sleeping?"

Claudia rubbed her tired eyes with the heels of her hands. "It's always the same. The unblemished man — and Pontius determined to kill him. I tell him not to. But he doesn't listen. He's not himself; he's monstrous."

"When we were leaving Italy," Veronica said, "we heard stories. A man called Pontius a butcher."

Claudia fluttered her hands in front of her face, as though fighting a plague of mosquitoes. "That all happened before I got here," she said. "He meant to impress Caesar with how ruthless he could be. On advice from Sejanus. He realizes his error." Claudia nodded as though trying to convince herself. "He's better now."

"But you're no better," Veronica said. She stroked young Pontius' foot. "This should help, don't you think? Both of you?"

"I'll bandage the foot," Claudia said. "I'll make sure he doesn't see it."

*   *   *   *

"In all honesty," the Doctor said, "I'm never really sure how long to leave eyes bandaged. But, you're anxious, I understand. If the light hurts your eyes, we'll put the wraps back on."

"That's if I see light," Longinus muttered.

"Many blind people do," the Doctor noted. He led Longinus from the doorway across the room. "You think they sit in total darkness, but not true. It's a pervasive grey. Like fog at midday." He touched the Centurion's shoulder, bidding him to sit.

"That sounds worse."

"True," the Doctor agreed. "We are creatures of the day, and we grow up fearing the night." Longinus felt him touch the side of his head. He heard the coarse snipping of the spring scissors near his temple. "But by a certain age, we reconcile ourselves to darkness. We understand it's our adversary; when the sun sets, we steel ourselves and gird our loins. Much more disconcerting is perpetual uncertainty."

Longinus felt the pads of cloth lifted from his eyes.

"I can't open them," he said.

"They're fairly crusted over, my friend," the Doctor said. Longinus felt a cool, wet cloth gently stroke his lids and lashes. "That should do it."

His lids fluttered. A shaft of light flooded his consciousness.

"I see light!" he declared. A blazing orb approached. He squinted against it until it retreated, falling to the side. A soft clink suggested the Doctor had placed a lamp on a table.

"Can you see me?" the Doctor asked.

There were only dull colors in front of him, without form or substance. They shifted.

"Wait — did you move?"

"Yes. You saw that, did you?"

Longinus placed his hands in front of his face. He could follow their movement vaguely, but not discern their shape.

"What does it mean?" Longinus demanded.

"At the moment, your pupils are dilated. It's like you're stepping out of a cave into the sunlight, only your eyes aren't adjusting. I worry about those surface scratches. I think of the eye's surface like a pool of water. When it's still, you can see the pebbles on the bottom, but when the surface ripples, it's all distorted."

"Is this permanent, then?" Longinus asked. When the doctor hesitated, Longinus stood abruptly. "Thank you, Doctor." He scanned the room, got no visual cue, but stepped towards where he remembered the door.

"I'd replace those bandages." The doctor tugged his arm. "The pupils. They might, in a couple of days —"

"*Might*, Doctor?"

The Doctor released his arm. "Have you ever known a man to look into an eclipse? It's dark, so his pupils open wide, but the sun is there, burning into him. He can go blind in a matter of minutes. Let's bandage your eyes for a few more days."

*   *   *   *

Veronica slept half the day away. She exited her quarters just as Miriam was handing young Pontius over to Claudia. The poor boy was on the verge of a tantrum. He didn't understand the point of the bandage; he wanted it off immediately.

"Miriam," Veronica called, "may I speak to you?"

"I'm sorry, Mistress, but Lady Claudia has given me leave for the festival. I've so many preparations for the meal."

"I won't hold you," Veronica assured her. "But I must see the Prophet again. I've heard he's coming to Jerusalem for Passover."

Miriam shook her head apologetically. "No one knows. He's keeping it a secret within his closest circle. Some say Bethany. Others that he's already in Jerusalem."

"Please send word when you know."

Miriam tied her headscarf tightly. She nodded. "*If* I know, Mistress."

As Miriam headed for the servants' exit, Veronica felt the need for fresh air. She left the family quarters for the front entrance, curious to see what might be happening at the Temple compound. She walked into the atrium outside the Perfect's office to find it lined with soldiers. She stepped onto the portico and there were more soldiers still. Spears in hand, they lined the ramparts all along the Palace and drilled in the forum below. Veronica imagined that Pontius had recalled every man in Judea and half of the forces north to Syria. And with good reason: the Temple mount was crawling like an anthill with men from all over Palestine. The Romans were greatly outnumbered, though they had the advantage in armor, weapons and horses. And they had a leader who would not hesitate to strike with all the brutality required.

Veronica imagined the city in rebellion with men flooding the forum and charging the portico. They'd be fully exposed to archers from the ramparts. They'd lose hundreds before anyone reached the steps, where they'd meet line after line of shielded Legionnaires, pressing them back at sword point. She couldn't imagine anyone being foolish enough to launch such an attack. The Zealots had occasional success in sneak attacks, but they could not sustain an assault against such fortifications.

Content that she and her loved ones were safe, Veronica thought again about *him*. Actually, she had two men on her mind: the Prophet who fired her imagination and the Centurion who by turns warmed her heart and infuriated her. She scanned the ranks, finding him just off the portico. His eyes were still bandaged. She approached as discretely as she could.

"Ave, Centurion," she said gently.

The man opened his chest and lifted his chin. "Mistress Procula."

"The Prefect told me. Of your heroism."

He smiled slightly. "You mean my folly. Obviously you were the better tactician; you were safer without an escort."

"Or just lucky," she proffered. "I admire your devotion to duty."

"During the festival, the Empire needs straw men as much as soldiers."

"You discredit yourself, Centurion." An awkward silence followed. Veronica felt the eyes and the ears of the ranks upon her. She spoke lowly. "What shall you do afterwards? After the Passover, I mean?"

"I imagine I'll be paroled. I'll return to Rome. I have some land allotted in the Provinces that I've... never seen."

Veronica was getting anxious. What she wanted to say required privacy. "Perhaps," she said, "if, this evening, after your post..."

"I spend my evenings in the barracks," the Centurion blurted.

"I understand, but..."

"No mistress," he whispered intently, "you do not understand. I lead men. I am not led."

"I'm sorry," Veronica said. "I would never presume to... I guess you're looking forward to Rome."

The Centurion spoke coldly; there was suddenly no trace of emotion. "No, Mistress. All I'm looking forward to is the end of this accursed festival. When I can take the hammer in my hand, and crucify the man who blinded me."

Veronica recoiled. How had this man made his way into her heart — the same heart that warmed to Jesus' radical love? He was choking on bitterness, on the violent hatred spoiling the world from Rome to Palestine. Veronica felt her own throat constrict. She suddenly felt very afraid — not for her physical safety — but for something more precious, her spirit. She hurried down the line of troops, each staring blindly forward. The line seemed to go on forever.

Chapter 27

The Centurion's bitterness nagged at Veronica the rest of the day. When she'd approached him, she had wondered, *Couldn't Jesus also heal this soldier?* She couldn't come out and tell Longinus; but she'd wanted to say something to give him hope. Once Jesus agreed to heal the Emperor, and he was on his way to Rome, it would be no more trouble to restore Longinus. Surely Jesus would not refuse; he didn't seem to refuse anyone. *But what of Longinus?*

Veronica recalled what Jesus had said — in Salim to the frail woman and in Bethany to her — *your faith has...* It didn't register at the time; the healing had been all *his* doing. But maybe the person healed, or an intermediary, had a role to play. *Someone had to believe.* Veronica's faith had sufficed for Pontius, but Pontius was an innocent; there was no cruelty in his heart. Could anyone's faith override the bitter hatred Longinus had expressed?

It shocked Veronica that this man, who had such a hold on her heart in spite of herself, could look forward to a crucifixion! She understood justice, and a criminal — a rebel, an assassin — had to be punished. And her heart went out to Longinus. *How terrible to be deprived of sight!* But how could he long to murder a man — even an evil one — who'd be helpless to resist? She recalled his threat to Jacob, to find a cross for him. She'd taken that for bravado, but now feared he'd been in earnest. Did he share the bloodlust, the deranged cruelty of Tiberius Caesar?

Oh no. Veronica's heart groaned. *Wouldn't Caesar, so bitter and hateful, be even more resistant to help, especially from a conquered foreigner? Would she get Jesus all the way back to Capri only to have him fail? Because Caesar could not have faith?*

Veronica knew the words of a mere girl could never inspire, especially a girl he'd conspired to kill. *But he might believe a soldier!* Oh, this was getting terribly complicated, but Veronica had to take Longinus to Jesus. Then he could testify so Caesar might believe. With the Prefect of Judea likewise attesting that his son was healed, Caesar might open his mind and soften his heart. More immediately, the man she — *oh, was it foolish to think she could love him? Yes, she could and did, but could he ever love again? More important than his sight,* Veronica decided, *was Longinus' heart. Could Jesus restore that?*

She'd have to act quickly before the festival ended and Jesus went on his way, probably back to Galilee. She'd have to get Longinus out of the Palace compound. He wouldn't do it by request, but he couldn't refuse a direct order!

That evening Veronica dined with Claudia and Pilate. It was as dreary and silent as the other meals, but the tension was no longer between the Prefect and his wife, but between the women. Pilate, as before, drank and did not engage. Yet Claudia had something she hoped could finally bring him back to her. She knew it, and she flaunted it, by actually bringing the boy to the table! To Veronica, it seemed as though Claudia were goading her husband to discover their secret. Claudia feigned innocence, but Veronica didn't trust her. Perhaps the only thing preventing Claudia from prodding young Pontius to dance on the table was her dread of jealous gods who punish mortals for being too happy. Veronica tired of Claudia — her antics only seemed to make Pilate focus more intently on his dinner — so Veronica spoke up to advance her own plan.

"Pontius," she said, "I was hoping I might have an escort tomorrow. For an errand in the city."

Pilate did not look up. "Whatever you need," he grumbled, "send Miriam, or another Jew servant."

"Oh, I'm afraid that won't do," Veronica protested. "They wouldn't understand. I really have to go myself."

"With the streets packed for this festival? Impossible."

"Doesn't it end tomorrow?" Veronica tried to sound as casual as possible, "I thought, if you had men that weren't essential, maybe that Centurion, Longinus...?"

Pilate dropped his knife and looked up from his plate. Veronica couldn't tell if he was angry or incredulous.

"Veronica," he huffed, "the man's blind. In that snake pit of a city, he'd be killed instantly." He pushed his plate away and stood. With a napkin, he wiped his mouth and then his brow. He stared harshly at Veronica as if trying to read intent from her purposefully impassive face. "If you have some personal interest in this man, I can't allow it," he declared. "I know you've been traveling in rough company. Perhaps you've gotten used to the lower orders. But you're a patrician. A lady of this manor. That man, even if he were whole — which he's not — the man's useless. He's a... *cripple*."

Pilate didn't — wouldn't — look at Claudia. Or his son. He threw his napkin on the table and stormed out.

*   *   *   *

The next morning a servant summoned Veronica to attend to Claudia. She found her cousin lying face up on her bed, like a corpse ready for the pyre.

"She's too despondent to move," the servant whispered.

"Fever?" Veronica asked.

"I can't tell. She won't let me touch her."

Veronica crouched on the side of the bed, took Claudia's hand in hers and felt her cousin's forehead. It was cool, but damp.

"Where's Miriam?" Claudia muttered.

Veronica shot a look toward the servant who hunched her shoulders in an exaggerated shrug. Looking back to Claudia, she asked, "No sleep again?"

Claudia wept, the tears streaming from the corners of her eyes to her temples. "Sleep is torture. Not sleeping is torture. I can't even wish for a peaceful grave; I've seen — what lies beyond this life is torture!"

"It's just a dream, Claudia," Veronica cried. "Your imagination. You want your dreams to be portents, but they're just dreams."

"No, no, no...!" Claudia seemed to be ranting. Veronica grabbed both her wrists. She couldn't help herself; either out of anger or frustration, or perhaps it was love, she told her cousin what she'd long held inside. "It was a way of getting close to Uncle Theo. Your father searched for omens, you wanted to give them." Claudia thrashed, but Veronica held her tight, speaking firmly, as to a child. "He lost his wife giving birth to you; you needed to be special to make up for that."

Claudia shrieked, "You call me a liar!"

"No," Veronica cried. "No. Just a child. But you're not a child anymore and your father is gone."

"Get your hands off me!"

Claudia pushed and Veronica slid from the bed, landing hard on the floor. Claudia pulled her legs underneath her, sat on her heels, then rolled forward onto all fours. Veronica spun away, fearing some animalistic attack. But Claudia rose calmly and smoothed her palla.

"Tell me this is merely a dream," she said quietly. She wiped the tears from the sides of her face. She stood wringing her hands over her heart, with her elbows tucked tight against her ribs.

"I saw a statue of a man, carved of white marble. Pure with no blemishes. Its shoulders were curved, its head hung, chin to chest. Then I realized it wasn't a statue; it fluttered, like the flame of a lamp. It entered a vertical shaft of light and rose. Then I saw myself, watching. I was kneeling in soft sand and started to sink, I reached over my head and a strong hand grabbed mine. Pontius. He was desperate to hold me, but I sank faster. He strained, but he was bound, shackled, prostrate on his back. Then fire rained all around us. And these... these winged creatures, bat wings and human faces. Children's faces with teeth like wolves. They fell on Pontius and devoured him. He cried horribly. His arm became slick with blood. And I slipped and disappeared into darkness."

Claudia closed her eyes. Veronica gathered her in her arms.

"Just a dream?" Claudia asked. Veronica had no answer. "It's always the same man. Spotless, blameless. Yet Pontius destroys him. And we... we suffer retribution. Oh, Veronica, I'm afraid. If there is a place of banishment in the underworld, the gods have destined us for it."

"No, Claudia, no." Veronica regretted what she'd said about Claudia's dreams. Now she needed her to believe they *were* portents. That might give her hope. "It could be a warning. To stay away from this man. You just have to think who —"

"He's no one!" she cried. "Or anyone. Oh, Veronica, there have been so many." She sat again at the edge of the bed. Veronica sat beside her. "Remember when you first came here? You said, *If ever a god walked on Earth,* and I begged you not to speak of gods?" Claudia cradled her hands in her lap and looked up at the ceiling. "A god would know how we've ruled."

As Veronica stroked Claudia's back, Miriam shuffled into the room. She curtseyed to the ladies.

"You're late," Claudia reproached her.

"Yes, Mistress. Sorry." She continued in deadly earnest. "There's been a commotion. The Prophet, he was arrested last night."

"Jesus?" Veronica gasped.

Miriam explained, "The Sanhedrin held a Council. Accused him of heresy. They're bringing him to the Prefect now."

Veronica rose in shock. She bolted from the room and ran from the family quarters down the hallway to the Prefect's office. The atrium was crowded with soldiers, but she weaved her way through the ranks and files toward the threshold that opened onto the portico. She could see Pilate, flanked by his legates, looking out at the crowd gathered beyond the forum.

"It is not fitting for the Prefect to descend from his offices to cater to your scruples," a legate said. A flustered man, by his dress a Temple priest, stammered.

"Y-You cannot ask the High Priest to cross —"

"Caiaphas has visited my office multiple times," Pilate stated, practically stifling a yawn. "Tell him to attend me here, then attend to whatever ritual baths his religion requires."

The flustered man stuck his bearded chin out, but had no response. He turned brusquely and padded down the stairs.

"What happens now?" the Legate asked.

"Caiaphas will grant some ceremonial dispensation to the crowd, allowing them to enter our grounds without fear of angry god vengeance," Pilate said blandly. "Then we'll hear what this agitation is about."

During this intermission, Claudia found Veronica.

"What's happening?" she asked.

"Politics," Veronica muttered.

The crowd started oozing forth from the fringe of the forum. Sentries looked to the portico, and Pilate signaled them to withdraw towards the Palace. At the head of the mob was the man Jesus had called Caiaphas in the Temple courtyard. Veronica strained to see the man at the center of a tight mass. It could be Jesus, but she needed a clearer view. As the mob reached the base of the stairs, Caiaphas called out.

"Prefect. This man is speaking heresy. Under the law he must die."

Die? Veronica thought. *What could he possibly have said that merits death?*

Pilate, who'd been facing Caiaphas directly, turned left and wandered to the far edge of the portico. "And what does Rome care about your petty, religious squabbles?"

Caiaphas followed Pilate laterally, declaring, "He incites rebellion against Rome."

Veronica grabbed Claudia's hand and wove through soldiers in the atrium onto the fringe of the portico then edged their way across to the veranda. They found places at the rail, when Pilate, who'd paused looking bored off to the distant south, finally answered.

"Really?" he scoffed. "Isn't he a carpenter? Who calls himself a shepherd?"

Caiaphas blustered, "Who surrounds himself with Zealots and assassins!"

Pilate looked towards his Legate, who spoke calmly. "One Zealot and one Iscariot out of twelve. Not a high percentage for a Galilean."

Pilate walked briskly towards the lip of the portico. He stared down at Caiaphas. "Is he Galilean?"

"Yes, Prefect," he admitted.

"And isn't Herod here for your feast?" Pilate challenged. "Take him to Herod!"

With a flourish, Pilate gave his back to Caiaphas and the mob. The High Priest signaled his cohorts and they turned, pushing back against the throng, and dragging Jesus — *if it truly was him* — along with them.

At the sound of the name *Herod*, Veronica was on edge. When Pilate broke from the portico, she abandoned Claudia on the veranda and sprinted to the atrium, catching Pilate at his office door.

"Pontius. Uh, Prefect Pilate," she curtseyed, "a word, please."

Pilate paused, but signaled his Legates to continue past him. Veronica held her hands out, imploring.

"You can't send him to Herod," she pleaded. "Herod killed the Baptist. A holy man. And Jesus..."

Pilate's eyes widened and his jaw set tight. He stepped close and glared down on her.

"This is a matter of state," he spat. "And you must learn your place. Heed my word, or you'll get my hand, and then you'll get the rod. Is that clear?"

Veronica quavered, but held her ground. She did not lower her eyes this time. "Yes, Prefect," she said, but nothing in her tone implied submission. Pilate stormed into his office and slammed the door behind him.

*   *   *   *

Veronica and Claudia had retreated to the Lady's quarters. Veronica was torn between her apprehension for Jesus and her immediate concern for Claudia, who was on the verge of madness. Her rampant imagination, ever her ally, was now her deadly nemesis. Even the healing of her son was no consolation; so desperate was she to believe that some curse lay over her household. *How different our lives have been*, Veronica thought. She, exposed to every peril in the wilderness, had grown strong, while Claudia, pampered by servants and sheltered by the greatest fighting force on Earth, had aged into a frail hysteric. Veronica passed an hour or more stroking Claudia from the top of her head to the small of her back, comforting her as she fretted and moaned. Miriam entered with a pot of valerian tea Veronica had ordered to calm Claudia's nerves.

"They're back, Mistress," she whispered.

"Thank you," Veronica sighed.

"Who's back?" Claudia asked.

"No one," Veronica said, rising from her side. Claudia rolled over onto her elbow.

"Your Prophet. They've brought him back?"

Veronica glanced at Miriam, who offered a cup of tea. "The crowd, with the High Priest. They've brought the prisoner back for the Prefect."

Claudia pivoted, placing her feet squarely on the floor. "Let's see."

Again they made their way from the family quarters to the atrium — Pilate had not yet reappeared — then skirted the portico out to the veranda. Veronica noted that the mob was more aggressive. They raised their fists and chanted. She scanned the crowd for Jesus, finally spotting him strangely outfitted in a rich, purple cloak.

"Where is he?" Claudia asked.

Veronica pointed to Jesus. At their angle, he was indistinguishable from any other Jewish man, with a beard and long hair. But as the crowd chanted for Pilate to come back out, the lesser priests prodded him forward. He lurched towards the stairs, then straightened and held his head erect. Claudia gasped and fell backwards. She slumped against a pilaster and slid to the ground. Veronica abandoned the railing and crouched beside her.

"Claudia?"

Her cousin's eyes were bleary, yet frantic. Again she seemed to teeter on the verge of madness.

"That's him," she gasped. "The man from my dreams."

Chapter 28

"Are you certain, Claudia?" Veronica pleaded. A pair of soldiers was helping the Lady to her feet.

"Yes, I'm sure," she moaned. She steadied herself and pushed the soldiers away. "I've seen his face dozens of times. It's him!" Claudia wrung her hands and ranted again, "That Caiaphas wants him dead, but he wants Pontius to give the order."

"We don't know that for certain," Veronica cautioned.

"The charge is blasphemy. These barbarians stone people for it."

"Then why come here?"

"Because we put a stop to it!" she laughed. "The Sanhedrin can give out any punishment they want, except death. They'd only come here for permission."

The soldiers in the atrium parted and Pilate strode onto the portico with his Legates. He took one look at Jesus, bedecked in purple, and glared at Caiaphas.

"Is this a joke?" he demanded.

"He claims to be King of the Jews," Caiaphas answered. "He opposes Caesar's taxes, and incites rebellion."

Pilate seemed skeptical. "I'll question him." He nodded to his Legates, who descended the stairs and led Jesus around the base of the staircase toward the gate that opened into the Praetorium. Pilate himself went back through the atrium to his office. Veronica saw her whole plan falling apart. Her hopes for Longinus, for Caesar, for all of Rome were dashed. But worst of all, a good and innocent man was going to be stoned for challenging the corrupt practices of a scheming priest.

"We'll show him the foot," Claudia begged. "Come, let's get Pontius." She broke towards the portico, and Veronica dashed after her. Veronica gripped Claudia's hand and felt her cousin's nails dig in. *Can we do this*? she wondered.

"Miriam!" Claudia called. "Where's my son? Bring him!" Inside Claudia's chamber, Pontius was on the floor and on the verge of a tantrum.

"He won't keep the bandage on, My Lady," Miriam apologized.

"He won't have to." Claudia stooped and unraveled the cloth. Miriam's eyes widened.

"Praised be God!" she cried.

"Claudia, you can't!" Veronica said.

"Why not?" She hoisted Pontius into her arms. Veronica barred her way to the door.

"Jesus said we must wait *until all things have come to pass*."

"*All things*?" she sniffed. "What does that mean? I think enough has come to pass. An innocent man arrested? He couldn't have known that would happen. He's probably sitting in that Praetorium praying to his god that we intercede for him."

Veronica grabbed Claudia's shoulders and forced her cousin to look her in the face. "He knew this was Pilate's son," she said. "I never told him." Veronica lifted the boy from Claudia's arms and handed him to Miriam.

"What are we to do?" Claudia groaned.

Veronica glanced at Claudia's desk. "Here," she said. "Write him a letter. You can give it to the guard. Don't tell him about Pontius, just about your dream."

Claudia went to her desk, picked up a sheet of papyrus and began to write.

*   *   *   *

Longinus had been summoned to the Prefect early in the morning. The messenger gave no indication why Pilate wanted to see him, but Longinus assumed he wanted a report on his status. Longinus had peeled the bandages from his eyes and tried to bring the room into focus. His cell was flat, colorless. He reached for his armor, gripping only air. Extending his arm farther, he lifted the breastplate off the peg. Sturdy as it felt, it appeared formless, ethereal. Dressing clumsily, he made his way to the door, opening it out onto the forum.

The scene resembled a drawing in sand: indistinct, void of contrast, absent any depth. Soldiers — for what else could they have been? — drifted across the scene like apparitions, in and out of focus.

"Do you require assistance, Centurion?" the messenger asked. "Pardon, but the Prefect bid me wait in case you needed —"

"No," Longinus said. "You may go ahead. I'll be right along."

"Very well, sir," he answered. Longinus squinted to distinguish the figure of the messenger from the columns surrounding the forum. As the messenger retreated, he momentarily became more distinct, and the Centurion marched after him. Longinus was able to negotiate the level surface of the forum easily enough. He got to the base of the portico, but faltered as he misjudged the distance from the staircase, stepping up prematurely onto mere air. He righted himself, found the first step, and climbed without incident.

"Last step," a voice whispered. Longinus couldn't tell if the messenger had lingered, or if a Sentry and taken pity. He set both feet firmly on the portico. He sensed, more than he could see, the troops fortifying the Palace. The dark maw of the atrium opened before him and, feigning confidence but relying on memory, he strode directly towards Pilate's door.

Pilate's questioning was brief. "Can you see me, Centurion?"

"Imperfectly, Prefect." In fact, before Pilate had shifted on his cathedra, Longinus hadn't made him out at all.

"Well enough to serve?" Pilate asked.

Longinus searched for an appropriate, nuanced response. He must concede some present limitation, but did not want to make any admission that would jeopardize his career.

"How long until your parole?" Pilate continued.

"Three years."

"It would be a shame to forfeit your pension because of disability. With so little time left." Longinus followed the voice, more so than the form of Pilate, as he rose from his cathedra and stepped down from the platform. "A pity the Empire does not make exceptions for combat wounds. Though, informally, the Legion has traditionally taken care of its own. A sympathetic commander can find creative ways to keep a good soldier on the rolls."

"Prefect," Longinus interrupted. "I desire no special treatment, nor do I require —" Longinus felt a sharp slap against his cheek, followed by a crush of humiliation.

"Your reflexes are not what they were, Longinus," Pilate said.

A loud knock at the Prefect's door jolted the room. As the door opened, crowd noise flooded the chambers.

"Forgive the intrusion, Prefect," a voice called. "Caiaphas approaches at the head of a mob. His messenger requests an audience immediately."

"This will have to wait, Centurion," Pilate said. "You may remain in this chamber."

Pilate exited with his Legates. Longinus heard the door close, but even so, wondered if he was alone; the chanting of the mob muffled any sound within Pilate's office. The Centurion paced about, observing how his vision improved or diminished depending on the light. He tested his depth perception, but objects that appeared close were consistently beyond his grasp. The noise outside abated; within a few minutes, the door rattled again, and Pilate and his Legates were back.

Pilate dismissed the incident as "merely an overreaction to that nonsense in the Temple." His Legates seemed in accord.

"Caiaphas fears greater demonstrations to come," one said. "He wants this Galilean off the streets until the festival ends."

"He's got his own jail in the Temple," sounded another. "But then, any demonstration against his captivity would occur at the Temple."

"Well, we're not locking him up in the Praetorium," Pilate declared. "The sooner we repatriate this controversy back to Jewish authorities, the better."

"You were quite right, Prefect, to send them to Herod."

"Let's hope Antipas has grown a spine since last we saw him," Pilate joked.

"We cannot confirm your hopes realized, Prefect," a Legate chuckled "For I'm told he arrived reclining in a sedan chair."

Even Longinus joined in the laughter.

"Summon our agents who observed this Prophet in Galilee," Pilate commanded. "I want to know if there's anything they left out of their report." A Legate went to the door and dispatched a soldier to the Praetorium. Longinus realized what Prophet they meant: that Rabbi of the rabble. Before he could volunteer his thoughts, Pilate suspended that discussion and returned to the topic of his sight.

"You may not desire special treatment, but can you suggest duty for which you are fit?"

Longinus cleared his throat. "There is but one assignment I covet, Prefect."

"Yes, yes," Pilate muttered. "The crucifixion. What have we, five days left to this festival?"

"Yes, Prefect."

"If any crucifixion comes up before then, I'll put you on it. Practice makes perfect, after all."

Again there was a knock at the door. Again, an apology for interrupting. The rumble of the mob reached the Centurion's ears. A Sentry announced that Caiaphas was returning.

"Our Antipas remains invertebrate," Pilate huffed. "What now, compatriots?"

"The mob cannot be ignored," a Legate advised.

"But can they be placated?" another asked.

"Delay?" Pilate suggested, perhaps facetiously. "Keep them out in the sun and hope they wilt?"

"If Caiaphas is here," the first Legate said, "his agents are out knocking on every door, drumming up support. We can anticipate the crowd will flood throughout the day, rather than ebb."

"We can defeat them, despite their superior numbers."

"At what cost!" Pilate lamented. "Can we expect praise for putting a rebellion down, or censure for having let it happen?"

Longinus heard a knock at the door, and a soldier entered. "Prefect, your spies are not to be found."

"They are spies, after all," a Legate mused. "They may be out among the mob."

Pilate paced. When close to Longinus, he said, "You spent some time in Galilee. You know the people. You know Herod."

Longinus cleared his throat, "I know... of this agitator."

"Good, I'll want you close."

With that, Pilate and the Legates exited. This time the door remained opened. Longinus worked feverishly to recall every detail of his encounters with the Prophet and his entourage. This was perhaps his last chance to demonstrate usefulness. Pilate was back quickly.

"This door opens to the garden of the Praetorium. Attend me there."

*   *   *   *

Claudia wrote her message hastily to Pilate, saying, "Don't have anything to do with that innocent man, for I have suffered a great deal today in a dream because of him." She folded her note and sealed it with wax. Then she and

Veronica raced back toward the atrium. Finding the office door bolted, they headed across the portico and down the stairs to the Praetorium gate. The crowd had grown larger and angrier; Veronica's knees wobbled slightly as she descended the steps, but the soldiers lining the perimeter offered some security. Once at the gate, they peered through the iron bars to see Pilate and Jesus seated back in the garden.

Claudia addressed one of the guards. "You know who I am?"

"Yes. Ave, Lady Claudia."

"I have an urgent message you must deliver immediately to the Prefect."

"Prefect Pilate has asked not to be disturbed."

Claudia thrust the note into his hand. "Then see that you deliver it without disturbing him."

"Yes, Lady Claudia." The Guard signaled for the gate to be opened, slipped through quietly and walked with great trepidation toward the Prefect.

Claudia turned away, gripping Veronica's arm. Veronica shielded her from the crowd as they walked back to the Palace.

*   *   *   *

Longinus stood at ease during the Prefect's examination. The prisoner's voice was calm; he seemed not to grasp the enormity of his situation and spoke of dull philosophy.

"My kingdom is not of this world," he said. "If it were, my attendants would be fighting to free me."

"If your attendants were men, not sheep," Pilate replied. "You are a Good Shepherd, aren't you?" Pilate paused. Longinus assumed he was studying the prisoner for some reaction. He went on, "I make it my business to know what happens in Judea. And in Galilee when it might affect Judea. You might be surprised what people say about you."

Someone passed between Longinus and the Prefect. There was another brief pause before Pilate continued. "Even my wife seems to have an opinion. She says you appear in her dreams. I should execute you for that alone, but it's not relevant to the charges before us. What I want to hear from you, carpenter, is... Are you a king?"

"My kingdom is not here."

"Yes," Pilate groaned, "not of this world. But you *are* a king?"

"You say I'm a king."

"No," Pilate spoke firmly, exhibiting irritation, "I say, there is only Caesar."

The prisoner drifted further off point. "I was born into this world to witness to truth."

Longinus expected Pilate to slap some sense into this dreamer, force him to understand that his life was in the balance. But, after a considerable pause, the Prefect's tone was solicitous. He may even have been genuinely curious when he asked, "What is truth?"

*   *   *   *

They were too nervous to return to their quarters. The cousins hung on the railing of the veranda, watching the mob grow larger, louder and uglier. It struck Veronica as odd that the crowd in the Temple had been so supportive of Jesus, even as he overturned tables and lectured the corrupt priests, but this crowd was universally against him. She scanned the faces, hoping to find a few of the Prophet's friends. She found none. She wondered if Caiaphas had sent the Temple Guard to round up all of Jesus' followers, and if they were captive in some vault of the Temple.

"Do you think he read it?" Claudia asked.

"I'm sure he did," Veronica assured her. "Or will, before he comes back out."

"Still, showing him Pontius would have —"

"I know," Veronica sighed, "but we can't. Unless — we could ask him. If we got close enough, we could ask Jesus to let us."

"As if Pontius will let us near a prisoner!"

With that, the ranks of soldiers on the portico opened and Pilate strode through. The Legates followed, flanking Jesus, who'd been relieved of that ridiculous purple cloak. He stood in his simple Galilean tunic, with his hands bound at the wrists in front of him. His eyes had a faraway look, as though his mind had retreated to a place of comfort. Pilate paused on the lip of the portico, visibly confounded by the size and vehemence of the crowd. Their shouts had crescendoed at his entrance. He stared above them and waited as a lull came, then held his palms out, gesturing that he was ready to speak. Below, Caiaphas signaled for quiet.

Pilate was brief, "I find no fault in this man."

Heartened, Veronica and Claudia squeezed each other's arms. But the crowd roared in protest. Caiaphas signaled for more noise, and Veronica thought she saw Pilate flinch. As the lull came, Pilate raised an arm. Chafing, Veronica imagined, at the insult of a barbarian crowd making him wait to speak.

"It has been our custom," he cried, "during the days of your feast. To release a prisoner to you. I propose to release... the King of the Jews." As he gestured to Jesus, the crowd shouted disapproval. At the High Priest's signal the rumblings form a rhythmic chant. Pilate could not speak above them, nor, it seemed, could he make out what they were saying. Neither could Claudia.

"What is it?" she demanded.

"Give us... something," Veronica said.

- 263 -

Pilate conferred with his Legates, then dispatched one towards the Praetorium.

"Wait," Veronica said. "Not something. Someone. "Veronica pointed to where the Legate had gone. "That officer — Is the dungeon there?"

"Below the Praetorium," Claudia confirmed. "They're asking for another prisoner, by name?"

Veronica made out two Aramaic words. "It's Bar Abba. Bar means son, abba is Father."

"They want two prisoners?" Claudia exclaimed.

Oh no, Veronica thought. *It can't be. Not him.*

The gate of the Praetorium opened and the Legate marched out with a retine of guards. The crowd erupted. The exultation shook the veranda, but what followed was worse. The chant began again, louder and more distinct. "Give us Barabbas! Give us Barabbas!" And suddenly there he was, the gargantuan savage, raising his manacled hands over his head in triumph. Veronica's mind flashed back to the moment of the slaughter: to Valentius' pierced body, Adrianna's slit throat, Sabinus' crushed skull. To her Uncle's pummeled face, a pitiable, bloody mass. Then, a sword at her own throat.

This one is spared by... Barabbas.

Chapter 29

"You know that prisoner?"

Veronica choked on her answer. "He... He's the one."

Claudia blanched. "He killed Father?" The images of the attack flooded Veronica's mind again.

"He killed them all," she wept. She doubled over. The grief welled up from her midsection; she thought she might vomit, but she wailed, then sobbed. Claudia hugged her close.

"I'll stop this. I'll stop it now," she declared. Claudia tore at the ranks surrounding the portico. But by now, the Legion was shoulder to shoulder and four deep fortifying the Prefect. With the ranks closed against her, Claudia grew frantic. She pummeled the backs of the soldiers with her fists, but they ignored her. She announced herself to deaf ears. "I am the Lady Pilate, my husband will have you flogged!"

One of Pilate's Legates cut through the ranks to Claudia. He bowed his head and whispered to her. Her fury spent, Claudia crumpled and the Legate braced her shoulders. Veronica gathered Claudia and escorted her back to the veranda.

"It's all right, dear," she whispered.

"The Prefect requests you return to your quarters!" she cried. "The Prefect requests!"

The mob continued to roar, and Pilate, flush with rage, tried to shout over them. "Whom should I release?" he demanded. "This murderer, or this innocent man?" But the crowd just continued to chant, "Barabbas! Barabbas!"

The savage laughed, hoisting his arms high, inciting the crowd to a greater frenzy. In another moment, they might have charged the portico and liberated the monster themselves. But Pilate signaled the guards to unshackle him. Barabbas rubbed his wrists and smiled a slimy, yellowed grin. Sneering down on the Prefect and his Legates, he swaggered across the portico and descended the stairs.

Pilate watched the Gorgon melt into the crowd. The Prefect's shoulders flagged. Veronica watched him idle on the portico, perhaps believing the climax had passed. Yet, the mob did not withdraw. Barabbas cut a swath through the mob, but, heedless of his passing, they pressed farther towards the steps, forcing the line of Legionnaires to thrust their shields outward, as reinforcements scurried from the Praetorium and arranged themselves along the lower stairs. Pilate, acceding to the mob's aggression, gestured toward Jesus.

"What shall I do with him?" he asked. "The King of the Jews?"

Their reply was bestial. "Crucify him! Crucify him!"

The demand was so savage, it shocked even the conscience of Judea's butcher. "What has he done?" Pilate cried.

"Crucify him! Crucify him!"

Pilate would not compete with the crowd, so he tried standing stoically to at least retain his dignity. He waited for the mob to shout itself out, but the volume grew. The longer the standoff continued, the weaker the Prefect appeared. Pilate dispatched a Legate into the atrium. He glanced briefly at Jesus, then clenched his jaw and looked away.

The Legate returned with two soldiers who placed a table by Pilate on the portico. On the table was a pitcher, a large glass bowl and a white towel. Pilate held his hands over the bowl and the Legate poured water from the pitcher. Pilate picked up the towel and rubbed his hands dry. He balled up the towel and tossed it down. He then turned to the crowd holding up the backs of his hands.

"I am innocent of this man's blood," he declared.

Pilate turned to the guards, then, with shoulders stooped, hurried off the portico towards his chamber. The guards gripped their prisoner and took him down the stairs towards the Praetorium gate.

Claudia turned her bleary eyes towards the heavens. "He's not to blame," she chanted. "He's not. He's not to blame."

*   *   *   *

As the crowd noise had swelled, Longinus had drifted from the garden towards the Praetorium gate. A team of Legionnaires broke the tension with wry observations, clever quips and crude retorts. Longinus was able to construct a narrative of the scene from fragments of their exchanges. When the crowd started chanting for Barabbas, Longinus cleaved to the gate.

"Imagine turning that brute over," one Legionnaire said.

A second sneered, "Pilate should deliver him in pieces."

"If I know Pilate," said a third, "he'll slit the monster's throat and roll his carcass down the stairs."

Then Guards burst through the gate in earnest. *Had Pilate called for the prisoner?* Pilate wouldn't release Barabbas to placate a mob; he'd put their champion on display to taunt them. Maybe cut off an ear and throw it at Caiaphas. Strangle the animal. Roll his body down the steps like they did in Rome. But if that were Pilate's intent, Longinus wanted his rights in the matter: the death blow was his.

Longinus caught the brute's stench before his shadowy mass emerged. A cloudy blot oozed across the garden. It took all of the Centurion's discipline not to unsheathe his sword and dispatch the Zealot, but he deferred that pleasure, content that Pilate would not forget his promise. He'd send for Longinus. But the minutes passed and no call came. The mob continued to thunder.

"Can you believe it?" one Guard howled. "He's freed the swine!"

"What?" Longinus demanded.

"That Zealot scum, Pilate's turned him over."

Longinus quaked with rage. He gripped the iron bars, straining his hands, arms and back. If he'd still had his faculties, he'd hack his way through the mob like buckthorn and cleaved the Zealot's skull.

"Faith, Primus," a Legionnaire braced him. "He won't get far. The scoundrel was born for the scourge and cross."

Now the mob chanted for crucifixion.

"Whom do they want?" Longinus asked. "Not Barabbas?"

"No. A king," one Guard laughed. "Without a crown."

"Without so much as a horse."

A tense, few moments later, a Legate led the escorted prisoner through the gate.

"The Prefect sends his regards," the Legate told Longinus. "His apologies for the necessary release of your prisoner. He promises to have the brute back in custody after the festival."

"Convey my thanks," Longinus muttered.

"As consolation," the Legate continued, "the Prefect desires that you take charge of this execution."

"Understood," Longinus said.

"Understand this," the Legate declared, "the Prefect does not care for the impression that mob rule has come to Judea. He must placate the crowd, but he wishes to give them more than they bargained for: a spectacle to shock their conscience. To choke on the gore. In short, he has ordered you to give these Judeans the bloodiest crucifixion they've ever seen."

*   *   *   *

Claudia collapsed on her bed, moaning to the gods. Veronica cradled her face in her hands, trying to black out the world so she could think.

"We're damned," Claudia cried. "Damned for eternity!"

"Please, Claudia. Please, calm yourself."

"I will not be calm! I will not!" She punched her pillows. "Am I Pandora? Arachne[74], Io[75]? What is my crime? How have I offended that the gods should torment me!"

"Stop it! Just stop it, Claudia!" Veronica shouted, "Are you the one going to the cross?" Veronica was done with her cousin's histrionics. She knew where she needed to be.

*   *   *   *

Longinus walked through the garden to the courtyard outside the Legion barracks. Soldiers, awaiting orders, taunted the prisoner.

"A *king* is he? Where's his scepter?"

Longinus heard the air bend, punctuated by a loud crack. And again. These men had every right to vent their anger. They knew what this annual festival meant: hundreds of thousands of young men, drinking heavily, lamenting captivity. All it would take is one demagogue — one self-proclaimed Prophet — to whip the masses into a frenzy and provoke an assault. It didn't matter the rebellion would be doomed. There'd be losses. Not enough that Pilate would notice, but in the ranks, among simple men working for their daily wage, there'd be loss of life and limb — *sight!* — and all because some carpenter dared fancy himself a king.

"This king needs a proper crown!"

---

[74] In a weaving contest with the goddess Athena, the mortal Arachne wove a tapestry mocking the gods for their lascivious behavior. Athena punished Arachne for her arrogance by turning her into a spider.

[75] Io was a beautiful nymph who attracted Zeus' attention. Zeus changed Io into a heifer to hide her from his jealous wife, Hera. Hera caused Io, as a heifer, to wander the world aimlessly, plagued by gadflies that stung her into insanity.

Longinus heard a sword unsheathed, then a hacking sound as a soldier attacked a shrub. Longinus knew the plant, the gundelia, a flowering thistle with yellow blossoms and long spines. A soldier laughed. The light reflecting off his armor suggested he had bowed to scoop up the branches. He seemed to twist them in his hands, which Longinus assumed were heavily gloved. His figure floated across the yard toward the tight group of tormenters pressed a wreath of thistles tightly onto the victim's head. The prisoner did not resist, nor did Longinus hear even a murmur apart from the mockery.

That silence irked Longinus. *A mute rebel?* He could spread his seditious poison among simple minded fools, but confronted with his crimes, he suddenly lost his tongue? That might make sense if he still had a chance at life. He could play the philosopher of truth and hope to dupe Pilate, but now his die was cast, so why not rage? Return curse for curse, and at least go out like a man.

The centerpiece of the yard was a pillar. Longinus ordered the Legionnaires to strip the prisoner of his tunic, then shackle him with his arms wrapped around it.

"How many lashes, Primus?" a soldier asked.

"Until I call *halt*."

The scourging commenced with vigor. The scourge was a hideous implement. If Pilate wanted a bloody spectacle, this, more than the actual nailing of extremities to the cross, would produce it. The whir of air and the crack of leather on flesh chilled Longinus and made the hair on the back of his neck stand up. *This should loosen the rebel's tongue.*

"We've got two other condemned men, Primus," a soldier informed him. "They were to go after the festival. It's been suggested to the Prefect that three crosses would make a grander spectacle."

"Have we enough wood?"

"Good cedar from Lebanon," the soldier laughed.

"Get them out."

Longinus turned back toward the pillar. The scourge still buzzed the air, but sounded dull when it landed. By now it had been soaked with blood and its target was soft pulp. Had he eyes to see, Longinus knew that the white of the victim's bones would be exposed. Most condemned prisoners would scream in agony and curse the hand that wielded the whip, but this — *what had Pilate called him?* — this *good shepherd* said nothing. Longinus raised his hand.

"Halt!"

He heard the sound of chains dragged across stone. The two prisoners had been brought up. They saw the carnage at the pillar and promptly vomited. Soldiers lifted beams from the wood piles and placed them across the shoulders of the three prisoners. They lashed the men's arms to the beams with heavy rope. As the soldiers prodded the tottering prisoners into line and headed them toward the gate, two horses were brought from the livery.

"I'll ride alongside you, Primus," a soldier offered.

"You are Optaio for these men?"

"Yes, Primus," he said. "It's a good squad. They'll show no fear with this mob. They'll get the job done though you march to the gates of hell."

Longinus mounted the horse he was given. The gates of the Praetorium opened and the march began.

*   *   *   *

Veronica changed quickly into her Galilean dress, and returned to the atrium, where a solid wall of Legionnaires barred her way. Remembering that Claudia's room opened onto the veranda, she backtracked. As she padded quietly across Claudia's room, her cousin rolled over, perching on an elbow.

"Where are you going?"

"Out."

Claudia sprang up. "You can't go out there. That mob will tear you apart." She followed Veronica out onto the veranda. Veronica tucked her hair under her headscarf and tied it under her chin.

"I'll be all right." She slid over the railing, planted her feet on the ledge and looked down. It wasn't much of a drop, perhaps eight feet. She could crouch and grab hold, then lower herself down. She'd only have to fall about three or four feet.

"You've gone absolutely crazy," Claudia cried.

"Sorry," she said. "But Jesus needs me."

*   *   *   *

Just north of the Praetorium was a gate that opened onto the area known as Golgotha, a hill so commonly used for crucifixions that it was littered with unburied remains and had been dubbed *the Place of the Skulls*. That would have been the quick, direct route. But Pilate wanted a spectacle, a parade through the tight streets. He wanted the grisly procession to worm its way through the crowd, pinning the masses back against the high stone walls, so even in abject revulsion they must still bear witness to what they had wrought. He wanted the culpability for this horror to burrow beneath the skin of every barbarous cur who had chanted for blood. So they marched east towards the Temple; Pilate wanted blame for this atrocity placed firmly on the doorstep of Caiaphas and the god he served. From there they would turn north, then southwest, exiting the city and climbing to the place of execution.

Four soldiers led the procession, pressing the crowd back. The two able-bodied prisoners followed, bowed beneath the weight of their crossbeams. Then came the Galilean, prodded on each side by a Legionnaire with a horse whip. Longinus and the Optaio followed on horseback. Shredded by the

- 269 -

scourge, the Galilean teetered on weak legs, and fell immediately out of the gate. A stroke of the whip across his calves motivated him to stand and resume his march. But the procession stopped again. The Galilean seemed to be talking to a person who'd come out into the street. After a brief pause, the procession continued.

When they reached the bridge to the Temple, the light improved and Longinus could better discern the movements of the men. He concluded that the prisoner would never finish the march; he'd expire on the street. Pilate would not tolerate that kind of failure. It didn't matter that the prisoner would be dead; Pilate had ordered a crucifixion with all its potent symbolism. Longinus called a halt.

"Take the beam from him," he ordered. "Press a bystander into service."

The Legionnaires struck the beam with their swords, severing the ropes. The plank hit the stones with a resounding crack. As the Galilean fell to all fours, the Legionnaires plucked a tall man from the crowd and prodded him to pick up the beam.

*   *   *   *

Veronica ran across the forum toward the Praetorium gate. By the time she'd wriggled through the tightly pressed crowd, the last horse had passed and the mob closed in behind. Veronica trailed the horses, trying to catch a glimpse of Jesus. But the streets were so narrow and the crowd so dense, she couldn't see beyond the mounted soldiers. The bridge to the Temple was broader, so space opened along the sides. The procession stopped, and Veronica darted to the right of the horses up towards the captives. She flinched as the Legionnaires drew their swords and hacked. Jesus dropped, and the beam toppled from his shoulders. What Veronica saw horrified her. His tunic was soaked, redder from the cowl to the hem than any butcher's apron. On all fours, he panted, desperately struggling to rise again.

As the Legionnaires pulled a man from the crowd on the left side of the road, Veronica skirted the mob on the right and got closer to Jesus. As she crouched beside him, Jesus lifted his battered face. It was horrific; he'd been pummeled so badly his eyes were swollen shut. His nose, broken, listed to one side. His battered lips protruded. His head was wreathed in thorns that opened crimson rivulets that pooled in every crevice and congealed in his beard. This man, whose peaceful visage had been so soothing, was now a mask of carnage. In him, Veronica could see Tiberius Caesar, leprous under his cowl; her Uncle Theodosius, brutally beaten; the severed head of John the Baptist, with lifeless eyes lifted to implore a deaf heaven. The healer now seemed to embody Veronica's every experience of human cruelty in one shameful indictment of the species.

Helpless, Veronica still felt the urge to serve, to comfort, to heal. She removed her headscarf and gently wiped the blood from Jesus' eyes.

For a brief moment, Jesus seemed to swoon and Veronica cradled his face in her hands. She caressed him and blotted his sweat, his blood and his tears. As she finished, she glanced at the soldiers, then the horses and riders. The commander, Longinus, stared blindly toward the Temple, oblivious to what was happening below him.

"Please," Veronica whispered. "This is wrong. You can stop this right now. The Centurion is blind. Heal him. Please, it'll be over, I promise."

"Not my will," Jesus coughed, "but my Father's."

He's delirious, she thought. *How can I make him—* "Aaugh!"

A large hand batted her shoulder then reached down her arm and yanked her up.

"Let go of me!" she screamed. But Longinus pulled her close.

"You shouldn't be here," he whispered.

"And neither should you," she retorted. "He's not the one who blinded you!" She struggled to free herself, but his grip was too tight.

"Please, go," he implored. "Don't make me strike you."

"Don't be a fool; he can heal you!" Veronica felt her arm wrenched as the Centurion tossed her back into the crowd. She fell hard on her tail, grunting as a shock went up her spine. The crowd responded angrily, jeering Longinus. As he groped his way back to his mount, a Zealot bolted from the crowd and slammed Longinus sideways, knocking him into the flank of his horse. He twisted and fell at the horse's hooves.

The distraction gave Veronica another chance. She righted herself and crept again towards Jesus. But a hand grabbed her from behind and pulled her back into the crowd. Spinning to free herself and raising a clenched fist to strike, Veronica locked eyes with Salome.

Chapter 30

"You're crazy," Salome snapped.

"Leave me alone."

The Legionnaires cracked their whips at the crowd; Salome pulled Veronica back into a narrow alley. "Yuck," She exclaimed, wiping the crusted blood from her palm onto the stone wall. "Get rid of the thing; it's disgusting."

Veronica wadded up the veil and shoved it deep into her pocket. Another time, she might have shoved it down Salome's throat. Let her choke on this blood like she should have choked on John's.

"You can't stop this," Salome scolded.

"I stopped you from dying," Veronica snapped.

Salome pursed her lips, as if to spit with derision. "That was Herod. This has to happen."

"You're horrible," Veronica cried. "You're evil."

"Maybe," she admitted. "But this is God's plan. None of us understands, but Jesus accepts it, so we have to."

"So Claudia's right?" Veronica said. "We're toys and the gods are cruel? I won't believe in gods like that!"

"None of us like this," Salome told her. "His mother is here; how do you think she feels? But she'll tell you, *God is just and merciful.* But before there's mercy, there has to be justice."

"Don't you lecture me on mercy and justice!"

Salome hung her head for a moment. "I know I've lived — *wallowed* — in sin. I didn't know, but, there's a price to be paid. And only Jesus can pay it."

"You call me crazy?" Veronica stared at her, incredulously.

"Go home, Antonia," Salome said. "Just go back to the Palace." Then she crept from the alley and darted up the street. Veronica watched her catch up to a close knot of women trailing the procession. There were the two sisters, and the handsome woman who'd anointed Jesus — preparing his body for burial he had said. *Had she known this would happen? Had Jesus confided in her that he'd be executed? Oh, if he knew, why hadn't he fled?* Salome's speech about sin seemed fantastical. In Roman terms, Veronica understood that one god might gift Jesus with healing powers and another, out of jealousy, would plot to destroy him. Humans were pawns to the gods. But the idea that *one* God would endow him with miraculous powers, then allow evil forces to destroy him, just didn't make sense.

Yet, as the procession moved farther away, Veronica sensed her part in the drama was over. Jesus was the only person who could have stopped this, and he'd chosen not to. Veronica turned and retraced her steps towards the sanctuary of the Palace.

*   *   *   *

As soon as he'd tossed the girl aside, he'd regretted it. Not that Longinus feared Pilate. The Prefect would have been scandalized that his niece was in the middle of this mob, and had been interfering with his governance. He'd appreciate that Longinus — at risk to himself — had promptly dealt with her. Longinus just hated that every contact with this girl turned into a battle of wills. She refused to respect rank or a man's prerogative and constantly provoked him to use force, when his every instinct towards her was for tenderness.

What was she even doing out here? This was awful work even for a warrior, but necessary. If they refused to execute one traitor, how many more would rise up? Hundreds — *no, thousands!* — would die instead of the one. The girl could cry *this one does not deserve to die!*, but that Prophet alive meant many would die, and through his death countless lives would be saved.

The procession had continued without incident. The Galilean had fallen two more times, but, relieved of the weight of the beam, was able to continue the march to Golgotha. On the summit, Longinus sat his horse alongside the gallows as the soldiers assembled the crosses. A wagon had brought the long post beams from the Praetorium via the short route; soldiers laid them out on the ground near the oft-used post holes. The crossbeams were notched into the post beams and nailed into place. The gallows was a permanent structure consisting of two taller posts and a very long crossbeam, over which soldiers would toss ropes to hoist the crosses into place. The structure resembled the proscenium arch for a theatre. And theatre it was; spectators gathered at the foot of the hill and, Longinus imagined, also lined every parapet on the northern wall of the city. They watched as soldiers stripped the prisoners and stretched them out on the crosses. Longinus felt a mallet tap his thigh.

"Centurion?" a soldier asked. "The first blow is yours, I'm told."

Longinus shook his head. "No," he muttered. "That was... another man. You begin."

Longinus gazed at the cloudy landscape and listened to the hammers drive the spikes through flesh and wood. The struck planks reverberated, as did the wails of the prisoners, off the stone walls in a hideous cacophony. For once Longinus was grateful that the dull, grey film obscured his vision, sparing him more sensory evidence of the horror his duty required. Yet, his sharpened hearing seemed to play tricks on him: as the soldiers nailed the Galilean to his cross, Longinus thought he heard the man cry, "Father, forgive them. They know not what they do."

*   *   *   *

The forum, which had overflowed with riotous Judeans not a half hour ago, was now solely occupied by members of the Roman Legion. They stood at ease in broken ranks and hardly seemed to notice the Roman girl in Galilean dress approaching the steps of the portico. Veronica felt totally defeated. Adding to her gloom was a pervasive overcast that threatened to block out the sun entirely. As she crept up the stairs, a swirling wind began to moan. Feeling a sudden chill, Veronica dug her hands deep into the side pockets of her robe. She gripped the wadded veil tightly in her right fist. As morbid as it might seem, grasping the scarf made her feel closer to him, united with his suffering.

As she reached the portico, Veronica looked over her right shoulder. She could see the gallows on the crest of Golgotha. Just now, soldiers were pulling hard on the ropes, hoisting the crosses up. Once vertical, they dropped maybe two feet into the post holes. The bodies shook. The crosses tottered slightly until the soldiers drove wedges into the base. When the crosses were stable enough, the soldiers slackened and removed the ropes.

As the sky grew darker, Veronica turned Salome's words over in her mind: *God's plan. Justice and mercy. The price for sin.* In accepting that an innocent man must be tortured and killed, the girl was every bit as bad as Pontius.

*   *   *   *

The sky was now so dark that Longinus couldn't even make out the motions of soldiers in front of him. He heard them gambling, tossing lots for the prisoners' belongings. For some reason, the Galilean's blood-soaked tunic was highly prized. Longinus had served in the ranks with such men, who took morbid souvenirs of their killings. That type of fetish made his skin crawl. He turned his attention toward the crowd. They'd lost energy, if not interest, and the darkening of the sky at noon had created an air of foreboding. Naturally, a lull had come over the prisoners. After all, they were dying.

They'd been animated at one point. The two who'd not suffered the scourge still had energy. Flanking the miserable Galilean, they'd argued about justice. One seemed to hate life, the other feared what lay beyond it. The fearful one curried favor with the Galilean; he seemed to imagine this wretch who couldn't save himself could grant estates in the hereafter. The Galilean may have been in earnest when he promised paradise. He might also have wanted the rebel fool to shut up so he could die in peace. Peace would come soon, Longinus knew. It had been nearly three hours. The Galilean, so abused, should not have lasted three minutes.

Longinus heard a tortured wheeze; one of the prisoners was gasping for breath.

"Into your hands, I commend my spirit."

Longinus bowed his head. A surge of pity rose within him. No curses for his tormentors, and now with his last breath, a prayer. *This has been a good death*, he thought. *There was nobility in this Galilean.* A soldier touched his knee.

"Centurion," he said, "the King is dead."

Longinus was now free to expedite the proceedings.

"Dispatch the rest," he ordered. He needed to ascertain personally need that the Prophet was dead. He drew a lance from the scabbard of his saddle. It was a long, wooden staff with a sharp, iron tip. He held it above his shoulder, parallel to the ground, as he would if he were to hurl it. It seemed a well-crafted implement, nicely balanced. The Centurion swung down from the saddle and planted his feet firmly. He was in total darkness, but oriented himself according to the sounds he'd heard throughout the afternoon. He stepped across the bone-strewn terrain to the center cross. Touching the post, he positioned himself below the left side, then gripped the lance in both hands, preparing an upward thrust.

To his left and right, soldiers swung iron bars, fracturing the shins of the other prisoners. They hardly cried out; they'd soon suffocate. Longinus raised his lance until he felt some pliable resistance. He braced himself, then thrust upwards, piercing the Galilean's side. What followed was a torrent of blood, in a volume unimaginable for one who'd lost so much. Longinus heard a stream, then felt a mist spray across his face, wetting his eyes. He blinked, disgusted, and wiped his face with the back of each forearm.

Before he could open his eyes, the hill began to shake. A violent tremor pitched him forward, so he struck his head against the Galilean's pierced feet. Longinus dropped his lance and grabbed hold of the post with both hands to steady himself as the trembling accelerated. He heard screams and sensed panic all around him. Rocks scraped, cracked and fell. Longinus feared the earth might open beneath him and so wrapped his arms tightly around the cross. He imagined the parapets collapsing, spectators tumbling and all Jerusalem — *the Palace, the Temple, its mountain foundation!* — sliding towards oblivion. But then, suddenly, the quaking stopped.

Opening his eyes, Longinus snapped his head back. The pierced feet, the bloody post, were in sharp focus. He staggered from the cross and stared at the lifeless victim. The blood-streaked body sagged. The crowned head bowed. Longinus could see it in horrific detail. The cries of his men filled his ears, but Longinus ignored them. His eyes scanned upward toward the darkened sky to the sign those soldiers had affixed at the top of the cross: *Jesus of Nazareth, King of the Jews.*

"Truly," he uttered, "this man was the Son of God."

*   *   *   *

Veronica had drifted from the portico to the railing of the northern rampart. As sickening as the spectacle on Golgotha was, she could not turn away; that would be like abandoning Jesus in his suffering. Others grew bored and left the parapet, but for two hours Veronica clung to the rail, twisting the soiled veil in her hands. As the sky darkened, she kept her vigil. The gloom struck her as altogether appropriate, as if heaven itself wanted to blot out this abomination. Veronica watched Jesus droop. He could no longer hold his head aloft; his chin fell to his chest. *Oh,* Veronica grieved, *if heaven truly cared, it should shatter this hill. Flatten this Praetorium.* She turned her tear-filled eyes toward heaven.

"He called you Father," she cried, "and you let him die! I'll never believe in you!"

A shock knocked her back from the rail. She lurched sideways, slamming her shoulder and then her head against the wall. Tremors rolled through the city. Soldiers scrambled, abandoning the buildings and running to the open forum. Veronica lost her footing and sprawled forward, landing awkwardly on her wrist. Then, suddenly, the shaking stopped.

Veronica crouched, grabbing her wrist. She could feel it was going to swell up; she needed to wrap it tightly. As filthy as it was, her headscarf would have to do. Veronica unrolled the cloth and pressed it flat. What she saw startled and amazed her. The veil was clean, pristine, but deep in its fibers was an image — a portrait. Her veil bore the face of Jesus.

Chapter 31

Clutching the veil, Veronica ran from the rampart, across the crowded portico and into the atrium. She paused in front of Pilate's chamber, where several guards were struggling to take one of the doors off its hinges. Apparently it had split during the quake. *Oh, Claudia would be hysterical.* Veronica ran down the hall to the family quarters.

She found Claudia in bed, holding young Pontius tight to her breast.

"Oh, Veronica," she sighed, projecting great relief. "I was so worried." She placed Pontius on the bed beside her and gestured for her cousin to sit. "You didn't really go out there? Among the mob? Tell me you came to your senses." She veered from the overly dramatic to the supercilious. "You've just been wandering the grounds. Creating a scandal by talking to that Centurion." She laughed and fussed over Pontius. "I thought he'd be terrified from that quake — wasn't that shocking, on top of everything else we've endured? — but his eyes just opened wide, filled with wonder, and... what's wrong, dear?"

Veronica couldn't tell if her cousin's concern was feigned or fervent, and she had no patience right now for her eerie moods. She opened the veil and revealed the image. Claudia's mouth dropped.

"His image, woven into the cloth?"

"I caught up to him on the bridge," Veronica said. "I wiped his face."

"And this just appeared?"

"It makes no sense," Veronica admitted. "If he could do this, he could have saved himself." Veronica felt her heart ache again. "It was suicide."

Claudia shrugged it off. "He wanted to be remembered," she said.

"For what?" Veronica cried. "For *this* — an image on a rag? In the Temple he spoke like he was going to change the world."

"And now he's dead," Claudia stated flatly. "Not the first time death put an end to ambition."

Veronica shook her head. Roman history was replete with ambitious men who'd gone down to the dust. But who among them had resisted the temptation to power? None. And none would have submitted to vile abuse if he'd been able to escape it. Even Brutus, who was called noble had fled when the mob against him. No, this wasn't human ambition soured. *Somehow this is different.*

Veronica needed to get away from Claudia or surely say something she'd regret. She walked out and wandered towards the atrium when she felt a shock of recognition for an old man approaching Pilate's chamber. *It can't be*, she thought as she quickened her pace, but passing through the damaged portal was Joseph, the merchant of Arimathea.

Veronica crept into the atrium. Standing casually, she glanced through the gap where the door had been removed, then peered in to see Pilate pacing the floor. Joseph addressed him calmly and respectfully.

"Excellency," he said, "I've come to request permission to bury Jesus of Nazareth."

Pilate dismissed him with a brusque wave of his hand. "The law is the law. We do not bury crucified criminals." Then the Prefect checked himself. "Wait, you're saying he's *already* dead?"

"Yes, Prefect."

Pilate glared at his Legates. "Why haven't they reported?" he demanded. "Get me the Centurion."

Joseph persisted. "Consider, Prefect, that this is not a good time to hang Jewish corpses."

Pilate turned, indignant, towards the merchant. "Are you threatening me, old man?" He boomed, "You threaten Pilate, you threaten Rome!"

Joseph responded by lowering his voice, but not his gaze. "You've nothing to fear from me, Prefect. Nor from any follower of the Christ. But for the Zealots, well, corpses gather more than flies."

"I gave them what they wanted," Pilate protested. He wrung his hands, as if — washing having failed — he meant to tear the skin off. Finally, he groaned, "Take him down. Take them all down."

He turned his back on the merchant and retreated to his cathedra. Veronica saw Joseph nod to take leave, then she skipped out to the portico and waited for him. There she found some of his retinue, a few old men and the handsome woman who'd done the anointing. When Joseph came out, escorted by one of Pilate's Legates, they converged upon him.

"The Prefect has granted our request," he said. "Now let's hurry."

Veronica couldn't contain herself. She rushed forward, exclaiming, "Joseph? What are you doing here?" She hadn't intended to speak Greek, but that's what came out.

Startled, the merchant examined her from head to foot, before smiling and responding in Greek. "Veronica? How you've grown! And your father? No, your uncle!"

Veronica shook her head. "I'm afraid Uncle Theo... He's gone."

Joseph frowned wearily. "I'm sorry, child. He was a good man. But in answer to your question, I've come to claim the Lord's body."

"The Lord?" Veronica queried. "You mean Jesus, the Prophet?"

"Much more than a prophet," he remonstrated. "I'm convinced of it."

Veronica unfolded her headscarf. "You should see this," she said. "I wiped his face after he fell. What does it mean, Joseph?"

Amazed, Joseph stepped toward her, shielding the image from the Legate's view. He rolled up the veil, and handed it back to her.

"The Christ's story will not end in death," he assured her. "We wait in hope to know the true ending." He patted her shoulder then turned back to his friends. They descended the stairs and Veronica returned to the Palace.

The Christ Joseph had called him. *What did that mean?* Veronica recognized the Greek word for *covered in oil.* Had Joseph heard from the handsome woman how she'd anointed his head? That he'd thanked her for anticipating his death and burial? That seemed an odd distinction, unworthy of a title. Certainly, Jesus should have been known as *the healer*, or *the teacher*, or *the merciful*.

She returned to Claudia's chamber, but stopped outside the door. Pilate loomed large within the portal. He lectured his wife, who reclined on her bed.

"Of course, you have a woman's heart," he said. "That's why I married you. But men must rule. And that requires hard choices. Was this man's life worth a thousand? Or a hundred, or even ten that would be lost in a rebellion?"

He may have expected acquiescence. That's certainly what Veronica expected. But instead of lying prostrate to her husband's will, Claudia rose to an elbow and stared haughtily through him.

"You tell me, Pontius," she sighed. Claudia rose from her bed and crossed to young Pontius, playing with his toys upon a carpet. She reached for his foot and unwound the heavy bandage. His limb free, the boy stood joyfully and with confidence. He ran to his father, who, though dumbfounded, lifted the boy in his arms. He pressed the healed foot in his hand to assure himself it was truly so.

Claudia stood defiant and proclaimed, "The Prophet did it."

"Claudia, you shouldn't..." Veronica interjected.

"Why not?" she challenged. "It's over."

"You should have told me!" Pilate roared.

"I sent you a note."

"Not about this! With this you could have swayed my heart, instead you wrote about your infantile, imbecilic dreams!"

"It wasn't her fault," Veronica cried. "The Prophet swore us to secrecy."

Pilate glowered. "You conspired against me?"

Claudia lifted her chin and looked down upon her husband. Gesturing to Veronica, she commanded. "Show the Prefect what else the Prophet has done."

Veronica clutched the veil tight. *It hardly matters now,* she thought. *Claudia's revealed the greater miracle.* Jesus had placed no constraints on the veil. She unfurled it on the bed.

Pilate recoiled at the image, then lunged forward and snatched the veil. Pushing past Veronica, he hurled the veil into the fireplace, onto the low flames. Veronica dove after it, but Pilate grabbed her shoulders and tossed her onto Claudia's bed.

"Speak of this man again," he sneered, "and I'll charge you with sedition. You know the punishment."

Claudia laughed at him. "You can't execute a virgin."

"No one must know!" he shrieked. "They tricked me! They said I'd prevent a rebellion. Now they'll use his death to launch one!" He flushed crimson. Veronica thought the veins in his neck might burst. "But I will crush them," he declared. He shook his fist below Veronica's nose. "As I crushed him!"

Pilate broke towards the door, staring miserably into the hearth before escaping to the hall.

Veronica fell to her knees and reached into the fire. She grabbed a corner of the veil between her thumb and forefinger and yanked it out. She tossed it onto the bare stone floor and stomped the flames out with her sandals. Miraculously, though it had been on fire, no part of the scarf had been consumed or even singed. She quickly rolled it up and hid it in her pocket, as she heard Pilate barking orders out in the hall.

"Make sure they stay put!" he commanded. "No one is to see them."

*   *   *   *

Who was he? Longinus marveled. He looked up at the lifeless figure sagging from the cross, his every bruise and laceration now in sharp focus. Was it for this the ground had stirred? Was this man so loved by the elements that the earth itself cried out when forced to receive his blood? Did that blood have power in itself? Was that why Longinus could see — *an accident of contact?* — or had the Prophet intended to restore his sight? *It must be the blood,* he thought, *because his spirit had flown.* He'd heard the Galilean commend his spirit to his God. Would he then have had command over his physical nature? Yet, could his blood have retained its wondrous properties without his spirit? But if not, why would the earth tremble? These questions were beyond a soldier's learning, but Longinus suspected the miracle of the blood required participation from the spirit. Longinus concluded that this — *carpenter, rabbi, healer, prophet, rabble-rouser* — had wanted to repay torture with mercy. The Centurion bowed and convulsed with grief.

He did not deserve mercy. As a soldier, he deserved commendation for having done his duty. He deserved his pension for his time served. These were things earned. He did not deserve mercy, because he'd never shown it. He pieced together what he truly knew about this Galilean — starting with his name, Jesus of Nazareth — and concluded this Jesus must know some things about him. Surely, Judas Iscariot would have told him of their encounter. How he'd started to hoist the Iscariot to rip the arms out of their sockets. He'd know how Longinus had hunted a boy, and tried to deliver a death sentence to him. Whether he knew even about the Optaio, this Jesus must have known that, given numerous opportunities to show mercy, Longinus had always chosen the full measure of cruelty.

That full measure shone on the brutalized face that hung, oddly placid, from the cross. Nothing in its expression indicated rage against cruel fate or the hands that had dealt it. *Why?* Longinus had always thought that a good death had to come with defiance. Had he fallen in combat, he'd have wanted to slay as many of his enemies as possible, and to die with a curse for his assailants on his lips. *Why wouldn't you hate me, smite me? Why did you choose mercy?* It was a mystery, and its answer had died on the cross with him.

Having calmed his men, Longinus idled at Golgotha waiting for the other prisoners to die. The superstitious crowd had scattered during the earthquake, so it could hardly have been called guard duty. He eyed the city, intact, though some cracks showed in the walls and tiles were missing from the Palace roof. He scanned the countryside and what he perceived to be Mare Nostrum glistening far on the western horizon. Never had Longinus so appreciated the gift of sight. He'd been given his life back. Everything he'd hoped for his future was once again possible: he'd have his grant of land, find a wife, and raise sons and horses in Lombardy. But as attainable as all those distant things seemed, suddenly, remaining a soldier was inconceivable. How could he ever stretch another man out on a cross and drive iron spikes through his flesh and bones?

His ponderings were interrupted when the northwestern gates opened and a party of Jews approached accompanied by Legionnaires and one of Pilate's Legates.

"Centurion," the Legate called. "Pilate has given this man permission to bury his King. Please get him down from that cross."

Longinus eyed the man to whom the Legate referred. He seemed dignified enough, dressed as a member of the Council. Then again, that Council had condemned the Galilean.

"What do you intend to do with the body?" he demanded.

"What do you care?" a woman snapped at him. "Could we abuse him more than you?"

"Mary," the old man hushed her. Longinus looked at the woman, hiding reddened eyes beneath the low drape of a headscarf. He knew her: the lunatic woman from Magdala. *A zealot accomplice*, he suspected, *but surely she bore the Prophet some affection.*

"We wish only to give him the proper rites our religion requires," the old man said.

"All right," Longinus conceded. He ordered his men, "The center cross. Remove the spikes. Gently." He turned from the befuddled faces of his men, back to the Legate.

"What of the others?" Longinus asked.

The Legate stared at him skeptically. "Have a detail bury them in the Potters' Field. I doubt anyone will claim them."

"Aye, sir." Longinus turned to the center cross; one of his men had propped a ladder against the right side of the crossbeam and, having climbed several rungs, was hammering the tip of the nail to drive it out the other end. As he dislodged that spike, the right arm swung low, crossing the body as though to tumble to the dirt. The old man braced the corpus with his upraised hands, and held it there as the soldier trotted the ladder to the other side and began work to free the left hand.

Longinus broke towards the cross. He propped his lance against the post and, easing the old man aside, he supported the dead Prophet. The left arm still stretched unnaturally, and Longinus feared it might tear. With each blow of the hammer, Longinus flinched. *Why now?* he thought. *Why shudder at the rending of a corpse, when he'd felt not a twinge for the man?* The left hand fell free, and the prophet's body draped over the Centurion's shoulder. The feet proved more problematic; they were driven into a triangular block attached to the post.

"Bring an axe," Longinus commanded.

The same soldier chopped at the block beneath the feet until it split away, then dug into the post to free the long spike. Longinus lowered the feet to the ground. Two women had spread a white shroud over a litter on the ground. They took the Prophet's arms, a young man held his legs, and they lowered him onto the litter. A woman, draped in a pale blue head scarf, convulsively sobbed over the body. Longinus, remembering his place, retreated to the cross and reclaimed his lance.

"Centurion," the Legate asked, "has something occurred with you?"

Longinus said nothing. He gripped the lance tightly and twisted it in his hands.

"Accompany me to the Prefect, please."

The Legate gestured broadly toward the northwestern gate. Longinus had an impulse toward his horse. He thought of replacing the lance in the scabbard, but some corner of his mind overrode the impulse. He planted the butt of the lance on the ground and pushed off it, striding down the hill. He tapped the dry earth as he marched under the searing scrutiny of Pilate's Legate.

"You're a changed man, Centurion," he commented.

Longinus continued to hold his tongue. He knew the type of this Legate, the same as the Magistrate in Ptolemais. *An intriguer himself, he naturally looks for intrigue in others*. He'd devise some interpretation of this healing to discredit Longinus, to call his loyalty into question. He no doubt intended to report his suspicions promptly, to ingratiate himself further with Prefect Pilate. Longinus had no good answer to why he'd regained his sight and did not expect to arrive at one before he reached the Palace.

＊   ＊   ＊   ＊

Veronica did not take well to being a prisoner. She was determined to seize the first opportunity to slip from Claudia's chamber. As she paced back and forth in front of the fireplace, from the window to the door, Pilate's voice boomed through the hallway.

"Guards! Guards!" he cried.

As the guards outside her door ran up the hall to the atrium, Veronica skipped from Claudia's chamber. She thought only of retreating to her own quarters, until she heard the unmistakable voice of the Centurion.

"Prefect... what is this?"

"How is it you can see, Longinus?" Pilate demanded.

Impossible, Veronica thought. Yet, her spirit soared. She crept closer, peering between the soldiers encircling the atrium.

"I was healed," the Centurion professed. "I have no explanation. It simply happened."

"Liar!" Pilate cried. "Conspirator! Why didn't you object when I freed Barabbas? Didn't he blind you? But now that he's free, you can see again!"

"You marched a long way with Barabbas before arriving at Jerusalem," the Legate added. "And visited him in the dungeon often."

"Once!" Longinus protested. "To taunt him!" Confounded, he beseeched Pilate. "Prefect, I did not object out of loyalty. A soldier's duty. I can only say I was healed at the cross. The man we crucified —"

"More lies!" Pilate stomped and whipped his cloak in a grand flourish. "You fake blindness to claim a miracle?" he accused. "You want to incite the mobs? To rally your Zealot friends against us? To bring a mob — two, three times what we had today — straight to our doorstep? Well, you'll soon have no evidence of your miracle. When *I* put out your eyes!"

Pilate drew a dagger from his belt. The guards surrounding Longinus tightened their circle. Longinus backed towards the wall, crossing the lance over his chest.

"You can't change what happened," he warned. "I'll still testify."

Pilate flicked his dagger at the Centurion's chin, threatening, "Then I'll cut out your tongue!"

The guards lunged. But Longinus parried with the lance, sweeping several out of his way with unnatural strength. He stepped deftly, pivoting and dodging, then striking with lightning speed. As Pilate's guards tumbled about the atrium, the Prefect himself pulled a mounted sword from wall and closed in on the Centurion. His men followed suit, drawing their swords and charging Longinus, slashing and hacking at the lance that blocked and countered their blows. Incredibly, the wooden shaft held against the blows from the swords. As Longinus left more guards sprawled about the atrium, he started to back towards the portico. But that escape closed as scores of Legionnaires flooded the opening. Facing an entire army, Longinus gripped the lance tightly and slowly retreated to the center of the atrium.

"I've done nothing wrong!" he protested. "I've been loyal to Caesar!"

"But you take up arms against him!" Pilate declared.

Veronica watched Longinus, obviously flustered, struggle to explain the impossible. When no words came, he stooped and placed his lance upon the floor. At Pilate's signal, the men fell upon him. They forced Longinus to his knees. One soldier reached his arm around Longinus's throat and pried his head upward with a forearm beneath his chin. Another soldier snatched up the lance and handed it to Pilate.

Pilate gripped the lance and hoisted it onto his shoulder. He crept closer, the tip of the spear hovering. Veronica hung on the periphery, once again seeing a man on his knees, struggling against brutality. Again, she saw Pilate on the Campus, taking deadly aim at his target. Only this time, he couldn't balance the weapon. The tip descended as if pressed by some invisible force. The weight forced Pilate's shoulder down. He struggled to hold the spear aloft, but his arm wrenched downward and the weapon clattered on the floor. Bewildered, Pilate flashed his dagger, extending the tip toward the Centurion's eyes.

"No!" Veronica screamed and burst through the ranks. "Pontius, look at yourself!" She knelt in front of Pilate's blade, exposing her throat, but glaring defiantly. "You fear rebellion? What's come is much more. The blind see, the lame walk, lepers are cleansed, even the dead are raised. I've seen it," she professed. "It's joyous and beautiful, but you fear it. Why, Pontius? If men rebel, can't your men crush them? You're afraid, because this rebellion comes from God. And that you can't fight!"

Pilate grabbed Veronica's tunic at the throat and tore her away from Longinus. His dagger point creased the flesh beneath her chin.

"For love of your late uncle," he snarled, "I spare your life." He released her, then waved his blade dismissively at Longinus, muttering, "And his." Pilate sheathed his dagger and skulked back towards his office. He drew himself up rigidly and declared, "You have three days to leave Judea. If you're found after that, you will be killed on sight."

The soldiers released Longinus, who slumped briefly, then rose, squaring his shoulders as the men dispersed. Veronica crept gingerly towards him. His dark eyes shone with a marvelous intensity.

"It's true, then," she whispered. "You can see."

He turned to her, shyly at first, then smiling broadly as their eyes met. Suddenly her hands were cradled in his.

"Yes," he sighed. "I can see." But his face turned troubled and he asked, "Did you know — you knelt to minister to him — so you knew him?"

"Only a little. He helped me."

"Why?" Longinus asked.

"I don't know," she admitted. "He gained nothing, though he could have had anything. I think he just wanted to help."

"But why help me?" Longinus pondered. Veronica wondered herself. *Had Jesus responded to her prayer? Or had he personal reasons for helping his executioner?* Veronica caught Longinus gazing dreamily at her. He reached a hand tenderly towards her face, and swept a strand of hair from in front of her left eye. Veronica ducked away and combed her fingers through her unruly hair.

"Oh, I must look awful!" she gasped. But Longinus chuckled heartily and gripped her shoulders with his strong hands, tilting her towards him.

"I've seen awful," Longinus confessed. "And if I thought a god had restored my sight only to witness horrors, I'd pluck my eyes like Oedipus. But seeing you, Mistress Awful, I am very, very grateful."

Veronica wondered if this was what Jesus had intended, and continued to wonder as Longinus kissed her.

Chapter 32

Longinus left the Palace, clutching a hastily drawn discharge notice, and hurried to his quarters across the forum. He had very few belongings, but there were some gold coins he used to purchase horses for himself and Veronica. *Veronica!* Finally, he could call the young beauty by her name, and how it suited her! Odd, yet musical, it connoted truth. Certainly, she'd shown no guile in their encounters. Willful and determined, she'd revealed her mind so brazenly that Longinus had thought her unfit for any man, let alone one of lower station. But there had been truth in her kiss, too — true affection, true desire — and so he dared hope that, fate having thrown them together, she'd lose some measure of her defiance and allow him — if not to rule — at least to provide for her and protect her.

They'd agreed to ride from Jerusalem together. That's as far as they'd planned. Longinus favored a route directly west, stopping at Emmaus for the night, then on to Jaffa. From there they'd take the Via Maris up the coast to Ptolemais. There he'd collect the remainder of his meager savings. It would be enough to purchase a fishing boat or some acreage in the provinces.

He did not get halfway across the forum, before a swarm of his Auxilia overtook him.

"Primus!" one of his horsemen called, "What's happened?"

"We heard an alarm," exclaimed another. "If we'd known, we'd have fought with you!"

"Against the whole Legion!"

A chorus of affirmations and avowals followed, until Longinus raised his hands and called for restraint. "It's best you didn't, my good men," he said. "Drawing Roman blood would have cost your lives. Though, I know, you'd gladly give them in my service. But, as you can see, I'm unharmed, and face no jeopardy, provided I leave the province."

"Then we go with you!" a voice declared, followed by a wave of solemn pledges.

"No," Longinus remonstrated. "You men have your duty." Then, remembering Juvenal, he added, "You must serve the law, not the man."

"If you're going, Primus," the first horseman offered, "I'd be honored if you'd ride my stallion. He's finer than any you'll find in this forsaken country."

Longinus knew the horse, a powerful chestnut with a coal-black mane. Responsive to subtle commands and bold in a charge, it was an animal to be prized.

"I couldn't accept," he answered.

"Then take mine!" rose the chorus. Longinus felt his heart swell as his men pressed him from all sides, affirming their loyalty.

*   *   *   *

Veronica had virtually nothing to pack, but she did have to take leave of Claudia, who was immobile with distress.

"Apologize to Pontius," Claudia implored. "Beg his pardon."

"I've nothing to apologize for," Veronica said. "It's he who executed an innocent man."

"Stop saying that!" Claudia protested. "You'd think he condemned the whole world!"

Veronica could have continued bickering; after darkness at noon, an earthquake, a miraculous healing and an eerie self-portrait, this day might well prove fateful for the whole world. But she didn't want her last moments with Claudia wasted in a drawn out argument.

"I'll miss you," she said.

Claudia studied her with teary eyes and trembling lips. "I'll miss you, too, little sister." They kissed and hugged and cried over each other. Then, Veronica swept young Pontius up in her arms once last time.

"No, no, no!" he protested, and kicked until she put him down.

"He doesn't like to be held anymore," Claudia laughed. "He's a big boy now. Thanks to you."

*   *   *   *

Longinus trotted the horses to the steps of the Portico. He'd relented and taken the chestnut stallion, but had insisted on trading his armor. Now he wore a simple tunic and cloak, with no indication of rank. His weapons he'd kept; his sword was sheathed on his hip and the lance was in the scabbard on his saddle. For Veronica, he'd purchased a roan gelding from a soldier who'd assured him it was quick, but obedient. The sun had fallen below the Palace, and if not for their high elevation would have set by now. They might not have time to reach Emmaus before complete darkness. Veronica appeared on the portico and Longinus swung down from his mount. It astonished him all over again that his patrician beauty was running to greet him, and in time might truly be his. She had only a small bag that he took and hitched to the rear of her saddle. She petted her new horse affectionately and surprised Longinus by ascending to the saddle without any assistance.

Veronica trotted in a tight circle as Longinus swung onto his stallion. "Careful," he called. "She's willful."

"You're a cavalry officer," Veronica teased, "and you didn't know this horse is male?"

Longinus sidled up to the roan and whispered, "I was talking to the horse."

They left through the northwestern gate, turning left away from Golgotha and following the dusty path that would lead to Emmaus. They soon overtook a column of Palace Guards marching with a measure of urgency. Longinus hoped to remain anonymous, but Veronica aimed her horse straight toward the Captain.

"Sir, where are you going at this late hour?" she asked.

"Guarding a grave," he muttered.

"Whose?" Veronica asked.

The Captain seemed to stifle an urge to bark at her, patrician or not. "That King of the Jews. His followers may be plotting something."

Longinus pitched his head to the side, trying to draw Veronica away. She took notice and urged her mount off the road over a green knoll. They slowed, realizing they were at the highest point of a Judean cemetery. Monuments cast long shadows across the florid landscape. Down below, and farther from the road, was a whitewashed cave, a tomb hewn out of the soft limestone. Longinus recognized some of the assembly — the old man from the Council, the Mad Hag of Magdala, the woman who'd sobbed violently and the young man who'd helped with the body. Two other men, probably servants, bore the litter with the shrouded body and stooped to enter the cave. Longinus shifted in his saddle as the file of Palace Guards marched towards the tomb.

"Veronica, dear," he said softly, "we're losing the sun. The roads are much more dangerous —"

"I can't leave now," she interjected.

"But we must."

The old man urged the women back from the tomb and ordered his servants to roll a heavy stone in front of it.

Veronica shook her head anxiously. "Jesus said, *until all things are fulfilled*. Something else is going to happen. I have to be here when it does."

Longinus was incredulous. "Nothing is going to happen. His friends will mourn him, then go on with their lives."

The servants were unable to budge the stone. The guards halted at a respectful distance and the Captain approached. After brief, unspoken communication with the old man, he ordered a few of his men to roll the stone. Eyeing Veronica, Longinus realized that, as bold as she was, she was still very much a child. Lacking a man's discipline and discernment, she succumbed to emotion. He needed to deal with her firmly, yet, having no real authority over her, he must be diplomatic. That was not his forte.

"Dear, I understand your distress," he said gently, "but we need to face reality. I've served with men of strength and daring; you'd think were immortal. It's a shock to find that they're not. But once a warrior has fallen —"

"I should have shown you this," she said. "I showed it to Joseph — the old merchant down there — and he took it as a sign of things to come." She pulled a rolled up cloth from the pocket of her tunic.

"What is that?"

"It's the scarf I was wearing," she said. "I used it to wipe his face."

Longinus watched her unroll the white cloth. It bore the image of that tortured face.

"Put that away," he said.

"But, Gaius —"

"Please." He'd seen enough of his handiwork back on Golgotha. Now he wanted that body entombed and the memory of the tortured wretch banished from his mind. Was this his recompense? That the woman he loved would forever carry a morbid souvenir of the torment he'd inflicted? Did his love come with a constant reminder of his brutality towards a man who'd shown him mercy?

Veronica tried to coax him. "We're sure this means it doesn't end here."

"It does for me," Longinus declared. He tightened his grip on the reins, alerting the stallion.

"Wait," Veronica begged. "Don't leave me."

The stone scraped across the painted face of the limestone. The guards affixed a wax seal.

"They're making it rather official."

Longinus patted his horse on the neck. "As the Captain said, they may be up to something."

"His followers? Even Zealots wouldn't rob a grave, would they?"

Longinus shrugged. What the Zealots did or didn't do no longer concerned him. He needed to leave, and he needed to know if Veronica would go with him. He couldn't compel her, but neither could he dawdle with her. He pointed to the tomb.

"His friends are leaving," he said. He softened his tone, adding, "They'll forget him and you should, too."

Veronica shook her head. "You're wrong, Gaius." Then she tightened her reins, ready to ride, but aiming the roan in the wrong direction. "We need to stay. For a day or two. "

"We've got three days. Or death. "

"Don't you think I can ride?"

"It's two days of hard riding — for a man!" *Oh, she wasn't being sensible!* "I'm taking the road to Emmaus," he declared. "I'll wait —"

"No, Gaius, please!" She clutched his forearm tightly. "I don't want to fight you. Not again. Not ever. But after all Jesus has done for us, we can't just leave him."

"He's gone."

"I don't believe that. Neither does Joseph. Please, Gaius, let's join them. What harm —?"

"You want me to join a tribe of Jews? After I crucified their leader?"

"Jesus forgave you," she said. "Why shouldn't they?"

So now he should beg forgiveness? From barbarians? This was too much to bear. "I'll wait for you in Emmaus. Until noon tomorrow."

Longinus gave his stallion a kick and reined him toward the road. He vaguely hoped Veronica would ride after him, but knew she wouldn't. Perhaps in the morning she'd come to her senses. Or maybe she was too far gone, too deeply assimilated into this barbarian cult. Like the old, gouty Primus who'd built a synagogue in Capernaum, she'd never be fit to return to Rome.

*　　　　*　　　　*　　　　*

Veronica watched Gaius ride west and felt a part of herself go with him. But her mind was set, or rather, was so unsettled with questions she couldn't leave without answers. She yearned to know more about who Jesus had been, and what promises he'd made to his followers that even now they expected him to fulfill. She nudged the roan forward and followed the mourners. The silent procession heard the clopping hooves, and stepped aside to let the horse pass. Veronica headed straight to Joseph.

"Good Joseph," she called. "May I impose on your hospitality once again?"

The old man scanned the distraught faces of the women in his party. His impulse to be generous was constrained by his duty to those he regarded as family. *Would the women vote?* The young sister, Mary of Bethany, seemed ready to welcome her, but the others appeared in a state of exhaustion. Why, after their terrible ordeal, should they open their hearts to a stranger?

A woman with intense red eyes stepped forward. She wore a faded, blue mantle over long, dark hair threaded with grey. Like the woman who'd done the anointing, she'd retained her beauty though her youth had fled. Veronica knew immediately who she was and why the other women deferred to her.

"You are Jesus' mother?" Veronica asked.

"Yes, dear," she answered. "I'm Mary. And you're the girl from the bridge?"

"Yes."

"Thank you for the kindness you showed my son," Mary said. "Is there something I can do for you?"

"I'd like to know more," Veronica said, "about who your son was."

"We welcome you as he would," Mary said. Veronica felt a swell of gratitude, just as she had when Leah had opened her home. Only this time, Veronica thought she had something to offer in return.

"I've something to show you." she announced. She unfurled her veil, explaining, "The image appeared after I wiped your son's face."

Mary stepped closer to inspect the veil. "That's amazing," she smiled, her bleary eyes tearing again. She traced a finger along the outline of her son's face. "How wonderful for you!"

"I think maybe you should have it," Veronica offered.

"Oh, no, dear," Mary cautioned. "If my son granted you this sign, he meant for you to have it."

In a few moments, Veronica was back within the walls of Jerusalem outside a fine house, the sometime home of Joseph of Arimathea. A servant took her horse, and Mary of Bethany warmly embraced her. The young sister escorted her into the house and formally introduced her to the followers of Jesus.

"You've met Martha," Mary said, pointing to her sister, bent over the kitchen fire. "And this is another Mary," she continued, indicating the woman who'd done the anointing. "People get us mixed up, because of the name, even though she's from Magdala and I'm from Bethany and we're nothing alike!" Magdala Mary appeared lifeless, as though she'd literally gone into the tomb and was buried with Jesus. "And you know," Mary of Bethany went on, "Even Jesus' mother is a Mary; it can be very confusing. We call her Mother Mary."

A young man assisted Joseph rearranging furniture to accommodate the swelling household. He'd been at the cemetery, but Veronica recognized him from several encounters; she was certain he was the young man who'd passed the bread and fish to her circle in Galilee.

"That's John," Mary told her. "He's the youngest of the twelve who followed Jesus from the beginning."

"Where are the others?" Veronica asked.

Mary shrugged. The words appeared to catch in her throat and her eyes misted.

"Ladies," Joseph called, "It's time."

Magdala Mary protested. "Can't we spare the rituals even for tonight?"

Joseph spoke softly, yet with firm authority. "Our rituals guide us in ordinary times, but they guard us especially in times of crisis. Yes, Mary, we must."

The houseguests rose and filed into the dining room. Veronica noticed someone was missing: Joseph's wife. She hesitated, concerned that perhaps the woman had passed away, but felt she should inquire.

"She is in Arimathea," Joseph said. "She does not care for the crowds during the festival. Thank you for asking."

They were interrupted as the kitchen curtain parted and in waltzed Salome. She held a stone carafe of wine. She took note of Veronica, but did not acknowledge her. She whispered something to Joseph, then placed the carafe in the center of the table. Salome's presence unsettled Veronica; she felt welcome here and believed she belonged, and she didn't want any animosity poisoning this place.

Among the people gathered, an odd mood prevailed. There was shock and sorrow, to be sure, and all were emotionally exhausted. But they were not defeated; save for Magdala Mary's outburst, there was no hint of despair. In fact, it seemed that, if the mood was not quite hopeful, the group held a firm resolve, a determination to show the world that evil would not snuff out the light of Jesus' radical love.

Joseph returned his attention to Veronica. He smiled, lifting one side of his heavy brow. "Have you observed the Sabbath before?"

"Oh, yes," Veronica chirped, perhaps trying too hard to ingratiate herself with her host. "For many months I stayed with a kind family in Galilee. I learned their prayers by heart."

"Very good!" Joseph chuckled. He took a burning reed and reached to light the candles. "It is good to remember our traditions. But now we must add to them." Martha entered from the kitchen holding a pan with freshly baked flatbread and placed it on the table next to the carafe of wine. Joseph glanced at Mother Mary, then at Mary of Magdala. "We shall do tonight as Jesus commanded us."

*   *   *   *

Longinus spurred his stallion into the fading light. The speed, the power, the rhythm of the hooves — it all freed his mind from thoughts of her. *Obviously, the girl did not know what was best, what was logical; she did not even know her own mind. Her kiss had betrayed her; revealed her true desire. And yet — not an hour later! — distracted like a cat drawn to a shiny object! — she'd forgotten about the sword dangling over their heads, and — like the child she was! — had gone off with a tribe of bearded peasants to see the second act of a corpse —*

Longinus heard a crack, then an ungodly cry as the horse fell from under him. He pitched onto the road, slapping his palms, rolling onto his shoulder, slamming his hip and skidding to a stop on his back. He had no breath; his chest had fully collapsed. He rolled like a tortoise on its back, fighting to refill his lungs. Then they were on him, pinning his arms and legs to the ground. The horse continued to cry until Longinus heard a loud puncture. The beast stopped struggling; the thrashing of its hooves on the stones and the muffled cries from its throat ceased.

A hulking figure cast its shadow over him and the point of a lance — his own weapon, dripping fresh blood from his horse — prodded his chest. The Zealot Gorgon towered over him and laughed.

"Centurion. Again we meet."

Chapter 33

Veronica's evening passed uneventfully. Everyone was so fatigued, they had no energy for conversation or conjecture about what tomorrow might hold. Veronica hoped for some inkling, a hint gleaned from prophecy, to confirm she'd made the right choice staying here or should head out at dawn to rejoin

Gaius. But after the meal and some perfunctory cleaning, the household retired.

Veronica shared a small upstairs bedroom with the sisters from Bethany. Her cot was comfortable enough, and though images of the day flashed through her mind, she was too exhausted to pay attention and slept until morning. Martha was first to stir, and readied herself for the day without concern she might disturb her roommates. Feeling somewhat obligated, Veronica tried to rise, but her head and stomach revolted against her efforts. After lingering a few moments, she realized that remaining in bed would not ease her condition, but food or water might. She rolled to a sitting position at the edge of her cot and placed her feet on the cool floor. She felt unsteady, which did not bode well for her plans. If she were to rendezvous with Gaius by noon, she'd have to focus her mind and hope her body would rally.

"Good morning, Sister Veronica," Mary chimed. She stretched her arms wide across the bed she'd shared with Martha.

"Good morning, Sister Mary," Veronica answered somewhat dubiously. "I got the impression Martha wants us downstairs working."

"Well, I hate to disappoint my big sister," Mary grinned. "But it's the Sabbath. There is no work to be done."

Veronica found that hard to imagine; men got days to rest, but there was always work for women. She and Sister Mary got dressed and padded down the stairs to the kitchen, where they found three women in a rather heated argument. Martha and Salome had retreated to a far corner, while Mother Mary tried to calm the combatants: Magdala Mary and a pair of older women. These two had been at the cemetery, but had not stayed the night at Joseph's house. The taller looked like she might burst a blood vessel.

"Who is that woman?" Veronica asked Sister Mary.

"She's the mother of young James."

Veronica had no idea who that was. "What's her name?"

"Mary."

Veronica rolled her eyes. "Your people would save some confusion," she sighed, "if you came up with a few more names."

"I still don't know where James is!" the latest Mary cried.

The other woman added, "Or *my* James!"

"Cowering! That's where they are!" Magdala answered.

"I want to see John," the second woman demanded.

"Who is she?" Veronica whispered.

"John's mother," Sister Mary said, "Her name is —"

Before Veronica could say, *Don't tell me*, the argument escalated.

"John's made his decision," Magdala declared.

"I'm taking him home!"

"John isn't going anywhere!" Magdalene shouted. "You want to make him a coward? Have him desert Jesus like all the rest!"

"I just want my sons safe!"

"Safe!" Magdala scoffed. "You wanted them seated at the throne!"

"There is no throne!" John's mother wailed. "There's just a borrowed tomb." Her shoulders quaked as she sobbed. Mother Mary placed her hands on her, soothing her with a gentle touch.

"That's enough, Magdalene," Mother Mary said. "We all had our visions for how things would be. Some of us were aware this day would come. Others need time to adjust." She helped John's mother into a chair and spoke to her softly. "They struck at the shepherd, and the sheep have scattered. But the sheep will not be lost. In time, they'll be gathered back in the flock."

"And those who deny him," Magdalene grumbled, "He will deny."

"Call John," Mother Mary said gently. "Tell him his mother is here."

Magdalene pushed past Veronica, grumbling, "Jesus said you're his mother," and exited up the stairs. Mother Mary continued to console the other women, which struck Veronica as odd, since her son was actually lost; the others were merely misplaced. Still, the mothers' concern was warranted; they couldn't be sure if their sons were in hiding or if the Temple Guard had rounded them up. They could already be in the Temple jail awaiting their own trials.

Magdalene returned shortly with John and Joseph. The young man somewhat tenuously embraced his mother, who renewed her sobbing, and begged John for news of his brother. Of course, he had none. So she made him retell everything that had transpired since Jesus had been arrested. Veronica learned that one of their group, Judas, the supple purse-holder, had brought an armed mob to a garden where Jesus had been praying. They laid hands on Jesus, and he went with them peacefully. One of their group, called Peter, had followed. John and his brother James had run back to the Passover house to alert the others.

Joseph broke in to say he'd been called, as a member of the Council, to a trial. "When I got there, they had Jesus with his hands bound behind his back. I objected. Loudly. Trials at night are strictly forbidden! I'd have won some members to our side, too, but Caiaphas had me ejected. His guards brought me all the way here."

John's voice cracked as he continued. "The others wouldn't come. James, he… he said we needed a plan. *How can you plan*, I said, *when you don't know what's happening?* He said, *Peter will tell us. We'll wait for him.* Peter!" John wiped his reddened eyes.

"I didn't know where to search," John wept. "Had Judas done this for power? For money? Either Caiaphas or the Zealots had put him up to it." Then he chuckled bitterly, adding, "But Zealots have no money." He ground a fist into his other palm, recalling, "It was Caiaphas surely; the mob was his Temple Guard. If they meant murder, I didn't think they'd do it at the Temple, so I went to Caiaphas' house. Outside there were knots of spectators. I guess they'd seen the mob drag Jesus through the streets. They waited. Like vultures. I saw Peter by a fire and started towards him. Then a maid of the house screamed at Peter. She said, *You were with him. You're a Galilean. You should be in there, too*. But Peter said... He said he'd never met the man. He cursed the woman and ran off."

John stood bereft. It seemed that Peter's betrayal had affected him more than Jesus' arrest. "I just waited there," he concluded. "Waited until Magdalene, Martha and Mary came."

John's tale did nothing to put the mothers at ease. John's mother demanded that he leave with her to search the city for his brother James, a task for which John obviously had no stomach. When Joseph reminded John of his duty to honor his mother, John looked apprehensively at Mother Mary, as if his duty lay with her.

"I'll be fine, John," she said. "Find James. And Peter, too; he must be tormenting himself."

"All right," John nodded, though the mention of Peter elicited a twinge of disgust. He gestured toward the door, then led his mother and the latest Mary out.

Martha, stooped at the fire pit, opened a crock and started ladling out bowls of stew that had been kept warm overnight. Since the Jews were not permitted to work on the Sabbath, the household would have to get by on such leftovers and small morsels that required no preparation. Veronica accepted a bowl and a portion of flatbread. She found the stew — leftover Passover lamb simmered in wine with assorted vegetables — too rich for her stomach in its present state. But, realizing she needed strength for her journey, she ate as much as she could.

John's tale had convinced Veronica she had to move on. This group was fractured and in disarray. The threat from the Temple authorities was real, and Veronica no longer enjoyed the Prefect's protection. Mother Mary's lack of interest in the veil dispelled the notion that it was a sign for anyone other than Veronica herself. In short, she had no reason to remain here, and, with Gaius waiting for her in Emmaus, she had every reason to leave.

Mother Mary took Veronica's empty bowl and placed it in a basin with the others to be washed after the Sabbath ended.

"Shall we take a walk, Veronica?" she asked.

Startled, Veronica wondered, "Where to?"

"It doesn't matter," the gentle mother answered. "You wanted to learn about my son. I'm happy to tell you what I know."

Sister Mary placed a scarf on Veronica's shoulders, then lifted the folds to cover her head.

"You should talk to her," Sister Mary whispered. "She knew Jesus like no one else."

Veronica tied the scarf, tucking in her hair, then rose to take a walk with the mother of Jesus.

*   *   *   *

Longinus had struggled throughout the night against the heavy rope that bound him to the beam. He'd finally conceded that escape was impossible, so sleep would serve better than continued frustration. But with his arms stretched, his circulation mostly cut off, and his shoulders propped up awkwardly, sleep wouldn't come. As fingers of dawn scratched at the eastern mountains, Longinus stifled an urge to curse the light; he needed to appear composed before the enemy.

He heard the ground next to him crushed under the boots of that enemy. Barabbas loomed over him, blocking the early sun. In his hand the Zealot held three long, iron spikes. He dropped them one after another onto the Centurion's chest.

"Today you are blessed, Centurion," he laughed. "It is our Sabbath, so we are forbidden to work. It's true that killing you could be considered pleasure, but the rabbis frown on even the slight physical exertion our enjoyment would require. So, we cannot kill you today. But I make you this promise," he sneered. "After the Sabbath, we'll find a hill for you to climb."

*   *   *   *

Mary walked briskly through the narrow streets, saying very little. Veronica understood; they had to assume spies were everywhere. Outside the walls, Mary spoke easily, relating fantastic stories of her and Jesus' early life. These tales, too grand for the close confines of Jerusalem's streets, were marvelously suited to the expansive hills.

From an early age, Mary had had a voracious appetite for prayer. Eventually, she perceived that prayer was her vocation, and was willing to forego marriage and a family to live a life of contemplation. There were thoughts of taking sanctuary in the Temple, serving the priests and supporting the liturgies, but for whatever reason that did not come to pass. Instead, her parents arranged a marriage to an older man, a widower named Joseph, who was known for his piety. She would keep his home, and he would support her vocation to prayer. That plan nearly unraveled — incredibly — when a messenger from her God invited Mary to give birth to His Son.

"I was astounded," Mary admitted. "How could I give birth when I hadn't known a man? He said the Holy Spirit would come upon me and I would conceive."

"So your God would literally be the father?" Veronica asked.

"Yes," she attested, "if I was willing."

"Yours certainly isn't a Roman god," Veronica sighed. "They don't ask. They take." Veronica thought of all the Roman stories of great men, from Aeneas to Dionysius to Hercules, who were reputed to have been parented by gods. They had marvelous powers and all the mercurial, lusty and violent tendencies of their alleged sires and dames. By contrast, Jesus had been gentle, patient, kind, generous, but — as his exhibition in the Temple had shown — insistent about justice. If these were qualities of *the* God — as the Jews believed, the one, true, living God — that would change every assumption Veronica held about the world, a world that held one constant, which was Caesar. Augustus had ordered a census to enroll the conquered world as his subjects. And yet, as Caesar seemed to assert his dominion, the living God of the Jews had used him to achieve a foretold purpose: that the child would be born in a town called Bethlehem.

Mary related more stories, about how Jesus was born in a shelter for livestock (not exactly how Veronica would expect a king, a son of God, to enter the world), how shepherds told her that an assembly of angels had announced the birth in the hills outside Bethlehem, and how three foreign kings had visited them, bearing gifts.

Mary looked back toward the city, to the dome of the Temple. She told Veronica how the couple had brought their new son for the customary rituals and encountered two holy people who prophesied that he was the Messiah foretold in scripture. Though the seers predicted Jesus would save his people, they also saw great pain, which Mary would have to share. "My heart would be pierced by a sword."

From that harsh, but wondrous birth, peril followed: Herod, fearing a threat to his rule, dispatched soldiers to kill all the young boys in the Bethlehem area. Mary and Joseph, warned by an angel, fled Judea for Egypt. After Herod died, they returned from Egypt, but, learning that the new king was equally cruel, continued north to Nazareth in Galilee.

"Did you think you were safe then?" Veronica asked.

"Oh, no," Mary said. "I knew we'd been spared, because it wasn't His time."

They strolled to the top of a hill looking down on Jesus' tomb. Pilate's Palace Guard still kept vigil. This was the hard reality that tested everything that had come before. Could promises, hopes and prophesies survive in the face of cold death? Veronica had learned early in life that death is final. That knowledge had been reinforced time and again. Why did she now feel an inkling of hope? Was it only as Gaius had warned, her shock at learning a great man was not immortal?

Mary would not accept finality; she'd spent her life as a witness to God's unfolding plan. She looked up, as if protesting the sky's emptiness. "Simeon took my baby from my arms and held him up to heaven. And he cried, *Lord, my eyes have seen the Savior of your people!* Was he mad? Was I?" Mary took the corner of her sleeve and wiped her eyes. She stared hard at the tomb.

"That won't hold him," she affirmed. "No. If Lazarus... if Lazarus can walk out... It won't hold him." Mary composed herself, took Veronica's hand and left the tomb behind. Veronica was suddenly frightened for Mary. *Just what was she expecting?* She recalled what Jacob had said about Lazarus: he was probably buried alive and somehow recovered from his illness while in the tomb. Jesus was most definitely dead. He'd been mutilated, his body torn to shreds. There was no chance he'd recover.

Mary continued to seek open, expansive spaces. Perhaps this was her antidote for thoughts of a cramped, dark tomb. They followed a trail along a rise above a broad field. Veronica spotted a large tree, and welcomed a chance to rest briefly in the shade. As they got closer, they noticed that a freshly cracked limb hung feebly, its branches having plunged into the field below. Veronica cleaved to the trunk and peered down at the mass of tangled branches. There lay the broken body of a hanged man. His chest had ruptured from the fall and his blood had drenched the ground. Veronica thought she recognized Judas, the follower John said had betrayed Jesus. She turned to Mary for confirmation. The grieving mother's face hardened.

"We should go back," she said.

The sun was at their backs as they walked toward Jerusalem. *Too late to meet Gaius*, Veronica thought. But she had no desire right now to leave Mother Mary.

*   *   *   *

The Zealot gripped Longinus' lance as he stared at the darkening sky. The sun was low enough on the western horizon that early stars would begin to appear. He pointed the lance at a faint glimmer to the northwest.

"See that, Centurion?" he blared. "Do you know what that is?"

"Venus," he answered flatly. "A wandering star."

"The evening star!" he laughed. "Do you know when the Sabbath ends? When three stars are visible."

"What if it rains?"

Barabbas laughed and stomped about the camp. "There is the second!"

"When Venus appears," Longinus grumbled, "can Mars be far behind?"

"Ha!" barked Barabbas. "You speak of false gods. Idols!"

"They've done all right by Rome, considering who's been able to conquer whom."

"So you think, pagan," Barabbas spat. "But what you think is a lie. Because you worship stone. Marble. We worship the living God. And I am going to do you a great favor. I am going to introduce you to Him." He jabbed the lance at the sky again. "There it is! Third star!"

Barabbas signaled his men. They crouched on either side of Longinus and lifted the beam, hoisting him to his feet. Then they cracked a leather whip across the back of his legs and set him forth upon a stony path.

Chapter 34

Barabbas did not march Longinus up a hill; he drove him towards the low-lying towns at the foot of Jerusalem. Longinus opened his eyes to a world inverted: a barbarian general celebrated his triumph with a Roman trophy in tow. The Zealot roused the town folk from their beds and into the street to abuse his captive. Most thought the display repellant and turned back to their homes. Others were eager: boys who'd felt the butt of a Roman lance, widows who owed their state to a Legionnaire's sword, young men who dreamed of defeating an empire, old men whose lifetime of bowing had left them stooped towards the dust. They struck Longinus, spat at him and threw stones.

At first, the Centurion held his own, rotating his torso and sweeping the beam to drive the assailants back, or skittering in a quick sidestep to ram an attacker. But eventually, the lumber's weight and the dizzying motion wore him down and left him defenseless. The torrent of abuse bloodied his nose, split his lip and closed one of his eyes. Longinus raged against his helplessness. Barabbas might force him to reenact yesterday's spectacle, but he was no prophet, no celestial king. He would not fix his eyes on heaven and beg forgiveness — not for himself and much less for this rabble! He would die as he'd always imagined, cursing his enemies and drawing their blood. If only he could break these bonds, he'd show them fury like they'd never seen! But he was immobilized, an easy target for his tormentors' amusement.

After a third stop, the Centurion's rage turned to madness. His assailants were not Judean villagers nor strangers. As Longinus danced before an orange bonfire, figures drifted from the shadows. Men he'd killed in battle encircled him. *Their night of retribution? Let them come!* But no, they were to bear witness. They sent forth their champions: the boy from Chorizan, Joachim Ben Nasir, balled up his small fist — "You poisoned me!" he snarled — and cracked Longinus on the jaw. "What of it?" Longinus mumbled. "You survived."

But the Assyrian cook who'd fled Capernaum answered. "I didn't." He bared his side, pierced by Juvenal's sword. "Your man killed me to hide your crime," he said, and struck a blow to Longinus' sternum. The Centurion buckled; with the weight on his shoulders, he couldn't breathe. "I... I didn't order..."

"You didn't have to order," Juvenal said. "You knew my love for you."

Longinus tried to open his swollen eyes and focus them as one. "M-my friend," he stammered. At last, someone who'd show mercy. Longinus staggered — groping — towards Juvenal, but from the shadows, the Optaio drew a cudgel and crashed the side of his head.

"A spy?" he scoffed. He slammed the club to his solar plexus, dropping him to one knee. The other leg trembled. Longinus struggled to open his chest. He needed to lift his head, get onto his feet. He would not die on his knees!

"I was an officer of Rome! Are you greater than Caesar? Your conduct above reproach?" the Optaio demanded. The cudgel split Longinus' cheek; he tasted blood, sucked on a broken tooth and spat out the fragments.

The Optaio spat back at him. "You took my life, rather than have yours examined."

Longinus' other knee dropped. Humbled, he stared into the fire. Three steps away. He could charge the flames, leap and be consumed, cheat the cross and die quickly.

"Don't think of it," Juvenal warned. "They'll pull you scarred from the flames and nail you shivering to that cross." Juvenal knelt before him. He touched his face. "There is one way for you, my friend: the way of the One who went before you. Carry your sins as you carry this beam. Walk in his way. And surely as this beam shall be cut from your shoulders, your sins shall be lifted." Longinus wagged his head to clear his mind. When he looked up again, Juvenal was gone.

Alone again, Longinus admitted, "I have sinned." He'd never thought of sin before, or that actions against the tiny, the insignificant, were transgressions against an Almighty. But what was *the Almighty*? Not the gods, who wallowed in human vice. But *Almighty* might be that which wept — which made the Earth to quake — at the death of the righteous. *Almighty* was not violence that sustained tyrants, but strength for the meek, who could then banish bitterness and dispense mercy. Such mercy had touched Longinus. Mercy had planted a thought in his mind and brought forth an utterance: *Truly, this man was the Son of God.* Somehow, Longinus sensed the torture he now endured, binding his heart in humility to the One he'd made suffer, was a greater mercy than the restoration of his sight.

Walk in his way, Juvenal had said. Longinus had walked as one tormented, but not *in his way*. He'd sought to return blow for blow, as he raged against his tormentors. Could he walk, *truly*, the way Jesus had? Could he own his sinfulness and accept the blows as just — in fact, divine — retribution? He had poisoned a boy. He had set in motion events that cost innocent lives. He had ordered the execution — without trial — of a junior officer, relying only on suspicion rather than evidence. These were grave sins, and even if grievously he answered them, he'd still have to confess that justice — pure, even *divine* justice — was being served.

"Enough entertainment," Barabbas declared. The ogre gazed at the stars. "The night grows long. We must climb the hill."

A Zealot on each side lifted the beam and set Longinus on his feet. Now, his last march would begin. He recalled the awe he'd felt when the ground had shaken and he'd discovered he could see. *Truly, this man was the Son of God. He would walk in His way.*

*   *   *   *

Veronica had decided to stay another night, and roomed again with the sisters from Bethany. It was certainly foolish; she was running out of time to leave Judea. But if Joseph and Mother Mary were right, Jerusalem would shortly be transformed and Pilate's death sentence wouldn't matter. *Oh, but what might happen to Claudia and Pontius?* Veronica needed to see this story through, even if it meant letting Gaius leave Judea without her. She pictured him at noon, climbing into his saddle, taking one last look up the road, then turning and riding away. She rolled over and faced the wall and softly cried herself to sleep.

She had a vivid and startling dream just before dawn. People were stirring within the room. Veronica turned over and saw a man hovering by the sisters' bed. *Uncle Theo?* "She's over here," a man said, touching her shoulder. She thought it was Valentius' voice, but the hand had all five fingers. Yet — he bowed his face towards her — *it was Valentius!*

"It's good to see you, Mistress," the Equestrian smiled. He stepped aside for Sabinus. He was restored: not a bruise on him.

"I'm glad you're alive," he said, but then hung his head, ashamed. "I loved you so much," he said. "I was happy to die for you."

"You were so brave," Veronica said. With a glance at Valentius, she added, "All of you."

"No," Sabinus said, "I was selfish. After I died, I hoped... I wished you'd throw your life away. So we could be together always. I'm glad now you didn't."

"Thank you."

"You belong to someone else now," Sabinus continued. "He also gave his life for you."

Sabinus stepped aside, and Adrianna knelt at her bedside. Paenulus smiled over her shoulder. His eyes weren't cloudy; they sparkled. They kissed her and parted for Uncle Theo. He sat on the edge of her cot.

"Uncle, Theo, I don't understand."

"I don't expect you to," he said. "Not yet." His face was radiant. "But *the way and the truth*, all that I searched for my entire life — through supplication, divination and reason — I know now that it exists. And it shall be revealed to you and your friends."

"What?" she asked.

"The fulfillment of all things."

He kissed her forehead, and they were gone.

*   *   *   *

Longinus strained under the yoke of the crossbeam. His legs felt like granite and his back was so tight it might snap at any moment. Yet his spirit was *hopeful*. Barabbas might think he was marching the Centurion to his death, but Longinus sensed another... point of departure. What lay ahead was not an end, but a beginning. He could not explain this mood — or self-delusion, if that's what it was — other than to note that focusing on Him Who had gone before —Who had restored his sight! — made the journey easier. So it was not the crack of the whip on his back that propelled Longinus forward, but a determination to reach a place his heart had been seeking.

The long night and several skins of wine had slowed his captors. The lashes became less frequent. The taunts had altogether ceased. Again, it might have been self-delusion, but Longinus sensed a turning point in his encounter with the Zealots. He could not suppress his impulse towards mischief. He stretched his back, straightening to his full height, and eyed Barabbas.

"Do you ever think of the man who took your place?" he asked.

Barabbas snarled and beat his chest with a hammy fist. "No one could ever take the place of Barabbas. That's why I'm free." He smiled maliciously and his men chuckled.

"That prophet we crucified," Longinus continued. "Do you think of him?"

Barabbas waved away the suggestion. "Men like him make poor soldiers. Minds so set on heaven, they're no earthly good. You don't save Israel putting yourself on a cross. You save Israel by putting Rome on a cross." He prodded one side of the beam with the lance, tipping Longinus, who tripped on a stone and sprawled forward onto the ground. The Zealots laughed uproariously.

Longinus pulled his knees under his abdomen one at a time, then wrenched his torso up to a kneeling position. He spat out dirt mixed with blood.

"That's how I used to think," Longinus admitted. "That thinking made me blind."

"Ha!" the Zealot scoffed. "*I* made you blind!"

Longinus planted one foot, then braced himself to stand again.

"Yes, you did," Longinus conceded. "Funny how I'm not blind anymore, isn't it?" He groaned loudly as he pushed up onto both feet. He stood erect and eyed the Zealot giant. "And how I'm not afraid of you?" Barabbas set his jaw;

apparently, not being feared irritated him. "This Jesus, whom you think so little of," Longinus declared, "gave me back my sight."

Barabbas thrust the lance forward, catching Longinus below the chin and jerking his head upward.

"But now he is dead," he growled. His eyes blazed. "Didn't you kill him?"

* * * *

Veronica awoke before dawn. Martha was already dressed and was shaking her sister Mary. *Didn't that woman ever sleep?*

"Magdalene's leaving," Martha said. "So come now or don't bother."

"Why so early?" Mary groaned.

Magdalene leaving? Back to Galilee? Veronica wondered if she could travel with her.

"She's going to the tomb," Martha said. "Didn't anyone tell you? She says Jesus was buried too hastily. The rites weren't done properly."

"Who's going?"

"Magdalene, Salome and *Mary* — if she ever gets up!"

"I'm up! I'm up!" Mary declared, stretching her arms to the ceiling. "What about you, Sister Veronica? You can help us roll the stone away."

"The soldiers will roll the stone," Martha said dryly. "If they've any manhood about them."

"I'll go," Veronica said. "But what about Mother Mary?"

"Spare her," Martha said. "After what those Romans did to her son!" Her tone stung Veronica, and Martha quickly censured herself. "Of course, our people demanded it. Anyway, if you're going, go now."

"What about you?" Veronica asked.

"I'll see him in the next life," Martha said. "I want to remember him as I knew him."

Veronica slipped on her tunic and sandals, tied a scarf around her head and followed Mary downstairs.

* * * *

Barabbas straddled Longinus, pinning him to the ground with the tip of the lance at his throat, as his Zealot comrades cut the ropes that bound his arms to the beam. They pulled the crossbeam from under him and began fixing it to the post beam. They notched the two planks together and lashed them with heavy rope. Having assembled the cross, they grabbed Longinus, two at each arm, and forced him onto it. Barabbas tossed aside the lance and picked up a mallet and a spike.

"What do you gain by doing this?" Longinus asked.

"It's your practice," Barabbas said. "You tell me!"

*　　　　　*　　　　　*　　　　　*

The women made their way through the empty streets to the city gate. Magdalene and Salome carried jars of oil and fresh linen for the burial rites. They exited the northwestern gate and made their way toward the cemetery. Magdalene practically sprinted. If Veronica had known the pace they'd intended, she'd have ridden her horse. As they got close, the first golden strands of dawn inched across the eastern sky. Veronica could see the whited hull of the tomb, but there were no soldiers.

"Where are the guards?" she wondered.

"Oh, no," Sister Mary gulped. "Who'll roll the stone away?"

"Don't worry," Magdalene told her. "We'll think of something."

But as it turned out, the stone had already been rolled aside. The tomb was open! They ran as quickly as they could. Magdalene ducked inside, and piteously wailed.

"He's gone!"

Veronica instantly thought of the Zealots. But how could they have gotten past the Palace Guard?

"The Romans!" Salome exclaimed. "They must have taken him!"

"Why would they do that?" Veronica retorted.

"Because they could," she answered.

Veronica sat dejectedly on the grass with Mary, as Magdalene surveyed the area.

"Someone must have seen," Magdalene insisted. "A caretaker. A gardener. Someone."

"This early?" Salome asked. "Who'd have been here?"

But Magdalene went off to explore.

"Maybe it's a joke," Mary suggested. "I mean, on us. Jesus said, *Whoever believes in me, even if he dies, will live.*"

"So?" Salome dismissed her, but Mary pressed her thought further.

"*So,* maybe we shouldn't be looking for him around all these dead people."

Before Veronica could consider Mary's point, a cry went up behind the tomb.

"Magdalene!" Salome exclaimed. "They've got her!"

"Who's got her?" Mary gasped.

"Whoever robbed the tomb!"

What should they do? Three women against a band of Zealots, or an octet of Legionnaires? They couldn't run willy-nilly into the same trap, but neither could they stand idly by and lose Magdalene. Yet before they could act, Magdalene rounded the side of the tomb and came running towards them.

"I saw him!" Magdalene cried.

Mary and Salome grabbed up the linen and jars of oil.

"No, forget that," Magdalene laughed. "He's alive!" She veered away from them and continued running back toward Jerusalem.

"Wait!" Salome called. "Where is he? Magdalene! Where are you going?"

Magdalene turned and leapt, wrapping her arms around herself gleefully. "He said to tell Peter! I've got to find him!"

As Magdalene ran off, Sister Mary danced over to Veronica, threw her arms around her and kissed her.

"Risen!" she sighed. "Like my brother. God is so... *great!*"

Veronica was dumbstruck and struggled to understand. *Had the soldiers seen him, too? Is that why they'd run off?* She couldn't concern herself with that now, because Mary was tugging on her arms, pulling her away from the tomb and back... toward life!

*   *   *   *

Barabbas tramped over to Longinus' right hand. He stooped down and placed the point of the spike squarely in the center of his palm. He raised the mallet over his shoulder against the morning sky.

"There! Zealots!" a voice cried.

Barabbas looked south to the next hill. It was crawling with Romans.

The Captain of the Guard commanded his men to charge. "There are the tomb raiders! After them!"

The Zealots scattered, abandoning Longinus. Barabbas tossed the mallet aside and grabbed up the lance. As he leapt past Longinus, the Centurion rolled from the cross and seized the lance, jerking Barabbas towards him. He wrenched his weapon away from his foe, offered a glib apology — "Sorry, friend, this is mine!" — and, twisting it again, slammed the butt against the giant's jaw, knocking him down the side of the hill.

Then the guards were upon him. "I'm no Zealot, you idiots!" he cried. But he remembered Pilate's warrant, and sensed they may not have mistaken his identity. Holding the lance across his chest, he thrust both arms forward and tossed four guards back. He twirled the lance, gripping it low on the staff and sweeping the next wave of Romans out of his way. Sprawled on the ground, the guards looked up at Longinus, mystified by the power of his lance.

"The zealots!" one suddenly remembered.

"The zealots!" his comrades echoed. They sprang to their feet and ran past Longinus down the slope of the hill. They set upon the woozy Barabbas, trading blows until the giant staggered. They swarmed over him and he collapsed beneath the pile.

Longinus felt his heart lift. Just as he'd imagined, this hill had not been his final destination. Having tasted divine mercy twice in three days, he felt confident he had a long, wondrous journey ahead of him. He had no intention of making that journey alone. He shouldered his lance and marched back toward Jerusalem. He wasn't leaving without Veronica.

Chapter 35

Longinus wandered through the cemetery without a penny or a plan. He knew he could count on the sympathies of his Auxilia, but dared not approach the Praetorium. Pilate would probably interpret his continued presence as defiance, mockery or worse — conspiracy. Longinus hated to admit it, but his best chance to avoid detection and get the aid he needed lay with that tribe of Jews he'd derided. Veronica might still be with them, or at least they'd know where she'd gone. *But where to find them?* Longinus knew his first step was to orient himself, and the best spot to start was the tomb itself.

He had to be careful not to expose himself; Pilate's Guard would still be stationed there. From a distance he'd discover if any mourners came to pay respects. Then he'd follow the mourners and question them in greater safety. He needn't fear these followers; if anything they'd be afraid of him. Veronica might have been right about the followers accepting Longinus if they knew Jesus had healed him. But none had seen him blind, so how could he prove anything? No, they'd suspect him as one of Pilate's spies, there was no way around that.

Longinus glimpsed the whitened dome of the tomb and walked in a wide arc up a low hill to get a view of the front. There didn't seem to be any guards posted. Those he'd encountered must have abandoned this post to chase Zealots. Why became clear as he reached the top of the hill: the stone had been rolled away. The body must have been moved. *But how and by whom?*

Longinus did a quick surveillance of the area and hurried down the hill. The stone had been rolled all the way back, more than was necessary to slip in and pull out the body. Longinus bowed his head and placed one foot inside. He was instantly overcome by a feeling of awe and wonder. The tip of his lance bowed to the ground, and he found his right knee following. Involuntarily, as though some higher instinct had taken over, Longinus found his weapon laid to rest and himself genuflecting towards the spot where the *Son of God* had lain. His wonder increased when he saw the wrappings discarded nearby. *Why would grave robbers unwrap a body?* His mind rebelled against a fantastic conclusion — *could the healer who'd brought the poisoned boy back from the brink of death somehow have revived himself?* Grabbing up his lance, Longinus backed out of the tomb, squinting into the sunlight.

"What have we here?" a voice called. "Is it Primus Longinus under all that bruising?"

Longinus recognized the man in Galilean dress though his beard had grown longer and fuller: Pilate's spy, the one who called himself Zev.

"Come to check on your victim, Centurion?"

"No, I – I meant to leave Jerusalem, but I was attacked by Zealots. I was just passing —"

"Weren't you traveling with a girl?"

"Yes," he averred, "it's she I'm looking for."

"So you're looking for the living among the dead?" Zev chuckled. "I'm sure the Prefect would like to have a word with you."

*　　　　　*　　　　　*　　　　　*

It was a very strange day. In search of Peter, Magdalene had run all the way to the house where they'd had Passover. The widow who owned the house denied any knowledge of Peter's whereabouts — his transgression apparently was contagious — and tried to send her away. But Magdalene was so insistent, the widow sent her son, a youth named John Mark, to the upper chambers to fetch Peter. Shortly, the burly fisherman descended the stairs shamefacedly to suffer what he thought would be a blistering attack on his manhood. Instead, he got astonishing news which he refused to accept, since it not only came from a woman, but from one particularly noted for fervor, not to mention demonic possession. Fortunately, young John was also there. He warned Peter that if Jesus had, in fact, told Magdalene to deliver him the news, his failure to respond would reinforce the denial he'd made, which was something he should wish to amend rather than compound. So, the two set out, and Magdalene returned to Joseph's home, where she gave the household her report.

The followers were in a frenzy, interpreting and debating the portents. If *all had been fulfilled*, then this world, as they knew it, would shortly cease to exist. The Son of Man would descend from on high and take his seat on the throne of David. Veronica did not know enough of their folklore to grasp their vision for the new age — or to trust that she'd have any share in it — but she knew what Jesus' resurrection meant to her personally: death was *not* permanent.

All her life, death had taken people from her abruptly, cruelly and irreversibly. Her father. Her mother. She'd watched as agents of Caesar had used the power of death to intimidate and enslave everyone around them. She'd seen a sick, frustrated, unloved boy wantonly kill sparrows and cats and claim that his power to bring death made him a god. In Herod's Palace, in the hills of Galilee and on Golgotha, she'd seen evil employ death to strangle goodness. Death had always been the ultimate force. The final word. But it wasn't anymore. So even if she couldn't prophesy what lay ahead for Judea or Rome, Veronica felt like celebrating.

Not so her companions nor the visitors who came and went surreptitiously throughout the day. They were apprehensive and in some cases more fractured by long-simmering resentments that had erupted during the late crisis. So, it was a weird day with the followers waiting — white-knuckled — for Jesus to show up and dole out punishments and rewards and somehow transform Jerusalem. Most, no matter how loyal they'd been, seemed to anticipate some horrible reckoning. It seems Jesus had warned them that to have a share of his kingdom, they'd have to *pick up their crosses and follow him*. They now understood how literally he might have meant that statement.

*   *   *   *

Longinus narrowed his gaze at Pilate's spy. Zev wore only a short sword; he was no immediate threat. *But could he cry out and summon a platoon?*

"Rest assured, Longinus," Zev said, "I've no intention of turning you in. I'd like to solve this mystery for my own sake. Come, I'll tell you what I know."

They left the cemetery towards the east, but then wove south and west, entering the city through a gate Longinus hadn't even known existed. They made their way from the upper city to the remote Essene Quarter via circuitous back streets until Longinus thought himself completely lost in a tight maze. Along the way, the spy divulged his story. At first he'd taken cynical delight in his assignment to spy on the Rabbi, but in the intervening year or so, he'd seen so many wonders and heard such profound teaching, he and his partner had started to wonder if Rome shouldn't open its ears to the man. When he'd been arrested, Zev hadn't been overly concerned, since the Jews needed Roman approval to execute anyone and the case against the Rabbi was weak. They never imagined the High Priest could assemble such a mob or that Pilate would show such weakness.

"Oh, that's the High Priest's house, by the way," he said, pointing to a palatial residence squeezed in among the simple brick structures. "We're almost there." Zev said he regretted that he and his partner had seen to their mission — observing the followers — rather than reporting to Pilate right away and advising him not to harm the Rabbi.

"It was apparent his followers were frightened rabbits, and were not about to come out of their holes. But," he stated with sadness, "we kept watching those holes while Caiaphas whipped up the masses." He pointed to a simple wood and brick home in the middle of a narrow street. "That's the house. A widow lives there; she's been sheltering some of them. Come with me."

They slowed their pace and strolled casually down the street.

"Shortly after first light, a woman, one of the entourage, came frantic to the house. She pounded on the door demanding admittance, calling for Peter. He's a big lout, but you wouldn't want him in the ranks. Complete coward. Came here absolutely whimpering the night of the arrest. So this mad woman" — Longinus nodded along, knowing exactly whom he meant — "is pounding on the door until finally they let her in. Shortly after, this Peter and a young boy come sprinting out. Naturally I followed them."

They arrive at a door directly across the street from the widow's home. "You'll excuse me pausing here, I don't want to have to repeat myself." Zev rapped on the door and was admitted. Inside was Zev's partner, Eli, whom Longinus remembered for his humor.

"Longinus, yes, I remember you. My beard was just growing in. Now tell me, exactly what is going on out there?"

"All right," Zev continued, "I followed Peter and John — did they come back here?"

"Yes, much quicker than you," Eli grumbled.

"Well, I did more investigating," Zev retorted. "I followed them to the tomb. It was deserted. Not a guard in sight. And it was open. John got there way ahead of Peter and waited for him before going in. It was like watching an Arabian stallion race a pig. So they get there and they're shocked. *Where's the body? Where are the guards?* I wanted to know where the guards were, so when they left, I looked around. I found a couple of them combing the cemetery and scared witless. They told me every member of the Guard, to a man, had fallen into a deep slumber, and when they'd awoken, the tomb was empty and the body was gone. They have no explanation and they fear Pilate will decimate[76] them. I returned to the tomb and that's when I found Longinus."

Eli shook his head. "You know what they're saying here? That he's come back to life."

"How did you hear that?" Longinus demanded.

"The fisherman was shouting it. When he got back to the house, he exclaimed quite loudly, "Jesus has risen!" but, quaking as he was, I couldn't tell if he was jubilant or terrified." There was no humor in Eli's recital. "Now," he asked in earnest, "is that the raving of an hysterical madman, or...?" He couldn't finish his question.

The Son of God has risen from the dead. The thought came upon Longinus as if someone outside of himself were placing it there. "Did you know I was blind?" he asked.

"What?"

"No."

---

[76] Decimation was a punishment in the Roman army where one in ten of the men in the ranks would be executed for the failure of their group

Longinus nodded. "I was blinded in battle. But his blood, raining from the cross, washed my eyes and restored my sight."

"You, too?" Eli gasped. "We've seen healings by the hundreds. We refrained from reporting them, called them *apparent* or *supposed* lest Pilate think us mad. But he healed you? His executioner?"

Longinus shrugged his heavy shoulders.

"We've got to get you out of Jerusalem," Zev declared. "Pilate will say you didn't kill him. He'll say you conspired to fake it."

"He's already accused me of faking my blindness."

"We'll get you a horse."

"I've got to find Veronica," he said.

"What's that?" Eli asked. "*The true image?*"

Zev rolled his eyes at his partner. "Get your mind off miracles for a second. He's talking about a girl."

*   *   *   *

When evening came, Joseph gathered the household for prayers which again included the ritual of bread and wine that Jesus had said they should do in his memory. That communion seemed to pacify the spirits of all who were gathered. They'd wearied of trying to predict the future, and were content to leave it to Jesus, who had never failed to demonstrate his love for them. The meal that followed was sumptuous; Joseph insisted they celebrate what he proclaimed was *the greatest victory the world had ever seen.*

"Not only has death been defeated," he said, "but that which brought death into the world — sin itself — has no more power."

Veronica cheered that sentiment, ate the rich food and even toasted with a glass of watered-down wine. But in her heart, she felt uneasy. Perhaps Joseph had gone too far. *Sin banished from the face of the Earth? Had word of that traveled to the slave market in Rome? Or into the Coliseum?* To look at Mother Mary — her face radiant, her fondest wish fulfilled and all her anxieties dispelled — Veronica could imagine a world without sin. Yet stern Martha still glared reproachfully at her dreamy sister, and Salome, off the slightest provocation, reverted to the petulant sneer she'd worn at Herod's Palace. And then there was Magdalene, who ate hastily and slipped from the house without so much as a word to the others. Veronica couldn't help wondering how deep and lasting an effect Jesus' resurrection would have, even on this band of devout followers. But it wasn't their place in Jesus' ultimate plan that gnawed at her; it was her own. *How did a Roman girl fit into the Jewish plan for salvation?*

Veronica suddenly felt the need for air. She walked through the kitchen toward the door to the garden behind the house. As she opened the door, she felt a light rap on the other side. Closing the door, she discovered a sparrow lying on the stones of the walkway. Lifeless, its neck had been broken.

"Bring it to me," a soft voice called.

Veronica turned to see a small fire burning in a pit in the middle of the garden, halfway between the house and the stables where Joseph kept his animals, and where Veronica's horse currently resided. A man, dressed in simple Galilean robes, sat warming his hands over the fire. *Was this a follower, perhaps Peter, getting up the courage to enter the home?*

Veronica stooped and picked up the bird. "If you're thinking of roasting it, you'd do better to go inside."

"No, no," the man chuckled. "Just hand it here." Shadows from his cowl obscured his face, but as Veronica extended her hands towards his, she saw the wounds. His palms had been pierced.

"Jesus?"

He took the bird from her and closed it in his hands.

"Why did you leave the party?" he asked.

"I don't know," she answered. "I kept thinking... of many things, but mostly of you."

"But the party's in my honor," he smiled. "Even if just two or three friends honor me, I am there."

"You mean *out here*," Veronica teased. Then, earnestly, she asked, "How am I... *your friend?*"

Jesus shrugged. "Maybe because, even with all you lost, you knew there was a God that cared about sparrows. And you never stopped looking. You opened your heart to that God, with courage and compassion."

She looked again at the wounded hands that caressed the dead bird. "Not that it did any good."

"It was good for him," Jesus said. He opened his hands to a flutter of wings and released the sparrow into the air. "And it was good for me."

Of course, Veronica knew the sign Jesus had left on her veil was an expression of his gratitude. Still, she couldn't help thinking she'd failed, because she couldn't prevent an innocent man — *her friend* — from being killed. Had he come back now to ease her conscience? After all he'd suffered, he continued to console? He lowered his cowl. The crown of thorns was gone, but the red incisions remained.

"Why did you do it?" she asked. Immediately she felt impertinent, but Jesus just smiled.

He folded his hands and touched his knuckles to his chin. After a breath, he divided his hands, placing one on each knee. He turned to Veronica and asked, "What's the greatest good you can think of?"

Veronica's eyes welled up and her throat got tight. She wiped her cheeks with her sleeves and answered, "Loving and being loved. Being with people I love... knowing... someone cares."

Jesus nodded. "Then perhaps this is how you can understand the last few days. The God who created the entire universe is so in love with you that he'd die to win your love, then come back from the dead to tell you he'd do it all over again." He touched her chin and lifted her eyes to his, saying, "You are worth more than infinite sparrows."

Veronica wiped another tear. She coughed. "That may be more love than I can bear."

Jesus laughed. "Then you'll have to give some away."

* * * *

True to their word, Zev and Eli found Longinus a horse. They also brought further news of Pilate. He'd had several members of the Guard tortured, but not one had changed his story. Meanwhile, word was starting to spread that Jesus had risen from the dead. Curiosity seekers had flocked to his open tomb and the tombs of many others that had come open, undoubtedly due to the earthquake, but now attributed to some general resurrection of the dead. To quell these rumors, Caiaphas had paid large sums to the Captain and other guardsmen to spread a story that they'd withdrawn from the tomb and Jesus' followers had stolen the body.

"We'll see how that one plays with the rabble," Eli laughed.

The horse they'd found was a yearling, not quite broken and slow to answer commands. He'd never have ridden such a filly on duty, but for the roads to Ptolemais, she'd do. He'd have her completely trained by then and she'd fetch a good price at the garrison.

There was still the problem of finding Veronica. He'd spent the whole day hiding in the spy house — tending to his wounds and catching up on sleep — and nothing his new comrades had discovered pointed to her. He'd told them she'd gone to a man named Joseph, a member of the Council who'd claimed the body. But they thought that man lived in Arimathea, and though he had a house in the city, they knew not where. Now the sun was going down and Longinus had to ride out under the cover of darkness, with or without Veronica.

"We can keep looking for her," Zev said.

Longinus peered again through the curtained window to the widow's house. For all the excitement Zev and Eli claimed was going on elsewhere in the city, this house had been oddly quiet. Since early morning, no one had left or entered. It seemed that Eli's observation about Peter had been correct: jubilant, but petrified, the man and the group of followers he dominated had turned to stone.

Longinus wondered *Why not knock at the door? Break the door in.* Would the rabbits suddenly grow claws? They'd be so afraid of arrest, they'd instantly inform on Veronica. But would that rash course expose Zev and

Eli? And would Pilate then connect them to him? He couldn't betray his new comrades.

Longinus turned from the window, thanked his hosts and headed out the door. The filly tossed her head upon seeing him, tugging the reins away from the iron ring embedded in the brick wall. Longinus stroked her neck to soothe her. He slipped his lance into the scabbard on the right side of the saddle, then ducked — painfully — under the taut reins crossing to the filly's left side. He reached his right arm around her neck to steady her as he untied the reins with his left hand. His battered ribs sent shocks through him as he steadied the anxious horse. She nickered apprehensively, but eventually stood still, allowing Longinus to swing into the saddle. The filly scampered back and threatened to buck, but Longinus, fighting waves of pain and dizziness, brought her under control. Pulling her reins tight, he got the filly's nose pointed up the street.

The abrupt spin startled a woman walking on the far side of the street. Longinus meant to reassure her, until the flash of recognition. The Mad Hag bolted back in the direction she'd come, and Longinus spurred the horse after her. He easily cut her off, pinning her against the side of a house. Longinus tamped his pain down with a show of bravado.

"Do you remember the last time I hoisted you onto my saddle?"

"I don't know what you're talking about."

"You bit me. I'm not going to give you that chance again." Longinus grabbed her arm and pulled her toward him.

"I never spoke to you before the crucifixion." She struggled and the horse sidestepped.

"No, but Septimus did," he groaned. His words registered on her face, a shadow of shame that she tried to dismiss. "You saw me in Magdala, in Capernaum and on the plain outside Ammathus."

"What of it?" she spat. "Our country's crawling with Romans. And, anyway, you've lost. Your weapon is death, and death has no meaning anymore."

"That's what I need to talk to you about."

He let her go. Given the intensity of his pain, fighting two irate females was out of the question. He breathed deeply to make his tortured body relax, then slid gently down from the saddle. He stroked the filly's nose until she was calm. The Magdalene leaned against the wall rubbing her arm.

"I'm sorry if I hurt you," he said.

"Others have done worse," she said. "And you've done worse to others."

"True," he admitted. "I crucified your King. But he healed me." He waved a hand in front of his bruised face. "Not from this; I was blind from battle and his blood restored my sight."

"I don't believe you," she scoffed. "I think Pilate tortured you, the way he tortured the guards from the tomb. Then he set you free to try to trap us. You see, you're not the only ones that have spies. We have eyes and ears in the Palace and the Temple."

"Well, I didn't believe you were mad," Longinus said. "I thought it was an act. Part of a conspiracy. But your — *Prophet, Lord, King, whoever he was* — showed mercy. And I know he's the Son of God, even if that's all I know about him."

The Magdalene's face softened, ferocity yielding to tenderness.

"I was tortured," she calmly revealed. "Relentlessly. What you — *we* — do here on Earth is nothing compared to what the true enemy does in the world unseen. Jesus freed me. Now he's freed us all. If you believe, truly, as you say you do, he's also freed you."

Longinus nodded in agreement to everything the Magdalene had said. The last few days had proved her testimony. He immediately felt ashamed of his anxiety to flee Jerusalem, especially at the cost of losing the one person he loved. He was no better than the scared rabbits in the widow's house.

"I'm sorry I bloodied your nose," he said. Puzzled, the Magdalene dabbed at her face. "I mean, when you were Septimus."

"Oh." Her lips curled in a wry smile. "I'm sure Septimus deserved it."

Longinus took a breath. He couldn't believe how much his ribs ached, but even more incredible was this conversation with a barbarian. He inwardly laughed at what he was about to say. "Mistress, if you could, I need your help."

*   *   *   *

"Your friends expect you to change the world," Veronica said.

Jesus smiled. "That's something we might do together."

Jesus noticed something hanging from her belt and extended his hand, beckoning for it with his fingers. Veronica removed the veil and passed it to him. Unfurling the cloth, Jesus scrutinized it with an arched eyebrow.

"Considering the swelling about the eyes and mouth, it's not too a bad likeness," he averred. "And I can't think of anyone better to show my face to the world."

"To the world?" Veronica queried.

"But first, we have to get you safely out of Judea." Jesus pivoted left, opening up Veronica's line of sight all the way to the stables. She heard the clop of hooves on the stone-paved road. Gaius Longinus, bruised and bloodied, emerged from the alley riding a small mare. He looked like he was returning from war. *What had he endured?*

Jesus gave Veronica a gentle squeeze on her shoulder, saying, "It would be better if you didn't go alone."

Gaius spied Veronica's horse. He eased himself down from his saddle and tied the reins to a post. *Should she go to him?* Veronica reached for Jesus, but *he was gone!* Did he go into the house? Should she run after him? Ask him what to do?

"Well!" the Centurion's voice boomed. "Here's someone else without the good sense to leave Judea."

Veronica ran to him. Longinus crossed his arms over his chest, and she realized his rib were probably broken. She tenderly touched his wounded face and looked for a spot that she could kiss.

Chapter 36

Damascus, 37 A.D.

"Dearest Claudia,

"I am sending this letter ahead of you to Misenum, in the hopes that you will read it and take heart before your audience with Caesar. Word has reached us in Damascus that Pontius has been recalled to Rome — or rather to Misenum, where Tiberius now resides — to answer charges of corruption and cruelty. Know that Gaius and I are flying to you as fast as the winds can carry us, to bear testimony that, in regards to followers of The Way, persecution emanates from the Temple, not the Praetorium. Please don't think me rash, Cousin; I know that Macro is the true power, and I know the ill will he bears our family. But we of The Way have a sacred duty to testify to Truth, and we dare hope that Truth, illuminated with the divine light of Christ, might change even the hardened heart of one such as Macro.

"Oh, but I'm sure my words appear strange to you. I've written often of my life in Christ over these four years, but your silence seems to confusion or displeasure. Or perhaps my letters never reached you. If so, let me briefly summarize my life since I fled Jerusalem.

"Firstly, you should know that the rumors are true: Jesus of Nazareth did, in fact, rise from the dead. To that I am a witness. I spoke with him and touched him. He had substance and was not a ghost. You may find this incredible, but recall those miracles you know to be true: your son's withered foot was healed and Gaius regained his sight. Do not dismiss His resurrection as too fantastic, when it is the natural extension of the healing you've witnessed.

"On the day of the crucifixion, Gaius fell victim to Zealots and though through the grace of Our Lord he escaped, he was too injured to ride. We traded our horses with our friend Joseph for a mule and wagon, and drove north to Ammathus, where that kind family had nurtured me when I was alone. We told them what had happened in Jerusalem, encouraging them to walk in The Way. Gaius worked as a fisherman; sharing his knowledge of Roman galleys, he was able to make our friend Reuben's boat swifter and safer during squalls. I learned to weave.

"The disciples soon returned from Jerusalem, saying that Jesus had appeared and told them to return to Galilee. We spent many inspiring days with them and though they frequently reported that Jesus appeared and even ate with them, neither Gaius nor I ever saw Him again. One day the disciples passed through Ammathus on their way back to Jerusalem. It was such a sad procession, we thought they intended to carry their own crosses to Golgotha. But Peter said Jesus had made His last appearance; He'd gone to take His place with the Father. Jesus had told them that He would send an advocate and they were to wait in Jerusalem. Gaius and I wanted to join them, but Peter discouraged it; Jesus had only called the Twelve and we were still under Pilate's death warrant.

"But later we'd gotten word that the Spirit of God had descended upon them, like fire from the sky. They'd been transformed; they proclaimed Jesus' teachings openly and worked miracles in His Name. When we heard this, we had to go to them to learn everything that had been revealed.

"Oh, Cousin, you would not believe what transpired. Peter laid hands upon us and an awesome feeling — which had to be the essence of life itself — rushed upon us. Oh, how I wanted to run to the Palace — to you, my dearest — and profess all I had experienced. But, Peter forbade me. We might all be called to the cross in time, he said, but we had work to do first. Oh, what torment it was to spend each day in the Temple listening to Peter preach, knowing you were so close and so in need of Our Lord's comfort.

"Peter then suggested we go to Damascus where more and more were coming to The Way. Gaius thought the city would suit him, since he could work with horses, which — other than soldiering — had been his vocation. He promised to buy me a loom if I went with him.

"I should mention that in all this time, Gaius and I have lived as brother and sister. Yes, dear Cousin, we do love each other, but in this time of uncertainty, when this world may soon pass away, it seems more urgent to expend our energies in extolling the virtues of The Way, and gathering more followers who would know salvation. I sometimes feel I'm cruel; he is a passionate man and dutiful. He should have the comfort of a spouse. Yet, he never complains. There may be time for marriage and children later, but for now, we belong to Christ first, and each other second. To that end, we tell our stories. We show our artifacts: my veil and his lance. We do that sparingly, lest simple people get the impression they should worship objects instead of the living God. Though Gaius has found the lance useful in convincing young men, as foolish and impassioned as he once was, for as he's demonstrated so many times, only the righteous can hold it steady or hurl it with any accuracy.

"Damascus was very exciting. Rumors of our arrival had preceded us, and we were greeted by hundreds of enthusiastic followers of The Way. Within hours it seemed we knew everyone within the city walls. Before sundown, Gaius had a promise of employment and I had a loom. But it wasn't long before trouble followed. A Pharisee named Saul, a bitter and ambitious Temple official, had obtained warrants to arrest all followers of The Way. He was coming to take us back to Jerusalem in chains. The townspeople flocked to Gaius, begging him to ride with them against Saul. They were certain that if *the Lance of Longinus* led the charge, they would prevail.

"But Gaius told them, *We are not dealers in death. We are people of the Way, the Truth and the Life.* He urged them to pray that Christ would turn the heart of Saul. Then, if it was God's will to do battle, he would lead them. But Jesus did intervene for us, blinding Saul with a flash of light and revealing himself so dramatically that Saul entered Damascus a changed man. He now preaches conversion to The Way more fervently than all the rest.

"That is why I tell you not to despair, Cousin. Our Lord can change the hearts of even the most vicious men. Gaius jokes that he was one of them. I'm sure you are distressed, and believe that your situation is dire. But we hold that all things are possible with God.

"Until we meet in Misenum, I am,
"Your loving cousin,
"Veronica."

*   *   *   *

Longinus took the coins and placed them in his purse. Veronica wiped her eye and stifled a sob.

"Why are you crying?"

"That's the first gift you ever bought me."

Longinus thanked the merchant who'd been kind enough to buy Veronica's loom. He thought she'd have been happy to be rid of the contraption. Sitting on a stool, weaving threads of wool for hours at a time, had never suited her. It had been something she'd wished to enjoy, never something that truly settled her heart. Veronica had a restless energy, better suited to managing multiple tasks, or perhaps, chasing a brood of children around a home. Ah, but that was wishful thinking on *his* part. As he led her to the livery where their wagon awaited, he reminded her, "I bought you a horse in Jerusalem."

Veronica shrugged. "That wasn't a gift. It was a necessity. You bought me the loom so I'd go away with you."

"I bought the horse for the same reason."

Veronica sighed loudly. He knew his logic, in the face of her sentimentality, was annoying her, but he couldn't help himself; he had to keep his own emotions in check.

"I had to leave Jerusalem," she cried. "I didn't have to come with you to Damascus."

"True," he admitted. "You could have lived in Ammathus." He let Veronica set her features defiantly, before adding, "And never thought about Rome."

That line stung. Veronica looked away, hanging her head. "I hadn't thought of Rome," she said. "Not for many months."

Longinus shook his head. "You've never *not* thought of Rome. You play the contented provincial girl, sitting and weaving. But you're still every bit the patrician and not a day goes by that you don't long to return to Rome."

"Now you're just trying to hurt me," she said.

"I'm being realistic," Longinus insisted. "And you should, too. You should realize why you're returning. It's not Claudia, it's Rome, despite what you've written."

"Every word I've written is true."

"There's more truth in the words you haven't written."

They reached the livery. Longinus inspected the wagon and the horse. They had little baggage, but they wanted to make good time to the sea. They wanted an animal and a vehicle for speed rather than strength. Satisfied, Longinus tossed their bags into the wagon and laid his lance with reach.

"You think I don't love you," Veronica finally said.

Longinus paid the stable keeper. He gestured for Veronica to step up onto the wagon's bench. She took his hand and stepped up, scooting across so he could sit beside her.

"It's not that I think you don't love me," he said quietly. "I know a part of your heart belongs to me, a part belongs to Our Lord. I don't mind sharing with Him, but there's another part that is unsettled and uncertain. That part is... troublesome."

"Then why go with me?" she snipped.

"Because I love you," he said, "and because the only way you're going to settle your heart is to finish whatever you must do in Italy."

Longinus cracked the reins and the horse sprinted forward.

*   *   *   *

Veronica clung to the rail as she strained to see the Emperor's city. Misenum was tucked into a northern inlet, a bay within the bay that cut an arc into Campania province. It was the largest naval port in Italy. So, in that sense, they were flying into Caesar's teeth. Veronica was conscious of a great irony, that six years ago she'd fled Caesar to be with Claudia, and now concern for

Claudia was bringing her back within Caesar's grasp. She'd been a frightened child when she'd left. Back then she was determined to return, triumphant, her family vindicated. But in the intervening years, she'd lost her desire for Rome. Or rather — as Gaius suspected —was afraid to acknowledge the desire still burned. Now she was returning a grown woman, and for the first time in years she felt frightened.

Veronica was determined never to deny Jesus, but she was not anxious for martyrdom. It wasn't that she doubted the resurrection, but she loved her life. Perhaps she had grown spoiled in Damascus, where The Way had thrived the last three years, but she saw no reason why she couldn't keep her faith *and* her skin. Jesus couldn't expect everyone who professed his truth to climb upon a cross, could he? Who would spread his good news? Of course, when her time came, she would try to meet it with courage and stoicism, but she prayed that would not be necessary and that it was not imminent.

Gaius was funny about it, as he was about this whole trip. When Veronica mentioned her apprehensions, he simply shrugged. "I don't think martyrdom is much of a concern. If Caesar kills us, it will be pure spite, nothing to do with Christ or The Way." Veronica admitted he was probably right, but she preferred martyrdom; *if death must come, let it not be small and petty, let it have meaning.*

But what was truly the meaning of this trip? Her dread fear was not of death; she was afraid of a desire deep in her heart — to return to her life before she met Jesus. She remembered how Peter, when he returned to Galilee after the resurrection, simply wanted to fish. He wanted things to be simple again. But Jesus wouldn't let go. And, of course, Peter gave up his desire for comfort to love the Lord and feed his lambs. Veronica didn't know if she was strong enough to do that — to return to Rome and still keep her Lord first in her heart. In that sense, she was afraid of betraying the two men she loved most: Jesus and Gaius.

Gaius placed a hand on her shoulder and pointed east toward the mountains rising above the shore. They undulated like a giant serpent.

"The highest mountain is called Vesuvius," he said. "It spews lava from time to time. Legend says that it flooded the plains with fire and released giant bandits that raided the countryside. Hercules during one of his labors pacified the area."

"And you're telling me this *why?*" Veronica asked.

"Perspective can be comforting. We're only confronting a man," he chuckled. "And with more than a mythical titan on our side."

Veronica rested her head on his shoulder. Yes, Caesar was only a man, and a sick, lonely man at that. During all the weeks they'd traveled, Veronica had reminded herself of her duty to imitate her Lord's attitude towards his persecutors: *they know not what they do.* She prayed that, if it be God's will, lightning might strike Tiberius as it had Saul of Tarsus. Yet, there was a darkness stirring within her, in what Gaius had called the unsettled corner of her heart. Anger. Fear? For the first time in years, she'd started feeling the same impulse to destroy she felt during her first time in Ammathus, after her family had been killed. Slowly Veronica began to realize that part of her longing to return home was a desire for revenge. She knew she couldn't destroy Caesar, but he'd be old and sick, and at least she could watch him suffer. Such thoughts troubled her deeply. But this time, there was no Leah to soothe her. And in her simmering rage, she felt an ever-increasing distance from her Lord. Only Gaius was present. Yes, she could have turned to him for tenderness, but how cruel would that have been? She knew he loved her, and desired her. But she could not give herself to him with a divided heart.

Misenum rose in three tiers from the sea. The first level was the port where too many ships to count lolled on the waves. Larger warships, hexaremes and quinterimes, were moored in the center of the bay, while the lighter, swifter scout ships occupied slips in the wharf. Transport vessels were also docked, and stevedores labored to unload cargo. Above the port, the town had been carved out of the hillside. Small, whitewashed homes with terra cotta roofs sat on a long, narrow shelf that ran from one end of the inlet to the other. High above those humble structures sprawled Caesar's villa. Its magnificence, achieved at the expense of the mountain that supported it, declared nature itself subservient to Caesar. But moreover, Misenum seemed to be a living diagram of Roman society: its foundation was a robust, even rapacious, military, its apex an opulent oligarchy, and in between lay a stretched and squeezed middle class of laborers and merchants whose lives were not their own.

The sail was struck and the ship coasted alongside the pier. Seamen cast lines to dock workers who strained to tie the ship in place. Others hoisted the gangplank into position. Veronica braced herself to take the fateful step into her past. Would she be able to hold strong to who she had become, or revert to the frightened child she had been? When her feet touched the Italian shore, would all that had transpired in the east vanish like a dream at daylight? She gathered the folds of her robe about her. She'd woven it herself. The cloth was coarse, substantial, real. She took Gaius' arm as he offered it. It was firm, lean and muscular. She patted the outside of her tunic's pocket, feeling the familiar wad of folded cloth, the veil, the true image of her Lord. These were her reality. Fear of Caesar — of his command over hearts and minds and world events — that was the illusion. Veronica strode down the gangplank with Gaius at her side. She walked from the wooden pier to the stone-paved streets.

"Why are you laughing?" Gaius asked.

"Am I?" she giggled. "I guess I am. Because... the sun is shining. Because... the beauty of God's creation and the energy of his creatures is all around us! Because —"

"Because Christ belongs here, too?" Gaius concluded.

"Yes," she echoed. "Christ belongs here."

*   *   *   *

The porter asked where to take their bags. He knew of a taberna for travelers of modest means, but recommended a villa above the wharf better suited to a lady. Veronica pointed to the Emperor's villa.

"That's where we're headed."

The porter's eyebrows rose and his jaw dropped in equal distances. Veronica couldn't tell if he dreaded the climb or the close proximity to Caesar.

"You are guest of Caesar?" he joked halfheartedly. He tried again to sell them on the local villa.

"I don't think we'll take a room," Gaius said. "You see, we're going to be arrested."

"After which," Veronica added, "we will be guests of Caesar."

Veronica and Gaius welcomed the ascent; it gave them a chance to stretch their legs and get their hearts pumping. Gaius tapped the stony path with his trusted lance as Veronica rambled on about Claudia: *Had she and Pontius arrived? Had they seen Caesar? Had sentence already been pronounced?* Gaius thought not.

"From what I know of these proceedings," he said, "when there's no evidence, authorities like to sweat the accused. They hold him, but they never call him. They lead him to believe he might be dragged out and executed at any time, hoping he breaks under the pressure and confesses."

"Do you think Pontius is likely to break?" Veronica asked.

Gaius paused, gripping the staff with both hands and staring out over the sea. "I think our brother has a heavy conscience. He may feel such a need to unburden himself that he'll confess to anything."

Veronica gripped his arm and they continued climbing. They could see the waters of Mare Nostrum lapping against the shore of Capri. Why had Tiberius left his island sanctuary and returned to the mainland? Did he desire more engagement with his people? Or was it Macro's decision, an exercise of power he'd usurped?

Caesar's villa was more magnificent up close: Carrara white marble pillars, a Rosalia marble plaza. An officer of the Praetorian Guard stopped them on the portico.

"We have business with Caesar," Gaius informed him.

"Do you?" he laughed.

"Sir," Veronica asked, "is Pontius Pilate is here? And his wife, Claudia Procula?"

"You are?"

"I am... the lady's sister. Veronica."

"Prefect Pilate awaits his audience with Caesar. For the past month."

"Well," Gaius smiled, "Perhaps we shouldn't be getting our hopes up about our own business?"

"I shall send word to Praetor Macro," the guard offered. "If you'll come this way, I'll direct you to Prefect Pilate."

*   *   *   *

Veronica found Claudia beneath a quince tree. She clung to a gnarled limb, her head resting on an upraised arm and her palla swaying in the breeze. Veronica stood close enough to breathe on her, yet to Claudia she was invisible.

"Claudia, are you all right?" Veronica asked.

Gaius raised his lance and struck at a high bough, knocking loose a ripe quince. He caught it and halved the fruit with the tip of his spear. He presented the fruit to Claudia.

"Perhaps this will open your eyes."

"I don't want them open," Claudia mumbled. She looked at Veronica. "I got your letter. You shouldn't have come."

"How could I stay away?" Veronica asked. She put her arm around Claudia's back and stroked her arm. Claudia loosed her grip on the tree, but wriggled away from her cousin's embrace.

"You've damned yourself coming here," Claudia said. "Whatever life you had — *Damascus, wasn't it?* — you should've clung to it. Here is only slow, soul-sucking death."

"Where is Pontius?" Veronica asked.

"Waiting to die."

Gaius cut some pulp from the quince and handed it to Claudia. She relented and tasted it. Perhaps the sweetness jarred her; she seemed refreshed.

"Is Pontius afraid?"

Claudia laughed. "Months ago he might have been afraid. Now? He's impatient. We've been here five weeks! Every day Pontius sends his petition to the Emperor, imploring him to hear his case. And every evening we're told, *Not today.* So Pontius drinks. He paces. He lashes out. He almost welcomes death. Death at least would bring peace."

Veronica thought of all the people she'd seen meet death. If peace was there, they hadn't perceived it; they'd fought for every breath and pulse of life.

"He asks me how he should request it," Claudia continued. "Should he accept to be strangled, or insist on beheading? Perhaps beg a dagger from his guards and fall on it himself? Is this what a wife wants to hear?"

Veronica knew no words could console her cousin. But she searched her memory for happier times: jousting in the atrium, feeding finches in their aviary, chasing foxes on horseback in Tuscany... it all seemed so trivial.

"You loved Pontius from the first. Do you remember? You led us from the party to the Field of Mars to watch him pitch his lance. Remember?"

"Yes."

"We hid in the thicket. And giggled."

"I remember."

"You still love him, don't you?"

Claudia lifted her face. Veronica saw hope there; she anticipated an outburst, some effusive declaration of love. But Claudia was stifled. Veronica heard heavy boots on the gravel. Macro stood before her.

"Mistress Procula."

"Praetor," she responded.

"It's many years," he sneered, "since your uncle abandoned Rome."

Veronica glanced at Gaius; he seemed ready, save the grace of Christ, to throttle this arrogant martinet.

"It was Rome that turned on him," she answered.

"Well, you were a child," he said. "I'm sure that's how it appeared. I imagine you've come to sue for clemency?"

Veronica smiled with closed mouth. After a beat, she answered, "We've come to see the Emperor."

Macro breathed deeply, feigning disinterest. "The Emperor is a busy man."

Veronica arched her left eyebrow. "Busy making decisions of state? Or gasping for breath?"

Macro stood stock still, but in his eyes Veronica perceived him reeling back and fro. She kept her eyes locked on him, forcing him to concede: "The Emperor is quite aged."

"Then we ought not dawdle," she said. She waited. After a moment Macro's austere façade crumbled and he laughed to release the tension.

"Perhaps I should have said, *the Emperor is dying*," he declared with finality.

Veronica set her jaw, tilting her chin up slightly. She locked her eyes on Macro's, stating simply, "Then you have nothing to lose."

Chapter 37

Veronica hugged Claudia and encouraged her to be strong. Then Macro led her and Gaius into Caesar's villa. Immediately Veronica sensed something was amiss. Despite the open shutters and high ceilings, the house was airless, and Veronica discerned a faint odor of waste, as if the servants were composting indoors. The smell increased as they walked deeper into the interior. The hallway grew dark; heavy drapes drawn over shutters in the side parlors blocked all evidence of the sun.

"Caesar complains that light hurts his eyes," Macro said.

Veronica could have said as much about the stench; her eyes watered. The drapes must have absorbed foul odors for years, sealing in the dank, fetid air. Veronica began to anticipate horror; the source of the rot and decay was getting closer. It could only be Caesar himself.

Macro lifted a velvet curtain and Veronica reeled. Gaius braced her, but even he had to cough, as the putrid fumes burned their eyes and throats. Veronica peered into the chamber, lit dimly by an oil lamp whose yellow flickering cast ominous shadows on the curtained shutters. Veronica eyed the bed. It looked as though, amidst the twisted, silken sheets, Caesar had dissolved. His raw flesh, black in the yellow light, glistened with puss. His swollen face was a mass of tumors, blisters and eruptions that reduced his eyes to slits and his mouth to a drooping chasm, forced open by a black and bulging tongue.

Macro continued to hold the curtain aloft, staring icily at Veronica, as if daring her to enter.

"So it was leprosy," Veronica whispered.

"It would appear so," Macro stated. "Though I could have you flogged for suggesting it."

Gone suddenly was any desire for revenge. Or any thought of satisfaction from his suffering. But Veronica felt no compassion. She felt nothing except Macro's smug condescension; he was daring her to enter. Of course, there was no point. Sue for Claudia and Pontius? Caesar could not possible be lucid. The rot attacking his flesh must surely have infected his mind. Why talk to fetid meat? Or petition decay? But she'd come this far; she would not turn away, if only to deny Macro the satisfaction. Gaius placed a firm hand on her shoulder and nudged her forward. He was of the same mind; Veronica ducked below the folds of the curtain and Gaius followed. Macro sighed haughtily and let the curtains drop.

Veronica found it hard to breathe. She became light-headed, but inched her way toward the bed. Caesar's face was repulsive; of all the brutalized, ravaged faces she'd seen — the Baptist's dumb mouth opened in final lamentation, Uncle Theo beaten, Jesus bloodied and mocked with a thorny crown — of all those horrors, Tiberius was most loathsome. Veronica wanted so much to dismiss him, to declare *This is justice!* and be done with Caesar forever. But she couldn't. She quaked with pity for a lonely, isolated man, and she fell on bended knees.

"Ave, Emperor," she whispered.

She perceived a flicker of life in Caesar's rheumy eye. He moaned.

Veronica felt an impulse — she knew not from where — and removed the veil from the pocket of her tunic. There was a pitcher of water and a basin on Caesar's sideboard. Veronica unfolded her veil and asked Gaius to pour some water into the basin. He placed the full basin on the floor beside her. Veronica wet the veil with the cool water and reached to dab Caesar's forehead.

Caesar writhed and reached his feeble arm upward, trying to push her hand away.

"How dare you!" he rasped.

"Please, Emperor," Veronica whispered. She held down his arm with one hand and continued to wash his face with the other. He struggled.

"Slave!" he croaked. "I'll beat you. Bloody."

Veronica washed the hand that gripped her, replying, "As you wish, Emperor. My life is a trifle." She stroked his outstretched arm with the veil.

His eyes flared open. "You dare mock me, slave! I am your master!"

Calmly, Veronica dipped the veil, immersing it completely, and wrung it out.

"You are Caesar. And you are master of most of the world. But you're not mine."

She pressed the wet veil to his chest and wiped up to his neck. Tiberius grabbed her wrist. His grip was firm. He twisted her skin painfully. He even raised his head and shoulders off the bed, as he demanded, "If Caesar is not your master, who is?"

Veronica stifled a laugh. Tiberius responded with fury. He lunged forward, grabbing both of her arms. He kicked his tangled sheets to free his legs. Gaius pulled the covers away, and Caesar rolled, planting his feet firmly on the floor. He stood, shaking Veronica, who giggled madly.

"Why do you laugh, fool! Why?"

"Because," Veronica smiled, "my Master is so wonderful."

"Imbecile!" Caesar huffed. "Lunatic!"

"Caesar," Gaius interrupted, "do you notice anything?"

The Emperor froze. His eyes widened and he stared at the backs of his hands. They were plump, without blemish. He patted his arms: they were firm and muscular. He touched his fingertips to his cheeks and traced the contours of his face to the tip of his chin. Then Caesar's face opened in awe.

"Incredible!" he exclaimed. "How did you do it?"

"I didn't," Veronica confessed. "My Master did." Veronica unfurled the veil and revealed the image. Tiberius stared at the tortured face of Christ, and tears streamed down his cheeks[77].

* * * *

---

[77] The cleansing of Tiberius is contained in The Golden Legend.

Tiberius skipped through the breakers, kicking up foam. He lifted his face up to the sun and stretched out his arms as if he'd take flight, and he spun in mad circles. His attendants watched with apprehension as the gleeful Emperor whirled like a drunken gull over the surf. Longinus, with Veronica at his side, strolled behind them. Euphoric over the miraculous healing, Longinus slipped his hand into Veronica's, lacing his fingers among hers.

"Heal the Emperor, and heal the empire?" he teased. Veronica tried to suppress her smile and feign annoyance, but failed. Instead, she tugged on his arm, dragging him into the breakers.

"If Caesar can act mad, why not his citizens?" She leaned towards the waves, threatening to soak them both.

So, on a mad impulse, Longinus wriggled his hand free and sent her flailing into the surf. Laughing, yet somewhat shamefaced, he trotted over, stooped and pulled her out of the foam. "That's what you get, *slave*," he declared, "for mocking your Emperor!"

"I should slap you," she groaned, but just slumped contentedly forward, leaning against his chest. She wrapped her arms around him dreamily, adding, "Gaius, we may be the most fortunate people living — in the most fortunate time in all of history."

Longinus lifted some wet strands of hair off her face. He caressed her cheek with the back of his fingers. "This was your dream," he said.

Veronica nodded. "It was."

"Then I should never wake you," he said. "Except," he hesitated, "do you have room for another dream?"

He could tell Veronica gathered his meaning, though it had been months — no years! — since they'd discussed it. Perhaps he should not have spoken now. He should've let this moment exist on its own, without making it the impetus for something more. Yes, he was headstrong. But Veronica had no cause to hold that against him. When she'd told him about Claudia's plight, he hadn't hesitated. He knew they'd be marching into Caesar's lair, but his resolve had been unshakeable. As he saw it, this crisis could have been God's way of provoking what had to be; Veronica's gift and Rome's dire need converging. When Christ had left His image on that veil, he'd also painted her destiny. And, yes, Longinus admitted, he'd had personal reasons for supporting this mission. He'd wanted Veronica to settle her heart. Now she'd fulfilled her destiny in Christ, and they could be free to pursue their own lives. They could surely count on Caesar's gratitude; he'd grant Longinus his pension and land. Despite their extraordinary blessings, they might yet live ordinary lives. There could be love, blessed with children. Of course, they'd raise their children in The Way. Shouldn't that be sufficient for their Lord?

Now Longinus feared he'd lost the moment. He'd rehearsed it in his mind, but faced with reality, he'd faltered. He considered how a soldier might pledge undying loyalty, but simply took Veronica's hand in his and knelt in the sand.

"Veronica," asked, "would you honor me...?"

"No!" she cried. "No, no, no!"

Veronica broke from him and ran desperately down the beach. Tiberius had fallen, and was flailing in the surf. His attendants, who'd retired to the road where Caesar's carriage was stopped, ran towards him. They gathered around, trying to lift him up as the waves hit. They carried him from the breakers, gasping for breath. Longinus ran ahead of Veronica and saw that Tiberius was choking; he pushed through the wall of attendants and stooped to help. He put his fingers in the Emperor's mouth and tried to clear his throat. Caesar wheezed. His body went rigid.

Longinus could sense Veronica over his shoulder; he heard her pray frantically, "*Please let Caesar live!*" He bent Caesar forward at the waist and struck him on the back to force him to cough. Then the tight knot of attendants opened and Longinus saw a file of the Praetorian Guard running towards them. Veronica cleaved to Caesar's side. She gripped his hand, pressing it to her cheek, his gold signet pressing into her skin. Longinus felt the tension in Caesar's body release — *he was breathing again!* — and lowered the Emperor gently to the sand.

Then the Guards were upon them. They thrust the attendants aside, and laid a litter on the sand. They pushed Longinus out of the way and lifted Caesar onto the litter.

"Wait," he objected. "Let him rest."

"Leave him!" Veronica cried. "He's tired."

But they hefted the litter off the sand and marched, double time, up towards Caesar's carriage. That's when Longinus saw another coach. Standing beside it were Macro and a younger Roman, whose fine dress seemed only to accentuate his homeliness. Tall, lanky and stooped, the young man had exceptionally hairy limbs, yet was thinning at the crown. The Guards dropped the litter at the young man's feet.

"No, not him!" Veronica gasped.

"You know that boy?"

The homely, young Roman crouched to inspect the Emperor, took him by the hand and wrested the signet from his finger, placing it on his own.

The Guards knelt and saluted, thrusting their right arms forward, "Hail, Caesar!"

Veronica stooped, clenching — not just her fists, but — her entire body. She bolted towards the Emperor, screaming in protest, "No! He's not dying! No!"

Longinus overtook her and dragged her to the sand. Veronica stared murderously at the young Roman — *the new Caesar?* — until Longinus grabbed her shoulders and turned her towards him.

"What—? Who is that?"

Veronica's lips trembled, as though she dare not speak the name. "It's... Caligula."

Chapter 38

The guards loaded Tiberius into his carriage with a pair of attendants. One of them lifted Longinus' lance out of the way, and seemed to consider tossing it into the road, but, finding room to sit, held onto it. Longinus kicked the sand in frustration, and a guard whipped the team into a gallop, whisking Caesar away to the Villa. Macro and Caligula followed in their coach. The remaining guards herded Veronica and Longinus onto the road, so for the second time that day, they made the arduous climb up the mountain. This time they felt no elation, only drudgery and defeat. But at least they weren't in chains — yet!

At the Villa, Veronica strained for a glimpse of Claudia, as the Guards ushered them into what would have been Caesar's receiving room, if Tiberius Caesar had ever received anyone. Macro sat at a desk, slightly elevated on a platform, busily drafting papers. Behind him, higher still on an ornate throne, was the odd young man Veronica knew as Caligula. On the way up the mountain, she'd told Longinus all about *Little Boots*: how he'd killed small animals, how he'd delighted in executions and how her uncle had forbade her to be alone with him. Longinus had known men like that in the ranks; the killing aroused them. They preferred shedding blood to wine, to food and to women. Their minds were so sadly twisted, no one could trust them, not on the battlefield, nor even in the barracks. They didn't last; no matter how skilled in combat, they fell, purged by their cohorts. That would certainly be Caligula's fate; the only question was how long it would take. But for now he was Great Caesar, the Emperor in whom Longinus had once said "the law and the man are one." How could he ever have been so naïve, to assume that, *somehow*, petty men who grasped for every shred of power might possess virtue enough to justly wield it?

Longinus watched Caligula shift uncomfortably, as if balancing on a narrow perch. He toyed perplexedly with the Centurion's lance. He drew his heels up under himself, bobbing on the balls of his feet as he hefted the spear above his shoulder, testing its balance and feebly pantomiming a forward thrust. Confounded, he lowered the spear tip to the floor. He pulled his knees up to his chest, wrapped his hairy arms around his hairier shins and rested his chin on his knees.

Macro dropped his stylus, checked Longinus and then leered at Veronica. "That was quite a miracle you worked on the Emperor's appearance," he said.

"I take no credit," she answered.

Macro chortled, pushing back from the desk. "Certainly not now. That he's dead." He waved as if dismissing a gnat, then feigned sympathy. "Oh, I suppose that was something your *Lord* didn't see coming." He held up a sheet of paper, and read in a mocking tone, *"'...we dare hope that the truth, illuminated with the divine light of Christ, might change even the hardened heart of one such as Macro.'"* He sneered. "Ah, *truth*. Yes, the truth, Mistress, is that your *Lord* was religious lunatic attempting to incite rebellion. Prefect Pilate executed him for it — end of story — and no amount of seditious nonsense can alter that fact. Including your claim to be a witness to some sort of resurrection."

"Do you deny Caesar was healed?" Veronica asked.

Macro flushed. "I affirm that Caesar is dead," he stated. He held his breath for an awkward moment before adding dismissively, "Tiberius was old. It was his time."

"How good of you," Veronica chaffed, "to help keep his appointment."

Macro laughed. "Well, it's my job to make arrangements. As to yours —"

"I want to see my cousin," Veronica declared. Her voice quavered as she added, "And then, we shall be going home."

Macro picked up his stylus and returned to his papers. "You have no home, Mistress. Your uncle's estate was seized when he absconded." He was attempting to belittle Veronica by ignoring her, but to Longinus it seemed that Macro was under siege. Could the cleansing of Caesar have shaken his spirit? A healthy Caesar might have judged Macro as cruelly as he had Sejanus. Macro couldn't risk that, so he'd murdered one tyrant to put another in his place, one he probably viewed as a malleable fool. But he had to assume his actions had offended Caesar's healer; whoever that was — a dead lunatic, a risen Lord or a willful, defiant girl — he took risk in provoking. He'd mocked the notion that the Lord could soften his heart — as any cold murderer would — but that's just what appeared to be happening. Thus Macro's tone changed, and he attempted to shift the focus from himself. "If only Tiberius had lived, you could have petitioned him. Of course, there's always his successor." Macro gestured over his shoulder to the hairy vulture perched behind him, then tipping his head in condescension, he added, "But you hardly showed the enthusiasm for his ascension."

"Hardly," Caligula soughed. After a beat he mumbled, "Your uncle hated me."

"That's not true," Veronica protested.

But Caligula asserted, "He let Sejanus take me away."

Veronica gaped, obviously flustered. Longinus squeezed her elbow gently, to caution her against arguing with a madman. Macro wanted no further argument either. He folded his papers and poured wax from a candle to seal them. Glowering at Veronica, he declared, "Your ship leaves this evening for Valentia. Gaul."

"You're exiling me?"

Macro snorted. "Emperor Caligula is granting you land in the provinces." His eyes darted to Longinus. "You as well. In Phrygia."

"Asia?" Longinus blurted. "My land's in Lombardy."

It was a ridiculous statement; he knew as soon as he said it, and so did Macro.

"Be grateful the Emperor doesn't have you strangled for desertion."

"Yes, be thankful," Caligula echoed. "I have to spare her; her family still has friends in the Senate. But I've no reason at all to spare you!"

Macro stood and gestured to the Guards, who closed ranks in front of the desk. He handed the sealed orders to one of the Guards, who then turned and handed the papers to Longinus and Veronica. "You will be escorted to your respective ships. They leave immediately."

When neither Longinus nor Veronica moved, Macro narrowed his eyes, "Is there something else?"

Yes, Longinus thought, *you can't separate us! Christ has joined us* — but Veronica spoke first.

"My cousin, Claudia," she said. "I wish to say good-bye."

"How fast can you swim?" Macro taunted.

"I put her on a boat to Spain!" Caligula chortled. "With her worthless husband." He was standing on the throne with his nose in the air, perhaps imagining the statue he'd erect to himself for valor in the face of women's backtalk. Longinus draped an arm around Veronica's shoulders. The girl, brave as she'd been, was in agony. In a few short minutes, she'd gone from the heights of ecstasy, having conquered Rome for Christ, to the depths of homelessness and exile. But it did not have to end this way; they did not have to submit to Macro.

"I'll fix this," he whispered.

"What now?" Macro demanded.

Longinus squared his shoulders and answered casually. "My lance."

Macro arched an eyebrow, feigning insult. "That's rather brazen, asking your Emperor to return a gift."

"You gave it to Caesar," Caligula squawked, "and what was Caesar's passes to me. His heir. You think I sat around this horrid villa all these years, watching him turn to pus, for no reason?"

"Of course not, Great Caesar," Longinus intoned. "And if I'd made a gift of my lance, I'd wish you to keep it. But I never did. I simply left it in Caesar's carriage when we went for a walk on the beach."

"Well, then," Macro interjected, "we can solve this problem. Simply make Caesar a gift of the lance now. In gratitude for your life."

"Why shouldn't I have it?" Caligula whined. "Pilate says it's a great weapon, with awesome powers. Pilate says it makes a man invincible."

Longinus felt his throat constrict. *Oh, Spirit, guide my speech at this moment of trial!* Caligula took up the lance again, fumbling with it before resting the staff on his shoulder.

"Who should have such a weapon?" Macro chided. "Great Caesar or a deserter and coward?"

"Were Pilate's words true," Longinus answered, "Caesar should lay claim to the lance. But Pilate spoke only to ingratiate himself with Caesar. He presented a fraud, hoping for clemency."

Longinus felt Veronica's fingernails dig into his wrist; she must have sensed where the confrontation was headed.

"Pilate said the lance cannot miss," Caligula objected.

Longinus peeled Veronica's fingers off his arm and backed her away.

"Don't do this," she whispered. "I can't lose you, too."

"You've already lost me," he said, "if I let them win."

Longinus separated from Veronica and faced the throne. Caligula tottered there, pushing the lance up and out in phantom thrusts. Longinus rolled his shoulders back, opening his chest.

"Let Caesar test what Pilate has told him."

Longinus heard Veronica gasp. *Good, that should get Caligula's blood lust flowing.* In fact, the salacious boy actually ran his tongue around the corner of his mouth. He struck what he must have imagined was a javelin thrower's pose and aimed the spear point at the Centurion's heart. Off balance, Caligula thought better of his perch and stepped gingerly down from the seat to the platform. With his empty hand, he waved Macro farther to the side, then refocused, pointing the flat, open hand at his target and pulling the throwing arm back.

It would be an easy toss, no more than twelve feet. Caligula was so close, Longinus could make out individual beads of sweat on his sloping brow. The hand came forward; the spear flew, then plummeted, sticking in the floor between Longinus' feet. Longinus grabbed the staff, but Veronica hugged him, pinning down his arms.

"This isn't the way," she implored.

"It's the only way."

Longinus pulled the staff toward himself, freeing the point. With a quick upward thrust, he could skewer Macro, then toss him aside and run Caligula through. God had endowed him with this weapon; at some point He must have intended him to use it. *What better time than now? Caligula would fall to an assassin eventually. Why not now, before he caused more misery? Kill these two tyrants and Rome is free. If another vulture takes the throne, kill him, too. Just keep killing the evil, the malignant, the malevolent...* Dark thoughts flooded the Centurion's mind: images from his night bearing the cross. He saw himself on the precipice of a black abyss — nothing but emptiness and despair — and his toe poised to step. He dropped the lance and held Veronica tight. He lowered his forehead to her shoulder and wept.

"I can't lose you," he said. "I can't let them take you away."

Veronica wiped his tears with the heel of her palm and combed her fingers through his hair.

"Take these women away," Macro barked. "They can keep the useless toy."

Longinus snatched up his lance. The Guards separated him and Veronica and ushered them out the door.

*   *   *   *

They rode in silence in Caesar's carriage. The wheels rumbled and the scenery flew by. They'd be at the wharf in no time. An octet of horsemen followed, to ensure the prisoners boarded their assigned vessels. Veronica nestled her shoulder under Gaius' arm and laid her head on his chest. She knew how badly his pride was wounded, but she hoped Gaius would talk to her. She didn't want to leave him without saying all that had to be said, and hearing what was in his heart. She grieved for him: he was a better man than Macro or Caligula, and if this contest could have been decided by warfare, Gaius would have prevailed, with or without a charmed lance. But God had a different plan for them.

That realization crushed her. Kneeling at Caesar's bedside, she'd felt the Spirit move her to bathe him. That inspiration had made her confident Jesus would bless her actions; Caesar was cured, and Rome would be next. They'd come so close, and had it all snatched away. Veronica knew it wasn't true, but at that moment, Jesus seemed as cruel and capricious as any Roman god. Veronica pulled her veil from her pocket; she wanted to see his face and cast her scowl upon it. She unrolled the veil and stretched it out on her lap.

"What are you thinking?" Gaius asked.

She dug her fingernails into the veil. "I want to go home!" Her eyes welled, she turned her head and dabbed her tears on Gaius' chest. The carriage reached the first tight turn, a switchback down the hillside. Veronica clung tightly onto Gaius.

"I've never told you this," he said, "But in my first encounter with Jesus, He undid my plan."

Veronica lifted her head Gaius looked away.

"I poisoned a boy," he confessed. "I'd intended to kill him, because he had accidentally killed one of my men. So I poisoned him. The Primus, my superior, thinking the boy was ill, took me to see this healer. The Primus knew

Jesus couldn't come to the garrison without causing a scandal. He told him, *I am a man who understands authority, I tell my men to do this and it is done*. He was lecturing me as much as he was informing the Rabbi. But he said, *If you order this done, I know it shall be done*" When we got back to the garrison, the boy was healed."

The carriage turned sharply again, winding the other way.

"Perhaps," Gaius continued, "Jesus expects as much from me as a soldier as the Primus did. That when he says, *Go here, do this,* I must go."

Veronica pressed her cheek against his chest again and hugged him tight. She loved Gaius more in that moment than she ever had.

"When I lost my sight," he continued, "the first thing I thought was, I'll never see that Senator's niece again."

Veronica trembled. "As I recall," she spoke coolly, "you were fighting for your life."

Gaius touched her beneath the chin, and lifted her face to his. "And if it were still my life, I'd like to give it to you." He kissed her sweetly, then brushed his hand through her hair.

"Obviously, it's not my life either," Veronica said. "But it's not Macro's. He may think he's punishing us, but... I remember something Mother Mary told me, about when she was with child. She was to have Jesus in Nazareth, where she and Joseph lived. But Caesar Augustus issued a decree, that all should be enrolled in a census. So they had to travel to Bethlehem, and Jesus was born there, just as the scriptures said. Caesar thought he could order the world, but when he tried, he simply made God's plan happen. Maybe that's true of us. We wanted what we wanted so badly, we thought it must be what Jesus wanted, too."

"I thought about that," Gaius admitted. "In the chamber with Macro and Caligula, I thought, *let me be done with Christ. Let me slay these villains, and take this beautiful girl for my own. And let me live whatever days are left, with her... and without Christ.*"

"But you didn't."

Gaius shook his head. He squeezed her hand and look out at the sea. "Because I know I can't love you, truly, outside of Christ. I've known that for some time. Before Christ entered our lives, I was arrogant. You were willful. There was passion between us, but no harmony. The passion would have burned out and left us miserable. I can only love you as I should through Jesus."

The carriage stopped. Veronica could see two ships at the wharf, both huge quinterimes. Gaius picked up his lance and hopped from the carriage. He gave Veronica a hand and she stepped down. He then pulled out their bags and hoisted them onto his shoulder. Veronica linked her arm with his and they walked to the pier.

"You know," Veronica said, feeling a little more optimistic, "I don't have anything left in Rome. No property. And certainly no one who'd understand my relationship with Jesus. So, maybe Gaul will be better."

"Or Phrygia," Gaius chuckled.

"I just wish I wasn't going alone."

A young officer approached, ignoring Gaius and speaking directly to Veronica.

"Mistress," he declared, "the Captain reports winds are favorable to launch." He gestured to the first quinterime. Gaius handed Veronica's bag to the officer, then, dropping his own bag, he gave her one last embrace.

"Show his face to the world," he said, then picked up his belongings and strode down the wharf to the other ship.

"We shall!" the officer called after him. He pointed to the ship's mast, where seamen raised a red standard, already emblazoned in gold with Caligula's profile. "Nothing strikes terror into barbarians like the image of Caesar." The young man gestured for Veronica to proceed, and she made her way toward the gangplank.

This officer struck her as very much a boy. He was probably a patrician, and this could well be his first tour of duty in the Roman navy. Yet, he may have been well traveled and might know what was happening in in the world.

"Have you heard any news," she asked, "out of Judea? Strange events?"

"None," he assured her. "Of course, they've been conquered, so the less we hear, the better." He gave Veronica his hand and escorted her up the gangplank. Veronica stepped onto the deck and cast about for a place to sit.

"I'm sure you're right," she told him. "But we mustn't close our minds to possibilities." He looked at her quizzically. "I mean, that things are happening in other places that we should know about." The young man nodded politely and stepped away. Veronica inwardly groaned. She clutched at the veil wadded in her pocket. She was being much too forward. They had a long voyage ahead. No sense causing a disruption that would prompt the Captain to flog her. Or chain her to an oar. She sat on a bench toward the stern as the ship cast off. Looking over her shoulder, she searched the wharf for some sign of Gaius, but couldn't find him. Gazing upward she saw Caligula's red and gold standard; the wind was strong and steady and stretched the pennant out against the blue sky. As the officer had observed, that was the face of fear. Veronica felt a chill, but she refused to be afraid.

The officer came back to check on her.

"Are you comfortable, Mistress?" he asked. "The wind can be fierce."

"Yes," she replied, "I'm fine." But no, she wasn't comfortable; she was bereft. The love she'd borne for Gaius had been true and... *good*. What could Jesus call her to that would be a greater good?

"Very well then." The young man bowed to take his leave.

Feed my lambs.

"But!" Veronica blurted. Her face must have looked panicked; she'd startled the young man. Veronica collected herself and continued calmly, "If you have a moment to sit, I have something to show you."

Acknowledgments

There are several people who provided invaluable assistance in getting this novel ready for publication. Tim J. Peterson gave constant encouragement, read the first draft enthusiastically and offered important insights and criticisms. Matthew Murray reviewed the final draft, made important corrections and pointed out several instances where there was still room for significant improvement. I am tremendously grateful for their input.

I would also like to thank the guest bloggers at MakingLentMeaningful.com — Ed Gillespie, David Marcus, Allen Matthews, Tim J. Peterson and Tim Ferguson — who took pressure off me during a critical point in my writing process and offered compelling witness to our shared longing for peace in Christ.

This work is a product of my imagination, but rests upon a foundation of research. While I used a multitude of sources for the historical background, from Plutarch and Suetonius to Wikipedia, two works stand out as being especially helpful. The first is Ann Wroe's excellent study of the Prefect of Judea, simply titled *Pontius Pilate*. The other is a rich collection of apocryphal tales from early Christianity, *The Golden Legend*, compiled by Jacobus de Voragine and translated by William Granger Ryan. I have woven several incidents from this collection into the narrative of Veronica and Longinus.

Some may object to the inclusion of apocryphal tales — and even the imaginings of a 21st century writer — within a larger Gospel narrative. I have attempted to eliminate any elements that might cause confusion among the faithful in composing what I hope is a lively adventure, rich in wonder, that communicates the timeless Christian truth of a loving God intervening in human history to redeem His creation.

Made in the USA
Middletown, DE
10 November 2014